Animate Me

by
Ruth
Clampett

ILLUSTRATIONS BY JUAN ORTIZ

Except Chapter Three by Vince Musacchia and

Chapter Thirty-One by the author

Cover illustration by Juan Ortiz

Photography by David Johnston

Design Jada D'Lee

The beautiful hands belong to

Erik Odom & Anais Mendoza

For my Dad who taught me to set my imagination free
and that an artist needs to takes risks with a brave heart.

For my Mom who showed me that strength of character and kindness
will lift you out of darkness.

But most of all for my daughter, Alex...my inspiration, my best girl.
From the day you were born I knew we would share a brilliant journey.
Your shine has led the way.

Animate Me

Animate Me / Chapter One / I'm in Love

an-i-mate *verb* \'a-ne-met\ 1. to bring to life 2. To give spirit and vigor to 3. To make appear to move for a cartoon

There you go with the breasts too big again.

I rub my eraser over the sketchbook page and brush the crumbs away before reworking my lines over the ghosted image. With each stroke of the pencil my dream girl comes to life, her heart-shaped face graced with huge blue eyes and plump bow lips.

Oh, how I want to kiss those lips

My pencil trails down to define her shapely thighs leading up to her small waist, just below the finale of her perfect breasts. I erase the rough sketch lines under the final clean pencil. Yes…there, she's just right. I may not be so comfortable talking to girls, but I sure know how to draw them. I hold my sketchbook up to admire her before setting it down next to the cash register.

At least I'm over my huge-breast obsession. Holy hell, during the months where I had newly discovered online porn I just kept drawing them bigger and bigger. If those girls had been real, they would have toppled over. Picasso had his blue period; I had my breast period. Eventually I got bored with the mechanical episodes of online porn. Now I've matured to studying vintage pin-up girls and reading graphic novels that still leave something to the imagination. As a result, my work is more refined, well, not really…but at least in that regard. My girls are safe from toppling over now.

Hearing a cough, I push my glasses up my nose and look over at the kid still transfixed in the new release section of the Playstation 3 aisle. He handles each cellophane-wrapped game like it's a treasure, a sacred gift from the video game gods. I have a fondness for this kid, Theo, who comes to the store every Saturday while his mom gets a manicure on the other end of the strip mall. He reminds me of myself at that age, a social misfit who couldn't look people in the eye. Now I chat with customers when I ring up their purchases. This is certainly progress for a guy like me who didn't start talking until he was four.

I let Theo fondle the packages knowing full well that he hasn't saved enough allowance to make a purchase this week. He blew his wad last Saturday on the latest *Dragon Age* release. When a car honks just outside the door, he turns to me and waves.

"See you next week, Nathan," he calls out before he runs through the door and slips into his mom's SUV.

When I was his age, I spent my Saturdays with my parents at my brother Curtis' various sporting events, grateful to have my sketchbook and pencils while I sat through hour after tedious hour of games. I learned early on how to get lost in the page and create worlds in my head where I could escape. Nothing's changed, just now I'm getting paid to draw as a studio animator, and I sure as heck don't have to go to sports games.

I pull out my colored pencils and start back in on my drawing when the door rings indicating a new customer. I look up in time to see a flash of female before she heads down one of the side aisles. A rush of adrenaline surges through me.

No…it couldn't be. Not her. She is not *here shopping at Jimmy's Geek World. Impossible. No.*

I close my eyes and count backwards from ten to try to calm myself. Around four, I give up and lean forward to see if my imagination was playing tricks on me.

She steps into the center aisle and strides towards me in slow motion, the sway of her hips distracting me from her black leather boots that lace all the way up to her knees. She has on a short pleated skirt and a vintage looking T-shirt with faded type that says *The Sex Pistols*. I sway and grab the edge of the counter to steady myself.

"Hey," she calls out with the bow lips parted just so. "Can you help me?" Her long auburn hair looks like spun silk and cascades down her back like those happy girls in shampoo commercials.

Can I help you? I repeat to myself, confused. Brooke Tobin, the woman of my dreams, my obsession from afar, appears to need me. I note that this is where my fantasy usually starts, before it ends with me fondling her in the stockroom. Today it is real and I must rise to the occasion.

"Sure, what can I help you with?" I cringe. My response is a little too enthusiastic but she seems unfazed. I can tell she has no idea who I am.

"I need a cord thingy for my computer, and I'm not sure which one."

Thingy? I smile as I step out from behind the counter and move authoritatively towards the *thingy* section. "Do you need a USB?"

"What's that?" She arches her brow and folds her arms like I've asked about a sexually transmitted disease instead of her port entries.

"A USB cord? The USB connection simplifies the process of connecting peripherals to the computer and offers much higher data transfer rates." I push my thick, black–framed glasses back up my nose hoping she's impressed.

Her hands move to her hips, and she steps closer then leans towards my chest. My breath catches until I realize that she is reading my name printed on the lip of my pocket protector.

"Na-than?" she half questions, half confirms. "I think now's a good time to tell you that I don't speak tech geek. Can you give it to me straight so I'll know what you're talking about? I just want a cord thingy so I can hook my old computer to my new one."

Considering my track record with impressing women, I shouldn't be surprised that she doesn't appreciate my vast technological know-how. Looking down at my feet, I desperately wish the phone would ring or something so I could step away for a moment and gather my thoughts, but the store is quiet as a tomb.

I've imagined talking and being with her for so long that my misstep has me unraveling. I don't want to mess up my one big chance to make a favorable impression. I fear she's already concluded I'm a freak.

When I look back up she has a broad grin on her face. "Cord thingy, Nathan?"

I reach for the USB's. "This is probably what you need. Do you know if it is a male to male connection?"

"I highly doubt it. Not my computer," she snickers.

Oh God, she thinks I'm being suggestive with her. I want to disappear. Where's my cloak of invisibility? I try to regain my composure.

"Well, you can always try this, and if it doesn't work you can bring it back," I offer.

She twists a lock of hair with her perfect fingers and considers what I've said. "Okay."

"Anything else?"

"Nope that's it."

We move towards the register. Sensing she's right behind me, I can smell her perfume, subtle and quiet like pears on a summer morning.

She pulls a wallet with a dangling Hello Kitty charm out of her little purse with the really long strap. "How much do I owe you?"

"Twelve forty-nine," I respond after double-checking the register's screen.

When she starts to set her money down I realize that my sketchbook's still open. I yank it off the counter so fast that the pencil and eraser take flight. Then I snap the book closed before she has time to really study the image.

She tips her head sideways. "Was that your drawing?"

"Yes," I mumble.

"Are you an artist?"

I can't lie. She may recognize me at work now. "Yeah…well, actually, I'm an animator."

She lights up, her eyes bright and happy. "Really? I work in animation."

"I know. I work at Sketch Republic too. You're Brooke in development, right?"

Good, that sounded cool…believable—like I don't dream about her all day and draw her naked late at night.

"Oh, you work there too. Sorry I didn't recognize you. Yes, I'm in development even though what I really wanted was to be an animator. I just didn't have the talent for it so I focused on what I'm good at. What show are you on?"

"*Bernie and the Beaver Patrol* with Joel's team. My buddy, Nicholas, is the head writer."

"Oh, I love Nick," she enthuses. "He's so damn funny."

"Yeah, everyone loves him—he's a riot," I grumble jealously.

"So what are you doing here?" she asks, waving her arm across the rows of games and accessories. "Don't we pay you enough? I thought animators did pretty well."

"Oh, it's not that. My friend's dad owns the place, and I've been helping them out while their manager is out for a few months recovering from knee surgery. I've only been doing it on Saturdays."

She nods. "Well, show me your work." She reaches for the sketchbook. "Are you good?"

I quickly step back, making my sketchbook out of her reach. "I'm *really* good," I state confidently. After all, it's the one thing I know for sure. I have talent; all my CalArts teachers told me so, and I got a studio job right out of school. "I'd love to show you my work, but this is just my scribbling. I want to show you the good stuff."

She puts her hand up. "Okay, when you're ready, I'd be happy to look at your work. You know where to find me."

Yes, I'd be happy to find you. If she only knew how long I've admired her.

"Will you remember me if I ask to show you another time? I mean, you must see a lot of artists' work."

Her lips curl up with delight. "Yes, I'm very sure I'll remember you, Nathan. You're pretty distinct."

I dig my wallet out of my back pocket, open it, then pull out the colorful rectangle. "Here, let me give you my card just in case." I feel suddenly grateful to my dad who taught me to always carry business cards because *you just never knew when opportunity would strike.*

It curls ever so slightly in her palm as she holds it close to read. She flips it over and studies the art on the back. "Nice card," she affirms before sliding it into her wallet.

"Thanks," I respond, trying to read every shade of her expression.

She looks up at me and studies me for a moment. "So what's with the bowtie? Is this a fashion statement?"

I can feel my face get red as I reach up and touch the bowtie that is sewn into my polo shirt. "No, this is the uniform. Can you believe it? And just in case the employees don't look geeky enough, this outfit seals the deal. We can't even wear jeans. It's high-waisted corduroy pants or twill slacks only. When my friend's dad, the owner, is here, he makes us tuck in our shirts."

"Oh, that's priceless!" she says. "It reminds me of those wild outfits the girls wear at Hot Dog on a Stick."

"You don't really think I'd wear a pocket protector of my own volition do you?"

"I wasn't sure. It's actually kind of sexy in a weird way. I bet you pick up some interesting hotties in that get-up. I bet there's one waiting for you in the back room."

My imagination comes to life as I think of Brooke in the back room.

"Yeah, we better hurry this up so she doesn't get jealous," I reply with a smile, pleased that I'm bantering. That book I read on how to talk to women seems to be paying off.

"What's she wearing…your hottie in the back room?" Brooke is very provocative.

"Not much."

She laughs. *God, I love her laugh.*

"Is she tied up?"

This isn't helping tame the fantasies I already have about her. *Jesus, hold it together man.* "Maybe." I cough nervously.

"You animators are all pervy," she snickers. "I love it."

She suddenly gets a look in her eyes and leans in closer. "You know you have great teeth. I'm really into teeth…for about five minutes in high school I thought about going to dental school. But when I realized that I wouldn't just be in sexy mouths like yours I dropped the idea immediately."

"Thank you." I smile broadly so that my teeth are showcased nicely. Her off-handed comment about being in my sexy mouth is creating some wild visuals in my head, but I try to refocus.

She appears to like, or at least tolerate geeks, and she definitely likes my teeth. I'm on her radar now, so winning her heart, although unlikely, is no longer up against insurmountable odds. Now it would just be equivalent to winning the lottery and people win the lottery all the time…right?

She reaches toward me to take the bag and her change. "So maybe I'll see you at work."

"Yeah, let me know if your connections work…you know the male to female thing."

Her resulting smile would melt glaciers, and I feel my heart swell inside my chest. I've never felt like this with anyone before. I swear this is love; what else could it possibly be? I want to pull her into my arms and never let her go.

"I'll do that," she says, then turns on her heel and walks towards the door.

I watch every move, committing it to memory…my fingers itching to wrap around a pencil and capture her on paper so that she'll always be with me.

Her pale, slender hand reaches for the door, and as she pulls it open she turns back toward me, self-assured enough to know that I'm still watching her. "You know, Nathan, don't let the cool clothes fool you. Deep down I'm a fan-girl geek…always have been, always will be. All my favorite people are too. Us geeks are the cool ones, because we are who we are; we don't try to be anyone else. Right?"

Although I am doubtful of her declaration, I nod and smile at her before she steps from the shadow of the doorway into the sun. The girl I adore glows in the warm light, brighter than anyone else passing by. As she shimmers and moves away I realize that there is no question in my mind, even if it defies logic or reason.

I am in love.

Animate Me / Chapter Two / Chivalry 101

"Pinky, are you pondering what I'm pondering?" "Yes Brain, but why does the chicken cross the road if not for love?" ~ Pinky and the Brain[i]

I pull into the parking garage and scan the reserved spots looking for Brooke's metallic, pale-green Prius. I usually come in before her, and today is no exception. Yet this morning the feeling of seeing her empty spot is different. Now that we've made a connection, I feel protective of her, curious about where she is and what she's doing.

It occurs to me that she could be with that idiot Arnauld, who she's rumored to be dating. The jealous beast roars inside of me. Arnauld's an asshole, and he doesn't deserve the perfection that is Brooke. I notice his space is empty as well, and my stomach tenses as I realize that there is every possibility that they are together right now: in the final throes of morning sex, or soaped up and showering together, or perhaps arguing about who finished off the last of the milk for their Lucky Charms. *Damn him.*

I sigh heavily as I blend into the group of employees streaming out of the parking structure and marching towards the building.

I feel so different today as I go through the main entrance and walk past the neon-lit Sketch Republic sign. I am different; I want something now that I gave up wanting a long time ago. The idea of wrapping my arms around a girl and kissing her has suddenly become tangible. I want Brooke to be that girl, and that feeling's like stretchy cellophane pulled tightly around me.

So when I reach my desk, I'm grateful to have a challenging scene to work on. For all the exuberance of animation, it's an exacting process that requires complete concentration. I'm hoping this focus will keep me from obsessing about Brooke, but I'm doubtful.

Joel likes to assign the most physical scenes to me because he says I'm old school Tex Avery in my animation style—adopting the master's stretch and squash flair. This week's assignment involves a fight between Bucky and Bernie Beaver after Bernie breaks Bucky's video game remote control. Before I start, I picture in my mind what I want to do with the characters.

I may be a quiet guy on the outside, but my work is always full of energy and expression. A surprised eye may stretch a foot long, or an open mouth's jaw can drop to the ground. I sharpen my pencil, attach the animation paper to the pegs on the light table, and fall into my work. All of my anxiety and excitement flows through my pencil, and the resulting drawings are particularly energetic.

"Hey dude, what's up?" Joel leans into my cubicle, and I look up at my desk clock to realize it's almost noon. I peel out my earbuds while pulling a drawing from the stack that I know he'll like.

"Is this what you had in mind for this scene?" Bucky has hit Bernie over the head with the broken remote, and now it's lodged in his forehead like a horn. Bernie's eyes are large X's and Bucky's smile extends freakishly past the edges of his pointed face.

"Oh, yeah," he howls. "That's perfect! You always make it even better than I've pictured it, Tex."

Referring to me as animation great Tex Avery is a sure sign that he's getting ready to ask for something. He usually isn't so complimentary, and I can hear it in his voice. I raise my eyebrows and tip my head waiting.

"Listen, no pressure or anything but management is demanding all the animators do seven feet this week since we are behind schedule."

The news is worse than I thought. "Damn, that's over forty drawings a day. We aren't a factory pumping out widgets."

"Sorry. Arnauld is all over my ass because I wanted to redo that scene last week. I'll bring lunch in for you guys today."

I tense up and pop my earbuds back in. *That jerk, Arnauld.* He always expects us to work faster and get the work done cheaper. "All right, well then I better pick up the pace."

By the afternoon my whole body is stiff from bending over the table, and I realize it's almost four o'clock. This is our magic Starbucks time when a group of us walk over to refuel on caffeine to get us through the rest of the day. The bunch gathers near the elevator and then we pack in when it arrives. I'm squashed in the back corner with rotund Andy, in his *Elmo for President* T-shirt, pressing into me.

Nick groans loudly when the elevator stops at the next floor. My heart surges though when the doors part and Brooke is revealed with her hands on her hips, focused on figuring out how she will fit into the overcrowded space.

"Come on Brooke, we won't bite," Nick teases, as he steps to the side and she slides in next to Genna.

"Yeah sure," she responds. "Last time this happened, I ended up with a 'fragile' sticker on my ass."

"Well, that wouldn't have been me, darling. You're one tough cookie— anything but fragile."

She smiles at him. "So where are all of you going anyway?" she asks, craning her neck and scanning the group.

"Our afternoon Starbucks run," he responds. "It's the only way we can survive the tedium of this animation chain gang."

"Oh, you poor, poor animators!" she says, rolling her eyes. "Go work at Disney then. They serve Starbucks in the break rooms. Of course that means you may have to do Mickey Mouse and that princess stuff."

"No!" yells out crazy Andy, like he's just been stabbed in the gut. "Anything but that!"

"Well, why am I not invited on these coffee runs, huh? Are you too good for me?" Brooke asks.

"Look, guys, the development queen wants to hang with the hired help. Well, come with us, your majesty," says Nick.

She frowns. "I can't. I have a meeting. A really, really important meeting."

"Uh huh…" he says playfully.

"Your job may depend on me being at this meeting. No worries though, our mutual caffeine fulfillment is far more important."

Nick turns to Andy. "See…she's such a tease. And I bet she drinks one of those stupid drinks too, like a half-caf soy caramel macchiato with two pumps of sugar-free vanilla and a Splenda very, very gently stirred in."

"Three pumps," she responds before she makes a grand exit when the door opens on the second floor. My eyes bug out as she steps out to head down the hallway. Her slacks hug her round bottom perfectly, and she turns back with a pivot to look in the car. Our eyes meet for a moment and she smiles, recognizing me. "Later, kids," she says happily before she turns away. My heart is thundering like a tribal drum.

Everyone's chattering so much in line that they don't seem to notice until we are almost back to the studio that I'm holding two drinks.

"Are you double fisting these days?" Nick asks, studying my two cups.

"No," I say, blushing. "This one's for someone else."

"Really?" Nick asks in an exaggerated voice. "And who, pray tell, would that be?"

"Ooooo," taunts Kevin.

"Does Nathan have a secret luva?" Andy taunts.

"I didn't think you wanted people to know about us, Andy," I respond. Since he is the only one without a coffee, he's the perfect foil. His purchase was a huge brownie that he usually washes down with his jumbo Coke left over from lunch.

"Ha! Gotcha," Kevin laughs and smirks at me. "So you're his secret luva taking the place of his life-size vinyl doll?"

Danielle's eyes grow wide as we step back into the elevator. "He has one of those vinyl life-size dolls? Yucko!"

"You said it," Nick agrees. "I wouldn't put my prize in one of those things."

"Hey, don't knock the doll, dude," Andy responds. "She's really good to me."

"We should all pitch in and get Nathan one," Kevin responds. "You two could double date!"

Thankfully Nick moves off topic and starts talking about the latest botched recording where the voice artist doing Bernie showed up coked out. While they're distracted, I slip away, grateful for an excuse to escape their torture. I head towards the executive offices, and when I see Brooke's, I notice that her assistant is away from her desk so I boldly step inside. I'm so nervous I'm trembling, but a flash of courage comes over me, and I go with it.

Her office is large, with a sitting area including a large couch. *Maybe one day I'll sit there next to her,* I happily imagine. The couch faces huge windows that look over the Forest Lawn Mortuary and part of the

Warner Bros. back lot. As I step closer to the window to check out the view, I notice something different about her office compared to the other executive offices I've seen. Instead of large framed posters on the walls of Sketch Republic's productions, she has an eclectic gathering of art in styles that look familiar to me. As I step closer, I realize that they are original works from some of our staff artists. *How cool.* I wish she had one of mine up, too. I also notice a print I've never seen before from one of my favorite animated movies from another studio. My girl must have a bit of rebel in her, I suspect, grinning. No idiotic Bernie the Beaver posters in here.

It brings me back to the beginning of my infatuation with Brooke. About two years ago, we were at our monthly company meeting in the building's auditorium/screening theater, and Brooke got up to talk about projects in development to our group of over four hundred employees. It was immediately apparent how smart and clever she was, but it was the warmth in her voice as she talked about the artists and new characters that impressed me so much. I'd never met an executive who seemed to be an actual fan of the work we do. It's not unusual to have young executives in animation, but Brooke was like fresh air blowing through the place. From that moment on, I paid attention to everything I heard and observed about her.

My growing impression was that she was the coolest girl ever...not just at Sketch Republic, or in Los Angeles, but the coolest girl in the entire world. As a result, my infatuation went from a wispy shadow on an overcast day to a sharp electrical current surging through me. I did a Google search and Facebooked her. I sat enraptured when she spoke at the monthly meeting. I even searched for satellite pictures of her house, hoping to see her stretched out on the chaise lounge in her back yard as we voyeuristically soared over her hillside condo.

Snapping out of my revelry, it suddenly occurs to me that Brooke could walk back in here any moment and see me stalking. Anxious to complete my task, I take out a black Sharpie from my pocket and write her name on the cup. It looks so ordinary, so I draw a little caricature of her face, which essentially is my B-Girl character. Right as I am about to set it on her desk I hear the rustle of papers.

"Well, hello, Nathan," she says happily. "What's up?"

"I brought you your coffee," I respond, trying not to blush. "I mean, I know you wanted to come with us but you had a meeting, so I thought I'd get it for you."

"That's the sweetest thing ever," she says. "Thank you. So that *was* you in the back of the elevator. I almost didn't recognize you without your bow tie and pocket protector." She grins, and I shyly smile back.

"Yeah, that was me."

"I just stepped out of the meeting to get my projections." She reaches over and pulls a folder off her desk. I'm mesmerized by her every movement, and the sound of her silver bracelets clinking together is music to my ears.

She's a bit taller today. The boots she's wearing under her slacks must have higher heels as she almost comes up to my chin now. My vision drifts to her delicate neck where a fine chain weaves along her pale skin before falling into the wide neckline of her floaty top. I can't help but notice that when she bends forward to reach a second folder placed further away on her desk, her shirt falls away from her body. It's just long enough for me to get a glimpse of her bra and the top part of her beautiful breasts. I blink nervously.

Folders retrieved, she straightens then lifts up the coffee to take a sip. As she squeezes the cup some foam oozes out onto the lid. In slow motion I watch her tongue slide out between her rosebud lips and lick the foam off the lid with a flourish.

"Mmmm," she sighs.

Oh, her pink, wet, perfect tongue! Between the foam lick and seeing her breasts, I am undone. My blood starts pooling where I don't want it to, and of course, the beast comes to life.

I casually try to hold my coffee cup low like a paper shield covering what's happening in my jeans. Thank God my coffee's a Venti.

She looks up at me, smiling, and raises her drink. "If Arnauld saw you got me this, he would insist that you're flirting with me, but I think you're just a really nice guy. Which is it?"

Turning beet red, I sway a bit before I drop my Sharpie and scurry around to try to find it on the floor. By the time I straighten up, she seems to have decided not to press me for an answer.

"Well, whatever the reason, thanks so much." She reaches over and grasps my arm for a moment. "I think you're cool. I've got to get back to the meeting, but let's talk again, okay?"

"Sure." I smile big enough to show my teeth and her eyes twinkle knowingly. I grin all the way back to my cube.

Of course when I get there I discover a surprise taped to the front of my computer. It's a caricature of me looking particularly geeky with an arrow coming out of my butt cheek. The fast rough sketch has my eyes rolling like I've lost my mind. A flying cherub with Andy's ugly face is holding a bow with one hand and fist pumping victoriously with the other. There are hearts floating around my head. Scrawled at the top are the words, *Nathan's in Love.*

I look around to see if I can figure out who's in on the joke. Did someone see me take the coffee to Brooke? I think it's Kevin's work, but I can't be sure. All that surrounds me is radio silence. *Damn crazy animators*, I silently curse knowing I can't say much really since I'm one of the group and have done many such drawings of them.

I carefully peel off the sketch and place it in my lower drawer where all the good stuff goes. This one, as infuriating as it is, is a keeper. After all, satire and caricatures work so well because of the truth behind them.

• • •

The next day's coffee run is uneventful, and this time no one questions the second cup. When I get to Brooke's office, her assistant eyes me suspiciously, but I explain that I'm just dropping off her coffee. When I step into the doorway, Brooke looks up and smiles.

"For me again?"

"Sure, it's no big deal…really," I assure her, trying to play it cool. Suddenly it occurs to me…*what if I'm bothering her?*

"You really don't have to do this."

"You don't want it?" I ask, trying not to look crestfallen.

"Oh, it's not that; I just don't want to take advantage of your kindness," she says with a wink and a sexy smile.

Is she flirting with me?

My stomach flip-flops as I try to think how to respond. Then I remember a line I heard once.

"Okay, I'll make an agreement. I'll only do it when I want to."

Hey, that sounded smooth. I smile as I shift nervously from foot to foot, watching for her reaction.

She smiles at me then lifts the cup to study today's drawing of her. This time I've sketched her on the cup with a "B" on her chest like Superman's "S" and a cape flapping behind her.

"How did you know I was a superhero?" she asks teasingly. "That's top secret information."

"Well, I'm one too, so of course I sensed it with my super powers."

"Yes, of course," she agrees, playing along. "How's the show coming along?"

"Oh fine. We got stuck with extra footage this week but it's do-able. At least I like this script…it's got good timing and some really funny stuff."

"That's great," she responds happily.

Wow, this is like a real conversation.

Then there's an awkward moment of silence as my mind races with what to say next. "By the way," I stammer, pointing at the print above her desk. "I love your *Iron Giant* artwork. It's a great design with the cold-war propaganda look. I am a huge fan of that film and Brad Bird, the director."

"Oh, me, too," she agrees. "You know I worked with him on *The Incredibles* when I first got started in the business."

We easily fall into a conversation about Brad and his brilliance. I'm doing great until I realize that I'm doing great and that makes me clam up again. She senses I'm struggling, but she seems confused as to why I'm trying so hard.

I look down at my shoes as I desperately try to figure out what to say next. Defeated, I finally give up.

"Well, I better get back to work. "

"Okay, thanks again, Nathan."

• • •

That night, after my dinner of nachos and carrot sticks, I make a list of things to talk to Brooke about so I'm better prepared for our next meeting:

1. Are you from L.A.?
2. Do you like living in L.A.? This can lead into the loaded question:
3. Do you have a roommate? If she's vague I can ask more directly:
4. Is Arnauld your roommate? *Scratch that. You can't ask her that... Besides, these questions are forgettable. You want her to remember you.*

I start again.

1. Do you have any tattoos?
2. Do you like Halloween?
3. What cartoon character are you most like?
4. Does Arnauld remind you of Homer Simpson? *Scratch that...I don't want to come off like an asshole.*
5. Do clowns frighten you?
6. What's your favorite ride at Disneyland?
7. Do you like nachos?

This leads to me imaging Brooke eating nachos with me, and I become too distracted to finish the list. Just the idea of the melted cheese on her fingers and watching the salsa trail over her lips gets me so worked up that I have to take my shower earlier than usual.

The next afternoon I do a more elaborate drawing of Brooke on her Starbucks cup. She's charming as usual and there's a cute little gremlin character from the new show she developed perched on her shoulder.

I dress a little nicer today, wearing my newer jeans and the green button-down shirt that my Mom says matches my eyes. I even cleaned the dust off my Chucks before I left the house, all with the hope of impressing Brooke.

This time her assistant rolls her eyes as I approach, but she doesn't stop me from going right into Brooke's office.

"Special delivery!" I say cheerfully since she's looking tense.

Brooke glances up. "Oh, hey, thanks so much for the coffee. I can really use it. It's been a crazy day, and I'm worn out. Please, at least let me pay for it."

"No" I insist, feigning offense at the suggestion. "I've been taking a class on chivalry, so this is coursework. You're helping me out actually."

"Really? And where does one take such a course?"

"Chivalry University. It's up in the attic of this building. They do it for the artists because we are typically so bad at this stuff." I'm impressed with the crap I can make up on the fly like this.

"Really? What other classes are you taking up there?"

"Conversation skills," I offer, hoping she will never know exactly how much I could use such a class. "Here, can I practice with you? I'm trying to learn to talk to someone besides animators."

"Sure, I've got a minute. I'm all yours," she says encouragingly.

I think for a moment about how she talks to Nick, and I realize that she's being gentle with me...as if I needed another reason to love her. My mind reels over the previous night's list, but I'm flustered so I say the first thing that pops into my head.

"What's your favorite ride at Disneyland?"

"Okay, that's a little random, but let me see...I'd have to say Haunted Mansion. What's yours?"

"Mr. Toad's Wild Ride," I reply without a pause. "The imagery and color is trippy...that ride always freaks me out. In a good way...I mean."

"Well, that's an unusual choice."

"Yeah, I guess I'm not your typical kinda guy."

She smiles and tips her head, waiting to see if I'll ask anything else.

The next question slips out of my mouth before I can stop it. "So, is Arnauld really your boyfriend?"

She looks slightly amused. "Well, have you been listening to the rumor mill or was that a question this University gave you as part of their coursework?"

"Maybe a little of both, why?"

"Just curious. Yes, Arnauld and I are involved. I must warn you: typically you would wait until we are closer friends before you ask those kinds of personal questions."

"Okay, that's good to know," I stammer, trying to recover from my faux pas. *Damn, and I was doing so well.* I mentally flog myself.

She waits, sensing my anxiety and kindly tries to help me recover by teasing me to get the conversation going again. "So, since we are all over the place with the questions, do you also want to know what I had for breakfast, or the name of my childhood pet?"

"My technique's that bad, huh?" I smile, embarrassed. All I can hope for at this point is that she thinks my goofiness is charming.

"Well, let's just say you could use some tutoring in that class."

I shrug my shoulders and nod. "Thanks for letting me practice on you."

She leans in closer to me and gently squeezes my arm. "You know, you shouldn't be nervous to talk to me. I'm not going to bite you. I'm just a girl—an ordinary girl who happens to love cartoons."

Does she have any idea what those words do to me? *There's nothing ordinary about you, Brooke.*

She smiles at me as she reaches for her pad and the coffee. "It's been fun chatting, but I've got a pitch to go hear. Thanks again for the coffee."

"Sure, see you later," I manage to say evenly before wandering out of her office. I start to panic on the way back to production so I stop in the bathroom to try to gather myself.

Damn, why did I ask about Arnauld? What the hell is wrong with me? Why did I have to act like such a loser?

As I splash water on my face and take several deep breaths, something comes over me. I arch over the sink, and when I finally rise up I catch my reflection. Underneath the dripping water and pale complexion, there is a look of fierce determination. It's all clear to me in that moment. Screw Arnauld, and everyone at Sketch Republic who doubts me.

I will win Brooke Tobin's heart, if it's the last thing I do.

Animate Me / Chapter Three / Buttering Her Up

"Ah, my little darling, it is love at first sight, is it not, no?" – *Pepe le Pew*[ii]

It's past ten p.m. when I erase the stray lines from my finished drawing and hold it up for closer inspection. *This is the best cover yet,* I think proudly as I date the bottom. Even though I've been self-publishing my own comic book on the side for over a year, each new issue of *The Adventures of B-Girl in Wildsville* feels like my first.

There are times I have almost given up on the project. The time and money I've spent are ridiculous. I keep doing it because these are *my* characters created with *my* vision, and I don't have to compromise a thing for anyone. My co-workers and friends at Sketch Republic know about it, and many buy and read them. They may not say it, but I think they admire that I have the focus and energy to do this after working so hard at the studio.

My inspiration for this issue's cover was the movie *Doctor Strangelove,* so B-Girl is straddling a large rocket about to shoot into space. Yeah, it's very *ride 'em cowgirl,* but she looks really hot which is how I like to see her…and incidentally won't hurt sales either. My friend Billie, who works at my favorite comic book store, says that girls like sexy heroines too. She keeps track and says my books sell almost equally to girls as guys. I love that.

Before turning off the lights in my home studio, I open my online calendar to capture today's most noteworthy events. I write one entry: *Took B coffee and discussed chivalry school.* On Saturday there was only one entry too: *Talked to Brooke at Jimmy's Geek World.* Monday, Tuesday, Wednesday…Brooke was the only thing that mattered. The best part of all is that she's even more wonderful than I had imagined during all this time I've admired her from afar. She's kind and approachable, creative and fun, a cartoon expert…hell, she's my dream girl…and to top it off, she's beautiful and sexy too.

I'm getting worked up just thinking about her. Within less than a week she has become the brightest star in my universe. It already feels like I'm orbiting around her.

Brushing my teeth, Brooke's favorite pearly whites, I prepare to slide into bed, my iPod fully loaded with my latest self-improvement download from the master, Dr. Wayne Dyer. I adjust my ear buds as I turn on the recording from my motivational guru. Wayne's encouraging words always help me focus on the bigger picture. What do I dream of? What do I really want?

I've got an extremely vivid imagination. So as I lie in bed, I'm completely living in the scenes I'm creating in my head, and Brooke quickly becomes the star of tonight's show.

Thoughts are things my friends. Never underestimate the power of your mind. The first step in achieving your life's goals is to visualize yourself already doing the things you dream of.

Okay then, I'm *visualizing* doing the things I dream of with Brooke and a lot of those things aren't rated PG. What's key is that in every scenario she gazes at me with adoration, as if she cares about me the way I care about her.

As Wayne chants away in my ears, I have to wonder if I'm weird for wanting her to not just want to be with me physically, but to love me too? As unlikely as this idea is, I'm not going to stop wanting it all… every part of Brooke, her heart most of all.

When I roll over to turn on my alarm, I decide that I'm going to continue to listen to Wayne and apply his positive thinking techniques while picturing Brooke in my arms. I fall asleep imagining that I'm spooning her instead of the king-size pillow my arms are wrapped around.

• • •

I'm about ten Bucky drawings into my day when Dani slips into my cube. "Have you seen this?" she says. "They've asked me to color it. Kevin is planning to make it a storybook. He's already done a dozen drawings."

"On the company's time, I bet." I sigh and I reach out for the drawing.

"No doubt," she agrees.

It's a straightforward view of the couch in Andy's apartment. I know because I recognize the Darth Vader poster hanging crooked on the wall. In the drawing Andy and I are sitting with our two life-size vinyl girlfriends. He is lovingly brushing the hair of his babe, and I've got my hand firmly planted on the large breast of my plastic vixen. Judging from the 'O' shape of her open mouth, she's rather pleased. My eyes are bugging out behind my glasses, and my cheeks are red.

I make a face, but frankly I was expecting to see a drawing of this the moment Kevin suggested it. It's just too juicy of an image not to do a caricature.

"Please tell me this is the only one that includes me," I urge Danielle, or Dani as she prefers to be called.

"Yeah, your solo appearance," she confirms. "As for Andy...well, let's just say that he will never live down letting it slip that he had to send Brandy back to the factory for some 'tightening.' I mean, for fuck's sake, I almost lost my lunch."

I shake my head solemnly, "Yeah, not one of his brighter moments."

"Hey, for real — do you have one of these at home too?"

Thankfully Dani has always felt like one of the guys to me, otherwise I would have passed out in embarrassment. "No! No matter how desperate I ever get I cannot imagine doing it with a doll."

"Okay, I overheard one of the assistants mention that when she dropped something off in your cube she saw Google open with the words *vinyl dolls* in the search box."

"That's because I collect the little Japanese vinyl cartoon dolls…they're collectible, like the ones you can get at Comic Con."

"Oh, I love those!"

"Hey, what the hell was this assistant doing reading my computer screen anyway?"

"Probably scoping you out. The assistants have a pool going about whether you're gay or not since you haven't hit on a single one of them."

"Are you trying to kill my afternoon or what? They remind me of the mean girls who bullied me in high school. You know, I was in a good mood until you brought all the rainbows and sunshine into my cube."

"Sorry, I just like to know what people say about me, and thought you may feel the same. Just disregard and delete, and we'll move on." She turned to leave.

"Hey Dani," I call out when she's a few steps away.

She turns back and looks at me.

"Can I get a good copy of that after you've colored it? I'm going to frame it up for my Mom for Christmas."

She knows I'm teasing her but she smiles anyhow, "Sure thing, Nathan!" And she all but skips down the aisle.

As unflattering as that drawing is, it's still a keeper.

At four-fifteen I'm half-way into Brooke's office when Brooke's assistant, Morgan's, shrill voice pierces my calmness.

"She's not here, Evans."

Evans? What have I done to her?

I try to push down my embarrassment. "Okay thanks, Morgan, do you know when she'll get back?" I ask politely, looking down.

"Not for the rest of the day. She, Arnauld, and the other execs had a meeting with the management team that came in from New York."

My expression falls as I stand with the drink and wonder what to do next. I need to see her and get my Brooke fix, and it hadn't occurred to me that she wouldn't be here.

"I'm onto you, you know," Morgan brags in her irritating voice.

"On to me?"

"These afternoon coffee visits, you're buttering her up for a pitch. Do you think she's stupid? I'm sure she knows what you're up to and it won't work."

"But I'm not doing that." My stomach starts churning realizing that if Morgan thinks that, there's a chance that Brooke does too.

"Sure, sure," she taunts. "Okay then, if you're not working her up for your pitch, then what are you doing?"

"We're becoming friends," I say quietly, realizing that I sound like I'm in the play yard of elementary school.

"Friends? You do realize that her boyfriend is the president of our company, Evans?"

I nod, and turn to leave before I lose it with the demon spawn. Right as I start to step away, I manage to have a flash of brilliance, and I turn back towards her.

"Hey Morgan, would you like this drink? It'd make me happy if you'd enjoy it."

Her expression immediately softens. "Yeah, I'd like it, thanks. I can't afford this stuff very often on *my* salary."

"It's a caramel macchiato. Is that okay?"

"Mochas are my favorite, but this sounds good. Thanks."

"You're welcome. Thanks for your help."

She smiles, and I get a sudden strong sense that giving her that drink will pay off for me big time somewhere down the line.

• • •

On Friday the building feels more relaxed with all the executives still off site at meetings with the corporate bigwigs. There are open boxes of doughnuts everywhere and impromptu games of table football, and waste bin basketball. I even witness the *pin the tail on Arnauld* game that comes down from the break room wall almost as quickly as it went up. Around two-thirty, word spreads like wild fire that management has returned so everyone gets back to work.

Around an hour later, Dani wanders into my cube and slides the color copy of the finished double-date caricature onto my desk. She's put some serious time into it, certainly more than I would've expected.

"Hey, thanks," I enthuse. "It's a work of art…a masterpiece."

"Oh, yeah." She rolls her eyes and folds her arms before hitching herself up on my desk. I watch her swing her legs back and forth a few times as I wait for her to spill whatever is on her mind.

She lifts her hand to her mouth and bites her thumbnail nervously. "Hey, does Nick ever still talk about me?"

"You mean since you guys broke up?" I ask.

"Yeah." She watches me carefully to see if I'm going to dodge the question.

"Well, remember that day you didn't show up and didn't call anyone?"

"Yeah, the hangover from hell the day after Zara's bridal shower. We got a little wild with the guys at the strip club."

"Spare me the details. Just believe me that he was really worried about you. He made me call you over and over until you answered your phone."

"And all this time I thought you had the hots for me."

"You did?"

"Well, no, not actually, but I have noticed that I'm the only girl around here you talk to."

I scratch my elbow, and consider her words. "That must be 'cause you've always been one of the guys."

"You are so friggin' charming, really." She watches me lift a heavy pile of reference books off my desk to get them out of the way so I can get back to work. "Hey, do you work out a lot? You're pretty built for a such a tall, lean guy."

I blush, but am secretly pleased to have someone finally notice all my efforts. Between running on my treadmill, playing tennis and lifting weights, like Curtis showed me, I'm in the best shape ever.

"Yeah, I work out. Thanks for noticing."

Suddenly I realize that she's stopped listening and I look up to see her surprised expression. I then turn to see Brooke at the entrance to my cube. She looks out of place, and very uncomfortable. My heart thumps so loudly I fear she can hear it.

Oh wow, what's she doing in my cube?

"Hi Brooke," I say. "This is Danielle."

"Dani," she corrects me as she slides off my desk and waves to Brooke. "I need to get back to work anyway. Nice to meet you."

"You too," Brooke responds and then looks back at me. "I'm sorry I interrupted you, but I thought it was time to return the favor. I brought you a coffee."

I grin like an idiot. "Wow, thanks," I say, stunned and unsure what to do. I finally step forward and gingerly take the drink from her.

"Of course, I had to guess what you drink…"

"And?" I start to turn the cup to read what's been checked off.

"Venti Cappucino with extra foam." She watches for my reaction.

"Extra foam?" I laugh, before my mind goes to dark places. *Does she think I'm wimpy?*

"The foam is my favorite part. Isn't it yours?"

"Well, it is now." I smile. "Thanks, this is perfect." I lift the cup up and carefully take a swig, watching her the entire time.

"So I talked to Nick about you."

My mind starts reeling. *Good God, no.* I can only imagine what embarrassing stuff he could say about me. "Really? What about?"

"Actually, he said you're the best animator here."

"Really?" I shake my head in disbelief. I know Nick likes my work, I overheard him once discussing me with Joel, but this is too much.

"As a matter of fact he said you're one of the best he's ever seen, and that you and Joel make a great team. You are the Rod Scribner to his Bob Clampett."

"You know Rod Scribner?" I ask, not masking the awe in my voice. "He's my favorite Looney Tunes animator from the golden age, when they really knew how to make cartoons."

"Sure, he was a brilliant animator who worked with Bob. They made magic together."

I'm one crazy guy, when talking about the greats of animation excites me like this. My emotion overcomes me and I bite my bottom lip to stop from saying anything stupid.

Her profound compliments have forced me to lose all logic and reason. For a moment I flash to an image of me falling to my knees and begging. *Marry me, Brooke. We can honeymoon at Comic Con, and have our very own* Three Little Bops.

"I warned you that I'm a geek. I'm a huge cartoon buff."

She can't be real…she's just too good to be believed.

I struggle to gather my thoughts.

"Well Scribner and Clampett are two of my heroes. I know Joel fancies us as a great cartoon duo: the human versions of Ren and Stimpy, Fred and Barney, or Beavis and Butthead. I swear, if we're a duo we're Pinky and the Brain, and I'm definitely the Brain, whether he accepts that or not."

Brooke laughs and looks over, noticing the caricature of Andy and me on the couch that Dani's left on my desk. Before I pull it off the table to hide it she asks, "Is that your girlfriend on the couch with you?"

"No!" I say abruptly. "That's just a stupid joke the guys were playing on me and Andy."

"That's one elaborate joke," she comments suspiciously as she steps back. "Well, I've got to get going. I just wanted to bring you your coffee."

I fear she's mad at me, so it takes all my courage to look her in the eye and smile. "Thanks again. That's so cool you got *me* coffee."

"You're welcome, Brain," she replies smiling, as she heads down the hallway.

Of course as the afternoon wears on, I get more and more agitated remembering the awkward moment of Brooke coming all the way to my cube with coffee only to find another girl practically lying across my desk. Then to top if off, she sees an elaborate drawing of me grabbing some whorish looking chick's tit. *Damn it all.* She must think I'm a complete and utter asshole.

By five forty-five I face the reality that I'll go completely mad if I don't talk to her again. I slowly stalk my way over to the executive offices, and happily discover that Morgan appears to be gone for the weekend. I peek into Brooke's office to see her typing away on her laptop. I knock gently on her open door to get her attention.

She looks over at me. "Hey, Nathan. What's up?" She says. I can hear the exhaustion in her voice.

"Can I come in? I want to clarify something."

"Sure," she replies pointing to the couch. "Have a seat; I'll just be a sec."

I slowly approach the couch and realize that I had pictured sitting with Brooke on this couch the first time I was in her office. Well, this at least is a step in the right direction.

I clear my throat as she appears to finish up an email.

"What's on your mind?"

"Someone asked me if I have been bringing you coffee to butter you up for a pitch. I just wanted to let you know that I would never do that. That's not why I've been talking to you, and you know…bringing you coffee."

A gentle smile transforms her tense expression. "Okay, then why have you been bringing me coffee and talking to me?"

I'm dumbstruck for a moment. What do I say without sounding like an idiot? "Well, because you're the kind of girl…I mean, when you give your talks at the company meetings I always…" I stop before I dig a deeper hole.

"Yes?"

I look down before blurting out, "You're just really nice and interesting. And I never thought you'd talk to someone like me…I mean, you're an executive, and I'm just an animator. You're so cool to talk to." I twist my hands nervously in my lap.

You're batting a thousand here, bucko. I inwardly roll my eyes.

"Just an animator? Please. Give yourself some credit. You guys are what really matters around here."

I can't tell if she is just trying to make me feel better, or if she means it. She has a magical way of always making me feel important—like her equal, even though I'm not.

"Well, it wasn't the most impressive meeting seeing me at Jimmy's Geek World in my bow tie and all." Something suddenly occurs to me that I had completely forgotten. "Hey, did your USB cord work?"

Her cheeks flush as she makes the cutest face at me. "Can you believe I haven't even checked yet? The rest of my weekend and this week have been crazy busy."

"Okay," I reply a little disappointed that the object of our union had been pushed aside. "Tomorrow's my last day covering for Bill there, so if you have time to check it out and there's a problem, you know where I'll be."

Her phone rings, and although she doesn't answer it, it reminds me that I should let her get back to work.

"That's good to know. Thanks."

I stand up to leave and push my floppy hair off my glasses. "Can I ask you something?"

"Sure."

"I'm curious…how old are you?"

She puts her hands on her hips and tilts her head. "I'm going to have to talk to the dean of the Chivalry University—they obviously don't know what they're doing. Hasn't anyone ever told you not to ask a woman her age?"

My head drops, forcing me to push my glasses back up my nose. I start backing out of her office with my hands up.

"Sorry, sorry…just forget I asked." I'm so embarrassed…*why am I such an idiot?* I'm going to have a stiff drink tonight and try to get over this.

"Hey, chill out…I was joking. I'm thirty. Why?"

I stop in her doorway, and try to catch up with the change in mood. *She was just teasing me.* I think for a second.

"You just seem so young to be so successful." *Good recovery, dude.*

"I guess so," she agrees. "How old are you?"

I pause for a moment before I fess up. Will she have an issue with being older than me? "Twenty-six."

"You're so young! So I could say the same. Look how much you've accomplished."

Although I don't believe I'm a success yet, I take the compliment. "Thanks." I turn once again to leave. "So if I don't see you tomorrow… then Monday?"

"Sure, it's your turn for the coffee. Just saying…" She grins.

I nod and push my hands in my jeans. "See ya." I give her my best tooth-flashing smile and head back to my cube. For all the twists and turns of that roller coaster ride, I step into the elevator feeling victorious.

Brooke brought *me* coffee! Progress has been made.

Animate Me / Chapter Four / Goodbye Geek World

"When you get a little older, you'll see how easy it is to become lured by the female of the species." ~Batman to Robin[iii]

I stand in front of the mirror, pushing my hair around hoping it ends up in some acceptable shape. I have never been able to control the unruly mess, and I usually don't even try, but today is different. Today belongs to Brooke, and I've got to look my best.

It's making me nervous how hopeful I am that she will come by Geek World since it sets me up for a tremendous let down if she doesn't show up. However, logic is escaping me, and my emotions have broken loose and are bouncing off the walls.

Looking in the mirror one final time to check my teeth, I notice my uniform's faux bow tie is crooked. I study my reflection trying to imagine what Brooke would see when she looks at me, and with one brisk movement, I grasp the bottom of my shirt and pull upwards, yanking it over my head. I'll tell Jimmy that I spilled coffee all over it or something, but I can't wear that shirt today. I've made tangible progress with Brooke, and I don't want her to be reminded of me as that completely awkward geek from a mere week ago.

I spend the morning helping customers while Jimmy works in the stockroom. At lunch he brings me back a burrito from Taco Bell to eat at the cash desk since I don't want to risk missing Brooke. I've just wiped the final remnants of refried beans off my fingers when the door opens, and everything that is tilted in my world suddenly straightens.

Oh good God, what is she wearing? She has this black stretchy get-up on that makes her look like a cross between Catwoman and one of those Zumba dancers on TV. *Does she have any idea what she's doing to me?* She strides right up to the cash register and pushes her sunglasses onto the top of her head.

"Hey, Nathan! I'm so glad you're here. How's it going?"

"Hi, I wasn't sure if I'd see you today." I smile happily.

"Well, guess what?" She pulls the Geek World bag out of her oversized purse.

"The thingy didn't work?" I ask.

"Nope, I guess my computer is gay after all. I think I need the male-to-male connection. It must be all that gay porn I watch on my computer."

"You watch gay porn?" I question, feeling aroused at the idea of Brooke watching porn—even if it's gay porn.

"Sure, don't you?" she teases.

"No," I stutter. "I'm not gay."

"Yeah, I know. I was kidding, and I've only seen it a few times. Don't judge me because I love men and their beautiful naked bodies. With that stuff, you get double the fun."

"If you say so. I mean, there's nothing wrong with porn. I've been known to enjoy it once in a while." I feel the flush burn up my neck and across my cheeks, but I try to maintain my cool. If Brooke can talk so casually about something so private with me, I want to be able to do the same.

She smiles. "See, that just means you're a healthy young man."

I bristle on the word *young*. Does she really see me as someone too young to ever be in her league? She's only four years older than me, but I have to admit she must have a lot more experience.

She looks down and starts to open her shopping bag, so I step out from the counter and head over to the cables and accessories section with her. "So male to male?" I ask.

"Yup, two outties. No innies."

I pull the correct cord off the spindle rack before I turn back towards her. "That's some outfit, if you don't mind me saying so."

"Oh, this? I just came from the gym. Arnauld says I'm getting fat, and I need to work out more." She turns and looks back at me over her shoulder. "Do you think my ass looks too big?"

"Too big?" I swallow nervously. My eyes move over the perfection that is her bottom. It may be ample, but it is a thing of beauty…round and robust.

Down boy. It would be so wrong to get aroused in Geek World. I try to refocus on what she's saying.

"Yes, that's what Arnauld said. He called me a fat-ass this morning."

"Ah…no," I stammer… "I think your bottom looks great…really great."

"See, this is why I should be dating someone like you…someone who appreciates my ample ass."

"You're pretty much perfect if you ask me," I confirm. "I can't imagine how he could possibly think anything less."

"Oh, you!" she sighs. "You're so sweet. As for Arnauld, I suppose this is what I get for dating a gym addict. He has such an incredible body, but it makes him expect everyone else to have one too."

I crumble inside. No, I don't want to hear about Arnauld's incredible body and what that does to Brooke. I wish he were a sloth with a beer belly and hair on his back. "Does he have hair on his back at least?" There I go with my verbal diarrhea. I need a filter for my big mouth.

"No…he gets it waxed. Please don't repeat that. He'd look like a monkey if he didn't."

"I don't have any hair on my back," I point out.

"Noted," she smiles. "You've got that smooth skin, don't you?" She asks as she innocently runs her fingers over my cheek.

I close my eyes for a second to try to capture the feeling of her caress in my mind. Then I snap back to the present, realizing that she just called me smooth.

"Well, smooth in a manly way," I proclaim in a faux macho voice.

"Well, then, your girl must be very lucky."

And once again I am tongue-tied. Do I tell her that I don't have a girlfriend? That I haven't since college? That will make me look like an even bigger loser. As the debate volleys in my mind, she looks down at her watch.

"Damn, I better get going. I'm meeting a friend for a late lunch, and I don't want to show up in yoga pants and a tank top."

I bite my tongue and follow her to the register. As I enter the exchange and wait for the receipt to print, an idea occurs to me. "Do you have someone helping you with your data transfer?"

"No," she admits. "If I did, it'd be done by now. My usual IT girl has been doing a job up north and hasn't had time for me."

"Well, I'm pretty good with that stuff, so if you need help, please call me."

"Really? That's so nice of you."

"I mean it." I pull out my wallet. "Here, let me give you my card again; my cell number's on it."

She puts her hand out to stop me. "You don't have to do that. I still have the card you gave me." She slides it out of her wallet and shows it to me.

And something about that, the fact that she had held onto my card and carried it with her all week, makes me unbelievably happy.

She grins widely and shoves the bag with the gay cord in her purse.

"Thanks. I guess I'll see you Monday."

"Okay, but promise me you'll call if you need help."

"Oh, I will." She turns to leave, and all I can think as I watch her walk away is *thank God for yoga pants.*

Soon after she leaves, Jimmy can see that I'm totally distracted, so he pushes me to take a break. Perched on the stool in the back room, I think about our conversation and the contrast of how much easier it was to talk to Brooke since even a week ago. I can't help but wonder if she likes me, even if just the littlest bit. A few times I've noticed her looking at me like she's interested.

Thanks to the newest *Mortal Kombat* release, the afternoon is busy so the time flies by. It's almost time to leave when my cell phone goes off.

"Nathhhhaaaaannnnnn!"

"Brooke, is that you?" I ask concerned.

"I'm ready to throw this piece of junk out the window! No matter what I try, nothing works. I've just spent two friggin hours, and I've gotten nowhere."

My hand tightens over the phone. "I'm sorry, you should've called me earlier. Can I come over and fix it for you?"

"You really don't mind?"

Oh, let me help you, Brooke…please let me help you.

"Not at all. I'm done here in thirty minutes, and then I can come straight over if you want."

"That'd be so great. I'll run over to Whole Foods and get some stuff from their deli in case you want to stay and eat."

I smile and silently fist pump the air, yet try to sound laid back. "Yeah, that'd be cool."

By the time she's done giving me her address and instructions how to get there, I'm completely amped. It's only day seven, and I get to see where she lives. If this isn't serious progress, I don't know what is.

When I get in my car though, I start to panic. I do the only thing I can think of and call my brother, Curtis.

"Hey, Bro, what's up?" He sounds like he just woke up. He's always following the stock market and doing weird deals at all hours, so his schedule is impossible to figure out.

"I've met someone. She's the one."

"The one? That's awesome, dude! Tell all."

"Her name is Brooke, and she's perfect…smart, beautiful, sweet, and so sexy. And you won't believe this; she loves cartoons, I mean really loves them."

"No way. She sounds like your dream girl," he laughs.

"She is. There's just one issue." I can hear the big lug breathing in the phone as he waits for my revelation. "She doesn't know she's the one."

"Doesn't know? Do you mean she isn't ready for a commitment, ready to settle down yet?"

"No. Actually she has a boyfriend. She doesn't like me that way…yet. We're just becoming friends."

His heavy breathing stops for a moment, and I can hear the concern in his silence. "Dude, that sounds a little fantasy land. I mean if she has a boyfriend, you shouldn't go engagement ring shopping yet."

"I know." I sigh. "I can just feel that it's going to happen. I'm headed to her place right now to fix her computer."

"That's not exactly a date, dude. You need to take a reality pill."

My spirit is sagging, but I'm not giving up. "Before I get there, you just need to tell me. How can I win her over?"

There's a long pause, and I can tell he's thinking what to say.

"You need to be super chill. Don't let her think you like her—just that you want to be friends. Be a good friend to her, but don't pressure her. That's the best thing you can do in this situation."

"You think that will work?" I ask anxiously.

"Well, how are things with her boyfriend?"

"I can't tell, really. They've been together for a while, but they seem to live separate lives."

"Well, you can try to give her whatever he doesn't."

That idea rings true in my mind. My brother's smart, and he has always seemed to understand the female species. He's had a good track record with some really cool women.

"Okay I'll try that. Hey, thanks."

"Sure, I'll see you at the house tomorrow. Meanwhile good luck with *the one.*"

It's only a few miles from quiet Burbank to Brooke's condo in the Hollywood Hills, but it feels like another world. With Brooke's perfect instructions, I wind my way up the narrow roads and park my Mini-Cooper with the tires turned all the way towards the curb. All I need is for the parking brake to give out and my car to slide down the hill. After I shut the car off, I take a minute to calm myself, taking deep breaths as I rest my hands on my knees.

Each of the four units appears to have their own entrance, and when I ring the bell just outside of Brooke's wrought iron gate, she buzzes me in. Her front patio is paved in terra cotta tiles. Her wooden door, like the rest of the exterior finishes, is Mediterranean in style. There's a wild menagerie of potted plants and a little sitting area. It looks cozy and peaceful, and I wonder if Brooke spends much time out here.

When she pulls open the door, she's backlit from the sun pouring in through her huge picture windows. Her hair is down now, loose around her face, and instead of the yoga pants, she has on a skirt in a vintage-looking fabric. She steps forward and pulls me into a big hug. I try to hug her back without seeming too stiff and awkward, and her warmth and sweet scent surrounds me.

"Thanks for coming. I was about to pull my hair out."

"Don't pull your hair out," I exclaim as we pull apart. "You've got beautiful hair. Besides, I'm more than happy to help."

"Do you want something to drink first?"

"Some water would be great." I follow her into her kitchen where she pulls a glass that looks hand-blown out of the cupboard. While she pours the water, I step over to her kitchen desk, noticing the collage of postcards and artwork on the bulletin board. I'm also intrigued by a collection of antique lady head vases lining the back edge of the desk, the holes in their wide brim hats holding miscellaneous markers, pencils and scissors. They have actual little strings of pearls around their necks and dangling from their little ceramic ears.

"Those are cool," I comment. "Where'd you get them?"

"I used to go to the Rose Bowl swap meet, but now mainly from Ebay. Arnauld doesn't like flea markets. Do you collect stuff?"

"Yeah, I'm a collector," I confirm. *If she only knew.* My figurines and vinyl doll collections have taken over my living room. "Ebay is addictive, but it certainly takes the adventure out of the hunt."

"I couldn't agree more," she says intently. "We should go flea market shopping one day. It'd be fun to go with another collector."

"That'd be great," I agree, remembering Curtis' advice. I look back to the bulletin board and notice a photograph of her and Arnauld, and something occurs to me. I suddenly straighten up. "Is Arnauld here?"

"No, he went with his buddies to Vegas this weekend. Regardless, he doesn't live here. We have separate places."

"Oh, I see," I say calmly. Luckily she can't see my internal happy dance.

She leads me down a narrow hallway to her home office. The walls are painted a buttery yellow, and the room is bright and cheerful with a window looking over a portion of the canyon.

"So here are the little monsters that have been torturing me."

I move towards the laptops confidently. This is something I know, and I'm happy to be her tech savior. Hopefully it will make her understand that she can count on me.

I sit down at her desk and open the first laptop. "Okay, I'll need your password."

"Buttercup," she replies without hesitation.

"Like the flower?"

"No, like the Powerpuff Girl."

I laugh. "I would have taken you more for her sister, Blossom. Buttercup was kind of mean."

"You don't know my dark side yet. I can be quite nasty."

"Really?" It's hard for me to imagine. "You aren't mean at all; I just know it."

"No, not really," she admits. "But my Dad used to call me Buttercup, and I *can* have a smart mouth." She steps closer. "Hey, take off your glasses."

As soon as I do, she slides her hand up my forehead and pushes my long bangs back. "I knew it! You look like Professor Utonium! You're tall like him and have that sculpted face and sharp jaw line. I always had a thing for him…he was so loving with his girls."

"Watch out, your boyfriend Mojo Jojo may get jealous."

"Are you calling my boyfriend a monkey?"

"Well, you're the one that talked about his monkey's back."

"And he does want to take over the animation world," she admits.

"Besides calling me the Professor isn't so great—he was clueless after all," I say.

"Don't knock the Professor; he was brilliant in the lab," she admonishes me.

"Yeah but he was clueless when it came to the girls," I remind her, laughing.

Brooke smiles at me warmly, and I turn back to the computers and start my diagnostics.

Over the next hour while I check the systems, update her software, and transfer her data, Brooke sits on the daybed in the office and keeps me company. She tells me stories about growing up in West L.A. where her mom worked for a chiropractor and her dad owned an organic food co-op, years before organic food became a trend. She describes herself as bookish and self-conscious because she wasn't part of the "in" crowd at her middle and high schools. Other kids thought her obsession with cartoons and comics was weird, especially for a girl. She ignored the naysayers and took every kind of drawing and cartooning class until she finally had to accept that she didn't have the natural talent for it. It wasn't until she got a chance to intern one summer at Animation Magazine that she found her calling. She ended up earning a scholarship to the USC film school where she focused on the administrative and marketing side of the business. The contacts she made there served her well once she was out of school.

"You know, my first job was with Nickelodeon as an assistant in development, and that's where I first met Arnauld. He'd come in to pitch a joint production between our studios. The project never happened, but Arnauld and I did. Within six months, he got me hired for a higher level position at Sketch Republic."

"Management didn't mind that you were involved?"

"They didn't seem to," she admitted. "We're very professional. Sometimes it feels like more of a professional relationship really."

As hard as it is to hear about Arnauld, these are the little nuggets I'm gathering in my arsenal to win over Brooke.

Later when Brooke serves me a platter full of weird non-food, like barley salad and brown rice with lumpy tofu gravy, we take our plates outside to enjoy the view. From her balcony, you can see parts of Hollywood and downtown. We are just about to start when her cell phone rings and she sees it's from Arnauld.

"Do you mind if I take it? We've missed each other several times today."

"Sure," I agree as I watch her step a few feet back into the house. She's close enough that I can hear what she says.

"Hey, baby.

Yeah, that sounds like fun. Is Stuart behaving himself?

Yes, I went to the gym, and you'll be happy to know I took the class and did my full work out. Now I'm eating that crappy healthy stuff you like from Whole Foods.

No, not alone…I'm about to eat with my friend, Nathan, from the studio. He came over and helped me set up my new computer.

Yeah, okay, get going. I'll talk to you later. Don't lose too much at the tables.

Okay, me too. Bye."

She slips back into her chair and stabs a tofu nugget with her fork before wrapping her lips around it.

"Does he mind that I'm here?" I ask nervously. If Brooke were my girl, I'd go atomic to hear another guy was at her house having dinner with her.

"No, not at all. He knows you're just a friend, but even so—he isn't the jealous type. Besides we have an open relationship; we're both free to date other people."

"You do?" I ask horrified.

"Last month I hooked up with an old boyfriend I hadn't seen in years. We only went out a couple of times, but it was fun."

I don't know if I should be happy with this news or discouraged. She can date other people, but I'm just a friend. I push the nasty food around on my plate as I consider everything.

"You don't like it?" she asks, nodding towards my meal.

"No, not really. I'm not a health food kind of guy. Don't worry, I'll order a pizza when I get home." I grin at her.

"Oh, thank God!" she laughs as she pushes her plate away. "You're so fit looking that I figured you ate like Arnauld does. Well, to hell with this crap. Let's order a pizza! I even have some beer stashed in the back of the fridge."

"Now, you're talking." I didn't miss that she called me fit. Buying that damn treadmill now really seems like the best investment I ever made.

We dump our food in the trash and tease each other about what toppings to have on our pizza. I draw the line at artichokes…nasty little buggers. They look like alien food.

A couple of hours later, we're sprawled out on her couch, watching a compilation DVD of independent animated films from the Annecy Animation Festival, and we're getting a little tipsy from our third round of beer.

"Okay, that one didn't make any sense at all. Did you understand it?" she asks laughing.

"The story? Was there one? I was too distracted by the weird animation with the wobbly lines." I moan holding my head with my hands.

"Have you ever submitted a film to a festival?"

"No, but I've thought about it. There is a short I did during my first year at Sketch Republic that with a few edits and new titles could be a possibility."

"Do it!" she yells out.

"Okay!" I yell back, and we both break into a fit of laughter falling back against the couch. I feel so happy just hanging here with her that I'm giddy. I don't ever want to leave.

When she finally catches her breath she turns to me. "I hope your girlfriend appreciates you."

47

I'm so relaxed and content that I open my mouth before I've thought it through. "I don't have a girlfriend."

"But I thought..."

"Nope!" I announce assertively, shaking my head. "Who has time for a girlfriend? The only girlfriend I've got is the one I draw every night for my comic book."

"How did I get the idea you had a girlfriend?"

"I have no idea."

"But don't you like someone? You must have your eye on someone? You're amazing and there are a lot of cute girls at Sketch Republic. What about that in-betweener, Genna?"

"Oh, I like someone, but she doesn't know it." I take a swig of my beer, and my head spins with my daring proclamation.

"Oh, this is exciting! I know, I know who it is...it's that adorable Dani who was in your cube the other day, isn't it?" She's practically bouncing off the couch.

"Oh, yeah...Dani," I say sarcastically, but I must be too subtle since she continues along this misguided path.

"I bet she likes you too. What's stopping you? Have you taken her out?"

"We've gone out," I admit, omitting the fact that the only time Dani and I went out is with Nick and the gang. I begin to wonder why I'm digging this hole. I guess I don't want her to fully understand yet what a social freak I am.

"Well, did you kiss her? That gives a pretty clear message...hard to miss that, even if she's clueless."

My head falls forward as I begin to put all my attention on peeling the label off my beer bottle. My stomach is rolling. "No, I haven't kissed her. I'm the world's worst kisser, so that isn't even an option."

"What in the hell are you talking about...world's worst kisser?" she slurs. "That's impossible."

"How would you know?"

"I can just tell. You're creative, and creative guys are the best. Plus you've got those lips with that sexy mouth. Hell, I would kiss you just to get closer to your amazing teeth. It's just impossible." Her arms are waving dramatically.

"Well I love that you think I'd be great to kiss, but according to Rachel...."

"Rachel?"

"My girlfriend at CalArts...she hated kissing me—refused actually."

"Do you have bad breath or something?"

Before I can respond, she practically crawls into my lap and puts her nose up to my surprised, open mouth.

"Wow, your breath is sweet, not bad at all." She falls back to where she was sitting on the couch.

"Gee, thanks. No, my biggest problem is that I'm just stiff and awkward."

"Oh, please..." She jumps up and reaches out for my hand. "I know I'm tipsy but never mind that. Do you want me to help you?"

"Sure, how?"

"I'm going to help you get over this crazy idea. Come on, stand up."

I take her hand, and she pulls on me until I push myself up off the couch. I steady myself and smile to see her so serious, her fists perched authoritatively on her curvy hips.

"Okay," she instructs. "Pretend I'm Dani and we've just had a date." She starts pulling me forward.

Oh, good God, I moan inwardly. This is really getting out of hand. I need to stop it, but like a car crash that you know you should avoid looking at, it seems beyond my control.

"So Dani is walking you to her door to say goodnight. What do you say?"

"Um, I had a great time?"

"No, that's too generic. Make it about her. 'Dani, I hope you know how much I love spending time with you.'" She takes my hand, as we get closer to the door. My fingers tighten over hers.

"Dani, I hope you know how much I love spending time with you," I repeat, my heart thumping wildly with a mix of anticipation and fear.

"Can I see you again?" she asks in a low voice as we reach the door.

I swallow hard. "Can I see you again?" I whisper.

She pushes me against the door, and the look in her eyes undoes me. I forget that she is acting, demonstrating this scene for my benefit. All I can feel is this overwhelming passion I have for her. I'm already excited. *Can I, can I?*

"Can I kiss you?" she asks with those beautiful eyes searching mine.

"Yes," I whisper as she steps forward. I feel her hands rest on my chest first before they move up to my shoulders. A second passes, and then she's so close to me that I can feel the heat from her skin, her full breasts skimming my chest. *Oh, Brooke.*

What if, like every other time in my intimate history, I'm disappointing? What if she gets disgusted and gives up on me? I'm overwhelmed with fear, but I close my eyes and reach for her with my heart and soul. I say a silent prayer that this will be a moment where my life changes course, all my wrongs with girls will be right…this will be the kiss that'll change everything. Or will it?

Animate Me / Chapter Five / Closed for Business

"Any more at home like you?" ~Lois Lane "Uh no, not really." ~ Superman[iv]

The minute her perfect lips touch mine the room goes black, but not in a good way. I gasp and my body seizes into one rigid mess. I'm an awkward statue, a frozen failure.

Her tender hand wraps around my neck, and her lips soften and coax mine, but the ship has sailed. The weight of every horrible kiss from my past slams into me, and the little sign in the window sadly flips forward, *closed for business.*

She presses on one more time, a hint of desperation and refusal to accept failure. This only makes things worse, and I pull away from her and raise my hands to cover my face. *No, no, no.*

I must have actually said the words because I instantly hear her shift in voice and tenor. "It's okay, Nathan, it's okay. Please don't freak out."

I blindly reach out for the doorknob to make my escape. I twist and pull, but she sees what I'm doing and she pushes back.

"No," she insists.

"Please, please…just let me leave. I'm so embarrassed. Please…" I moan.

"No," she says with more conviction. "This is my fault. I pushed it, and I want to fix it."

I open my eyes wide, and frustration washes over me. "You can't fix me. I'm just messed up. Something's wrong with me, and I'm just not meant to be like this with anyone normal." My chest is heaving, and I can't look at her. My eyes are focused on the door leading into the hallway.

"Please," she begs, and I hear the tears in her voice before I finally look at her and see them trailing down her cheeks. I take off my glasses, and rub my eyes.

"Brooke, please don't cry." I feel even worse, if that's possible.

"Will you just sit with me for a minute please?" she asks, gesturing towards the couch.

I nod and follow her over, and as I sit back down she turns off the TV and puts her iPod in the dock. The Cure comes on in their dreamy atmospheric splendor. *Oh great, emo music*, I think shuddering. A minute later Brooke hands me a small glass with clear liquid.

"What's this?" I ask.

"A shot of vodka, drink it please. It'll help relax you."

I knock it back without a thought. She has me now, even if I'm worthless. I would probably do anything she asks. I look up and imagine I can see the wheels turning in her head. Like Geppetto from *Pinocchio*, she's trying to figure out how to fix her broken toy.

She crawls onto the couch and curls up next to me, taking my hand and gently rubbing it. Just when I figure she's given up, she speaks.

"Where is your favorite place to relax?"

Huh? *She's pitching out of left field.* I'm confused, but I still want to please her. I think for a moment.

"Well, probably my hammock in my backyard. I like to lie in that and think of story ideas while I sway in the breeze."

"That's good. Is it under a tree?"

"Yes, it's in the shade, so it stays cool."

"Good, okay." She scoots over even closer to me, practically sitting in my lap. *What the hell? Could this night get any stranger?*

She runs her fingers through my hair, and then starts rubbing my shoulders. "Close your eyes, Nathan. I want you to imagine that you are lying in your hammock, in the dappled light on a warm summer day."

Her voice is soothing and soft, much prettier than Wayne Dyer's. My head falls back on the cushions as her fingers move back up into my hair, and start massaging my scalp. No one has ever done this for me. It feels so good that I start to moan softly.

"Isn't it wonderful in your hammock?" she asks.

"Yes," I moan. *Keep rubbing Brooke.*

She works over me for a long time. I am vaguely aware of one Cure song shifting to another, and the burn of the vodka spreading through my veins. I'm so relaxed that I'm somewhere between sleep and the waking world.

When she senses how far gone I am, she starts up again. "Now I want you to imagine that Dani is curled up next to you," she says softly.

My stomach lurches, but I quickly remind myself to replace that image with Brooke, and I relax again. Her magic fingers are unraveling me. One hand moves back to my shoulder, and the other lightly strokes my neck, and then skims across my cheek. "You pull Dani closer as the breeze blows over you. She gently touches you, and with each stroke you relax further."

I take a deep breath as I feel Brooke's soft hands move over my chest. I feel my body relaxing, sinking into the couch.

"Now imagine her lips kissing your face gently." I feel Brooke's lips on my forehead as her hands weave through my hair. I'm not sure if I've ever felt this great. Every touch stirs and soothes me. She is a witch of unspeakable potions and spells, transforming me under her magic hands.

"Brooke," I moan.

"Dani," she corrects with a whisper.

Her lips brush across my cheek, and over my closed eyelids. I reach out and rest my hand on her hip.

It doesn't fully hit me that she's kissing me until my lips have already molded to hers in the most natural way. Her fingers work across my scalp as her tongue eases in, and suddenly my mouth understands the language it was meant to speak.

This is completely different in the best way, and we move together like the most graceful dancers. The push and pull, the building of passion, I am Gene Kelly to her Cyd Charisse. She makes me feel like I'm leading this dance even though I'm not. For these precious moments I am passion and romance, debonair and suave. I am the man I was supposed to be, and it's so great.

My fingers sink into the flesh of her hip as I pull her closer one last time before we part. "Oh, my," I moan, looking up at her.

"See, Nathan. I knew it was there all along, you just needed to quit thinking so much."

"I just needed you," I say unguardedly.

"Well, I'm glad I could help. You had me worried for a minute." She runs her hand across my head and I see the warmth in her eyes. She does care about me. Maybe not in the way I want her to, but maybe more than I realize.

She eases off my lap until she's sitting next to me on the couch. "But just for the record, you're an amazing kisser. I forgot I was Dani for a moment."

"Really?" I ask, trying to hide my happiness. "I kinda forgot you were Dani too." I admit.

She looks at me but doesn't say anything, as if she's torn. She finally smoothes out her skirt, and sits up straight. "Well, I should get to bed. I've got an early morning tomorrow with my trainer at the gym. I'll have to work off all that pizza and beer."

"Okay," I say. I stand up and follow her to the front door. Before I can figure out what to do, she pulls me into a hug. "Thanks again for fixing my computer. I really appreciate it."

After we part, I shove my hands in my pockets and shuffle my feet. There's so much I want to say, but I decide to keep it simple. "Hey, thanks for not giving up on me."

"I had a good time tonight. *I hope you know how much I love spending time with you.*" She smiles as I realize she had just repeated my lines for Dani.

"I hope you know how much I love spending time with you," I whisper.

"So I'll see you at work Monday?" she half states, half asks.

"Four twenty-five, with a half-caf Soy caramel macchiato with three pumps, and a Splenda gently stirred in."

"I like it sweet," she teases.

I grin. "I know you do."

As I reach her gate she buzzes me out, and I turn back one last time and wave. As happy as I am, my legs feel like lead with each step I take to my car. I don't want to leave her. It's as if a huge magnet is trying to pull me back. And as my car slowly winds down the road, I realize that everything I want is perched on that hill. All the way down, I memorize every turn and landmark, so I'll always be able to find my way back to her.

"Mom," I yell as I step through the door.

"In the kitchen," she yells back.

I find her at the center island cutting up fruit. I kiss her on the cheek, and take a strawberry.

"How's my boy?" she asks, looking up at me. I see something in her eyes. It's curiosity mixed in with that all-knowing mom look. "You look different."

"Different how?" I ask, a bit creeped out from my mom's innate intuition. Can she tell I'm in love?

"I'm not sure yet, but I'll figure it out," she says confidently. "How's work?"

"Good, the same. They always want too much done in too little time. Guess what though? I was contacted by Sharper Edge Comics about my comic book."

"Really, what did they want?"

"They're interested in publishing it for me. That would be a wider distribution and more promotion."

"Oh, that sounds great. Make sure and talk to Dad's lawyers before you sign anything."

"Don't worry, I will. By the way where is Dad?"

"He and Curtis are already out playing."

I start to head out the door.

"And Nathan, if he tries to get you to test the ball retriever out, watch your ankles. He hasn't worked out all the kinks yet."

"Okay, thanks for the warning."

As I head over to the tennis court, I laugh at the idea of my dad working on a ball retriever. He loves tennis, but hates bending over to pick up balls. Dad is the wacky inventor who's had great success with his unusual ideas. He's invented countless things over the years and owns dozens of patents, but it's a small group of his ideas that actually made him rich.

He isn't an extravagant man. He still drives his old Honda Civic and shops weekly with my mom at Costco. He likes space around him, so their home in Pasadena is large and on a big piece of land. When the doctor told him he needed more exercise, he took up tennis, and built a court at the edge of the property. Now Curtis and I join him every Sunday to play.

"So you finally show up!" Curtis calls out with a grin when he sees me open the gate.

I look at my watch. "Hey, I'm only ten minutes late," I respond. "Besides, you were a half hour late last week." I turn towards Dad. "Hi, Dad."

"Hi, Son. You ready to kick his butt?"

"I'm sure going to try."

Sadly the game goes as it always does, Curtis beating me, and Dad too while hardly breaking a sweat. He's an athlete through and through, definitely a deviant in our family gene pool. I've always been more like my dad, non-athletic, quirky and a loner, slow to connect with people. If he hadn't met my mom, he probably would've ended up one of those eccentric old guys with tall piles of newspapers stacked all over his house.

Mom serves brunch out on the patio since she doesn't want our sweaty bodies on her nice upholstery. Big mouth Curtis pipes up before I've even taken a bite.

"So Nathan has made a new friend at work...a girl."

"That's nice. What's her name?" my Mom asks politely.

"Brooke," I say before giving Curtis the evil eye.

"What does she do there?" Dad asks.

"She's head of development," I answer cautiously.

"So I'm hoping something will develop for you with this head of development," Curtis responds.

My mom raises her eyebrows, and looks back and forth between Curtis and me.

"We're just friends," I insist. No need making my parents hopeful. I know they worry about me. I was a mess after Rachel and I didn't work out. I think they feared I would never date again.

Dad pipes up out of the blue. "The mathematical odds of meeting someone at work who would be appropriate for a significant relationship are favorable. Consistent exposure is key."

Thanks Dad, for the warm fatherly advice.

"Okay, it's great to have new friends," Mom says carefully, trying to protect me. "Why don't you bring her to brunch some time?"

And subject her to the strangeness of my family? No thank you.

"Well, let's see how it goes first. We've only been friends for a week."

• • •

The next afternoon, Brooke waves me over to her computer like I just left her office. I've been a tangled mess all day waiting to see her, but she's cool as a cucumber and looks really happy to see me. "Hey, come look at this," she says.

I step up behind her and lean forward. There's a color image of a girl with big eyes that looks like artist Keene's work, surrounded by little creatures holding a row of lollipops. It's freaky, but in a good way. "That's cool. Whose work is that?"

"Sarah. She's an in-betweener on Bruce's team. There's so much talent here. People have no idea."

"I know you're right. A lot of the artists have a hard time promoting their own work."

"That's why I'm starting a website where all this art can be featured. I'm also going to do a rotating gallery show in the lobby of the building."

Like I need another reason to love this woman. She turns back to see my reaction, and I smile happily at her. "That's a great idea…really."

"You like it? Arnauld thinks it's a stupid idea. Well, not so much stupid, but that it is distracting me away from my job. I told him I can do most of it during my off hours."

"Can I help you with it? I've done several websites. You wouldn't have to pay me."

"That'd be great. I could really use the help. You shouldn't do it for free though. Hey, I know…I could feed you. How would that be?"

"As long as it's not that healthy crud."

"I promise." She laughs. "How's Thursday after work?"

"Sounds good." I set her coffee on her desk and walk around to the front. "Unfortunately, I've got to go, Joel called a four-thirty meeting in the conference room. There's a problem with the storyboards."

She looks up at me concerned. "Nathan, are you okay? I mean after Saturday night, are we okay?"

"Okay?"

"I'm just worried I pushed you too hard. I fretted about it all day yesterday."

I push my glasses back up my nose, and run my fingers through my hair. It occurs to me that she looks vulnerable when I'm the one who was such a mess that night.

I smile at her and hope she can see the gratitude in my eyes. "No, you were just right. I needed to be pushed."

She lets out a deep exhale. "Oh, I'm so glad."

"So tomorrow, four-twenty?"

"I'll be here," she says, before I regretfully leave for my meeting.

On the way back from the conference room I stop in Dani's cube. Her earbuds are in and she's in the zone. It looks like she's working on some character designs for an upcoming episode. I wait a minute, and when she doesn't notice me I finally tap her shoulder. She pauses her iPod, and turns to me.

"Hey, Nathan. What's up?"

"I was wondering if we could talk about something?"

"No can do. This is supposed to be done by six. I can talk after that, though."

"Okay, just come get me. I'll be in my cube."

She nods and turns her iPod back on.

It's about six-forty when Dani finally show up.

"Sorry dude, he asked for last minute changes."

"No problem, I have a pile of stuff to do here anyway." I stand up, and see that Andy is still working in his cube next door. "Hey, let's find somewhere to talk outside."

In the elevator down we chat about the show, and rumors that Joel is over budget again.

"He better watch that shit," Dani warns. "I don't care what kind of genius he is; for the suits, it's all about the money."

When the elevators open we step out and head for the door. Right as I pull it open for Dani, I catch someone in the corner of my eye, and turn to see Brooke holding her work-bag and heading our way. She has a huge smile on her face, and it hits me that she thinks I'm making progress with Dani. I hold the door open longer, until Brooke can pass through.

When we are all three outside, there's an awkward moment.

"Hi Dani," Brooke says politely.

"Hey."

"Are you guys heading this way?" She points to the parking structure.

"No, we were going to go sit down for a while," I explain nervously.

"Okay, cool. I'll see you guys tomorrow." I watch her walk away, before turning back to Dani.

"She seems really nice," Dani observes.

"Yeah, that's kinda why I needed to talk to you. I've got myself in a mess and hope you can help me out."

She raises her eyebrows. "What kind of a mess?"

"Well, Brooke and I have become friends, and I was helping her Saturday night with her computer." I twist my hands together. "So then we had pizza and beer, and she got it in her head that I like someone at work."

"Really? And who would that be? Because it's very clear to me that you have set your sights on Ms. Brooke. Am I right?"

I can feel the blood rush to my face. "Please don't make this any harder than it already is." I stand up and pace a few times before I sit back down. "I'm so screwed. She thinks I like you."

She throws her head back and laughs. She laughs so hard; it's almost insulting.

"I'm so glad you find this amusing."

"Well, so why didn't you straighten her out? Oh yes, there's a little complication. She's got a boyfriend who happens to be the PRESIDENT of our company, Nathan. I mean, what the fuck are you thinking? You want to get black-balled in our tight-assed little industry?"

"I know. This is really bad." I double fist my hair and pull hard, groaning.

"You're whacked. Besides what in the world makes you think she'd go for you? Don't get me wrong, you're a kick ass artist, but socially you're a wee bit stunted."

"Thanks so much. Now that we've talked, I'm feeling so much better about things."

"There is one more thing I don't get. How does telling her that you are after me, help things along with her?"

"She wants to help me win you over, so she's going to teach me things and improve me. She's doing a *My Fair Lady* on me. And the lessons are really…enjoyable."

"You're full of shit—you're not that big of a loser, are you?"

"Well, actually…"

"And what do I get out of this?"

"Maybe it'll make Nick jealous, and he'll see the light."

At first her eyes roll, but then I see a fire light up in them. Maybe that isn't the craziest idea. He has taken his time going back to Dani, but if there is a challenge, he may feel the urgency for them to be reunited sooner. They both know they are destined to be together.

"I'm going to have to think this over. I just don't know."

"This isn't a flat out 'no,' right? You'll at least consider it?"

"Yeah, I'll consider it…let's talk again tomorrow." She picks up her backpack and slings it over her shoulder.

"Thanks, Dani, I appreciate that. Until tomorrow then."

I decide to sit and gather my thoughts, and my mind starts to spin. Just over a week ago my life had a predictable pattern. Every day blended into the next, like a loop of animation being repeated again and again. Now, the loop has torn, and the film is flapping under the hot light of the projector. I have no idea how the next scenes are going to play. The result is a mix of exhilaration and terror. At this point, all I can do I keep the projector running, and hope for the best.

Animate Me / Chapter Six / Yoga Pants

"It's very hard to be brave when you're only a very small animal." - Winnie the Pooh[v]

"Soooo…" she says, grinning ear to ear. "How'd it go?"

I hand over her coffee and today's cup illustration is one that only the two of us would understand. It's two ends of a USB cord meeting for the first time. They have little cartoon faces on them with mustaches and outie plug heads. They're both looking at each other with concerned looks and question marks floating over their heads.

Male to male connection, indeed.

"How did what go?" I ask.

"Your date with Dani. Did you kiss?"

I'm embarrassed, but I try to keep my cool. "Oh, we didn't have a date. We just talked. There was definitely no kiss."

"Oh." She looks surprised. I can't tell if I'm reading her wrong but she looks kind of pleased that she's the only one I've really kissed.

I hold up the cup in front of her so she can see the drawing. Her resulting laugh lightens up the room. "You should at least do these drawings on the cup sleeve, you know. Then at least I could flatten them out and keep them."

"Oh, you want to keep my cup art," I tease, hardly able to contain my thrill.

She walks over to one of her built-in cabinets and pulls open the door, then does a Vanna White wave of her arm. Each of my Starbucks cups since day one are lined up like paper soldiers. "As you can see, I'm running out of room. I rinse them out and everything." She snaps the door closed and walks back to her desk.

"You're making me feel special."

"Well, your custom Starbucks cups make me feel special," she teases back, but I know she means it.

I tip my head down embarrassed, despite the fact that her words make me really happy.

I suddenly feel the energy change in the room, and I turn to see Arnauld in the doorway, leaning against the door jam with his arms folded. He speaks to Brooke like I'm not even there.

"Ready to go over the presentation?"

"Sure, but first, say hi to my friend, Nathan. He's the animator I told you about on Joel's team."

"One of the beavers." Arnauld snickers. "Hey man, thanks for fixing Brooke's computer." He nods at me in that manly, confident way that reeks of masculinity. He's one of those guys who knows how good-looking he is, and expects everyone to appreciate it. What a schmuck.

"Sure, it was no big deal," I reply quietly. This is painfully uncomfortable. "I'll see you later, Brooke."

"Okay, thanks Nathan."

When I pass Arnauld, he nods his head again, but all the while he is watching Brooke with a look in his eye. It feels territorial, and I hold my breath until I've stepped out of her office.

Morgan gives me that damn knowing look, like I just got caught with my hand in the cookie jar. Well, don't worry Morgan, *I sure didn't get any cookies today.*

• • •

The next day Dani and I slip into a conference room for a private moment. Now that she's had some time to mull over my request, I'm nervous she's going to turn me down.

"Do I have to kiss you?"

Leave it to Dani to be thorough. My mind starts imagining different scenarios, and I'm not sure how to answer her.

"I don't think so, but maybe."

"Do I have to sleep with you?"

"God, no. The worst it would be is some type of PDA, you know public display of affection."

"How long are we talking here? It can't be some ambiguous time frame. We need a firm start date and end date for these shenanigans."

"Does this mean you're going to do it?" I ask, hopeful.

"What can I say? I'm a sucker for the underdog. Besides I get a really good feeling about that Brooke, and Arnauld is an asshole. He doesn't deserve her. You, on the other hand, are one of the good guys. You're definitely worthy of her."

"Oh, Dani," I give her one of my stiff hugs. "Thanks so much."

She looks at her watch. "Today is the twenty-fourth. You have eight weeks. On the twenty-fourth, month after next, I turn into a pumpkin, so you better be done by then. Agreed?"

I nod nervously. The clock's running, and its quiet ticking is pounding in my ears.

At lunch time, we head over to Outer Limits, our local comic shop that's walking distance from the studio. I've been so distracted by Brooke that I'm actually behind with my reading. Spiderman could have had a love tryst with the Green Lantern, and I wouldn't have even known it.

Billie looks happy when we burst through the door because the Sketch Republic crowd means money in the cash register.

"So, you finally show up. What's the matter Nathan, don't you love me anymore?" Billie drapes herself over the trading card case and pouts her lips. She knows how to fluster me.

"Of course I do," I mumble, trying to be cute, but from me it sounds awkward and insincere. It doesn't help that Andy pushes me towards her, and the guys are chuckling. All of them have a thing for beautiful Billie, but for some reason I'm her favorite.

"You didn't visit me last week and I missed you so."

"Missed me, or my wallet?" I surprise myself by challenging her.

"Well... your wallet. But only just a little bit more. It's true that your open wallet is one of the reasons I put up with you."

Yeah, that's Billie.

"Hey Billie, is that a new tattoo?" Joel asks stepping closer. I can't imagine how he would notice it from several feet away considering that both her arms are entirely covered with tattoos. I didn't think she had any space left. But she lifts and twists her arm and shows off Wonder Woman deflecting bullets with her silver cuffs.

63

"Wonder Woman kicks ass," moans Andy. "That's so hot."

"Glad you like it," she purrs, admiring it herself. She looks at me and winks. "Hey guys did you see that Nathan's new issue of *B-Girl in Wildsville* is in?"

"Is that the one with B-Girl painting a ladder to climb out of the maze of doom?" Joel asks. "I remember Nathan working on that one."

"That's it," she confirms. "Now go young warriors, and seek many treasures."

They take off in different directions throughout the store while I linger behind. "Thanks Billie. It's no surprise that your store sells so many copies of my books."

"Don't get too full of yourself, dude, I wouldn't be doing it if I didn't love it. B-Girl is the bomb. You keep it up and she'll be my next tatt."

"Well, I'd be very honored. I'm sure I'll be extra inspired when I work on tonight's pages."

Dani brings the latest Sailor Moon manga graphic novel up to the register.

"Hey Billie," she says, pulling out her wallet.

"Dani! Where've you been girl?"

"Working too much. All work and no play is making Dani a very dull girl, but did Nathan tell you? He's taking me on a date this weekend."

I flush like a smacked bottom.

"Really?" Billie says in an exaggerated voice that is way too loud. "I would never have pegged him as your type."

"Me neither," she giggles.

I'm horrified. I step close enough to whisper in her ear. "What're you doing?" I ask nervously.

"What does it look like?" she whispers back. I can see Nick off to the side watching us.

"So where are you two going?" Billie asks playfully like this is a game. *If she only knew.*

"I bet somewhere romantic," Dani teases. Just then her phone rings, and she scrunches her nose after looking at the screen. "Sorry guys, love to talk about our date but I've got to take this...gotta step outside." And she moves quickly out the door.

"What the fuck is that all about?" Billie asks me, her eyes squinting suspiciously.

"Billie, please," I half whisper. "Not now, I'll tell you about it later."

"You better," she warns. "Or else."

Billie scares me enough that I believe her. She'd make a great dominatrix.

I nervously move over to the New Release section, hoping if I buy some more stuff it will distract Billie from torturing me. I follow our group out of the store fifteen minutes later with two shopping bags, one hundred-fifty bucks less in my wallet, but my dignity still intact.

Late that night, as I put the final touches on the fifth page of the latest B-Girl story I think about the complicated mess I've made with Dani and Brooke, and now Billie is going to stir things up and regularly give me shit about it. I get exhausted just thinking about all the ways things could go wrong. Before I know it, I'm pulling on my hair and my pencil is frozen over the drawing. I make a few more attempts to focus before surrendering and turning off the lights. I hope that tomorrow things will look better.

• • •

The next evening Brooke and I sit at her dining room table with a sketchbook and two beers. It occurs to me that it's amazing how comfortable I've become with her. "Can I ask you something?" I say.

"Of course." She smiles softly as she watches my pencil move from one side of the paper to the other.

"I know we talked about this once before, but people are still gossiping and it bothers me. Have more people been telling you I'm buttering you up for a pitch?"

"Is this where the title goes? Or do you think it should be in the center?" Her perfect finger points to the vague shapes I have sketched out.

"Brooke? Are you avoiding my question?" I ask, the insecurity seeping into the tenor of my voice.

"Oh, buttering me up? Yeah, maybe…particularly Arnauld. But I don't mind. It doesn't mean you don't genuinely like me. That's just how business is done."

"But this…" I wave my hand between us. "This isn't business to me. It's a lot more than that to me." I immediately feel the burning across my cheeks. I sound like such a pussy. On top of that, now I want to kill Arnauld for wanting Brooke to think that about me.

"How do you know I'm not just being nice to you so that I can keep getting those fabulous soy caramel macchiatos every day?"

"Actually I thought you wanted me for my cup art." I inwardly smile, pleased with my pussy-free rebound.

"That's what I'm talking about; you can see right through me. Do you know today Arnauld asked me why I didn't bring him coffee? Something about the snarky, entitled way he said it, made me want to kick his teeth in. But you…well, you overheard my ridiculous drink mentioned in an elevator, and you wanted me to have it. Now look at us. We're besties."

"So it is the Starbucks then." I smile at her, but inside I ache knowing being besties is a one-way ticket to endless frustration for me. "You may have had an agenda, but you still really think about me, Brooke—not just the development chick."

I push the pad aside and grip the edge of the table. "It's just important to me for you to understand that I'm not going to pitch you."

"What, now I'm not good enough for your show ideas?" she teases.

"It just wouldn't be right. So you can beg and plead, spoil me with more of these amazing dinners…"

"It was just take-out Thai."

"Don't interrupt me. You can beg all you want but I'm not pitching you. Understood?"

"I guess so—if it means that much to you. But if you have some great idea, and take it to another studio and they make it, and it's it big hit; I will hate you forever. But if you're willing to take that risk, I guess I'll be willing too."

I groan and let my head fall into my hands, my floppy hair falling across my face.

"Hey you," she says, shaking my shoulder. "Snap out of it, we have a website to design."

We work too long but I'm not ready to leave yet, I'm on my third beer again. I guess I'm headed toward alcoholism or at the very least a beer gut, but if it means more time with Brooke, it's worth it.

On our final work break of the evening, we are sitting on the balcony looking out at the view. Brooke seems lost in thought.

"What're you thinking about?" I ask softly, nervous to be too nosey.

"For some strange reason I was thinking about my parents. Do you know that if they'd stayed married they would've been married thirty years by now?"

"They got married after you were born?"

"Yeah, my mom didn't even want to but the families kept pushing. A lot of good it did; they always fought, and finally divorced when I was thirteen."

I feel sad for her. As weird as my parents are, they love each other deeply. I can't imagine what my home life would have been like if they didn't.

"I think that's why I'm with Arnauld. I purposely picked someone who is as adverse to commitment as I am. He doesn't ever want to get married or tied down to just one person."

"And you feel the same?" I boldly ask. "You couldn't be happy with just one person if you loved them?" I hold my breath waiting for her answer.

She examines the beer bottle intently before taking a swig and looking back out at the view. "I don't know. I've never felt that strongly about anyone. It's hard for me to imagine, but I guess that with the right guy it could be possible."

I turn and look at the view mulling over what she's revealed. Again, the lottery odds and my willingness to gamble on her drift into my mind. She only left the lowest odds with her answer, but that doesn't mean I won't bet all my chips on her anyway. What choice do I have? She's all I want.

We finally carry our beer bottles into the kitchen and I gather up my things.

"Oh," she moans, rubbing her tummy. "All that beer and I'm stuffed, my jeans feel tight."

"Next time we do this just wear your yoga pants, they're stretchy," I suggest in my most innocent voice…the sex fiend inside of me howling with delight.

"Oh, you just want to ogle my ass," she teases.

What does she expect? Her yoga pants have become a visual cue to my sexuality. "So what if I do? Anything wrong with that? I'm a guy, you know."

After all…now that I've seen Brooke in yoga pants…I have seen the light.

She steps behind me, puts her hands on my shoulders and starts massaging as she pushes me to the front door. "Speaking of which, when is your date with lucky Miss Dani?"

"Saturday," I lie. I haven't even set the faux date up yet.

"Where are you taking her?" Brooke's hands work harder digging into the knots under my shoulder blades.

"I don't know yet, do you have any suggestions?"

"Let me think about it when I'm not beer buzzed."

"Okay, I'll ask again tomorrow when I bring you your coffee."

As much as I hate to end the massage, I turn around to hug her goodbye. "Thanks. I had fun tonight."

"Working on my website was fun?"

"Well, yeah, you're always fun."

She pushes my hair out of my eyes in a gentle way and smiles warmly.

As much as I know I shouldn't say anything, being this close to her does something to me.

"Hey, would you mind if I practiced with you one more time? You know, to get ready for my date with Dani."

"You want me to kiss you?" she asks, not sounding against the idea.

"I thought maybe this time I could try to kiss you. You know, learn to be more assertive."

"Are you going all alpha-male on me?"

"Well, I thought I would try. But if you don't want me to…"

"No, I'm committed to the cause here. We are sacrificing for the greater good. Go ahead and pretend I'm Dani. Pull me in your arms and kiss me, you fool."

"Okay," I bite my lip and try to figure out which angle I should work from. "Are you ready?"

"Don't ask that. It's not sexy to ask a woman if she's ready. Just give her the look and if she gives the look back, go for it."

I repeat that advice twice in my head so I won't forget it. "Okay, the look." I narrow my eyes at her.

She giggles. "You look pissed. Why don't you take your glasses off?"

I pull my glasses off and carefully fold them, slipping them in my pocket.

"Wow, your eyes are amazing!" she exclaims. "We're going to take you contact lens shopping soon."

She loves my eyes. I'll put up with sticking painful plastic discs in my eyes just to hear her swoon like that again.

This time I just look at her without trying to be cool or suave and I can feel the difference. I'm looking at her with my heart not just my eyes, and I think she sees it too.

Her eyes say yes back. She settles against the wall right next to the door and waits.

I lean down and move forward, leading with my lips as if they're a missile slowly heading towards a target. When they land I remember how soft and warm she felt last time we kissed, and I relax into her and let my instincts take over.

She's tentative, seemingly not wanting to take over, but lets me give my best effort. If I were being graded, I probably would've gotten a C plus, not stellar, but a far cry from my previous total failure.

When we part she looks up at me and smiles encouragingly. "Once, more," she instructs, "but this time we'll get your hands involved."

She takes one of my hands and perches it on her shoulder, the other on her hip. "Okay, that's good," she affirms.

Wow. What a difference; I'm stunned. Maybe it's just because the kiss warmed me up, but it feels like there are sparks firing from her body right into mine. It's a super-hero force field. Surely if we harness this, we could save the world.

Deep breath, I look in her eyes...they are sparkling and saying, *oh yes, kiss me.* I note the green light, and go.

This times when our lips touch the melting begins immediately. I don't even think about it, the hand on her shoulder slides to her back and pulls her into my arms. The other hand winds across her hip to her lower back, just above her bottom. I press her even closer as our lips move together. When I feel her hand twist in my hair my tongue gets involved...very involved, and so does hers.

I'm kissing Brooke, and it's so hot. This has to be at least a B plus. *Hot damn.*

I only pull apart when I worry that if I don't pull my hips away I won't be able to hide my growing secret. He's that happy, the guy in my pants, and I'm not ready for Brooke to meet him yet.

I open my eyes to see that Brooke's are still closed, and her lips flushed and swollen.

"Wow," I whisper and she smiles lazily.

"Yeah, wow. You're a fast learner."

"Well, I have a great teacher." I grin, trying to keep her attention focused above, so she doesn't see what's happening to my body below.

"Keep kissing like that, and no girl will be able to resist you."

"Okay." I nod my head. I desperately want to forget that in her mind this was intended for Dani, and she was just trying to help me.

She pulls the door open. "Thanks again for your help with the website. Can we do this again next week?"

"Sure," I say as I step outside. "So, see you tomorrow afternoon."

"See you," she says softly, smiling.

I'm almost to the gate when she calls out to me.

"Hey Nathan, when you go to Starbucks, do you buy Dani a drink too?"

I should probably lie, but I just can't. Not about this. It's Brooke and my special thing…just ours.

I shake my head and push my hands in my pockets.

Her smile is big and bright. If I didn't know better I would think that she was really happy about that.

"Just wondering," she calls out, before buzzing the gate and waving her final goodbye.

Later, about a mile from my house, I drive by my local Starbucks and smile. It's closed, but its sign's still lit, glowing against the dark sky. That green and white circle is the bright light in my murky afternoons, my very own Brooke-beacon of hope. In my quest for Brooke, I have come to believe in its power as we move forward, one caramel macchiato at a time.

Animate Me / Chapter Seven / I am Clark Kent

"There's nothing better than a little old-fashion Smurf Power!" - *Hefty Smurf*[i]

Just past noon Joel sticks his head in my cube. "I think the Incredible Hulk is looking for you."

I find my tall, well-built brother, Curtis in the lobby chatting up one of the producers, Dawn. His charm is irrefutable. Dawn is pretty serious, yet he has her giggling.

"Hey Nathan," she says as I approach. "Look who I found."

"I found you," he corrects her. "And you can bet I'm going to come looking for you again."

She blushes, looking down. "Okay, well it was nice meeting you Curtis." She scurries off.

"Do you know I've seen at least a dozen cute girls since I've been here, dude. You should be hitting this stuff hard."

"Thanks for the brotherly advice," I say, trying not to smirk. "Hey, you still want to see my work before we have lunch?"

"That's why I'm here," he responds, nodding.

I lead him back to my cube and he starts looking at the drawings on my animation desk. "I still can't figure out how you learned to draw like this. It's not like we have a single artist in our family."

I click on my computer screen. "Here, check out this pencil test of a scene I've been working on."

A sequence comes on of Bucky chasing Bernie through a flea market and strange items like sombreros and suits of armor attach to them as they run.

"Where's the color and why are they floating in space?" he asks, leaning into the screen.

"I'm working on the animation part. When I'm done, the character lines are digitized and the colorists digitally paint the animation. Then the backgrounds are created separately by a different set of artists, and the work is then layered together."

"That sounds complicated," he says, rubbing his chin.

"Yeah, and that's not the half of it. There are sound effects, music, editing. Not to mention the writing, storyboarding and timing and voice recordings at the front end. These days most studios do most of it overseas, so I'm lucky I still get to do it this way."

"All of that for a fucking cartoon," he shakes his head in disbelief.

"Well, I could say the same for what you do—all that bullshit for some fucking money."

"Don't pop your cork, bro, I'm actually really impressed." He pats me on the back. "Let's go eat. I'm starving."

I decide to take him to Mo's in Toluca Lake because the burgers are almost as big as his head. Big C still eats like he did when he played football in high school.

"So how's it going with Beth?" he asks before taking a handful of fries.

"Brooke," I correct him. "It's going fine, well better than fine, I think."

He raises his eyebrows like he can't believe a dork like me can be doing fine with a girl. "Are you being chill, like I told you to be?"

It occurs to me that in his eyes my plan may be a good one, so I test the waters.

"Really chill. As a matter of fact she thinks I like another girl at the studio, and she's going to help me get her."

"What the fuck are you talking about? I told you to be chill, not insane."

"Don't you see, she feels safe now spending time with me. And she's like my dating coach, she was showing me how to kiss Dani...the other girl."

"No shit, that is bizarre. So she is kissing you to show you how to kiss someone else when she doesn't know that you're actually really kissing her?"

"Exactly!" I exclaim.

"You are one crazy fucker. So tell me Einstein, how do you see this playing out in the end? Or did it occur to you to figure that out first?"

"No, the whole thing just sort of happened. I'm figuring it out as I go along and it seems to be working just fine." I am getting irritated with his doom and gloom. It's a black cloud lingering over our table.

He shakes his head. "But in the end—no matter what—she will know that you lied. You deceived and manipulated her. And in my vast experience with women, that's usually a deal breaker."

I spend the rest of lunch watching him eat, since I've completely lost my appetite. As we go to leave I ask if he minds us swinging by Outer Limits since Billie wants me to pick up my special-ordered vinyl Harley Quinn collectible figurine that goes with my Joker. It's the last one she has and she's sick of people eyeballing it despite the fact that my name is on it.

Billie is standing near the door rearranging a display when we enter the store. She turns towards us, and her eyes widen when she sees Curtis. For almost any girl, you would hardly notice the gesture, but with hard-ass Billie it's like the earth has tilted off its rotation. He must be wearing that pheromone cologne or something, since I appear to be witnessing textbook instant attraction.

"Hey, Nathan," she says, never taking her eyes off him. "Who's your friend?"

Curtis steps forward. "Hi, I'm Curtis, Nathan's brother. And you are?"

"Wilhelmina." She smiles. "But you can call me Billie."

I move to the back of the store, disgusted that in ten seconds he has scored with Billie-the-ball-buster. Everyone but me has asked her out and she usually just rolls her eyes and punches them on the arm.

When I finally head back to the front to see what's going on, Billie has her shirt hiked up and she is showing Curtis the tattoos on her lower back. He is running his fingers over her skin and quietly charming her with his admiration.

Curtis wins yet again.

I'm quiet for the first part of the ride back to the studio, but then I can't help myself. I need my suspicions confirmed. "When?" I ask.

"Late this afternoon, after work."

"Really?" I grumble. I'm not jealous, just frustrated. Everything is always so easy for Curtis.

"She told me that she wants to know everything about me…if you know what I mean."

I take a sharp breath. *Damn.* We weren't even in there twenty minutes.

"I can't even believe how I feel," he says. "There's no bullshit with this girl. She serves everything straight up, and it's a revelation compared to the other women I've known. Our attraction was completely visceral." He shakes his head in wonder.

• • •

Later in her office, Brooke gives me a soft smile as I present the latest Starbucks cup to her. "Do you know how much I look forward to seeing what you're going to create for me?" She asks.

"Well, I like drawing them for you," I reply. "I hope you like this one."

She turns the cup and grins when she sees that I've rendered one of her collectible lady-head vases on the cup, but this time she's the lady head with pencils and a pair of scissors coming out of the top of her head.

"Oh, Nathan...I love it! I'm going to set this cup next to my collection."

"I'm glad," I say. "It was fun to do." I let out a sigh as I sink down into her guest chair.

"Hey, are you okay?" Brooke asks as she notices me pull my hand through my hair.

I can't hide anything from her. "Not really." I admit. After my loser lunch with Curtis I've convinced myself to tell Brooke the truth and cut my losses.

She walks over to her office door and closes it.

"What's up?" she asks after sitting on her couch and motioning for me to join her.

"I just have the worst feeling, like everything's a mess and I'm not sure how to fix it. Do you ever feel that way?"

"More often than I'd like," she says nodding.

I look over at her and notice that her face looks drawn and pale.

"What about you? Are you okay?"

"Not really, no. I had something really disturbing happen earlier."

"You want to talk about it?"

She suddenly stands up and goes over to her desk, grabbing her purse. "Come on. Let's get out of here, I need a drink and it sounds like you do too."

Morgan doesn't say a thing when Brooke tells her that we're leaving to take care of something. I keep as neutral of a face as I can, despite the fact that I am nervously thrilled to be running off somewhere with her. The excitement distracts me from the feeling of doom that was weighing me down only minutes ago.

We stand quietly in the elevator, and when we stop on the sixth floor Kevin joins us holding some storyboards.

"Hey, Nathan," he says before turning to look forward.

Something suddenly occurs to me. "Um, Kevin, will you do me a favor? I need to run out and take care of something. Can you let Joel know? Tell him I finished the revisions."

"Sure, no problem." Kevin nods. I don't think he's associating me with Brooke who is standing quietly in the corner.

For a moment I'm grateful he's the one that I ran into. Andy or Nick would have asked me twenty questions.

Once in Brooke's Prius we head out without a word. After a long quiet minute I finally speak up.

"Where are we going?"

"Smokehouse, over by Warner Bros."

I smile at the odd choice. It's so old school that it's cool. Despite the traditional decor, and older clientele, there's something about the place. I'm sure a million film and cartoon deals have been made there.

"I saw Frank and Ollie there once eating soup."

"Disney's Frank and Ollie?" I ask with reverence. They were a famed part of what was termed *Disney's Nine Old Men*, the brilliant animators who worked on all his key classic films.

"Yup, I almost asked if I could join them."

"I bet they would have loved that, such a beautiful woman fan-girling all over them."

She looks up at me surprised. Is it because I called her beautiful? It can't be since that fact is irrefutable. Maybe she's just surprised that someone as dense as me noticed.

"I wish I had." She responds after the pause. "Now they're both gone, and I could have told them what Bambi and Dumbo meant to me as a young girl."

After being sat in a deep booth in the corner of the room, we decide to order serious drinks so Brooke gets a martini and I, a double Jameson on the rocks. We start out talking about the cartoons we grew up with. The Smurfs are on both of our lists and I laugh telling Brooke about the twisted caricature I remember seeing of Hefty Smurf doing inappropriate things with Smurfette. Brooke practically spits up her martini.

"You're so evil," she laughs. "I'll never be able to look at those little creatures again without having that idea in my head!"

"I guess that's the point, revising animation history, one disturbing caricature at a time." I can tell, as I watch her face warm up, that the drink is doing its magic. She looks much happier and relaxed now than when she was in her office.

"Oh, I'm glad we did this," she exclaims, stretching her legs out under the table so that they pass in between mine. "I was ready to kill Arnauld, and now I barely give a fuck about him and his *agenda*."

"Agenda?" I ask, too curious to stay quiet.

She rubs her hands over her face and moans.

I take a long sip of my drink before setting it back on the table near hers. "What did he do? It must have been bad to get you so upset."

She plops a green olive in her mouth and watches me as if she's trying to decide whether to tell me a secret or not.

"He tried to whore me out."

I grip the edge of the table and my back goes rigid. "What? Did I hear you right? You have to explain what you mean by that."

"Okay, I've told you that we have an open relationship, right?"

"Yes." That's one bit of information I'll never forget.

"Well, we had our network meeting today and they've been working us over hard, both with content and budgets. It's so aggravating to always feel like you're on your knees for them…at their mercy in every way."

This is a side of the business I never hear about, and from the sounds of it I'm lucky to be shielded from it.

"So the key decision maker, Stephen, is this prick with a bad comb-over. And lucky girl that I am, Stephen seems to have a thing for me. The looks he gives me during meetings are so inappropriate. He's even suggested that we go out a few times to 'go over business' but I always turn him down." Her hands curl into fists and press into the table. "Arnauld knows all this; he knows how I feel about him."

My stomach's churning, and our waitress brings over our second round. I take another long sip, as does Brooke.

"So the meeting ends, and as I'm packing up, Stephen slithers over to me and asks me to lunch. I lie and tell him that I have a lunch meeting with Arnauld and our directors. The words have just left my mouth when Arnauld jumps in and assures me, in front of Stephen, that they will be fine without me and to go ahead and have a nice time with Stephen."

"He threw you under the bus," I say quietly, anger in my voice.

"And removed my panties before he did," she agrees, disgustedly.

"So Stephen says he will meet me in the hallway after a pit stop, and Arnauld pulls me aside and encourages me to charm him into getting the deal through."

"Hell no, what did you say?"

She leans forward into her drink and sighs. "I was so stunned, so completely stunned and furious that I couldn't say anything. I just turned and walked away from him. Besides, I couldn't exactly start screaming at him since we were still in the building."

"I understand," I say sympathetically. "When I'm surprised I'm dumbstruck, that is my reaction more times than not."

"And I got to spend the next two hours listening to Stephen talk about himself and avoiding his slimy advances."

"Are you okay?" I ask, worry etched across my face.

"Yeah, but it was nasty. I had to abandon *polite Brooke* early on, but of course he liked that challenge. I did everything to dissuade him but kick him in the balls. That ass is persistent. And it's beyond me how any of that could have helped Sketch Republic's cause. The whole thing made me sick to my stomach. I will never be put in that position again."

"I'm so sorry." I look down and feel so frustrated that I can't do anything to take that memory away. "So what are you going to do now to Arnauld? Let's think of something deserving of the offense," I say determinedly.

"Something really evil," she agrees. But just then her phone vibrates telling her that she has a new text and I can see on the screen that it's Arnauld trying to reach her.

"*Where are you?*" she reads off the screen. She laughs and then slowly types the answer. "*Exactly where I want to be.*" After hitting send, she looks at the phone and curses, "Fuck you, Arnauld."

I smile, hoping she really means that. She turns and looks at me. "Have I ever told you that his real name isn't Arnauld...it's Arnold?"

"Arnold?" I choke out, almost spitting up my drink.

"Yeah, isn't that rich? I discovered his high school yearbook once and found his picture. I called him Arnold once when we were having a fight and he stormed off like a big baby." She grins.

A second later her phone prompts again.

She reads his response aloud. "*What are you doing?*" Her fingers fly over the text keys to respond. I imagine I can see the steam rising out of her ears like what happens to Yosemite Sam when Bugs Bunny really pisses him off.

"I thought you knew. I'm bending over. If he fucks me again I really think I'll be able to close this deal."

Why did she have to read that to me? It makes me sick and yet arouses me at the same time. I'm in pain, and I down the rest of my drink. The room tilts as a result.

She reads his response with a mock angry face. *"That isn't funny, Brooke.* Oh, hairy back is getting angry," she slurs.

"No, it really isn't," she types while reading aloud, then shuts off her phone. She waves for the waitress, who comes over warily. "Another round, please."

You go, Buttercup!

I sit quietly wondering what to say. Finally I offer my best idea. "You want me to beat him up? My brother, who's looks like the Incredible Hulk, would help and it wouldn't be pretty."

"You're so thoughtful, and for the record that's really hot."

"I mean it," I say. I want her to understand I mean business.

"I know you do and that means a lot to me. Still I have to say no, but thanks. Look, I'm a little loaded and enjoying venting, but for all my bitching I know he didn't really want me to sleep with him. Charm him, yes, but not fuck him."

"It's still disgusting," I insist.

"Yes, it is." Her head drops and we sit silently for a minute before she looks back up. "Look, enough about me. What happened to you today?"

I realize that I shouldn't tell this story drunk, but I'm overwhelmed with the urge to let out this gnawing frustration.

"Oh, I'm having envy issues. I'm so pathetic."

"What happened?" she asks sympathetically.

"I had lunch with my brother today. After lunch we stopped at the comic book store, and I introduced him to my friend, Billie. She runs the place and is exceptionally good looking. And of course they had an instant love connection."

"But I thought you liked Dani, why does him liking Billie, and her liking him, bother you?"

"I don't know, probably because they're most likely in bed right now. Women always fall all over Curtis and drag him to bed. He has amazing sex all the time, and I don't. Things never work out that way for me."

"Really?" she asks, looking disappointed for me.

"Sorry," I groan, letting my face falls into my open hands.

"You don't? What do you mean you don't? You make it sound like you've never had great sex or something."

I look up at her and blanch as I watch the blood also drain from her face.

"Oh my God," she chants. "You're not a virgin, please tell me that you're not a virgin."

I'm already the worst kind of loser and I don't even care how it looks anymore. Defeated I lean into my drink and take another long sip. "Well, technically I may as well be for the lack of fun I've had."

"I don't understand. Is something wrong with you physically? I would imagine not since you felt more than healthy when you were holding me last night."

I'm horrified and dumbstruck. I can't even look her in the eye. "I'm not sure I'm comfortable talking to you about sex, or I mean my lack of hot sex, Brooke. It's so humiliating."

"First of all Nathan, I love to talk about sex. It's my favorite subject. So please don't be shy."

She scoots over closer to me and reaches over, putting her hand on my knee. "You have to understand, I was raised by free-love hippie parents who were very open. By the time I was in high school, my mom left a candy jar full of condoms by the front door and tried, to my horror, to show me the best way to perform fellatio on a banana. Hell, all she ever talked about was sex. So there's nothing you could say that would change what I think of you. This is a subject I'm very comfortable with. Besides, I bet I can help you."

I look down into my drink and nod. "Okay."

"Let's take a step back for a moment. I knew about the awkward kissing issue, so is it similar with sex? Did you try, but not like it?"

"I don't know where to start." I pull on my hair in frustration.

"How about at the beginning?" she suggests gently.

"Well, I think I already told you that I was really shy in high school with the girls. My senior year I ended up going out with my friend's

80

sister for a while. We fumbled around and did stuff a few times but she was even more uncomfortable than I was about it and it wasn't very satisfying. We really didn't have any common interests, nor did we have good chemistry together so that didn't help. We finally just gave up. Later when I got to CalArts I met Rachel, another animation student and within weeks we were involved."

"She's the one that didn't like to kiss."

I nod. "Yeah, but she's so great in so many ways. We felt the same about animation and we talked about it non-stop. Before you knew it we were glued at the hip, together all the time. I was so happy to finally have that with someone."

"That sounds great."

"It was. Plus she was my biggest supporter, always telling me that I was the most talented in our year…that I was going to have a great career."

"How sweet." Brooke nods, encouragingly.

"It was so confusing though when it came to sex. She was very physical with me, always touching me, holding my hand, sitting on my lap but whenever I would try to initiate anything more she would just freeze. It started with the kissing. She hated the kissing. So finally I gave up with that."

"But I had needs you know. I loved her and wanted to be with her… really be with her. So I just kept asking and finally she gave in, agreeing to try making love."

"Well, that's good, right?" she says, smiling.

"Honestly, I don't know what I did wrong. I thought since we were in love it would be different than high school. But no matter how I touched her she didn't react the way I expected…the way I'd seen in movies or read in books. She just laid there. And then when I tried to, you know, go inside of her, she said it hurt and she stopped me."

I realize that my hands are twisted together painfully, and I pull my fingers apart and flex them while sighing.

"I cared about her so much. It took me weeks to get over that first time."

"That's awful," she says.

"The next time I tried, I got us drinking first thinking it would relax her and the situation. Instead it just made her emotional. She started crying when I was only halfway inside of her."

"Damn," she mutters.

I nod. "You can imagine how I felt."

"So I started doing research on how to please a woman. I desperately needed to figure out what I was doing wrong. I was obsessed. It was like I was trying to crack a secret code. I put together an arsenal of techniques and a plan of seduction…and the only thing that seemed to work was… you know…" I can feel my face on fire.

"When you went down on her?" She gently asks.

I nod, and look down embarrassed. "She was crazy for that and I got really good at it."

"But what about you?" I can't help but notice how sad Brooke looks, and my heart sinks even further.

"I loved making her feel good so it wasn't the end of the world. Sure I wanted more, much more, but what could I do? And that is when I finally just accepted that I just didn't have it — that indefinable thing that men should have to make women want them."

But suddenly Brooke's mood seems to shift, and she even looks a bit angry.

"Why are you making this all about you? What you did or didn't do? Did you ever consider that she was just frigid when it came to full on intercourse?"

"Not really because she said she had a boyfriend in high school who really made her feel good. She made it clear it was me; whatever it was, I was lacking. Besides, my experiences hadn't been good in high school either."

Brooke huffs and folds her arms over her chest. "Really? Maybe she was lying about the boyfriend. She could've made him up to cover for her issues. Did you consider that?"

"No, Rachel wouldn't do that to me. She loved me; I know she did. We stayed close even despite all that."

"Do you still see her?"

"No, other than seeing her once last year; but we still talk. She took a job at Pixar and moved up North."

"Does she have a boyfriend now?"

"Not that I know of, but that doesn't prove anything. I don't have a girlfriend either."

"You're unreal, Nathan." She shakes her head with disbelief. I can hear the martini drawl in her tone. "Maybe I should just sleep with you and show you what you're capable of. You need to know what good sex is."

Oh, good God. My heart flip-flops at the idea of it. Yet, despite the absolute thrill and how much I want her, this isn't how I would want it to happen for us. I need her to desire me…not have sex with me to help me.

"Do you think that's a good idea?" I ask carefully. "I mean, that's really generous of you but are you sure you'd want to do that? I mean, you aren't even attracted to me."

"How do you know that? Maybe I'm wildly attracted to you? Maybe I go to bed every night thinking about you that way."

Okay…it's official. She's really drunk.

I know I'm beet red. No mirror is needed to confirm this. I'm also so painfully hard that I have to lean back in the booth and pivot my hips to adjust myself. "Brooke…" I stammer.

"Okay, I'm sorry…I'm being crass. My point, poorly made, is that I want to help you. And if showing you how to have fun in bed helps you, I'd like to do that. I think you're amazing, Nathan. I want you to understand how beautiful sex can be. I don't want you to have all these negative images plaguing you. You aren't ever going to be truly happy until you get past this."

Our waitress comes over with her hands on her hips. "Can I get you two some food? Looks like you could use it. Today's special is prime rib with baked potatoes, how about that?"

We both nod at the same time. When she leaves to put the order in, Brooke reaches over and rests her hand on my arm.

"Don't worry, we'll take this slow…one small step at a time. All right?"

I nod, still completely confused about what I've signed up for. Am I getting a baked potato and Brooke in my bed? The whiskey must be playing with my head. I can't even remember if I told her that I had lied about liking Dani, when all I want is her.

After devouring our plates of food, and considerably more sober, we debate in the parking lot who should drive. She finally agrees to let me drive her car. Back at Sketch Republic the parking structure is empty except for my little red Mini-Cooper. I desperately don't want to say goodnight yet. I never get enough of her.

I am so done for.

After I park her car next to mine we both get out and face each other. She steps closer, and I step back until I'm against my car.

"Are you okay?" she reaches over and touches my wrist. It's the lightest touch, like a butterfly brushing against me. Yet still, the spot burns hot and wild.

"Shall we practice?" She steps closer still. There's nowhere for me to go.

"Practice?" I ask, my voice shaky.

"Our kiss, just our kiss," she whispers and a second later she is pressing up against me. When our lips connect my mind goes gloriously blank, forgetting the rules, the geometric optimal angle, just how incredible it feels when Brooke's tongue is tangled with mine.

Next thing I know my hand is in her hair and my hips are pressing into hers. *Oh yeah.*

"See," she whispers, in between gasps. "This is absolutely right…just as it should be."

I kiss her again, and again.

"Can I touch you?" she whispers.

I take a sharp breath. I can't help it; I want it so much. I think I nod, but I'm not really sure.

But next thing I know I feel her stroking me outside my pants.

"Is this okay?" she looks up into my eyes.

I swallow hard and nod.

"Let me tell you…you feel so amazing, just right. Do you understand?" The look of lust she gives me sets me on fire. She tightens her fingers over me for a long moment before slowly removing her hand.

My body is screaming for more, but I know we're done. She's pulling away. "That felt so good," I whisper.

"When you touch yourself later, remember how good that felt, okay?"

I nod with a grin as she gets into her car and pulls away. She looks a bit flustered herself. Could she be feeling aroused too?

As she passes through the lot gate I fight the urge to run after her like Superman, so I can pull my Lois out of the damn car and into my arms. But in reality I'm Clark Kent, bumbling and slow, and she's just turned onto San Fernando Road and out of my sight.

I quickly get in my car, anxious to get home and spread out across my bed. The vivid image of her hands on me, wrapped with her seductive words, echo in my head all the way home.

Oh, I'll remember all of this when I touch myself Brooke. Will you?

Animate Me / Chapter Eight / Hearts Unfolding

"You're afraid to tell Wilma, aren't you?" ~ Barney Rubble to Fred Flintstone[vii]

In Saturday's sober morning light I replay what will forever be termed "The Smokehouse Fiasco" in my mind. The single picture that will accompany this memory is of horror-struck Brooke, with her mouth gaping open, after I've revealed that I'm a sexual failure. I might as well have a flashing neon sign that says "loser" installed right over my forehead. The fact that she goes onto explain that she was raised in a sexually charged atmosphere only a few steps above a brothel didn't help. She is a writhing, pulsing, sexual creature while I'm an amoeba whose cell hasn't yet divided.

Not only did I not explain the faux Dani romance as I'd intended, but I agreed to a pity fuck so Brooke can fulfill her community service hours for the romantically and sexually disenfranchised, of which I'm a fully vested member.

I only crawl out of my cocoon long enough to grab a bowl of Captain Crunch. Then I go back to bed to eat and watch the *Spongebob Squarepants* marathon on Nickelodeon. The happy sponge in the little shorts is the only thing preventing me from falling into a funk. My phone rings just past noon and thanks to my curious nature, I surprise myself by answering it.

"So Nathan, what the hell is up with our date tonight? I haven't even heard from you."

"I'm sorry, Dani," I moan.

"If this deal is off, it's fine with me. I just need to know cause I need to get out tonight one way or another, and the girls are going clubbing."

I can't mess this up now. "How about a movie?"

"You're paying, right?"

"Of course. I'm a gentleman."

"A gentleman, now that's a novelty these days. Good for you. Keep that up 'cause I bet Brooke will get off on that too."

My head starts pounding. *How will I ever keep this up?* "So can I pick you up at seven? I ask. "We can eat something and then see a nine o'clock."

"Right-e-O," she confirms.

All in all it wasn't a bad first date, despite the fact that it really wasn't a date, the movie sucked and I spilled the popcorn. At least the Mexican food was good and Dani gave me the lowdown on the various love connections at Sketch Republic. Evidently there must be something in the air filtration system because lust sparks are flying all over the place, on every show. Leave it to me to be completely oblivious until it's spelled out for me. Even loser Kevin is getting it on with Beatrice down in editing.

At the end of the evening, when I walk Dani to her door, I start to laugh.

"What's so funny?" She asks, confused.

"Well, Brooke's been teaching me how to kiss you goodnight for our first date. The irony of all of this is just too much."

She puts her hands on her hips defiantly. "Wait, you said minimal kissing and I thought it was only for PDA's."

"Chill, I'm not kissing you."

"Why don't you tell Brooke that you chickened out and you need more training?"

"I may just do that," I tease her. *If I am ever able to face her again,* I groan inwardly. I reach out and give Dani a hug. "Thanks again for everything."

"You're welcome. See you Monday."

• • •

Curtis never shows up for tennis and brunch at the folks Sunday morning. When I call him he picks up his phone but I can hear Billie giggling in the background.

"What's up, Bro?"

"Aren't you coming?"

"Coming?"

"To Mom and Dad's—it's brunch time."

"No shit, it's Sunday already!" He appears to pull the phone away as his voice gets softer. "Baby, did you know it's Sunday?" She squeals. In a million years I would have never imagined hearing Billie sound giddy like that. Curtis gets back on the line.

"Hey Bro, will you tell Mom and Dad that I'm tied up and can't make it." More loud squeals from Billie. Holy shit, does she really have him tied up?

I swallow hard. "Do you mean literally tied up?"

"Wouldn't you like to know," he taunts. "Let's just say that Billie thinks I've been naughty."

"Too much information!" I yell into the phone. "I'll see you next week."

· · ·

Wary doesn't begin to describe my mood Monday morning. Three times I pick up the phone to call in sick so that I don't have to face Brooke yet, but I finally man up and head out the door. After all, I can't avoid her forever.

It helps that when I wander into the break room mid-morning to get more coffee that Dani and Genna are having a colorful conversation that totally takes my mind off my problems.

"He was hot Dani, really I would do him without a second thought," Genna says with wide eyes and a brisk head nod.

"Really, that dude from Tangled?" Dani responds. "From the commercials he looked obnoxious."

"Yeah, but he grows on you. And he's got the moves." Genna sighs.

I silently sigh too. Yeah, those animated leading men always got the moves.

"Well, haven't you ever seen a cartoon character you'd do?" I challenge Dani. I notice Nick at the back of the room trying to get a vending machine to work.

She thinks for a moment. "I would say Tarzan. Yeah, most definitely."

"Oh yeah, he was hot," Genna agrees.

"What a body. And I'd finally get to see what was under that loin cloth."

I notice Nick is lingering, leaning against the vending machine eating his newly purchased granola bar.

"So how about you Nathan?" Dani asks. "Who have you dreamed about, besides me of course."

Genna snickers, and Nick looks over.

"I bet you liked that Jessica Rabbit from *Who Framed Roger Rabbit*. Am I right?" Dani asks.

"Close," I admit. "My favorite is Tex Avery's Red Hot. Now that's a body...and the way she moved. She was hand-drawn sex for sure."

"So you like the girls with the curves, some meat on their bones," Genna says happily.

"Yes, I do," I say with conviction.

"If only more guys felt that way," Genna sighs. "I could eat more cupcakes."

"That girl in the movie Saturday was pretty lush," Dani points out.

"You guys saw a movie Saturday?" Genna asks surprised. I can feel Nick's eyes on me but I refuse to look at him. I'm going to need to talk to him as soon as I figure out what to say.

"Yeah, Nathan took me out on a date." She says dramatically.

We hear a rustle and all three of us turn to see Nick leaving the room. *Fuck.*

Dani gives me a knowing look. I can't tell if she's happy or scared.

Maybe I should go pick a fight with Joel now because clearly my life isn't quite complicated enough, and he's the only key person I haven't offended this week. I lower my head and stumble back to my cube.

Four twenty-five. I hold the warm cup in my hand with my marker poised in the air. What to draw? What to say?

I finally settle on Hefty Smurf scratching his head confused, while his intended conquest, Smurfette's head is peeking out from where she is hiding behind the Starbucks logo. I do the whole thing in a blue marker.

I give myself a pep talk and slowly head upstairs, praying that Brooke is in a meeting. I approach Morgan's desk warily, looking past her to see if Brooke is in her office. My stomach falls when I see that she is, but then a wave of relief hits me when I realize that she's on the phone.

Making a split-second decision, I set the drink in front of Morgan.

"Hey, Morgan, I see that Brooke's on the phone and I don't want to interrupt her. Could you just give this to her."

She stands up and takes the drink. "Actually she told me to interrupt her when you came by."

"No, that's okay. Don't interrupt her," I say as I take steps backwards, then turn to head towards the elevator. Of course this is one of those days where both cars are on the bottom floor and don't appear to be going anywhere. I squint and look up, searching the halls for an *exit* or *stairs* sign.

"Nathan?"

I push my glasses up my nose and turn slowly to see Brooke standing with her hands on her hips. Her body language looks angry but her eyes look sad.

"Can you come with me please?"

I nod and follow her silently. She's wearing heels and one of those tight business-y skirts that showcases her magnificent bottom. The sway of her hips with each step hypnotizes me all the way back until I'm in a trance by the time we're in her office with the door closed.

She turns towards me. "Morgan said you practically threw my drink down and ran down the hall. What's going on?"

I want to cover my face with my hands, but I can't hide from Brooke. She doesn't deserve that. I study the Iron Giant poster for a minute to think about what I can say.

"I'm just so embarrassed, Brooke. You know things about me now that no one else knows. And as okay as it felt Friday when I was drunk, now I'm just horrified that I told you all of those really personal things."

"So you are horrified and don't want to see me because I know you've had a disappointing sexual history?"

She whispered the question but it's like she's screamed in my ear. I nod, muted from the weight of that sober confession.

"Does that mean you don't want to be friends anymore? Is that what you're trying to tell me?" I look up and see her sad eyes are now veiled with hurt.

"Maybe we shouldn't be friends." I admit. "It's so unbalanced. You're helping me and what do I do for you besides the computer stuff? What do I bring to the friendship? I don't want you to feel sorry for me. It makes me feel like a bigger loser than I already am."

"You're not a loser, Nathan," she insists, but I can hear the defeat in her voice. She lets out a long sigh and sinks into her desk chair before putting her face in her hands and leaning forward over her desk. "I knew this would happen," she mumbles.

I notice a sophisticated arrangement of flowers on her desk. All kinds of fancy flowers: roses, lilies, stuff that girls like...stuff that I would've never given Brooke. My heart shrinks a bit more and I know I can never compete for her with guys like Arnold.

"Are those from Arnold?"

I notice the corners of her mouth turn up slightly when she hears me use his real name. She nods, silently watching me.

"Did you make up?"

"He spoiled me all weekend to make up for his mistake...dinner at Le Cirque, brunch in Malibu. This is my third delivery of flowers. Do you like my new earrings?" She flicks the dangling blue stone with her finger. "He got these for me too."

Her tone is weird. I'm not sure if his gestures did the trick or not.

"They're very nice. Well, that's good. You should be spoiled," I say quietly.

"But we really aren't going to be friends anymore? Is that really it, Nathan?"

"I guess not."

"I'm an idiot," she says, leaning her head on her hand, her elbow resting across a tall pile of business papers. "I should've never touched you. I pushed things too far and I worried about it all weekend. That was wrong of me. I care about you, and I like being close to you; that's where my intentions were. I didn't want to upset you. I hope you understand that."

"Of course, I do."

"But I was wrong. I'm sorry I touched you. Please just forget it ever happened."

"Brooke..." I stammer.

"It's okay. I won't bother you anymore. Let's just say goodbye now." She stands and walks to the door and opens it without looking at me.

"Brooke..."

"Please, Nathan."

Oh, I have really screwed up now.

"Okay, bye."

The door closes softly behind me.

Morgan doesn't even turn around.

I walk mechanically to the elevator like a wind-up toy. I'm in my car and half way home before it hits me that I'm supposed to be going over the upcoming storyboards with Joel right now. I walked out of the building and left my iPod on my desk and computer open.

I don't even hesitate. I can't care about any of that, and I keep driving. I just blew my one chance for true love, and it's taking all my focus to get myself safely home. Even if I could have Wayne's wise words fill my head, and some whiskey fill my unquenchable thirst, it still wouldn't do a thing for the hole I just blasted in my heart.

The next morning, everything is grey, and I feel dead inside but I do my damndest to get to the studio and catch up on my work. I don't want Joel to think I'm dropping the ball, on top of everything else.

Right before noon I sense someone looking at me and I glance up to see Nick waiting in my doorway. He looks very intense.

"Got a minute?" he asks.

"Sure." I slowly pull out my earbuds and pause my iPod. "What's up?"

"So what's going on with you and Dani?" He folds his arms over his chest and watches me carefully.

The direct approach… I gotta hand it to Nick, that's pretty effective. I can't believe his timing, but I suck it up because I know I should've faced him already.

"We went out Saturday. Does that bother you? I didn't think you'd mind since you aren't into her anymore."

"How do you know what I'm into?"

"Well, I presumed. It's been a long time since you were together. Dani doesn't think you like her anymore either. She told me that."

"Is that so? I'm just surprised that you didn't ask me first. I thought we were friends."

"We are friends. I'm sorry, you're right, I should've said something. You looked pissed off that night we all went out."

He watches me for a moment. "Okay, it's cool. You've always been clueless."

"So we're still friends?"

"Yeah, you idiot." He smiles, just slightly.

"But can I suggest something, Nick? If you do still like Dani you should try to work it out with her. You guys seem like you're still into each other."

"Really?" he asks with his eyebrows raised.

"I think she still loves you, dude. She's a really great girl, you know."

"I know," he says quietly.

"Well, so are you going to make me fight you for her?" I grin at him and he rolls his eyes.

"Yeah, how about a duel at sunset?"

"No, a video game at lunchtime is more my speed. You pick the game."

He suddenly gets serious. "The problem is that I don't want to screw with her. If we get back together it's gotta be for good—the white dress and diapers and shit. I just need to be sure that I'm ready to grow up 'cause right now I'm still a big, stupid kid and Dani deserves better than that."

"I think you're more grown up than you think," I say resolutely. "But if you insist, I'll keep dating her until you make up your mind."

"Just watch your step, asshole. If I hear that you've fucked her, I'll kill you."

"Noted."

I watch him walk away and I replay the conversation in my head. Either I finally did something right today, or I screwed up my relationships with two more people who I really care about. I'm such a mess; I can't decide which…all I can do is hope that I did the right thing.

• • •

There's finally a single ray of sunshine that afternoon. I get a call from Chris Carpenter from Sharper Edge Comics wanting to meet me for lunch to discuss the deal for the B-Girl series. He puts his assistant on and we set it up for next Friday in Studio City. I feel a surge of excitement pumping through me and even though the feeling quickly fades, I'm still grateful to have the meeting to look forward to.

Just after five I see Morgan wandering down our aisle sticking her head in each cube looking for someone. I consider hiding under my animation desk, but before I can fall to my knees she sees me.

"What happened to you?" She looks angry, tapping her watch impatiently.

"What are you talking about?"

"Where's her coffee? Her afternoon visit?"

I blanch.

"Did the pitch not go well and now it's payback time?" she sneers.

"Morgan, for the last time I wasn't going to pitch her, and I didn't. That's not what's happening here."

"Okay, can you then tell me why she left early yesterday without a word and I caught her crying at her desk a few minutes ago. Right after she'd asked if I'd seen you."

She might as well have kicked me in the stomach. "Really?" I ask softly. "She was crying?"

"I've never seen her cry before. It freaked me out. And yes, she's my boss…but I care about her. She's a really good person."

"I know she is, Morgan. She was just trying to help me, and I screwed up."

"Well then, fix it, damn it!"

Morgan's kind of scary when she's mad. I jump up from my drafting chair and grab my Sharpie. "I'll be up there in a few."

"Okay, hurry. She just got pulled into a meeting so I want it waiting for her when she gets back."

Other than the excruciating moments in the elevator, I run all the way to Starbucks. My hand's shaky when I draw on the cup but I do my best. I draw an eye, with a screw next to it followed by an apostrophe and the letter "d". Next I draw an arrow pointing up. *I screwed up.*

Then underneath I draw a little caricature of me with my hair in my face, big glasses, and the biggest frown. In small letters underneath I write, *I'm sorry* and just underneath, *I miss you.*

The barista has put those little green stoppers in the sip hole of the lid so I'm able to run back to the studio without spilling it all.

My heart is pounding as I run up to Morgan's desk and hand her Brooke's drink. "Did I make it? Is she out yet?"

"No, perfect timing," she says, giving me a thumbs up. "I think it's almost over."

"Good," I gasp still catching my breath. I set the second coffee on her desk. "Here Morgan, this mocha's for you. Thanks for your help."

She looks up at me and smiles. "You're welcome. Thanks for the drink. Here I'm going to put this on her desk so it's waiting for her when she gets back. I really hope this will cheer her up."

"Me too."

Everything hits me as I get into the elevator and almost sink to my knees. The emotional overload of the last couple of days is crashing down on me. I don't know how much more I can take. Maybe I was better off alone, with my predictable weeks, and small, reliable group of friends. I'm living Mr. Toad's Wild Ride now and it's terrifying. But just hearing how sad Brooke is breaks my heart again and makes me realize that I can't walk away from her…not now, not ever.

I get back to my cube and force myself to work knowing that Joel often walks through in the afternoon to see how our assignments are progressing. Sure enough, only minutes later he steps in to say hi and I show him the latest drawings. He doesn't seem to sense anything amiss and I breath a sigh of relief when he moves on to Andy's cube.

Just past five-thirty, I get a text. My heart leaps when I see it's from Brooke.

Thanks for the coffee, Nathan.

I'm so sorry for being an idiot, Brooke.

You're not an idiot. This would be a lot for anyone to deal with. I think you're very brave.

Well, I think you're amazing. Thanks for believing in me.

Do does this mean we can still be friends?

I realize how brave she is to ask this.

There's nothing I want more. Can I still come over Thursday night and help with your website?

95

I guess so, but only if you're sure you're comfortable with me. I promise not to touch you.

Why don't we talk about the touching part when we meet? I'm very comfortable with you, okay?

Okay, that makes me happy. I'll see you at seven.

See you then. I have a big smile when I hit the send button for the last time.

• • •

Thursday at six forty-five I play the Foo Fighters, *Everlong* really loud the whole way up the hill. I can barely breathe I'm so excited to see her. Even though I can't open my heart to her yet, I wish I could tell her everything…that I love her…that I want her to touch every part of me, as long as I can touch her too.

After I park, I lower the sun-shield and looking in the mirror, try to smooth out my crazy hair. Before I climb out of the car I take a few deep, calming breaths.

It's okay. It's okay. It's okay.

When she buzzes me in, I use my back to push the gate shut, as my hands are more than full. She pulls the door open and smiles. She looks hopeful and happy to see me.

I'm overcome. I want to cry out of frustration for almost messing this up. I want to pull her into my arms and kiss her until the sun sets over us, or something equally corny, but true.

Instead I lift my heavy arms and show her the twelve packs of Heinekens I'm holding in each hand. "These are for you. Well, for us." I say quietly.

"Thanks," she says, pulling the door open wider.

And then I realize why I'm the luckiest man in the world.

Yes! Yoga pants. Her curvy hips and lush thighs are sheathed in stretchy black magic. I almost pass out in excitement. My eyes trail up to her torso where Tom is chasing Jerry over the round, full swell of her breasts. It's almost too much — it's so damn good. I know she's worn this just for me.

Now I understand people with faith. God *is* Good…so, so good. Yoga pants good, and in my book there's nothing better.

I step right up to her and lay the beer at her feet like a sacred offering. She looks up at me and smiles, opening her arms and I step right into them.

The hug is long, our hearts unfolding. This is a new beginning and I'm going to be stealthy and hardy, brave and kind, everything that asshat, Arnold, isn't. I will do whatever it takes until my dreamy, cartoon-loving, Red Hot in yoga pants knows without a doubt that I'm the best man for her.

Animate Me / Chapter Nine / Extra-Special Best Friends

"That's a good little boy." ~ Betty Boop[viii]

When we finally pull apart from our hug she looks down at the beer, and then back at me with her eyebrows raised.

"Are you planning on getting me drunk tonight?"

"No," I stammer. "This is just proof of my intention to keep coming back."

"Oh," she smiles warmly. "I like that. Come on, let's see how many we can fit in the fridge."

I pick up the cases and follow her to the kitchen, enjoying the sublime yoga pants view. I don't know when I've ever been happier.

Tonight she's feeding me Middle Eastern food: beef and chicken shawarma, tabouleh, fattoush salad and hummus with pita bread. Although delicious, I note that this stuff is loaded with garlic. Is this an evil plot to avoid kissing me? I'm onto her strategy but I have my own. As we finish I pull out a stick of mint gum and offer her one too.

"So I'm meeting with Sharper Edge again next Friday about my comic book. Actually it's lunch with the publisher," I tell her while she takes a sip of beer.

Her eyes get big. "So this is serious," she says, grinning. "They must really want your series. Do you want this deal? It can lead to the big time."

I start to peel the label off my beer bottle while I think about it. "Well, I want the big time, but at what price? I've done a lot of research and I don't want to give up the rights to my characters."

She looks at me and shakes her head. "You know it's almost impossible to hold onto your rights. They will demand ownership unless there's a very compelling reason that they want your particular property."

"Well, then I may have to walk away," I say firmly.

"And you're willing to do that?" She asks studying me carefully.

"You bet."

Her face lights up and she lifts her bottle to clink with mine. "Here's to artistic integrity."

"Hear, hear," I agree, and we take long sips with our lips curled up. If I do what the studio wants, there are all kinds of possibilities for money and prestige. So the fact that she wants what is best for me as an artist, no matter what the cost, makes me love her even more.

Later in her home office, I show her the rough layout for the website. She leans over my shoulder, and the sweet smell of pears surrounds me. Normally if she were this close to me, she would rest her hand on my upper back, or brush her fingers against my arm, but I'm painfully aware that she isn't touching me. She's remaining true to her word.

"Oh, that looks so good," she moans. "Where'd you find that font?"

"Genna loaned it to me. She's a font expert."

"Well, thank her for me."

I turn towards her and smile, her face close enough to kiss. She swiftly pulls back and sits down on the edge of the bed. I ache at the distance between us. I want to kiss her so much.

She looks at me, then out the window. *What's she thinking?*

"Another beer?" she looks distracted.

"Sure." I nod.

When she returns from the kitchen and hands it to me, she's watching me intently. At times like these I worry that she can look straight into my heart and see that I'm hopelessly in love with her. And if she did learn that, I fear I would no longer be welcome here, no longer be part of her life. So I bite my tongue, and turn back towards her computer screen.

She finally speaks. "Nathan?"

"Uh huh," I reply while I wait for another image to import.

"I'm really glad you're here."

I turn towards her and tip my head, trying to figure out what she's really trying to say.

"What I mean is that I'm really glad that we're still friends," she says quietly.

She still likes me. Maybe I still have a chance. I grin at her and she grins back in response.

"Me too, Brooke."

Several beers later, and done with our work, we're sprawled out on opposite ends of her couch.

"When are you going to let me see your comic book? I'm waiting for you to want me to read it."

Damn. How do I explain to her that my main character looks like her? It never seemed like an issue when I admired her from afar, but now...

"Well, um..." I stutter. *Damn.* I can feel my face turning red.

"I just hope you know that the longer you make me wait, the higher my expectations are going to be," she teases, waving her beer bottle at me.

Despite the tension, the beer buzz gives me courage. "Hey, have you ever told a white lie to get something you really wanted?"

"A white lie?" she asks, her expression unreadable.

"Uh, huh."

She makes a face. "I hate all lies—white, black or whatever...always have. Besides if you have to lie to get something, you shouldn't have it in the first place."

I feel all the blood drain from my head, and I'm fairly certain my heart has stopped beating.

"Why?" She asks.

Good job, stupid. Okay...I'm completely screwed. She's going to hate me. And just like that I lose my courage.

"Sometimes I just have trouble saying what I really feel," I stutter.

"I know it can be hard, Nathan. But you always have to try. I know, why don't you tell me how it's been seeing me tonight after all of our ups and downs this week?"

I look over at her and she seems a million miles away perched on the far arm of the couch. I can't talk about the big lie now, but I can address the immediate issue. I look down at my shoes and my fingers curl over my knees. "It's been great seeing you, Brooke, but can we talk about the touching thing?"

"Okay, if you really want to." I notice her fingers tighten over the beer bottle. "But, I'm hands free from now on, I promise."

I swallow hard and push my hair out of my eyes. "But that's my point; I don't want you to be."

She looks at me confused. "But I thought that's why you didn't want to be friends with me anymore?"

"My problem wasn't because you've touched me. Believe me. I was just so humiliated to have you learn the most embarrassing thing about me. Only a complete loser would still be this inexperienced at my age. And because of that I felt like I couldn't face you again."

I close my eyes, folding my arms tightly over my chest. "But the last two days have been hell. Not facing you meant sacrificing your friendship, and that's far worse than you knowing what a total loser I am."

She crawls down to my side of the couch, pulls my arms apart and curls up under my shoulder. It feels so good to have her close to me. I guess the touching embargo is over. I take a deep breath and pull her closer.

"You're not a total loser, Nathan." She takes my beer out of my hand and takes a swig, then hands it back. "I think you're great."

I smile at her and her compliment encourages me to ask for more. "Besides," I continue, "you know the worst about me now, and you still want to be friends. If you don't care that I'm inept, than neither will I. If you want to help me, well then, I welcome it."

"Really?"

"I want you to help me, and teach me. The times you kissed and touched me made me feel so...amazing."

"Oh, Nathan." She smiles sweetly at me. "Promise me though, that you'll tell me when I make you uncomfortable."

"Like you drinking from my beer without asking?"

She elbows me softly.

"Just kidding, I liked your lips on my beer bottle. And as for sharing, from now on I'm really going to try to be an open book."

"Okay, me too then," she agrees.

Later at her door she wraps her arms around me.

"Are we okay?" she asks.

I nod, incredibly happy that things are good with us now.

"Am I your best friend again?" She teases.

"I would say so," I confirm. "Although I've never kissed my best friend. So I guess that makes you an extra-special best friend."

"Good, I like the way that sounds."

I look down at my feet. "Brooke, does Arnold mind that we're best friends?"

"He set these open relationship rules, didn't he? He can't complain about them now," she answers cryptically.

"You know, if you were mine, I wouldn't share you with anyone," I say softly.

"Really?" She smiles widely. "That's so sweet, Nathan."

She thinks I'm just trying to be nice, but it's true. It's another in a long list of reasons why I'm better for her than Arnold.

I'm almost to the gate when I turn around.

"Hey, Brooke?" I call out.

"Yes?" she asks.

"I just wanted you to know that I really, really love it when you kiss and touch me."

"Is that so?" she asks.

"Yeah, so please don't stop no matter how goofy I get. Okay?"

She laughs. "Okay, I won't."

• • •

The next afternoon in her office she pulls me over to the couch as soon as I pass through the door.

"Well, hello to you too." I say grinning, handing over her coffee.

"I forgot to ask last night, how your date with Dani last Saturday went. Did it go well?"

I blanch. That faux date seems a million years ago and completely insignificant now that Brooke and I are extra-special best friends again. "It was okay."

"Just okay?" she asks.

"Well, I was in a bit of a state after my big reveal at the Smokehouse."

"Oh...oh, yeah." She moans sinking back against the couch. "What bad timing."

"And the movie sucked."

"You saw a movie? You never see a movie during the first stage of dating."

"Is that so?"

"Well, was the kiss at least good?"

Oh for God's sake, she isn't going to let this go.

"We didn't kiss. I guess I'm still not comfortable kissing anyone but you." I say, hoping she doesn't realize how embarrassed I am.

"Well, I'm flattered, but I should feel guilty because that isn't very productive."

"Don't feel bad for helping me, Brooke," I insist. *I wish I had the courage to tell her how I really feel.*

She grins. She almost seems relieved that my date didn't go well.

"Hey, if I may change the subject? Dani reminded me that the Rose Bowl swap meet is this Sunday in Pasadena. Do you want to go? There may be some of those great vases you like…the ones shaped like ladies heads waiting just for you."

"As much as I'd like to check out those lady-head vases, do you really think I should go with you and Dani?"

"No, I was talking about just you and me. And I thought we could stop by my parents afterwards for brunch."

"Why don't you take Dani?"

"Because I want to go with you. We'll have fun."

I'm happy because I know this is something she loves, and I can give it to her when Arnold won't. I want her to understand that I really care about what she likes to do.

She makes a face at me, but I also sense that she's pleased and tempted.

"Besides, you and I are the real collectors."

"Okay, I'll go," she confirms. "It's been a while and I've missed going so much. The only thing is that I may be a little tired. I have a party I have to go to on Saturday night." I can see her mind figuring something out. "Why don't you let me pick you up?"

Yeah, I don't really want to pick up Brooke from Arnold's where he answers the door with a towel around his six-packed waist.

"Okay. I'll email you my address and directions. How's seven a.m.? You know you have to get there early to get the good stuff." A side benefit to an early start is the sooner I get her away from Arnold the better.

"Are you nuts? Eight, and not a minute earlier."

At three minutes after eight I look out my living room window again. What if she forgets and doesn't show up? It was pretty forward of me to ask her to come, but she did say we're best friends now. This is the kind of stuff best friends do…right?

A moment later I get a text.

Sorry-late, but in the car, be there in ten.

Relieved to know she didn't forget, I reply.

Great, see you then.

I go into the kitchen and get a dishtowel to wrap around her macchiato to keep it warm. I had them make it extra hot but that was twenty minutes ago so I want to make sure it's how she likes it.

Pacing back and forth through my house looking for things to straighten, I try to imagine seeing my place through Brooke's eyes. She loves cartoons so that's a plus since there are figurines and framed animation cels throughout the house.

I normally have Delia, my parent's housekeeper come clean my house only every other week to keep it from being a pig sty, but I had her make an extra visit yesterday just to make sure everything was clean. And before she came I took all the piles of junk lying around and shoved them in the closets. Thank God Delia does my laundry or I'd have piles of dirty clothes all over the house. As it is she always gives me a hard time for only having beer, milk for my cereal and Cheese Whiz in the fridge.

Despite my college dorm tendencies, I feel a sense of pride as I walk through the rooms. I love my little house, and I really hope she likes it too. I look out the window again just as her Prius pulls up in front and I excitedly go out to the front porch to greet her.

I watch her take in all the landscaping as she walks under the arbor and up the winding brick walkway. She stops to smell some roses and then looks up at me and smiles. "Wow, Nathan. Look at this yard!"

The only pieces of furniture in the room are two leather chairs and a coffee table covered with comic books. If it had been up to me it would have ended up crabgrass and strangely shaped topiaries.

"Like it? I love it!" she exclaims. "Was it like this when you bought the house?"

"No actually the yard was pretty awful when I moved in. But my brother Curtis was involved with an interior designer at the time, and her partner was a landscape architect. He did the designs."

"I love the funky painted garden gnomes. Are they your touch?"

"How'd you guess?" I smile watching her reaction to everything...so far so good. I jam my hands in my pockets nervously. "Do you want to come inside for a minute?"

"Sure," she steps onto the porch and gives me a hug.

When I open the door and we step inside, she smiles. "Oh my, Nathan, what's this?"

"My living room," I answer sheepishly.

She's reacting to the glass cases full of figurines that line the room. Each wall is a different bright color. The only pieces furniture in the room are two leather chairs and a coffee table covered with comic books.

"Who or what was your inspiration here?"

"Pee-wee Herman," I answer honestly. I go over and flip the switch that lights up all the cases. I always get a thrill when I do that. The spotlight on my bronze Rocketeer sculpture makes it glow.

"Wow! So this is Nathan's playhouse? Did the designer do this for you?"

"The designer quit the job because of this room. I was very insistent about what I wanted and she hated it. Actually I was glad when she quit because then I got to finish the house the way I wanted."

She smiles warmly at me. "It's like a gallery, or a collectible store. Have Dani or any of the girls you know seen this?"

"Nope, you're the first."

"Ahhh. Well, show me more."

The dining room has a space age Jetson's table and chairs that I found on eBay. Once I had them I went nuts with the theme. I also have a sixties starburst light fixture and vintage Disneyland Tomorrowland posters on the wall. I point out my framed Jetson's animation cel that hangs above the side table with pride.

"Look, it's signed by Bill Hanna and Joe Barbera."

She examines it closely. "Cool," she says softly. "I love how much thought and effort you've put into everything."

"Thanks," I say proudly. If she only knew how much it means to me that she likes my house. "Will you hang out with me here some time?"

She smiles, "Sure."

She's particularly interested in my home studio and studies the art on the wall and the way my animation table is set up. This is the room most out of control with piles of books and drawings on every surface. Luckily I've stashed away my B-Girl art in the flat files though as I'm still not ready to show her that.

"Is this where you work on your comic book?" she asks.

I nod. "But I put that stuff away. I'll show it to you another time."

She makes a face at me, but doesn't argue. She knows how to handle artists.

As we move to the end of the hall, I'm not sure if it's appropriate to show her my bedroom or not. I hesitate in the doorway and look down at my feet.

"This is…my room."

She looks up at me, and hesitates, but then wanders inside. She takes in the wall of windows facing the back garden. "Wow," she says quietly.

I give her a moment as she approaches my bookshelves and takes in the titles, along with my DVDs and CDs.

"Wow, you have really eclectic taste," she comments. "I'm impressed." She finally turns towards the elephant in the room. "And what a bed!"

"It's pretty grand, huh?" I ask happily. I love my bed. I even painted the dramatic headboard with my own design. "Here you have to test it out. Lay down."

She raises her eyebrows, but climbs up on the bed anyway. When she's all the way on she turns and sinks into the midnight blue velvet covered duvet. "Nice," she sighs.

"Wait till you see the best part!" I climb on and lie down next to her then reach over for the remote. "Ready?"

"I think so," she laughs.

I press a button and the foot of her side the bed slowly lifts, elevating her legs.

"Woooo," she hoots.

Next I press another button and the head of my side the bed lifts.

"Does it vibrate too?" she asks laughing.

I grin and press another button.

"Wo-o-o-o-Ho-o-o-o," she exclaims with the vibration in her voice. "Hell yeah…this is better than Disneyland! I'd never get out of bed. Let me try it!"

She reaches over for the remote but I pull it away as I keep pressing the different buttons. Next thing you know we've got an *I Love Lucy* episode going. The sides are quickly lifting at different times, while the bed madly vibrates. In her effort to get the remote we end up wrestling for it and my tenacity takes over. We're both howling with laughter and grabbing at each other.

But I'm stronger and suddenly I'm on top of her, pinning her to the mattress while one hand holds her wrists down over her head, and the other waves the remote over her head.

"Oh no you don't!" I taunt. "No one but me plays with the magic remote."

I suddenly realize that she's not laughing anymore, and instead her eyebrows are raised as she lifts her head off the mattress and looks down towards where I'm pressed over her. I take a breath and follow her gaze to see her legs spread wide open while my pelvis is pressed right there. As I shift I realize that I am completely aroused and rubbing against her. I freeze, embarrassed. We're still and silent, only the sound and movement of the vibrating bed filling up the room.

"Nathan," she whispers. I think I hear longing in her voice but I can't be sure.

The only thing I'm certain of is that Brooke is on my bed. Not just on my bed, but beautifully, seductively, gloriously pressed against me on my bed and I am dangling somewhere between panic and my supreme happy place. If I were a cartoon character my eyes would be bugging out of my head, and my tongue hanging to the ground while I howled. But I'm a man, and my lust soars as I look into her eyes and feel her thighs spread wide and her legs wrap around me.

Everything I want is underneath me. Do I roll away and apologize for being so forward or show Brooke how much I desire her in every way?

Animate Me / Chapter Ten / Right Girl, Wrong Time

"Oh! Oh! Oh! Oh! Gromit! There's a bomb in me pants!" ~ Wallace[ix]

All the times I've imagined Brooke in my bed underneath me, I never thought it would happen like this.

She looks up at me, watching me intently and I can't help it. I shift my pelvis and slide against her. She has to feel how my heart is thundering and know how preciously close I am to losing control.

But instead of pushing me away, she shifts her hips and rubs back. Her eyes close and when they open again I'm sure…it's *the look*…the look of wanting, needing, that in this very moment she belongs to me.

When our lips meet the kiss isn't soft and tentative, but heated and insistent. Her fingers wind into my hair and pull me closer. There's moaning, but I'm not sure if those sounds are coming from me or her, or both of us. I don't care. I just keep kissing her, pressing down, breathing her scent. I'm a desperate man on the brink of salvation.

When we finally break apart to gasp for air, I realize the ferocity of my grinding, as if my hips won't give up until we are actually joined. *Is it possible to bruise her down there?* I wonder horrified. But before I can worry another moment she takes control.

Her teeth scrape up my neck and her hands reach down and grab my butt controlling the rhythm of our rocking.

"Like this," she says softly.

I follow her lead and realize that with this shift her eyes flutter each time I stroke. "This?" I question, hopeful.

"Oh, yes," she confirms, her cheeks flushed.

I kiss her again, this time with even more confidence. I wonder if she could climax from just this friction. She's acting like she could, and it's making me wild inside.

"Touch me," she whispers her cheek pressed against mine.

My hand lingers, and she takes it and places it on her breast. I'm mesmerized by the feelings as I explore—firm yet soft, more than a handful, her nipple hardening to my touch. Even though I've drawn her breasts a thousand times, I could've never fully imagined how incredible they would feel.

"You're making me feel so good," she moans.

Oh God, she's so perfect. As my hand moves over her breast I can feel that her heart is thundering too. It's so intense for me that I pause. What do I do next? What's she expecting of me? As I continue to hesitate I fear that I've lost my game, and she senses it too.

She grazes her lips along my chin until they brush against my ear. "Are you okay? What do you want, Nathan?" she asks tenderly.

I must be doing something wrong; because I thought what I wanted was pretty damn obvious. Wasn't the pelvic thrusting a pretty clear indication? I search her face to see if I can figure out what she's trying to say.

She reaches up and gently pushes my hair out of my eyes. "What do you want...right now, this very moment?"

"You," I say quietly as I tentatively trail my hand along her hip. "I've never felt this way...ever."

She smiles, "I'm feeling pretty amazing too. But I want you to be sure you're ready for being this intimate with me."

I feel her run her fingers along the waist of my jeans and linger at the snap. I ache to feel her hands on me again. I want her lips on me, and I desperately need to be inside of her.

Am I ready? No, but I may never feel ready to get naked with someone as amazing as Brooke. How can I possibly live up to the other men she's been with?

"I don't know if I'll ever be ready," I admit as I look away embarrassed. "But I want to be."

Brooke pivots her body gently so that we both roll to our sides. We lay facing each other and she takes my hand and starts playing with my fingers before she looks into my troubled eyes.

"There's no rush, you know. The build up is half the fun," she teases.

"Half?" I question skeptically.

"Well, no, not really half. But I think you should be sure, you know?" She reaches for the remote and turns off the vibration mode on the bed.

I groan, and close my eyes.

She scoots closer and lays her hands on my chest. "You *will* be sure Nathan, I promise. When it's the right girl at the right time, you'll know."

I sigh an endless sigh. I have to imagine that she knows she's the *right one*, the only one. I feel her gentle hand rest in the center of my chest as I try to calm down.

The *right* girl's hand is placed over my heart. Every moment we are together she's guiding me in ways I can't yet understand. But until I have the courage to tell her the truth, all I can do is follow her lead. I hope one day I won't just be stumbling after her, but right by her side.

Somehow Brooke magically keeps things from being awkward by distracting me with flea market talk as we ease off the bed and get ready to leave. I try to push my failure out of my mind so it doesn't ruin our day.

Remembering our coffees in the kitchen, I smile showing her where I wrapped up her macchiato like a baby swathed in a blanket. Despite my efforts, the drinks are no longer hot so we nuke them before grabbing our muffins and heading out the door.

"I can't believe you made it to Starbucks before I even got here. You're a saint."

"Well, you warned me you'd be tired, and I need you amped up to keep up with me."

"So you're a serious antique-r then?" she asks, her eyebrows rise playfully.

"I've been known to knock over an old lady to get to something I want. One even tried to wrestle me for a Spiderman bobble head for her grandson."

"Who won?"

"No contest." I grin.

"Hardcore," she shakes her head. "I took a mini-Snoopy piggybank away from a kid once. I made him cry." She flexes her little muscles dramatically. "We'll make quite a pair."

"I'm sure we will," I agree.

"What's our strategy today?" she asks. "Divide and conquer?"

"No, I think we should stick together—see if we're flea market compatible. You know, you can't have a dawdler with a speed shopper."

"Absolutely," she agrees with a mock-serious look on her face. "If you are a dawdler, this will be our one and only Rose Bowl outing together… just saying…"

"Noted," I confirm as I pull into a parking space. My cheeks flush with treasure-seeking anticipation as we exit the car.

She extends her hand, and I take it.

"Excited?" she asks.

I nod.

"Let's do this!" We march towards the entrance buzzing with anticipation.

"Oh my God, oh my God…Nathan look!"

Alarmed I move quickly towards her. We already have several purchases between us.

I turn my nose up. "Why are you holding a Strawberry Shortcake lunchbox?"

Her eyes are watering. "I had this exact one Nathan! I remember that was during my stage where I ate peanut butter and strawberry jam for lunch every single day. It made my mom crazy."

"That sounds like the kind of memory you would want to forget."

"No! I loved the little freckled girl with the strawberry shaped hat attached to her head. And I loved The Peculiar Purple Pieman too."

"I've gotta warn you, your pedestal has some serious cracks right about now. That thing is trippy, like the artist was on acid," I tease her. "What's with those magic mushrooms anyway? If I were you I'd put the lunch box down and walk away."

"Hey, I didn't make fun of you for that Transformer toy you just bought."

"But that was cool," I argue.

She holds up the lunchbox to the vendor.

"Fifty," he shouts out.

"Too much," she says with a pout, and we move on.

Of course, when she takes a break to find the port-a-potties I run back to the booth and buy her the Strawberry Shortcake lunch box.

She rejoins me about three booths down where I've spotted a Mojo Jojo keychain mixed in with a bunch of random Christmas ornaments. I lift it up to show her.

"Hey look…you can get this for Arnold."

She gives me a dirty look. "Would you stop. He isn't that hairy."

I set it back down. "Can I ask you something?"

She nods, only paying half attention as she examines a case with Bakelite jewelry.

"How did you start going out with Arnold in the first place? You guys seem so different."

"Yeah, we're very different." She pauses and she turns to look at the table of depression glass. "Do you promise not to think less of me if I tell you why?"

I nod. "Promise."

She stops to think for a minute before she starts explaining. "I guess I've always felt like an outsider…my whole life, I was the girl everyone thought was strange. My grandmother made all my clothes, and I brought these weird organic lunches while everyone else ate the fish sticks and chicken nuggets from the cafeteria. But most of all I was weird because I was obsessed with cartoons and comics. They were my escape, they took me to my happy place."

I smile at her. Her past is yet another reason why we're destined to be together. I watch her pick up a cobalt blue vase and hold it up to the light. She sets it back down and turns towards me.

"Later when the hormones kicked in, I always had a boyfriend but they were outsiders like me. Arnauld would've never looked twice at me."

"But I'm sure you were always beautiful," I argue.

She smiles and shrugs. "I don't know, maybe like you, I blossomed late and once I was working at Nickelodeon I put more effort into how I looked so that I could fit in with the people in my department. The irony is that I always fit in with the artists, but I wasn't talented enough to be one, so I had to carve my own path. As I worked my way up I found myself in meetings…dealing with executives."

"Did changing the way you looked really help?" I ask, curious.

"Sadly, I think it did. As much as we hope it's not true, we are judged so much by how we look."

We move towards the next vendor who has a lot of vintage toys. I pick up a random Mickey Mouse faded plush so that I don't seem like I'm too fixated on what she's saying.

"Right around then I met Arnauld. From the moment I met him he made me feel like I was cool and part of the in-crowd. He'd take me out to hot clubs and the edgy, word of mouth bars and restaurants. Suddenly I was meeting a lot of people and had something exciting to do all the time. It was like I had walked into someone else's life, and I just went for it. He would even take me shopping and buy me clothes. And then when he started to help me professionally my career really took off."

She picks up a vintage Barbie in a little black and white swimsuit. "We had so much fun in the early days. It was crazy-fun for a long time."

Crazy fun? I'm sure I'll never make Brooke feel that way, and I'm actually not sure I would want to anyway.

"Is it still really great like that?" I look up at her hopeful that she'll say no. I'm searching for a sign that her passion for him has truly faded.

When she sets the Barbie back down her tiny shoe falls off. Brooke carefully picks it up and wiggles it back on her permanently pointed foot.

"You know what I've learned Nathan? All those people living the glamorous, hip life are really not that interesting even though they think they are."

"Really?" I ask. "You wouldn't rather be out with them right now than at the Rose Bowl with me?"

She laughs and loops her arm through mine pulling me along. "Oh Nathan, you're soooo much more interesting than those people. I would choose this over sitting in a chic café listening to gossip any day."

My hope flares brightly. It occurs to me that there could be no better time to give her my gift. "Hey, I got something for you." I step away and present the bag to her. "Go on, look inside."

She puts her hands on her hips and tilts her head. "What did you do?" she asks in a playful admonishing tone. She reaches for the bag and peers inside. She looks back up at me with big doe eyes.

"Nathannnn," she sighs and I can feel the emotion in her voice. She pulls out the lunch box and admires it, then clutches it to her chest. "You're too good to me."

I smile. "I could never be too good to you."

She steps close and wraps her arms around me and presses her cheek against my chest. "Thank you, you're the best."

I wrap my arms around her too and note that I'm no longer awkward and stiff when I hug her like this. It just feels right.

• • •

"So you grew up in Pasadena?" she asks, while we load up the car. We managed to scope over half of the flea market in just under two hours.

"Well, actually Calabasas, but it was the land of the evil beautiful blonde people. The kids really bullied me there, so my parents thought I'd fit in better in Pasadena. Besides my dad loves living so close to Caltech-nerd nirvana."

"So was the bullying better in Pasadena?" she asks having a hard time containing the distress on her face.

"A bit, but really only by a matter of degrees. The confident jocks can make high school a rough place for artists who love cartoons and comics."

As we pull up to the house I give her one more out. "Are you sure you're up for this? They can be very odd."

She turns towards me, and smiles. "They sound like my kind of people, Nathan…let's go."

She seems a little taken aback as we head up the walkway. "This is quite a house," she says. "What does your dad do again?"

"He's an inventor."

"Did he invent the Post-it Note or something? This is pretty grand."

I look up at the Greene and Greene craftsman style home and see it with a new perspective. "I hadn't thought about it, but I guess you're right."

I lead her around the side of the house, into the back and towards the tennis court. Right as we approach the gate I hear Curtis moan loudly.

When we step inside we see that he's playing against Dad and Billie, and they appear to be winning. Billie is doing some type of victory sashay across the court.

Dad sees us first. "Look," he calls out and points, "Nathan's here with his date."

Ugh.

"Dad, this is *my friend* Brooke, not my date."

He ignores me and steps up to shake her hand. "Nice to meet you Brooke, Nathan told us about you." He turns towards me. "You're right son, she's very attractive."

Can I die now? Can't a meteor fall from the sky and nail me, turning me into tennis court dust? I look over at Brooke and she's smiling, but right then Billie and Curtis approach us.

"So this is Brooke," Curtis booms. "Nice to meet you. Have you and Billie met?"

"Hey, I know you," Billie says surprised. "You've shopped in our store, right? It's Billie's Outer Limits on Olive near Buena Vista."

Brooke smiles. "Yeah. I almost went in last week to buy Nathan's book. He won't give me one."

"Don't be a dick, dude. Give Brooke a book," Curtis demands.

Billie's eyes light up as she studies Brooke. "Hey, I just realized...you look just like B..."

Panicked, I jump in and cut her off. "Can we talk about this later? I haven't introduced Brooke to Mom yet."

Billie gives me a look as I quickly lead Brooke back to the gate. Once safely inside the house, I can derive comfort in knowing that my Mom is the only one who won't humiliate me. When we step into the kitchen she turns and smiles.

"Hi Mom, this is my friend Brooke."

Mom comes over and warmly shakes her hand. "So nice to meet you Brooke. Welcome to our home."

"Thanks for having me, Mrs. Evans. Your house is amazing."

Mom smiles at her. "Thank you, and please call me Diana."

Wow, that was fast...I can already sense that she likes her.

"Nathan will have to show you around later."

"Can we help you get lunch ready?" Brooke asks.

I've never seen this side of Brooke. It's a revelation.

"That'd be great," Mom replies, as she pulls out some fruit. "Would you two mind cutting this up for me?"

I turn towards Brooke. "Do you mind getting it started? I just have to ask Dad about something. It'll only take a minute."

I hurry back to the court and when I step inside Billie comes right over and punches me in the arm.

"Hey, what's that for?" I grumble.

"Cheating on Dani, you swine." She gives me the ultra-bitchy Billie look. "And am I right, is B-Girl modeled after Brooke?"

Curtis joins us shaking his head. "I warned you dude, that this could get messy."

"Yes Billie, B-Girl is Brooke but please, you have to keep that a secret. Brooke doesn't know about it....she has no idea. Besides, she has a boyfriend already."

"Your boss's, boss's, boss, right, dude?"

Curtis is so damn helpful.

"Yeah, he's president of Sketch Republic," I admit defeated.

"Are you fucking kidding me?" she spews. "What are you going to do when she finds out about the drawings and that you're *so* in love with her? Cause from the looks of it that could be soon. Then her boyfriend will find out and you'll find your ass on the street like a cheap hooker."

I clasp my hands over my head and groan.

Billie pushes me. "And how could you do this to Dani, asshole?"

Dad steps up and joins us looking totally confused.

Curtis pulls her back. "Calm down, baby. Dani is in on this."

"What do you mean *in on this*?" Billie's face and neck are getting red. I notice her tattoos take on a different look as a result.

"Who's Dani?" Dad asks me, while watching Billie with a frightened look.

I take two steps back and fold my arms. "That's it…we're leaving. I should've known it would be a mistake to come here."

"Who's Dani?" Dad asks louder this time.

"Dani is Nathan's pretend love interest, that Brooke, his real love interest, is helping him hook up with," Curtis explains.

"What?" My Dad says with a faraway look as if he is calculating a complex math problem in his head.

Yeah, good luck with this one Dad.

"What, are you fucking kidding me! Nathan, I thought you were a smart dude," Billie says, shaking her head.

"Evidently not," I offer as I start walking towards the gate.

"Don't leave, Nathan," my Dad insists, trying to be the voice of reason. "Consider the ramifications, son. Leaving under the effects of provocation is only going to make things worse. How will you explain the deviation to Brooke? It defies logic which is intrinsically unsettling."

"Huh?" Asks Billie.

I can't blame her. You have to hang with dad awhile to get his particular form of geek speak.

He turns towards Curtis and Billie. "Let's just all agree to have a nice lunch and give Nathan a chance to recalculate and reformulate his strategy with Brooke another time, somewhere more appropriate."

"Dad's right," Curtis nods. "Besides, Mom'll be really bummed if you leave now."

I turn it over in my mind. "Okay," I agree. "But only if you promise."

They nod and so I go back in the house to rejoin Brooke where she and my mom are chatting away like long lost friends. Despite all the drama we just dodged, for a moment I allow myself to imagine Brooke and me in the future. I picture us as a real couple hanging out here on a Sunday with my parents, and I get a warm feeling in the pit of my nervous stomach.

Luckily lunch is uneventful other than my mom's obsessive staring at Billie's tattoos. Everyone is polite and talkative. Brooke seems particularly enchanted with my dad's stories about ideas he's pursued with his inventions. After lunch Curtis gives Billie a feral look and they disappear somewhere in the house while dad offers to show Brooke his work studio. I decide to stay behind and help Mom with the dishes.

"Oh, Nathan. She's lovely, really lovely. She's just the kind of girl I hoped you would find."

"But Mom, she's just a friend. She has a boyfriend already, and he's the president where I work."

"Perhaps," she states in that cryptically female way. "But clearly you two are meant to be together. She'll just need some time to work it out."

"You really think so?" I ask, not hiding the hope in my tone.

She firmly nods. "You're crazy about her, aren't you? I can see it in the way you look at her."

"I've been crazy about her for a long time," I admit. "But I never thought I'd have the opportunity to talk to her, let alone become friends. It's like the impossible doesn't seem impossible anymore."

"Like it's meant to be," she says with a dreamy look. My mom is such a hopeless romantic. I found a bunch of those erotic romance stories in the back of her closet once, leading me to believe that she can be well versed in suspending disbelief. That could explain her complete faith that Brooke will end up mine.

Brooke seems deep in thought on the drive back to my place. I try to relax and go with it, but finally I can't take it anymore.

"You're so quiet. What are you thinking?" I ask nervously.

"Just now I was thinking how much I miss having a family. I'm an only child, but before my parents got divorced we hung out a lot like your family does. And your parents are so cute together; they genuinely adore each other, don't they?"

"Oh yeah, they make a good pair. I'm sorry that your family is split up but you can be a member of my family. My parents both liked you a lot."

"Thanks." She smiles warmly. "Your Dad's pretty amazing Nathan. I'm knocked out by all the stuff he's invented."

"I'm impressed you got him to talk and open up so much, but I guess I shouldn't be. Look how much you've gotten me to talk."

She grins. "You're both really similar you know? Both of you have super creative minds."

"Well, we're both geeky and awkward. That's for sure."

As I pull up to the house Brooke looks out the window.

"So your Mom talked a bit about Rachel when we were making lunch."

"Really?" I'm not sure I want to hear this.

"So she told me that Rachel is living with a woman up North. You never mentioned that."

I pull into the driveway. "It didn't occur to me to mention it. I've only met her roommate once. Why?"

Brooke looks at me curiously. "Just wondering."

I open the trunk to my car and pull out our stuff.

"Do you want to come in and hang out?" I cringe at how stupid that sounds but I'm desperate. I'm so addicted to her that it pains me to think about her driving away and going back to Arnold.

She steps closer and runs her hands along my shoulder. "No, I've got stuff I need to do—girl stuff."

"Girl stuff? Anything I can help with?"

"Not unless you're good at mani-pedis."

"I could try," I offer. I'm an artist…so how hard could it be?

She wraps her arms around me and holds on tight. "No, I think we will leave that to the little woman with the sharp scissors. But thanks for offering."

I pause and look down at her lips with longing. "I suppose I used up all my practice kisses this morning, huh?"

"Yeah, mister, that was about a week's worth, but who's counting?"

She surprises me by reaching up and pressing her lips against mine. It's a sweet slow kiss, her tongue barely grazing mine. When we part I pause for a moment with my eyes closed not wanting it to be over.

I feel her pulling her bags out of my hands. "That was so much fun. Thanks, Nathan."

"Will you come with me again?" I ask, hopeful.

"How about next month? It's the second Sunday every month."

"Yup, it's a date then." I grin widely.

"So, see you tomorrow?"

I nod and watch her get in her car.

Inspired, I spend the rest of the afternoon drawing without restraint. Pose after pose, naked and clothed, stretched out and curled up. Laughing, pensive, smiling…every kind of beautiful.

Brooke.

Animate Me / Chapter Eleven / Man With a Tux

"We've been framed, Gumby. Never trust animated people." -Pokey[x]

At four in the morning I wake up suddenly and lay there stunned until it is time to drag myself to work. I watch the clock until the afternoon, when our group finally heads to Starbucks. Now I am minutes away from seeing Brooke again, signifying the impending conclusion of my restlessness.

I walk right past Morgan and into Brooke's office. Brooke is working at her computer, so I go straight up to her desk and sit down in the one of the visitor chairs. She looks up when I set down her coffee.

"Well, hello." She laughs but then stops when she notices the look on my face.

"Are you all right?"

I lean forward on my elbows. I gaze at the grain in the wood of her desk and finally ask the question that has tormented me for the last twelve hours.

"So that's it, isn't it…Rachel's gay?" I exhale long and slow, finally letting the air out of my chest. "It hit me in the middle of the night, and I've thought of nothing else since then."

She gets up and closes her office door, then returns to her chair. She pulls up close to her desk and leans in towards me.

"Well, that would explain a lot, wouldn't it?"

"I've wondered if that were the case from time to time. I even asked her once but she insisted that she wasn't."

Brooke has a sympathetic look on her face. I'm shaken even though I've agonized over the idea since four a.m., complete with visions of Rachel with other women dancing in my head.

"She must not have felt ready to admit it to you."

"Is that what my mom thinks too?" I ask anxiously.

"Shouldn't you ask her directly?" she gently suggests.

"I need to know right now. Come on, Brooke..."

She slowly nods, and I sigh.

"But please talk to her about it. I feel bad telling you."

"Why didn't I trust my instincts? Do you think Rachel was always gay, or did I make her that way?"

"Oh God, how could you think that? Of course she was born that way, but she must have cared about you enough to want to try men anyway."

"Oh, lucky me!" I say sarcastically. "So remember how I told you that she loved me, you know...giving her oral sex? I was thinking about that all day and how she would always have her eyes closed. Do you think she was imagining I was someone else...a woman?"

"Maybe," Brooke says sadly.

"Yeah, and her current roommate is kind of a tomboy. I swear, I'm so damn slow!" I press my fingers over my forehead in frustration.

"You just didn't want to see it. Didn't you say she was the first girl that you had a strong connection with? All things considered, I'm not surprised you didn't pick up on it since she had indicated to you that she was straight."

"You're just trying to make me feel better," I say quietly.

"No, I'm not. Give yourself a break; you aren't only attracted to gay women. Like what about Dani? I know she isn't gay. And you seem to enjoy me, and I'm not gay."

"But you're just helping me. That doesn't count."

"Sure it does, I'm not just helping selflessly. I always get really turned on with you," she says matter-of-factly, like she's talking about the weather.

"You do?" Suddenly it's like the clouds have parted. Rachel, and all her gayness, fades out of my mind.

"What? You can't tell? I thought it was rather obvious at your place yesterday morning. I've been very tempted to accelerate the education into advanced studies."

I blush and immediately feel my pants tightening. "Wow, I'd really love to sign up for that."

Oh, you're such an idiot! I shift in my chair, embarrassed that I opened my big trap.

"Damn…sorry, I'm just so clueless. I wasn't completely sure you really felt like that…"

She laughs. "Well then, you'll just have to take my word for it." She looks down at her coffee and lifts it to examine it more closely. "Now, what do we have here?"

"Brooke Berry Shortcake," I respond, smiling.

The drawing is of her perched like a sexy pin-up on top of a huge strawberry with a strawberry hat on her head. She's wearing yoga pants and a fitted T-shirt.

"Oh, this is awesome. I love it!"

I smile at her and then look down at the pile of projects strewn over her desk. "Well, we should get back to work." I slowly push away from her desk.

"Are you okay?" she asks, watching me carefully.

"I guess so. But I think I'll drink the hard stuff tonight."

• • •

Dani nails me near the break room.

"So I hear you and Brooke went to the Rose Bowl. What am I, chopped liver?"

"No, you're just not Brooke." I point out, confused that this isn't obvious.

"But I'm your pretend girlfriend. I need attention too."

I suppose she's right since she's the one trying to help me. "Okay, when should we go out again?"

"Well, a bunch of us are going out tomorrow night. Why don't you take me?"

"Is Nick going?"

"Yup," she says happily.

"I'm onto you, Dani."

"Screw you, Nathan. I'm onto you too."

The next day, just after lunch I get a frantic call from Brooke.

"Nathan, thank God you're there. I'm so screwed. I have a presentation in an hour, and my damn computer's frozen. I have documents I have to print out. I'd call the IT guy but he's a raving idiot."

"No problem. I'll be right up." I'm so excited she needs me that I take the stairs instead of waiting for the elevator.

She looks completely stressed when I arrive. She pushes away from the computer and offers me her chair.

"Thanks for coming so fast." There's relief and gratitude in her voice.

"Don't worry, I'll get you fixed up in no time." I settle in and get to work with complete focus. I need to make this work for Brooke.

About ten minutes into it, I've unfrozen the computer and located the documents, when Arnold comes into her office. I look up and see him regarding me with scorn.

"Do you ever work, man, or just come in here and bug Brooke?"

Stunned, I sit up tall and start to respond when Brooke jumps in.

"Lay off, Arnauld," she says harshly. "For your information my computer froze before I could print out the treatments for the meeting. He's helping me recover them."

"But I thought he was an animator. Why didn't you call IT?"

He directs his glare back at me. "Let me guess; are you one of those super geeks who stays up all night playing with computers too?"

He reminds me of the jocks who used to bully me in high school, and I can't let him do that to me in front of Brooke.

"No, I'm an animator who happens to be good with computers."

I hear Brooke snicker softly.

Arnauld rolls his eyes and turns to Brooke. "Whatever. Look babe, I've got a problem."

"What's that?" she asks impatiently.

"I've got a conflict now with Emmy night, and I'm not going to be able to go."

"What are you talking about? It's this Sunday! You're *supposed* to take me. This is a big deal."

I can't help but listen, and I take a glance. I'm surprised at how upset she looks. She must really want to go to the Emmys.

"I know this is your big night...after all, you are the one who discovered Lazlo and helped him develop *Danny Deletes*, but I've worked things out. Roger's offered to take you instead."

"I don't want to go with Roger," she all but shrieks. "He is the dullest man I know. He'll want to talk projections all night." She puts her hands on her hips and juts her chin out. "So, what's so damn important that you can't take me?"

He looks down and I know before he opens his mouth that it's bad.

"Zach got us ticket for *the* big fight in Vegas. Third row seats."

"Are you fucking kidding me? You're blowing off my big night for a fight?"

"Do you have any idea what it took for him to get those tickets, babe?"

"I don't give a damn what it took! I'm not going with that loser Roger so you better rethink your plans."

"Roger is CFO of this company Brooke." He turns and points at me. "What? Would you rather go with this dweeb?"

I turn around pissed off. Did that asshat just call me a dweeb in front of Brooke? "Hey," I challenge him, absolutely amazing myself.

"Don't worry, *toon boy*, she'd never go with you."

"Screw you, Arnauld. I'd love to go with Nathan." She turns to me. "Will you take me to the Emmys Nathan?"

Things are suddenly looking up. "Sure, when it is again?"

"Wait just a damn minute," Arnauld rages. "You can't go with him. Just look at him with those goofy glasses and floppy hair, you'll look ridiculous. I bet this geek didn't even go to his prom. Have you ever even rented a tux, man?" He folds his arms over his chest assuming victory.

"Actually I own one," I state calmly.

"What?" they both ask in unison.

They both look shocked. I can't begrudge Brooke for her surprise. It's unusual for someone like me to own a tux. But my dad dislikes renting anything. It's against his religion or something. So we all got tuxes for the black tie event when he won the National Award for Outstanding Innovations. He told me at the time that I would wear it for my wedding one day. I bet he never imagined that I would wear it to the Emmys too.

"Is it a Halloween costume or something?" Arnauld asks warily.

"No, actually it's an Armani. I got it at Barney's."

I'm sure that little tidbit impresses him, Mr. Hip Fashion guy. *Screw you, hairy back. I hope one of those boxers gets knocked out of the ring and lands on you, crushing that stupid look right off your face.*

Brooke's grin is priceless. I can tell she may break into a happy dance any moment.

"Well then, that's all settled. So if you'll excuse us Arnauld, we have some plans to make."

He gives me a death glare and I shrug my shoulders. He storms out of her office.

She walks over to me and kisses me on the cheek.

"What's that for?" I ask puzzled.

"That was priceless…I swear I love you, Nathan. You really perform well under pressure. How did you ever think up that tuxedo thing…and Barney's! That was brilliant!"

"But I really do have an Armani tuxedo from Barney's, Brooke." I explain, suddenly worried that she doesn't intend to actually go with me. "Can I still take you?"

She throws her head back laughing, and it makes me smile to see her so happy.

"Hell yes! Believe me, there's no one else I'd rather go with."

The next day I tell Brooke that I'm considering contacts.

"Is this about Arnauld mentioning your glasses? Don't think you have to change because of what he said."

"I know. But remember when you took off my glasses that time and told me what nice eyes I have? I actually started thinking about it then. I even talked to my ophthalmologist about it last week at my check-up."

"Okay, if you're sure. As long as you're going why don't I come and we'll pick up some stylish frames as back up. Lot's of girls love guys in glasses if they're cool ones."

"You'll come help me pick them out?"

"Sure, let's see if we can get into L.A. Eyeworks this evening. Arnauld gets all his glasses there." She scans through her Blackberry until she finds the number. "Do you have your prescription?"

"Yeah, I'm pretty sure it's in my book bag."

• • •

The highlight of my week thus far is Brooke picking out frames and gently easing them on me. Each time, she brushes my hair up off my forehead and steps back for a better view.

"Your green eyes are so gorgeous. They were hidden under your heavy old glasses."

I smile as she slowly pulls the third pair off. They're a sleek European design like the hipsters wear.

After the fourth pair, she shakes her head and mutters something to herself.

"Is something wrong?" I ask, pushing the new frames further up my nose.

"No, you just look really hot. You're going to have the girls lined up."

"A line of girls? Well, then...let's buy this pair. If you think I look hot, that's good enough for me."

She goes and talks to the technician while I study myself in the mirror. I don't see the big difference, but I'm used to ignoring my reflection unless I'm shaving.

She returns, stepping up behind me to study how I look again. I can't help feeling nervous; it's so important to me to look good for her.

"Well?" I question. Has she changed her mind?

"Very hot," she confirms.

"You think so? Would you be one of those girls in line?"

"Hell, I'd be first in line." She makes a dramatic *Dream Girls*-like arm motion. "I'd be all, watch out, bitches...he's mine."

He's mine? Oh God, that's making me wild inside.

I swallow as I watch her in the mirror's reflection. "How soon will they be ready?" I ask anxiously. *I need these glasses now.*

"You can take the contacts tonight. They'll deliver the frames to you tomorrow."

Thursday I suffer through the contacts only a few hours in the afternoon so Brooke can see me wearing them. It's as long as I can stand them, and that's with repeated eye drops. As it is I spend half of my lunch hour trying to get them in, after being too chicken to try in the morning.

I can't tell what's more painful, adjusting to the little discs stuck to my eyeballs or all the attention my new look is garnering. I have to wonder, why didn't anyone tell me I looked like a super geek in my old glasses? I always thought they were cool.

All the girls seem to be intrigued with me now. Even Morgan gives me *the look* when I go to Brooke's that afternoon.

"Hey handsome," Brooke says as she reaches for her macchiato. "Are you coming over tonight to help with the website? I'll show you my dress for Sunday."

"Sure," I say enthusiastically. "Do you want me to pick up dinner?"

"Nope, I've already ordered us a sushi platter."

"You were that sure I was coming?"

"Have I mentioned that I'll be wearing my yoga pants?" She teases.

I grin. "Well then, I'm coming for sure."

Brooke suddenly looks up and I turn to see Morgan in the doorway.

"Sorry Brooke, but Arnauld just called and he needs you in on this call. They are in the conference room across from his office."

She stands up and grabs her Blackberry and notebook. "Okay, thanks Morgan." She touches my shoulder as she steps away from her desk. "So, I'll see you later." She winks, and I nod, smiling.

On my way out of Brooke's office I pause at Morgan's desk.

"Morgan, can I ask your advice?"

She looks surprised, but nods. "Sure."

"As you know, I'm escorting Brooke to the Emmys Sunday."

She jumps in. "Yeah, before I forget, do you want the limo to pick you up at your place, or Brooke's?"

I have no idea how to answer that, but it occurs to me that at the end of the night I don't want to just have the driver drop her off. "Well, why don't I go to Brooke's and then they'll just have one stop?"

"Okay, then be there and ready to go at five. Oh, and you do know it's black tie, right?"

She must really think I'm an idiot, but I remember I need her help so I remain polite and calm.

"Yeah, thanks Morgan, I'm set with a tux. But Arnauld said my hair looks stupid and I don't want to embarrass Brooke. Do you know of a good barber I could go to who would make me look all right?"

I can tell that my question has pleased her. "Great idea. Let me do a little research, and I'll email you within a half hour. It's kind of late notice for the top people though."

"Well, I could do it any time tomorrow late afternoon, or Saturday."

Morgan makes notes on her pad.

"Also, I have no idea about these things…do I bring her a corsage or something?"

Morgan snickers. "No, this isn't the prom."

I blush, feeling humiliated. "Okay, so no flowers then."

"Well you could bring her flowers when you come to her place…you know, to congratulate her for her achievement. That would be sweet."

"Do you think roses?"

"Actually Brooke loves peonies. She orders herself an arrangement once a month because they're her favorite. I'll call her favorite florist, Mark's Garden on Ventura Blvd., and have them put together an arrangement. You should pick them up at four-thirty Sunday. I'll email you their address as well. You can pay for them there."

"Wow, thanks Morgan. You're amazing."

She glows with the compliment. Maybe she really isn't that bad.

"You're welcome. Take good care of Brooke. Okay, Nathan? This is a big night for her."

"I'll do my best." I assure her.

• • •

When I get to her house that evening the sushi's just been delivered, and I bristle at the young delivery guy checking out my girl in her yoga pants.

I'm wearing my new glasses that make me look "really hot" and to seal the deal I'm wearing a size large narrow black Gap T-shirt that I previously would have never considered wearing. Normally I wear extra large because I like my clothes loose and comfortable. But the contacts and new glasses have got me feeling bold, like it's time to break new ground.

"Hey, Brooke," I say stepping inside.

"Oh my," she says when she sees me and gives me a hug.

She steps back and nods. "I would strongly suggest you wearing that shirt and those glasses more often. They really show off how handsome you are."

I love how she says that so matter-of-factly.

"And look at you." I grin, gesturing to her outfit.

"Yes, my yoga pants have made another appearance just for you."

I sigh. "It's the simple things that make me happy."

She pulls me towards the kitchen. "Come on, I bought Sapporo beer to go with the sushi.

After dinner we clean up and start to head into the studio.

"Hey, before we start can I show you the two dresses I'm trying to decide between for the Emmys?"

"Sure," I agree. I may not know anything about women's clothes but I'd look at Brooke in anything. Who'd have thought I'd ever be judging fashion?

She disappears into her room and comes back out a few minutes later in a long black fitted gown of some velvety looking material. It's elegant and makes her look older than she is.

"What do you think?" she asks, sounding uncertain.

"You look beautiful, Brooke. It's really fancy."

"Fancy?" she smiles at me, her fashion idiot friend. What was she expecting?

"You look great. But you'd look great in anything."

She makes a face at me. "All right Mr. Picky, let me show you the other one now."

She's gone a longer time and she comes down the hall even more tentatively.

This dress is a deep red, almost wine colored and it makes her pale skin glow. The fabric sweeps over her curvy hips and thighs. I look at her long neck and then down to where her breasts nestle in the top folds of the dress.

"Wow," I say quietly. I can't stop looking at how pretty she looks, soft but sexy, shy but provocative. "Wow."

"Right?" she questions. "I like this one too. Here can you help me with this zipper?"

She steps close, turning around and I freeze as my gaze trails over her.

Her back is exposed all the way down to the top of her bottom, the softest white skin I've ever seen. My mouth actually waters as I fight the urge to run my tongue all the way up the length of her. I want to softly kiss her across her shoulders and then wind my hands around her until they are cupping her breasts.

"Zipper?" she asks looking over her shoulder to see what's holding me up.

With great focus I take the tiny zipper pull between my fingers and drag it up as slowly as possible without giving myself away. I desperately want to leave her back naked, smooth as a field of freshly fallen snow.

When I finally zip the dress closed she turns around and the fabric swirls, falling against her in an embrace. Her cleavage is revealed...well not just revealed but celebrated, her breasts round and full. My lips ache to skim over them.

The fabric cinches at her curvy waist and then molds to her shapely bottom. This dress is everything a dress should be, because all I want to do is take it off and make love to her.

She takes several steps back while smoothing the fabric over her hips. Turning sideways she pulls the fabric up where it cups her breasts, then runs her hands back down to her hips. I'm fully hard now watching her touch herself. I'm trying to contain my overwhelming desire.

When she turns around and smoothes the fabric over her bottom, I'm so aroused I can't focus. I take several steps back until I can sink onto the couch. I pull a throw pillow over the situation in my pants, hoping she doesn't notice.

"So? What do you think, this or the black one?"

"Are you kidding?" I ask stunned. "This dress was made for you. You look amazing."

"Really?" she asks like she's still not sure. "You're not just saying that?"

"It's perfect, seriously. It really shows off your great body, and the color's beautiful on you." I sigh and smile.

"This is my favorite too. I feel really good in it. But Arnauld said it was unflattering."

I can feel how tender she is all around her edges, and a powerful desire to protect her roars through me.

"What? He's nuts." I say, trying not to just go off on him and get her even more upset. But I'm so angry. It's like he tries to control her by messing with her head.

"I don't know why I let him get to me, Nathan. I'm normally so confident, but he's always pointing out what's wrong with my body and I guess it's worn me down."

"You know, I'm sorry to be selfish, but I'm glad Arnauld's going to Vegas for that fight. I may not know anything about fashion stuff but I'm a man and I know what I like. If Arnauld can't see how beautiful and desirable you are in this dress, then he has his head up his ass. I can't wait to walk in front of all those people with you on my arm."

"Really?" she asks studying me with her wide eyes.

"Yes," I say. "I'm so proud to be going with you." I take a deep breath and hold it, barely believing that speech came out of me. But that's what Brooke does to me. She inspires me to be more than I think I can be.

She stands there silently and I wait, not sure what to do next. But a moment later I realize that there are tears trailing down her cheek.

Despite the awkwardness of the moment, I sense what she needs. So I get off the couch and step right up to her. Reaching over, I wipe her tears away with my fingers and pull her into my arms.

And although I have no words left that can adequately express her beauty and how she affects me, I hope the way I hold her says everything.

Animate Me / Chapter Twelve / A Very Small Banana

"There's a very logical explanation for all of this." ~ Velma, Scooby-Doo[xi]

"Nathan," she sighs.

I'm rubbing her back, and I feel her relax the more I touch her.

"Are you okay?" I ask softly. "You really do look beautiful you know."

She looks up and smiles. "Thank you." She closes her eyes and leans into my chest.

"Do you want to sit down?"

"Yeah, I do. Let me take the dress off first."

She turns and I carefully unzip her, stealing one more glance of her flawless, alabaster skin.

"I'll be right back," she assures me.

I settle back down onto the couch. Only a minute later she returns, having changed back into her yoga pants. As she sits down next to me, I realize her expression has changed. There is fierceness under the outer layer of sadness. She leans towards me and puts her hand on my shoulder.

"Promise me something, Nathan."

"Okay?" I respond, wondering where this is going.

"When you've got your girl, promise me you'll treat her right and support her in feeling good about herself."

"Of course," I say quietly. "Isn't that what you do for someone you love?"

I feel her fingers tighten over my shoulders as if she's bracing herself for something that's building inside of her.

"Don't tell her that her ass is getting big and that she has chunky thighs, even if you think it. Just don't say it. Okay?"

Stupid ass, Arnold. "I would never do that, Brooke," I assure her. *If you were with me, I would worship every perfect part of you, every day.*

She finally relaxes and sags against the cushions, as if the air has gone out of her.

I reach forward and grab my beer off the coffee table, then hand it to her. "Here, I think you could use a drink."

She turns the bottle in her hands as she continues. "I've always believed that a woman should never let a man affect the way she feels about herself. So the irony of what his words do to me…"

"But it's hard not to be damaged by the things the people you care about say and do."

She nods slowly. I watch her take several long sips before she sets the beer back on the table.

"He wasn't always like this, you know," she says, a faraway look in her eyes. "He can be incredibly charming…he used to constantly tell me how beautiful and talented I was. In the beginning he swept me off my feet. No one had ever treated me the way he did, and he's still very charming at times. In fairness, I've only told you about his dark side. He's a complicated man."

"Yeah, the things you've told me make it very hard for me to understand why you're still with him," I admit.

"The way things have shifted between us…well, it happened so gradually that it's taken a while to realize the extent of it."

I look at her, noting her sad expression. She must still care about him.

"How have things shifted?" I ask, almost afraid of the answer.

"He's taught me so much about the business, and has given me opportunities no one else would've so soon in my career. But it's almost like the more confident and successful I become, the more critical he is."

"Do you know why he's like that?"

"Maybe he feels threatened. Maybe he was more comfortable when I looked up to him and was less of an equal. But the biggest turning point was when he demanded that I move in with him, and for us to be exclusive with each other."

I'm shocked and my stomach sinks, as I grip the edge of the couch. "He did? When was that?"

I don't know whether to be sick about the fact that he wanted more with her, or happy that she apparently turned him down.

She nods slowly. "Late last year. I'd gone out with this guy he apparently had issues with, and in a drunken tirade he proclaimed that our open relationship was over and that it was time to move in with him. Among many other issues, I was so pissed that his change of heart was prompted by jealousy and not by any desire to really develop our relationship further. Even if I had wanted more of a commitment, I knew he didn't really mean it. I didn't trust his intentions and refusing him is what started all the passive aggressive behavior. I think it made him crazy that he couldn't control me. So he'd do things like promote me, then criticize my work…tell me he loved my body one week, then buy me a gym membership the next."

"That's awful," I say quietly.

"Honestly, it wasn't until I met you, and saw the way you made me feel so special and appreciated, that I realized how much had changed."

As glad as I am to know that I've helped her, I'm still really concerned about her situation.

"Can you tell me what he said to you specifically to make you so upset when you tried on the dress?" I ask carefully, each word measured.

She looks away and her expression gets angry again. "He's pushing me to get lipo. He insists on paying for it so he doesn't understand why I won't do it."

"Liposuction?" I ask alarmed. "But your body's so beautiful, Brooke. Where would you possibly have lipo? Why?"

"My hips, thighs and ass," she explains. "He wants me to look like one of those skinny models. He did it for his love handles that he couldn't exercise off, so he thinks it's no big deal."

"What, no!" I respond alarmed. "Show me what he's talking about."

She gets off the couch and stands in front of me. But then she seems to have a second thought, and crawls onto my lap so that she's straddling my knees, facing me. "Starting here," she says quietly, as she takes my hands and runs them along the smooth black Lycra covering her inner thighs. She then drags my hands over her hips. "All along there." Finally our hands settle on the round part of her bottom. "And a lot here."

"No!" I moan loudly, without thinking. "You can't let him take your curves, Brooke! Is he nuts? You're perfect and sexy, and I'll never forgive you if you agree to that."

"This is who I am," she says quietly as she strokes her hips. "I used to like my curves."

It doesn't escape my notice that my hands are still on her butt, so I squeeze it gently. "I love your curves. Why do you think I appreciate these yoga pants so much?"

She smiles sadly at me. "Don't worry, I'll never agree to it. But I can't deny that it's getting to me hearing him suggest it all the time. And that's not all, you know."

"What else?" I ask, not sure I can stand to hear more.

"He wants me to get my breasts augmented...you know, bigger."

"Why? They're perfect," I huff.

"How would you know, you've never seen them," she teases.

"No, but I've held them. Well, technically one, but that gave me a pretty good indication. It felt so perfect to me." I grin.

"Well, to be honest, I've always loved my breasts. I think they're really pretty. Lately though, he seems to get off on huge breasts, and has no qualms telling me that."

"I bet your breasts are much higher ranked than pretty...more like stunningly beautiful or fucking unforgettable. And being a bit of a breast aficionado I think my opinion holds more weight, than Mojo Jojo's."

She grins and I'm encouraged that her mood seems to be brightening.

"So now you're an aficionado?" She teases.

"Well if you count studying them very carefully and drawing breasts thousands of times." I pause and move my hands to rest on her thighs. "You know you could show me if you want a second opinion on how spectacular they are."

"You want to see my breasts?"

"Yes, of course I do." My heart is pounding.

"Are you going to touch them too?"

I swallow hard. "If you'll let me." *Oh, please let me, Brooke. Please*

She leans back and eyes me playfully. "Is this educational?"

"If you want it to be." I'm getting nervous that she's changing her mind. I can't get this close to the Promised Land, only to find out that it's closed for business. I reach up and tug on the edge of her T-shirt. "Don't make me beg," I tease.

She smiles and grabs the hem and starts to slowly pull it upward. Her torso is just as glorious as her back, creamy dreamy smooth. My fingers itch to glide over every plain and valley of her body. But when the shirt finally peels away from her chest, my heart stops. Mojo is clearly on crack because these are the most exquisitely beautiful, lusciously plump, bewitchingly bodacious breasts I've ever seen.

"Oh, my." I state weakly. The sight of her without her shirt completely overwhelms me, and I'm rapidly losing my super powers. I'm now a mere mortal in the presence of perfection.

"That's it? After all that build up?…Just an 'Oh, my'?"

Has she not noticed that my eyes are bugging out of my head and I'm swallowing every ten seconds to control my salivating?

"Can we take this off?" I whisper, weakly pointing to her bra.

She smiles. "You want to help?"

I nod and as she reaches around to unhook the back, I gently slide the straps off her shoulders. She waits patiently for me, and my trembling fingers slide under that part in the middle that brings the two worlds together. I pull until the pale blue symphony of lace and straps falls away from her.

I can sense that she's fighting shyness, a temptation to fold into herself. But she stays strong and sits tall, with her shoulders pulled back.

"Oh, Jesus," I moan. "Oh my God." Evidently I've suddenly found religion. That's how incredible her breasts are. I glance once more at the perfection before my eyes roll back in my head.

I hear her take a deep ragged breath.

I reopen my eyes just in time to watch her slide further down my lap. Instinctively I react by pushing my hips forward to seek friction for the battle my hard-on is fighting with my jeans.

And as if that wasn't enough, she smiles and takes my hands, pressing them softly against her.

"Oh, sweet baby Jesus," I gasp. I have never felt anything so wonderful as her naked breasts, full and warm in my hands.

"I didn't know you were a religious man," she says with a sly smile.

"I wasn't. But I am now." I sigh as I marvel at them again in my grasp. I could sit here all night and just hold and admire them.

She laughs softly. "Are you all right?" She notices the serious look that has just flashed across my face.

"Never, ever, ever, let anyone tamper with this perfection," I insist.

Her smile is so happy, like I just brushed all the darkness and self-doubt right out of her mind.

"Promise me, please, Brooke," I beg.

She smiles. "I promise." She looks down at how I'm holding her, and then runs her hands along my forearms. "See, this is what I'm talking about," she explains. "This is making me feel really good."

Let's look at that scoreboard, I think to myself. *A touchdown for me, and Mojo has been sidelined. Looks like I'm winning and we haven't even reached half-time.*

Newly confident, I let my fingers explore, feeling the weight, and firm softness. My fingers circle her nipples and I notice that her body reacts in a really good way.

"I have to warn you Nathan, my breasts, especially my nipples are super sensitive. Don't be alarmed if I get carried away when you touch me."

Is she kidding? All I want right now is to make her get carried away. I want it really, really badly.

She scoots even closer, pushing herself firmly on top of my erection, finally giving me the friction I desperately need.

From the looks of how she's arching her back, she wants me to take her nipple in my mouth. My tongue leads the way, and after its tentative introduction with a circle and a flick, I surrender to my instincts. Brooke wasn't kidding about being sensitive. The minute my lips wrap around her she starts moving over me.

I guess in the back of my mind I'm always convinced that each time will be my last intimate experience with Brooke—that my lucky streak is finally over. So I'm hyper aware of every feeling, the way my heart skips when she winds her fingers through my hair and pulls me closer...the sounds she makes as I work my tongue over her, making me feel like I'm doing something really right.

Unlike Rachel, whose eyes were always closed, Brooke's eyes are open and she watches me doing everything I can to please her. Watching seems to arouse her even more.

Her fingers grasp my hair and she pulls hard as she rocks back and forth on my lap. I want to be inside her so badly, but I try to stay focused on not losing control. If she keeps rubbing against me like this I'm going to lose it for sure.

"Nathan?" she whispers, her voice hungry and raw.

"Mmmm?" I respond, as I look up, her nipple still in my mouth.

"I think I should warn you...I mean, if you keep doing that I'm going to come."

In that moment it hits me that *I'm* making her feel this way. I pull back and look up at her while my fingers tighten over her nipples. I'm arousing her to the point that she may come undone in my arms, and I want that so badly.

"I really want to make you come, Brooke." I insist, surprising myself with my boldness.

"You do?" She considers my expression while running her hand down my chest. "Is it turning you on to see what you're doing to me?" Her face is flushed and her breathing fast and shallow.

I nod. "You're so beautiful." I take her in my mouth again, with a desperate urgency and she groans, her head falling back. "...and sexy," I moan. "I'm so excited right now."

"Believe me, I know how excited you are. You don't know what you're doing to me."

"I'm not going to be able to hold on much longer," I warn her. I sink into her cleavage and my hands cup her bottom and help guide her rhythm over me. My heart's pounding.

But luckily I don't have to worry about jumping the gun because her erotic dance suddenly becomes a powerful force. Watching her orgasm is like taking an advanced course in the power of female sexuality. The look on her face alone could make me come.

"Nathan," she cries, her eyes fluttering, her body electrifying.

Oh man, I've never seen or felt anything like this. I just hold on tight and give her everything I have. I'm so focused on Brooke that my climax sideswipes me, hitting me with sudden impact. I gasp and surrender, as the wave hits me with astounding force.

I'm in the final moments of settling when I feel her lips against mine. The kiss is sensuous as her breasts graze against my chest.

"Good?" she whispers as she runs her fingers through my hair.

I grin. "Oh, yeah. You?" I'm so comfortable with her now that I'm not even embarrassed.

"Really great. I feel amazing."

"You do?" I ask, knowing, but wanting to hear it again anyway.

She takes my face in her hands and looks into my eyes. "You make me feel amazing."

She kisses me again, and as much as I don't want to delude myself, I know I feel something else, another feeling in that kiss—something sweet and tender.

When I go into the bathroom to clean up I'm so happy that I don't even care what a mess I've made getting off with my clothes on. I wipe up as best I can before I wash my hands and return to the living room.

Brooke is sprawled across the couch, and I smile at her. "Sorry about this, but I really need to take a shower and change. I can't work on the website like this."

"All messy from our fun?" she says, looking blissful.

"Yeah, pretty much," I admit grinning.

"Don't worry, I'm too relaxed and happy to focus on work anyway. I'm going to take a long hot bubble bath and go to bed. Come on, I'll walk you out."

She takes my hand and leads me to the door before hugging me.

With my hand in hers I realize that Arnold's lingering presence from earlier has completely faded.

"I'm sorry we made you messy."

"I'm not," I insist. "It was worth it."

"You are really something Nathan Evans. I hope you know that there's nothing more sexy than a man who makes a woman feel beautiful." She gently pushes my messy hair out of my eyes and off my face.

"So I'm sexy now?" I tease.

"You're a sex God, and I'm honored to be in your good graces."

"Gee Brooke, you sure know how to make a guy feel great." I grin. "So I'll see you tomorrow?"

Feeling entitled with my sex God crowning, I lean down and gently kiss her, savoring one more taste of her sweetness. When we part she smiles up at me. "Okay, tomorrow...I'll be waiting."

Between my thrill of pleasuring Brooke and anticipation of my meeting with Sharper Edge Comics tomorrow I can barely sleep. I pull out my iTouch and listen to Wayne, reliving every perfect moment with Brooke until I finally doze off.

There's a mile stretch on Ventura Boulevard in Studio City where just about every fifth storefront is a sushi restaurant. I get so confused by their similar names that I'm almost late for my meeting with Chris from Sharper Edge Comics. It doesn't even matter to me than I had sushi for dinner with Brooke last night because I'm probably going to be too nervous to eat.

Luckily when I get there Chris seems cool and laid back, not one of the "suits" who make a sport out of raking artists over the coals. He's even wearing jeans without his shirt tucked in, so I immediately feel more at ease.

After we've ordered and gone through formalities, he asks me what my long range plans are for both my career and the B-Girl Series.

"The thing is, Nathan, you're unique. You have a distinct, modern style with your art, combined with a very strong story sense and great character development. There's a need for people who can create compelling characters and story lines....it's a rare talent; where there are lots of 'hands' that can draw."

He's repeating what several of my Cal Arts professors told me, when they assured me that story and character development were my greatest strengths.

"But I like to draw," I insist.

"You haven't jobbed out any of the B-Girl pages yet to other artists?"

I shake my head. It seems sacrilege to have someone else draw B-Girl besides me.

"Well, that's impressive, but you'll have to when we pick up publication. It'll be impossible for you to keep up with the schedule otherwise."

"You're going to test it first for a while, aren't you, to see how it sells?" I ask, still tentative.

"Oh, it's going to sell. We've done our research. We're great at marketing and finding the book's audience. I think you'll be happy with what we can do for you."

All the way back to the office I allow myself to imagine what the future could be, huge B-Girl banners at Comic Con and fan girls walking around wearing home-made B-Girl costumes. That's when I'll know for sure that I've really made it.

• • •

That afternoon on the way to Starbucks, Nick breaks away from the group and walks with me. I'm wondering if he's going to say something nasty about the caricature that Andy did of Dani and I with Nick scowling in the background. But he surprises me instead with a compliment.

"You look happy, dude," he comments.

"Yeah," I agree. "I'm having a good day."

"Is it true you missed Kevin's birthday lunch because you had a meeting with a company about your comic book?"

"Uh huh, Sharper Edge Comics. I can't believe it but unless the lawyers get stupid, I think this deal can work out."

"Wow," he says slapping me on the back. "That's great, I hope it happens for you."

"Thanks." I say quietly as I smile at him. I know it means a lot for him to say this considering he's still not sure what to make about Dani and me.

His face suddenly looks troubled. "But does this mean you'll be leaving us?"

"I doubt it, and definitely not for now. It's going to take a while to see if the story has the potential in the market they think it does. But printing and distributing them myself has been tough for me to do. I'll never reach a broad audience unless I do a deal like this so I want to try it."

He nods and gets quiet, so I try to continue the conversation.

"Hey, how did it go with Dani after we all went out? She was so happy when you offered to take her home."

"We talked a little but she still seems very unsure about me. Maybe she thinks she can't trust my intentions."

"Well, then you'll have to prove to her that she can," I suggest.

"So, when did you get so fucking wise about women?" he teases.

"If I were wise about women, believe me, my situation would be a lot different right now."

"Really?" he asks, curiosity written all over his face. "Hey, has Brooke been helping you with your B-Girl comics? You've been spending time with her. I notice that you always bring her coffee now, and you're taking her to the Emmys and everything."

"No, she hasn't even seen one," I admit nervously.

"Really?" he asks, too shocked for my comfort level. "I almost called her B-Girl the other day cause she looks so much like your main character."

"Ahhh, please don't do that. I don't want her to get the wrong idea…I mean, it's just a weird coincidence." I don't even look him in the eye, fearful that I'll give myself away.

"Yeah, sure…coincidence." He laughs. "Well, good luck explaining that one."

Later when I walk into Brooke's office and see her dressed in a pretty navy dress that wraps all around her and shows off her curves, all the B-Girl panic is forgotten.

"Hey, you're dressed up. You look really pretty," I say as I set the macchiato down on her desk.

"Thanks." She smiles sweetly. "Arnauld took me to a nice restaurant for lunch. He's still trying to make up for the Vegas thing…and guess what?"

"He's not going to Vegas?" I ask, my nerves shattered to think I won't be her Emmy date. I knew it was too good to be true.

"No!" she huffs like that would never happen, and I breathe a sigh of relief.

She sits up straight and throws her shoulders back proudly. "I read him the riot act. I warned him if he tells me one more time that my ass is too big or my breasts not big enough, that it's the last time I'll be around to hear it."

I grin, happy to see her standing up for herself. "Oh, that's great. What did he say?"

"He was speechless. For the first damn time I can remember, he was completely speechless. He just nodded his head and kept eating his osso bucco."

"Ha! I'm sure you surprised him."

"That I did," she laughs. "You really inspired me. When I woke up this morning, I laid in bed and ran my hands over my body…and I felt so good…you know…sexy. It was the best I'd felt in that regard for a long time."

I swallow hard and look down. Does she have any idea what saying things like that does to me? Now I'm going to be distracted all afternoon imagining her in bed touching herself.

I clear my throat and look up. "Well, you're the sexiest woman I know, so I'm glad I could help. I'm also really happy that you set him straight."

Wow…if he keeps screwing up, maybe he'll be out of the picture soon.

She reaches across the desk and squeezes my hand. Her warmth lingers even after she pulls away to pick up her coffee. No matter how or when it happens, I love it when she touches me.

"Now what do we have today?" She turns the cup until my drawing faces her. This cup is so special that I had Starbucks give it to me empty ahead of time, so I could take my time rendering the image.

"Oh my God, Nathan! You need to draw this for me on good paper…I love it!"

I'm so happy she likes it; I put extra effort in to my illustration of an Emmy award and even used gold and bronze markers to fill in the drawing. In my version Brooke has replaced the winged bronze woman who normally holds up the sphere of metal. Brooke's little feet are attached to the base as she stretches upwards, her hair flowing behind her. I paid particular attention to capture all of her curves. Brooke is the prize I would be so happy to win.

She reads the line I wrote small, underneath. "You're always a winner to me." She puts her hand over her heart and takes a sharp breath. I'm surprised by the sudden emotion.

"Nathan." She sighs.

"Yes?" I ask tentatively. I hope I haven't upset her for some reason, or stepped over some boundary I don't understand.

"You're the best thing that's happened to me in a long time. I hope you know how much I adore you."

I smile, relieved and excited. I'm kind of flying and I'm going to need some time to think about what she just said.

"Well, I feel the same, Brooke."

Unfortunately, just then Morgan comes in with several messages and Brooke nods. I stand up realizing she must need to get back to work.

"So Sunday, at five." She smiles warmly.

"I'll be there."

On my way out of her office Morgan stops me. She looks concerned.

"Arnauld wants to see you. Go check in with his assistant."

"What does he want?"

"I have no idea," she insists, giving me a look. "He usually doesn't confide in me."

Great. It must be bad. She hasn't been sarcastic with me like that in at least a week.

"Okay, thanks," I respond politely, not wanting trouble.

"Oh, and you got the info for your hair appointment tomorrow, right?"

"Yeah, thanks."

"Now, make sure and tip Bradley twenty percent and give whoever washes your hair five bucks. I told you the consult and cut will be a hundred, right?"

I nod, still marveling at how a haircut could cost so damn much. But I'm not going to say anything because I've got to get this right for Brooke. "Is it really Arnauld and Brooke's stylist?"

"Yes, so be careful what you say. What are you going to have him do anyway?"

"I was thinking about a mohawk," I say with a perfectly straight face.

She laughs, or snorts. It's hard to tell. "Yeah, you do that Indian boy, and I'll pull a Pocahontas and nail you with an arrow from my bow on Monday. Now get your ass over to Arnauld's before he starts yelling."

I thank her and turn to head down the hall. *What the hell does Arnold want with me?* He knows I'm taking Brooke on Sunday so how bad can it be? It's not like he's going to fire me or beat me up until at least Monday, when I've completed my task.

I approach ice princess, Alana's desk. "I'm here to see Arnauld. I'm…"

"Nathan," she says with a pinched face. "Wait here." She stands up and moves with great efficiency into his office. A moment later she steps back out.

"Wait over there." She points to a chair in the waiting area. "He needs to take care of something first."

Okay, then what was the rush for me getting over here? Oh yeah, that's what "suits" do to toy with you.

About ten minutes pass where I imagine every possible horrible thing he could say or do to me before Alana picks up the phone. She does a hand motion like those guys on the tarmac giving signals to planes. "He'll see you now."

When I walk into his office he's tapping away on his Blackberry and doesn't even look up. So I pause in the middle of the office and wait. The only noise besides his tapping is the sudden closing of the door behind me. *How did he do that?*

I study him, marveling at why he pays so much for a hair stylist when his hair's so short—practically shaved. Joe, the guy I see on Magnolia in Burbank would charge about ten bucks for that. I note his strong features as he continues to text. I guess he's what women would call handsome. If only they could see his back right before waxing.

The ass who wanted some doctor with a mechanical straw to suck Brooke's perfect bottom away, finally looks up at me.

He gestures towards a chair in front of his desk. "Have a seat…" He's searching for my name.

"Nathan," I reply.

"Yes, Nathan." He pushes his chair away from the desk and leans back. "So I wanted to make sure things were set for Sunday, that everything is in order." He studies me for a moment like he's trying to figure something out. He finally seems to have an idea.

"Where are your glasses?"

"I got contacts," I reply, watching him continue to study me carefully. "And yes, Morgan helped me with the arrangements."

"All right good. And you weren't full of shit when you said you had an Armani tux, right? Because I picked out my girl's dress, it's an elegant black Valentino and I don't want you showing up in some burgundy polyester number."

So if you're so concerned about how Brooke and her escort are going to look, why don't you take her yourself, Mojo?

Then I remember the red dress. I internally smirk about the change in dress plans, but bite my tongue. If I tell him he'll surely harass Brooke about it.

"I wasn't lying, it's a black Armani tux."

"Make sure you comb that crazy hair too, you look like a rag-mop."

Gee thanks, asshat. At least I don't have a receding hairline forcing me to go for the Bruce Willis look.

"Yeah, I'm getting a haircut. Anything else?" I'm getting pissed and don't know how much of this humiliation I can take.

"Just don't do anything stupid. If you don't know what to say, stay quiet." He folds his arms over his chest. "This is a big night for Brooke, and I want it to go well. I have no fucking idea why she thought you should take her…you seem to be her latest 'project,' but I couldn't talk her out of it, so I'm just warning you."

Project? I feel a wave of panicked insecurity, but then remind myself that he doesn't have any idea about what is between Brooke and me. My back bristles but I force myself to speak.

"Warning me?" I grip the handles of my chair so hard my knuckles are white. "Is this a work related issue? If so, I think someone from HR should be here."

He gives me a threatening look and ignores my veiled threat.

"Don't fuck this up for my girl, Nathan. Do you understand me?"

"Perfectly," I say looking down so that I don't give him the death glare. If I were the Green Lantern *mister big shot* would be on his knees now, blinded by the rays from my powerful ring. "Can I go now?" I ask as steadily as my fury will allow.

"Yeah, get back to work."

The entire walk and elevator ride back to my cube I plot my revenge. The first gesture will be executed on company time.

Too bad he won't be seeing the caricature I've got planned for him. It will definitely be a pre-waxed Arnold in the Amazon, swinging from a vine with one hand, and a very small banana in the other.

Animate Me / Chapter Thirteen / And the Award Goes to...

"Every adventure requires a first step." ~ Cheshire Cat[xii]

Saturday morning I stand in front of a row of stores on Melrose Place confused. When I look to the right I see a designer's store called Stella McSomething and when I look to the left I see another expensive looking clothes place called Marc and Jacob but I don't see a fancy hair-cutting place. I study the address on the paper and look up again. Is this like Number Twelve Grimmauld Place in Harry Potter where you have to cast a magic spell for the buildings to slide apart and reveal your destination? Maybe it has a protective nerd shield. Perhaps it's a sign that I shouldn't be here.

Just when I'm about to give up I notice an antique looking gate between the two buildings. I approach it and peer through, revealing a courtyard with a fountain and all kinds of exotic looking plants. *Is this the place?*

I tentatively pull open the gate and step inside. Just on the other side of the fountain I see a wall of glass with busy haircutting people inside. I can almost hear Betty, the tiny woman who lives in my car's dashboard and runs my GPS, say, *"You have reached your destination."*

The minute I approach the reception desk I realize my life is no longer my own. I also realize that I should've dressed nicer.

"Hi, I'm Nathan Evans and I have an appointment with Bradley."

"Yes, of course," the glamazon purrs before stepping from behind the desk. "Come with me."

I walk behind her marveling at how she balances in those ridiculous shoes. They have big platforms and a mess of straps halfway up her calves. Her skirt is short enough that she probably can't bend over without a show. She stops in front of a door.

"You can change in here."

"Change?" I sputter. Am I getting a physical exam along with my haircut?

She squints and I can tell she's trying not to roll her eyes. She opens the door and steps towards a fancy antique looking wardrobe thing. Reaching in, she pulls out a black robe made of a thin fabric—definitely not terry or flannel. *I'm supposed to wear this?* Maybe this *is* Hogwarts.

"You take off your shirt and hang it in here, and then put this on," she explains like I'm a candidate for preschool. "Can I get you a cappuccino or a glass of wine?"

Wine? It's ten in the morning. This crowd must like to get the party started early. "Actually, some water would be great, thanks."

After she closes the door behind her, I pull off my hoodie and T-shirt and hang them up. As I slide on the robe I stop to look in the mirror noting that those new crunches and bench presses Curtis showed me are paying off. When Brooke put her hand on my chest Thursday night, I didn't flinch from embarrassment but welcomed it because I know working out has been worth the effort. Curtis has had me on a regimen for years, initially in the hopes that I would be able to defend myself when people picked on me. But I kept it up because it relieved the stress of bending over an animation table all day.

I tie the robe shut and venture outside. Another woman approaches me. She has her eyebrow pierced, light blue eyes and the blackest hair against her pale skin.

"Hi Nathan, I'm London. Let me take you to Bradley."

He must be the king of this castle because the throne-like chair she leads me to is in a private area facing the garden. Bradley sweeps in right after her and shakes my hand.

"So you are Nathan."

I nod.

"Morgan asked me to take good care of you. You are taking Ms. Brooke to the Emmy's tomorrow, yes?"

Ms. Brooke? I nod again, still overwhelmed.

He tips his head, examining me. I can tell there are a lot of thoughts running around in there that he won't be sharing, but I'm used to that feeling when people meet me.

"I looooove Brooke, so I am going to make sure you're the hottest guy at the event."

Really? I think skeptically. *Well, good luck with that.*

He steps behind me and watches my reflection in the mirror as he runs his hands through my hair, lifting and watching it fall.

"Can I show you something?" I ask, remembering my plan.

"Sure, do you have a picture of a cut you like?"

"Not exactly." I pull out my old glasses and put them on, then press my hair over my forehead. "This was my old look that Arnauld suggested could be improved. I thought it would be helpful for you to see it."

Bradley coughs and London hands him his bottle of water. He is pressing his hand on his chest and can't seem to talk, so I continue.

"Can I ask your opinion? I mean, is it really that bad?"

"Well, let me understand," Bradley asks once he has his voice back. "What is this, some kind of pseudo-intellectual, geekazoid grunge, pre-Mia Farrow-Woody Allen, *'I'm too busy thinking deep thoughts to do anything as frivolous as getting my hair cut'* look?"

I stare at him, blinking repeatedly, stuck on the creepy Woody Allen reference.

"Was any part of that what you were going for?" he questions.

I dig in my pocket for a folded paper and I open it carefully. "No, I was patterning myself after Roy Orbison in his later years. I hold up a picture of the singer who was popular in the fifties. "See the glasses and how he wore his hair swept down. He was so cool when he toured with the Traveling Wilburys."

Bradley holds it up and studies the image. "You think this is cool?" he asks, not hiding the disbelief in his voice. "Wait a minute, isn't this guy dead?"

"Yes, but…" I begin to argue before he cuts me off.

"Oh no! I don't do dead guy styles or Justin Bieber haircuts. I draw a hard line there. We all have our limits and those are mine."

He folds up the paper and gently removes my glasses and sets both on a side table.

"Nathan, did Morgan explain that I'm the best?"

"Yes," I lie. Morgan only told me how much he cost, which of course would imply that he's either the best, or people with money are stupid.

151

"You need to trust me Nathan. I am going to make you look hot. You have great hair, a great face…you need a style that compliments both."

"Okay," I say weakly. "I'll trust you. Just do what you think is best." Hair grows back after all.

"You've made a wise choice," he says dramatically. "You'll be glad you did."

I take a deep breath, glad that without my glasses everything is a little fuzzy when London takes me off to wash my hair. The full impact of what I've agreed to won't hit me until I leave the salon.

I can't imagine why it takes so long to cut my hair; I'm not Rapunzel or anything. But Bradley seems pretty damn serious about his work, taking steps back to consider his progress every few snips. I sense that we are done when London comes towards me with an oversized paintbrush and starts dusting me off like a knick-knack.

Immediately following he swings the chair face forward, and they both step on either side of me to study my reflection.

"Wow," sighs London. Her intonation is full of admiration, so I figure that's a good thing.

"Yes," Bradley agrees, nodding. "Yes."

I squint, and so London hands me a large hand mirror.

Wow, I look really different. "Hey, that looks good," I say, surprised.

"He looks hot," London says to Bradley.

"Sizzling," the master insists. "Now, Nathan…I'm tempted to not give you those glasses back because they must not be worn…ever again."

"Don't worry, I have contacts and new glasses Brooke picked out from L.A. Eyeworks."

Bradley smiles; I guess he approves. I leave my tips and thank them. Heading out, I'm so stunned from the whole experience that I almost leave with my robe on. Luckily I catch myself before I make it to the front desk.

The glamazon looks flustered as she runs my credit card. She keeps staring at me. It makes me uncomfortable, but there's nothing I can do about it now, the hair I always hid under is gone.

Once home, I end up taking many opportunities that day to stare at myself too. I put in my contacts so I can continue to break them in, and consequently every time I look in the bathroom mirror, I get a clear look of my new haircut. I'm less surprised with each glance, until by the end of the day, I think I like it.

• • •

"Ah, Mom," I sigh as she fusses over me.

She puts her hands on her hips and shakes her head. "All the times I've tried to get you to cut your hair, and you refused." But then she smiles. "It was that lovely girl…Brooke, wasn't it? You did it for her, didn't you?"

I nod, my face turning red. "I just hope she likes it."

"Oh, she'll like it," Mom responds with no hesitation.

"She'll see it tonight. Remember, he's taking her to the Emmys," Curtis explains.

"Are you wearing your tux?" Dad asks.

"Yeah, I'm so glad I have that tux, Dad." I watch him grin with satisfaction and nod his head.

"Outstanding! It looks like our calculated investment is showing the potential to pay off far beyond our original projections," he says rubbing his hands together happily. "And one can never underestimate the potential impact of an impressive personal presentation with a desired mate."

"Yeah, you're going to look so hot she's going to be all over you, dude," Curtis confirms encouragingly.

I can't help but blush and grin at their support. I know that they genuinely want me to be happy.

"Well, you must call when you get home and let us know how it goes," Mom insists.

"If it goes well, calling you is the last thing he'll be doing," Curtis snickers.

I can't get my hopes up like that, but the thing I know for sure is that I'll get to see Brooke in that dress again and be her date. Anything beyond that is icing on the cake.

Back home, I spend a couple of hours roughing out pages for the next B-Girl issue. I'm glad to have my time occupied until it's finally time to get ready to go. Once I've showered, fixed my hair with that stuff like Bradley showed me, and gotten dressed, it all hits me.

I'm taking Brooke to the Emmys.

As I study myself in the mirror I realize, for perhaps the first time in my life, that I'm not bad looking at all. Since these plans were made, I've desperately wanted to believe that I could look worthy of being with her tonight. And with my final glance, I actually believe that I do.

My stomach flip flops the whole way to the florist, because it means I'm that much closer to being with her again. As I park I wonder if she's nervous too. Once out of the car, I slide the tux jacket off the hanger from where it's hung in the back seat, and pull it on. I wish I could have sorted out my bow tie, but I'm sure Brooke will do a better job with it than I could. I roll my shoulders back and clear my throat before I ring the doorbell.

She buzzes the gate, but I'm all the way down the stairs before she pulls open the door. I stop in my tracks. Her hair is swept up and she's wearing the dark red dress, the fabric fluttering around her legs in the breeze.

She's a vision, and tonight she's mine.

"Nathan!" she gasps. "You've cut your hair."

I nod, noticing that her cheeks are flushed and her expression's bright. Her eyes move over me, from my hair, to my eyes—now unhindered by glasses—to the tux. "Oh my God, you look *so* handsome," she says slowly, each word pressing into me. I can tell she means it. "Wow," she whispers.

I'm speechless and while I'm searching for the right response, I manage to hold out the bunch of flowers.

"For me?" she says, stepping forward. "That's so sweet."

I watch her take them and look down into the swirl of dark and light pinks. "Peonies," she sighs. "How did you know these were my favorite flowers?"

"I did my research," I answer grinning.

She smiles, tipping her head as she studies me. I can tell she's impressed.

"Brooke..." I start.

"Yes?"

"You're so beautiful...I mean, you look so beautiful tonight...well, I mean both—you are beautiful *and* you look so beautiful tonight...but then you *always* look beautiful, not just tonight..." I ramble, horrified.

I've apparently lost all verbal ability, thereby making a complete idiot of myself.

She steps closer and touches her fingers to my lips, stilling me.

"Thank you." She pulls her fingers from my lips, yet still lingers close to me. It almost feels like she's going to kiss me, but then she turns towards the foyer.

"Here, come on in."

She turns and heads into the kitchen and I follow, noting that she's barefoot. She pulls out a vase, fills it, then deftly unwraps the flowers and quickly arranges them before pulling back to admire the results.

"No one has ever brought me peonies," she says wistfully. "Until you."

I smile, excited about how well things are going, but just then the doorbell rings.

"Can you get that? It's the driver; tell him I need a couple minutes."

The driver assures me it's no problem, and I go back inside to find Brooke bent over the couch struggling with her shoes.

"Ugh, I can't seem to get the hook thingy to fit in the little hole!"

"Can I help?"

"Please. These are the only shoes I have that will look right with this dress."

I kneel down in front of her and remove the high-heeled sandal and examine the strap. "Damn, those are tiny holes. Here let me give it a try." I slip her beautiful foot back into the sandal and thread the delicate strap into the buckle, and then carefully press the prong into the hole. It takes some force, but it finally pops through. When I finish I wrap my hand around her ankle and softly stroke her skin.

"How's that?"

She leans forward on the couch and looks down. I can't help put peek at her lush cleavage. I swallow hard and struggle to focus.

She smiles. "Perfect. Can you do the other one too?"

I repeat the action, but when I'm done I let my hand trail higher up her calf and back down marveling at her beautiful legs. When I look up at her she's biting her lip as she watches me. I lift up on my knees so my face is level with hers and our eyes meet. Can she feel how much I want to pull her into my arms and kiss her? But before I can, I feel her hand sweep along the side of my face.

155

"Thank you." She pauses as if she wants to say something else, but then sighs. "We better get going or we'll be late."

I nod, and slowly stand up and then take her hand, helping her off the couch. Right before we get to the door she stops me, "Hey wait a sec, I need to do your tie."

"Oh yeah," I stammer, embarrassed. "I'm no good at these things."

"Well, I am," she says softly as the steps up close to me and begins maneuvering the two strips of fabric.

I look down at her. She's so focused on what she is doing that it gives me the opportunity to stare. Her skin is luminous and her shiny lips slowly part as her hands flutter with the bow tie just under my chin. I'm so drawn to her that I don't know how I'm going to get through a whole evening without touching her continuously.

When we arrive, Brooke's movie star beauty is apparent to everyone. As we step out of the limo one of the security managers tries to usher us into the red carpet line. We notice our colleagues heading directly into the theater and we end up having to convince them that we aren't actors and aren't supposed to walk the red carpet.

Right before we step inside we are led to an area where we pose for press pictures. I gently slide my hand around the back of Brooke's waist until I wrap my fingers along her side and pull her closer. I feel incredibly proud to be here with her. My smile is genuine as the flash captures us right as she looks up at me and smiles.

The energy in the air's exciting but once we're seated and the ceremony starts it gets dull pretty quickly. I don't watch much TV so the nominees and shows don't mean much to me. I only spark up when it's announced that the animation category is coming after the commercial break.

"Are you nervous? I know we're favored to win," I say, searching her face for anxiety. If I were her I'd be a wreck.

"Yeah," she admits, twisting her hands.

"You'll do great, you're a natural. I reach over and squeeze her hand and she smiles warmly.

"I'm glad you're the one here with me, Nathan."

My heart's pounding when our category finally comes up, and two actors start announcing the nominees. When they announce *Danny Deletes* as the winner, Brooke looks over at me beaming and as we rise out of our seats, I give her a big hug. I don't sit back down until I know she is safely down the aisle and up the stairs to the stage.

She looks amazingly composed considering that I felt her trembling when I hugged her. *Damn, she's beautiful.* I'm so mesmerized watching her that I don't clearly hear her speech at first, something about accepting for the artist who created the show. But right before she ends, it seems like she's searching for me in the audience. Her words cut right through me.

"This is for the animation artists who quietly put their hearts and souls into their work to create magic for us all. I'm honored to be a part of their world."

I take a sharp breath and fall back against my seat. I can't believe the way she makes me feel. Every time I think it isn't possible that she could do or say anything to make me love her more, she proves me wrong.

She gives me a shy smile as she settles back into her seat. I lean in closer to her.

"Congratulations, Brooke. You were amazing up there."

"Thanks. I think your Starbucks cup drawing brought me good luck."

I smile warmly at her and whisper, "And just for the record, *I'm* honored to be part of your world."

Luckily the hair guy, Bradley, had warned me how boring award ceremonies can get, so I came prepared. Well into the second hour, I pull out my mini-sketch pad and pencil and start drawing little caricatures for Brooke of the different people we see on stage. She almost laughs out loud at the one of Ellen DeGeneres dancing with one of the guys from Glee.

When the ceremony torture is over we head over to the Governor's Ball for what appears to be formal dinner torture. Even though Arnold's an ass for abandoning Brooke, I'm starting to see why he didn't mind missing this endless event and all the industry small talk required. Everyone is standing around having cocktails, so I leave Brooke with some people from Disney Animation to go get us drinks at the bar.

When I finally get back there's some good looking guy standing too close to Brooke and handing her his card. I grip my drink so hard I'm lucky the glass doesn't shatter. As I step up he looks at me and takes his cue.

"Okay Brooke, call me next week and we'll have lunch."

I wish I were one of those guys who could just haul off and punch him, instead I watch him walk away.

"Who's that?" I ask carefully.

"Richard's from Disney. He says he wants to meet with me about a potential joint project between the studios for charity." She glances at me, watching to see my reaction. I can tell she isn't completely convinced of his motives either.

"Yeah, I bet he wants to *meet* with you. Are you going to go?" I hand her the drink.

"I don't know."

I feel a wave of nausea wash over me. It's one thing to know she's with Arnold, but if she starts seeing another man too, I know I won't be able to handle it. But before anything can get even more tense and awkward, Gene from Nickelodeon joins us and the industry banter starts up again. I just want to get the hell out of here.

When it is time to be seated Brooke looks at me and seems to sense that I'm at the end of my rope.

"Hey, are you all right?"

I nod, not wanting to reveal the jealous beast that is burning inside of me.

She takes my hand. "Come on. Let's get out of here."

"Are you sure? What about the people you should be talking to?"

"I don't care about that. I've done my bit. Let's go get a burger." She grins and my heart soars. I whip out my cell phone and call our driver.

Once in the limo we crack open the chilled champagne and clink glasses before settling back into our seats. Due to traffic and construction it's a slow drive back, so by the time we get to In-N-Out we're already buzzed.

There's nothing like the vision of Brooke in her evening gown, perched in a plastic seat, waiting for me to bring her a Double-Double, animal style. The Emmy sits grandly on the Formica-topped table. I can only imagine what the other diners think of us, but I don't care.

I undo my tie and the top few buttons of my dress shirt so I can breathe. We laugh as we eat, her doing goofy impressions of the speeches while I draw the corresponding caricatures in my little sketchpad. More than once she takes a napkin and wipes the ketchup off my chin. This is how I like my Brooke. This is how we should always be.

We're even more boisterous on the limo ride back to her house. We finish off the champagne and put our feet up so we are practically lying down. I open up the skylight so we can look at the stars. Something about the vastness of the night sky makes me feel like anything is possible.

When we reach her house I sign for the driver and walk her to the door.

"Thanks for letting me take you Brooke..." I start, hopeful that this isn't goodbye.

"You're not leaving yet!" she laughs as she takes my hand and drags me in. "I have some wine open in the fridge."

Yes! I follow as she pulls me along.

She hands me the bottle while she grabs two glasses and we head back to the living room. I notice she's walking a little funny.

"Are you okay?" I slide off my jacket and drop it over the edge of a chair.

"Yeah, it's just my feet are killing me. I can't wait to get these shoes off." She lowers herself onto the couch as I uncork the bottle and pour the wine. I hand her a glass and watch her lips skim the edge as she takes a sip.

"We need some music," she suggests as she settles against the cushions. "Do you have your iPod with you? I don't want to get up and look for mine."

I nod slowly. "Yeah, but I'm not sure there's anything you'd want to listen to on my playlists."

"Don't be so sure, handsome. Here, let me see," she teases as she reaches towards me.

I remove my iPod from the inside pocket of my jacket, then hand it to her. "Be gentle," I implore.

She takes another sip as she skims the many playlists. She grins widely and looks up at me. "*The Carl Stalling Project*? You have Looney Tunes music on your iPod!"

"Yes," I admit, my cheeks turning red. "I think it's cool. Stalling was brilliant."

"It is cool," she agrees. "But that's not the mood I'm looking for." Her eyes light up as she makes a different choice and then hands it back to me. She gives me a coy look with one eyebrow raised. "Very interesting playlists."

"Thanks," I murmur.

"The dock's right there." She points to a small table next to the wall.

I smile and take the iPod back and set it in the dock, without looking to see her choice. The sounds of Marvin Gaye's, *Let's Get it On* fills the room. I freeze, horrified realizing that she found an old playlist titled *Make-out Music* which I had made when I thought I still had a sexual chance with Rachel. *Damn! Why hadn't I deleted it?*

My mind races wondering how I can explain this to Brooke, but I look up and she's smiling and seems inspired. The buzz from the champagne probably isn't hurting my cause either. *Don't be an idiot Nathan; she chose that playlist after all.* It occurs to me to calm down and just go with it, so I give her an awkward smile back.

She sips her wine and then lifts her leg up and twists her ankle. "Help," she implores.

"So...you really need my help?" I'm teasing her so she teases back, making it sound so damn sexy.

"Badly," she suggests.

I step closer and lower myself to my knees in front of her.

The sound of her voice and the look in her eyes does something to me. I slide my hands around her ankles and rub my thumbs back and forth along her insteps. "Can I take these off for you?"

"Please," she whispers.

I carefully unhook the first delicate strap and then pull it open, before slowly easing it off her foot. I know that she thinks I will merely move onto the other shoe, but I start massaging her gently.

She moans softly. "Oh, that feels so good."

I smile and look down. Even her feet are perfect.

"Nathan?"

"Uh, huh?" I'm focused on her toes with their little painted toenails.

"I love your haircut. I especially love that he left some of that messy part on top; it's just enough to pull on." She reaches forward and winds her fingers in my hair, pulling gently.

If I wasn't completely turned on a moment ago, I certainly am now.

"You cut your hair for me, for tonight...didn't you?"

I nod, and shyly look up at her. Part of me doesn't want that information to make her uncomfortable, the other part wants her to know that I would do anything for her.

"You look so damn sexy in that tux. Will you wear it again for me sometime?"

"Whenever you want," I murmur as I caress her soft skin just above her ankle. I reach over and start to undo the other sandal.

"You know, Nathan, when the time comes I'm going to have a really hard time sharing you with another girl."

Oh Brooke, you didn't just say that, did you? I can't help but look at her shocked.

She must take my expression the wrong way because her expression falls.

"Oh, but of course. You're nothing like Arnauld. You probably couldn't be with more than one woman at a time. Could you?"

"No, I wouldn't want to be." I state firmly before I think how she will react.

She nods as she watches me touch her. With one hand tenderly massaging the ball of her foot, the other runs up her calf, each stroke just a little higher.

She closes her eyes and moans again. I notice her legs pull further apart, just slightly, yet the suggestion is there. She lifts the hem of her dress up higher. I'm so excited I can barely breathe.

I picture kissing her between her legs and desire rips through me.

Oh Brooke, can I? Please...please...

Marvin Gaye's seductive voice in the background is encouraging me to make my move and *get it on* with Brooke. When he sings how he's held back the feeling for so long I shake my head knowingly. I also know I may never have this opportunity again.

My hands are now stroking each calf evenly and I take a deep breath and stop at her knees. I'm empowered, sensing the spirit of Marvin is with me. My fingers press into the soft skin, gently parting her legs far enough for me to fit in between. She opens her eyes just as I lean down and begin kissing her on the inside of her thigh, just above her knee.

Her sigh is ragged and wanting as I lower myself even closer. It gives me hope that she'll let me pleasure her this intimate way. Rachel always said this was something I was truly great at. Now if I don't get too nervous and fumble, it will be Brooke's turn to find out why.

Animate Me / Chapter Fourteen / A School-Night Sleepover

"Ooh, what does this button do?" ~Dee Dee[xiii]

"Nathan," she moans. "What're you doing?"

I'm slowly trailing kisses up her inner thighs. I look up at her and smile, hoping she'll go along with my plan.

"It's a surprise," I tease as I run my fingertips higher and higher.

"I like surprises," she says softly as she edges her skirt up, her legs easing further apart.

Her skin is unbelievably soft; I savor every inch of sweetness as my lips feather over her. I'm intoxicated with the idea of having my tongue against her. It's making me so excited that I struggle to stay calm. When my fingers finally stroke along the silk of her panties, she moans.

"I really, really like surprises," she whispers.

She isn't resisting at all. If anything, I can feel how much she wants this. It's an unbelievable rush. I feel like Superman would if Lois had her thighs spread open for him.

I love the idea of Brooke's delicate panties just disintegrating in my superhero hands, but instead I carefully loop my fingers under the lace that runs across her hips and gently pull down. She lifts up to help me, and we work together until she is bare—and I mean completely bare. I almost pass out with excitement when I see that she's perfectly smooth between her legs. This is new territory for me that I've dreamed of navigating. I hope that I can live up to her expectations, since I already told her that this is something I'm really good at.

But once I start it all comes naturally because instinctively I want to please her more than anything. I quickly learn that the best part of exploring Brooke is how responsive she is. Her moans and whispers, along with the way she rocks gently against me tells me how good I'm making her feel. Every look and sigh is unbelievably motivating.

Do you have any idea what your reactions are doing to me Brooke?

I manage to resist the urge to unzip my trousers and get relief from the need to be touched. I have to resist, because this is all about Brooke…my chance to show her what my words cannot say.

I start out slow, my tongue, lips and fingers softly working over her. Every time she begins to accelerate I slow down. I can feel the building and then the easing back, and I want to push all of her sensations as far as I possibly can.

At one point she gets frisky as I do this particular thing with my tongue. All of a sudden she randomly cries out, "The dress!"

"The dress?" I question, pushing the fabric out of the way again, and lifting up to face her.

She's panting. "It's got to come off…now."

She won't get an argument from me. I lean back on my heels and rise, as she pushes off the couch and turns. My fingers work the zipper with astounding speed. Next thing I know the dress is off and then the bra.

Good God, she's naked before me.

And before I even have time to think about it she's kissing me, unfazed by the idea of where my mouth's just been, or the fact that she's naked and I'm still in my tux. It's like some James Bond movie.

My hands roam over every curve while we kiss: the swell of her hips, her soft breasts and her nipples tight with arousal. I discover a tiny dimple just above her bottom and I softly run my finger across it. Meanwhile I'm burning up with the sensation of her pressed against me. I can't believe the way she's kissing me…my God, I've never imagined kissing could be like this.

When we pull away, I gasp for breath, then stutter, "I-I-I'm not done."

"No, you're not," she grins, as she eases back down on the couch, her legs falling open as she pulls me down.

Again on my knees, I slide my hands under her bottom and pull her closer. She is warm and wet, pink and soft, a landscape to wander with my tongue as my fingers push into her. Every part of her is beautiful.

"Do you know how incredible you're making me feel?" she asks, her fingers weaving through my hair.

Her words give me the confidence that sexually I could be good for her. I've never felt like this before with anyone—not even close.

Inspired, I rise up higher to kiss her again. This time I'm more assertive, my arm wrapping around her waist and pulling her into me. Working my way down her neck, I take my time with her breasts before finally settling back between her legs. Within moments I'm lost in her again. I never want to leave.

"Oh, God," she groans. "You're amazing…ahhh…" She tugs on my hair, pulling me closer as her legs wrap around me.

Just about then it hits me: *I'm on my knees, between her legs, about to make Brooke orgasm with my outstanding oral skills.* It's almost too good to be true. This event will always be noted as one of the most satisfying accomplishments of my life. I groan loudly with pleasure and this seems to be the spark lighting her fuse.

Her power's astounding as she starts to climax, her fingers digging into my shoulders as her hips thrust forward. She's all passion and fire, more woman than I could've ever hoped for… a lit rocket, soaring past me into the dark night.

When her cries subside, I pull back and gently rub her knees, waiting for her to catch her breath. Her eyes are glassy, and her skin's flushed.

"Are you okay?" I ask, starting to worry a bit. She looks disoriented.

She laughs, and then as if talking to herself, asks, "Am I okay?"

"Brooke?" I ask again, hoping she can focus.

"Oh, Nathan…whatever am I going to do with you—Mister, *I've got a surprise for you.*"

"Do with me?"

But before she can answer, she pulls a throw blanket over her shoulders, slides off the couch and joins me on the floor.

"Were you really as into that as you seemed?" she asks as she leans her head back on the cushions watching me.

"Yes," I reply, looking down, suddenly embarrassed.

"Wow…just wow." She says happily.

She lifts my chin with her fingers, and looks me straight in the eyes. "You are wonderful," she says softly.

I grin ear to ear as she reaches out and takes my hand.

165

"Are you still hard?" Her blanket is bunched between us; otherwise my situation would be so glaringly apparent that she wouldn't need to ask.

"Are you kidding?" I groan, even more embarrassed.

"Show me," she whispers.

Show me? Holy hell, what's she going to do? I say a silent prayer to the oral sex Gods before I lift up and tentatively unzip my tuxedo trousers. While I fumble to push my pants and boxers down, she reaches over and wraps her hand around me. *Oh my God. Please, please, Brooke, don't let go.*

"Oh wow," she moans, studying me.

I gasp, watching her lick her lips, admiration in her eyes. I feel a surge of hope as she keeps touching me.

My head rolls back. "When you look at me and touch me like that... it makes me crazy. I swear, you're going to make me come."

She stills, her warm hand still holding me possessively.

"What do you want, Nathan?"

My heart's pounding, I'm too overwhelmed to speak. I want her to keep touching me. I want to see her slide me between her lips. I want to make love to her. I want everything. She's naked, apparently still aroused, and only inches away from me. But how can I tell her all the ways I want her?

Lucky for me she has her own ideas.

"Can I take you in my mouth?" she asks, with a taunting smile. Does she know she's just made me impossibly harder?

Oh my God. Do I want to be in her mouth? Does the Road Runner always get away from Wile E. Coyote? Yes, please, Brooke.

"Yes," I say evenly, trying not to sound desperate. I decide not to tell her that I've never had that done to me.

She looks extremely pleased and happily sinks down. I watch her, while I frantically try to suspend my disbelief. Just the look of her hand grasping my thigh and her soft lips wrapped around me is almost more than I can take. The last thing I logically remember before I tumble into a lust-filled state is her slowly running her tongue up my length from the base, and then circling the head.

She's moaning like she loves doing this to me... for me. It's so incredibly intimate; my heart is racing ahead before the rest of me can catch up.

"Oh, Brooke." I groan as I observe her mouth full of me, her beautiful breasts in full view just below. This time she moans louder and everything starts intensifying.

I'm lost in the hot, wet swirl of her mouth. She's moving like she intends to pull every little bit of pleasure out of me—like there's nothing else in the world she would rather do. It's all too much; my damn traitor body—it's happening too fast.

"I'm gonna…" I manage to say, as my hold slips. I'm dangling from the high wire.

Both of her hands grip me as she rubs the head across her lips before taking me in again. *Yes*, she nods, her mouth so full and her eyes smiling.

I let go, an explosion of surging intensity, and she takes it all. Her desire to satisfy me makes me crash past every moment I've ever felt wrong, because now I feel completely right.

When I eventually return to consciousness she grins at me and I grin back bigger.

Wow

A short while later I'm in her arms. She's in mine, and I don't ever want to let her go.

"Can I tell you something?" I ask cautiously. We've both settled down. She's put on a robe, and is tucked tightly under my shoulder.

She looks up at me and waits.

"I really don't want you to go out with that guy, Richard, from Disney."

"Why would it bother you if I did?" She runs her hand across my chest. "You almost sound jealous," she teases, smiling.

I can't smile or tease back because this is bothering me too much. "Maybe I am. I don't want you to date him, or even worse, sleep with him. I don't want him kissing you either."

"Is that because you think it will change how I feel about you?"

"Well that's part of it," I admit.

"Are you getting all possessive on me now?"

"Maybe I am. Does that upset you?"

"Well, what if I get possessive if you and Dani or another girl get closer?"

"That's not going to happen." I reply. "But would you get possessive?"

"Definitely," she admits softly. "Although I would try to be good. We should promise to always be friends…no matter what. Okay?"

"With benefits?" I ask confused.

"I want to be with you like this but that's up to you and the girl. Not everyone can handle the kind of strange set-up Arnauld and I have."

Not everyone would want to, I think. *If you were mine, I would never share you Brooke.*

Never.

Some time passes before I realize we haven't spoken for a while and we're both dozing off. I rub my eyes and gently rock Brooke.

"Brooke, it's late, I better go."

She blinks as I rise off the couch. As I take a step forward I sway, all the exhaustion and liquor of the evening hitting me. I drop back down onto the couch and run my hands through my hair. "I don't think I should drive." I find my jacket and fish the phone out. "I'm going to call a cab."

"Don't be silly," she insists, taking the phone from me. "Just stay here with me."

"On the couch?" I ask, not wanting to presume where I would sleep.

"No, just sleep with me. I've got a big bed and I promise not to take advantage of you."

Oh, please take advantage of me…take advantage of me over and over again.

"Are you sure?" I ask. "Tomorrow's a work day."

"So what? No sleepovers on a school night? Screw that." She stands up and takes my hand. "Come on."

We stop in the kitchen to grab bottles of water and then head back to her room. If I weren't so out of it from exhaustion, I'd probably freak out. I push off my shoes, socks and pants. And even though I have my back toward her, I can hear Brooke changing. When I turn and see her in her little tank top and matching tiny shorts I realize if I make it till morning without imploding, it'll be a miracle.

I slide under the covers near the edge of the bed, nervously waiting for her to join me. After doing stuff in the bathroom she comes out and gets into bed, acting like my being there is the most natural thing in the world. I try to close my eyes, but I can't stop staring at her. I watch her even once the light is off, and I only see her in dark shades of silver from the moonlight.

I'm spending the night with Brooke…in her bed…in my boxer shorts. We are only three small garments of clothing away from being naked in bed together. Wow.

She seems to fall asleep right away, but suddenly I notice movement under the covers half way between us. I slowly wave my hand around the linens to figure out what's going on, and I'm surprised to discover her hand searching for mine. When she finds it, she grabs on.

"Nathan?" she whispers sleepily.

"Yes?" I reply, feeling her fingers lace through mine.

"Thank you for tonight." She sighs happily.

"Which part?" I can't resist asking.

"All of it," she says without hesitation. "The beginning, middle and end. It was all better because it was with you."

I linger at her including "the end" part…and the idea that it was better with me. I'm doing an internal fist pump.

There's long pause while I consider if I should say what I want to. I take a deep breath.

"I hope you know Brooke that I'd go anywhere with you, do anything for you," I reply bravely.

She's quiet at first, but then whispers, "I do." She squeezes my hand gently one more time then settles further into her pillow.

I may not be able to see her smile in the dark of the room, but I can feel it all the way through me.

About four a.m. I stumble out of bed towards the bathroom, and when I return I laugh quietly, because Brooke is lying exactly where I was before getting up. I open the bottle of water, and take a swig as I observe her.

I sigh deeply. The moonlight falling through the window skims over her. Her hair's fanned across my pillow like it's blowing in the wind, her lips gently moving, whispering secrets I can't hear. She's so beautiful as she waltzes through dreamland.

I flex my fingers, fighting the urge to run my fingertips across her cheek.

I love you Brooke.

Do you think you can love me too?

169

Her eyelashes flutter, tiny butterflies. She looks fragile in her stillness, but I know she's tougher than most…certainly tougher than me.

Rather than disturb her, I decide to get in on her side of the bed. As soon as I settle in though, she rolls towards me, until she is pressed up against my body. I shift awkwardly and she curls into me, her cheek resting on my chest, her leg folded over my thighs. I wrap my arm around her and listen for her steady heartbeat until I am lulled back to sleep.

The next time my eyes open the room is glowing with the quiet morning light. Realizing that my muse's ankle is hooked over mine, I look over to see her arms flung over her head. If she were standing up she'd be reaching for the stars. With all her movement, her little tank top has hiked up high, the pale silk skin of her torso calling for my touch.

I slowly shift down in the bed until I can gently lay my cheek just above her waist where the skin is softest. I lie like that for a while, careful not to press down too hard. I like watching the subtle rise and fall of her breaths and this view of her shapely legs. Suddenly I hear a sigh and her legs shift.

I feel her hand rake through my hair, slowly massaging my scalp. *Should I move?* But before I can decide, she takes a fistful of my hair, gently pulling my head up higher. Her free hand pushes up her tank top, while the other leads me directly to her breast.

Am I dreaming? Either way, I'm going to go with it. I slowly brush my lips across her beautiful soft curves.

The moment I pull her nipple into my mouth she arcs under me. Her low moan is my undoing. Desire roars through me. I'm sure she's fully awake, and the rawness of the morning is revealing a hunger for me I could have only dreamed about. My hand wanders over her, and she pushes it down between her legs.

"Brooke?" *Show me what you want.*

"Like this," she whispers, sliding my hand under her shorts, her legs pulling apart, welcoming me.

Oh God, she's wet. She wants me. She wants this. My fingers move over her, in her.

I roll towards her until I'm pressed hard against her thigh. I can't help myself; I push against her, searching for friction while my hand presses on. Right before I move to kiss her other breast, I look up at her.

170

She's biting down on her swollen lips as she watches me. Her hair tangled and wild, the black smear of her eye make-up against her ivory skin renders her a gothic princess. I can only imagine that I look like the village idiot next to her. But the way she looks at me makes me believe she really wants me.

"Kiss me," she whispers, as her legs part, encouraging me to get in closer. I crawl over her and then lower my body until we are pressed together. She takes my face in her hands, watching me, waiting. Our lips meet softly until she wraps her legs around me and pulls me against her. Things quickly shift in intensity, and it's becoming clear to me what she wants...and it's even more than I hoped for.

"Are you ready? Do you want this?" she asks with a whisper.

"Can I have you?" *Please say yes.*

"Do you have condoms?"

Ah, she thinks I was only talking about wanting her sexually. It's hard to be disappointed considering I'm a winner either way. "No, do you?"

"I don't think the ones I have would fit you." She runs her hand down between us until she has me in her grasp. "No, definitely not."

My heart falls. Here's my chance and my lack of latex is crushing the deal. Why don't I carry a condom in my wallet like normal guys? *Damn it all.*

"But I'm on the pill, and Arnauld always wears a condom. And you're clean, so..."

"Really?" I was concerned about that, but I'm more afraid of disappointing her if I can't be the kind of lover she wants.

"Yes, I want to do this with you...so much."

"But..." I'm fighting my insecurities.

"Don't over think this Nathan. Let's just start easy—no fireworks with the heavens parting: just you inside of me—your Brooke. Even if it's just a few minutes, you'll be glad you did." She reaches up and kisses my neck, biting me gently.

My chest is heaving, and we aren't even doing it yet. She seems willing to accept so little, but I want to be everything to her.

Yet, she's right. I've got to stop over thinking. I'm going to talk myself out of sex, and right now I need to have this with her like I need water and air.

"You don't have to full on make love to me," she suggests. "Just do a test run. Like trying on new shoes."

Trying on new shoes?

"I know how much you want me," she murmurs, her tongue circling my ear as she presses against me.

"Can you show me what to do...I mean, how you like it?" I fumble.

"Sure," she whispers, smiling happily as she pushes my boxers down, while I try to peel her tank top off. We aren't too smooth, I was hoping for something seamless like I see in the movies. Instead we are fumbling and awkward. When I have trouble getting off her little shorts, we end up laughing. At least it helps my nervousness.

Finally completely bare, she lies down and stretches out seductively as she watches me. As I try to figure out what my next move should be she runs her hands up her thighs and over her breasts.

"Mmm, you must remember what your touching and kisses do to me."

I remember everything, Brooke. I blink several times.

"I need you, Nathan. Come closer."

I love that she can ask for what she wants. I lift up then lower myself over her and let my hands wander. My lips wrap around her nipples, her heated response encouraging me on.

"Yes, that feels so good," she moans. Her pelvis presses into mine, and my erection bucks, ready for action.

"Kiss me," she says so softly it's almost a whisper.

I nod, and shift up, until my lips are just an inch from hers.

"Are you sure?" I ask tentatively, wanting to make sure since this is a big step for both of us. I can't believe our big moment is finally here.

She nods with a sweet smile, "Please."

The moment our lips touch she wraps her limbs around me and pulls me closer.

She starts getting more assertive with the kissing, and I'm relieved. I'm not sure I could take the lead right now, even if I wanted to.

When we finally part, she pulls back and looks me in the eye. "Are you ready?"

I know she's also checking to make sure I can handle this. She cares about me being okay, and I love her for that.

"No...yes...but..." I'm silently imagining all the ways I can screw this up and ruin the possibility for future sex lessons from Brooke. I also realize that I'm scared shitless. What if this hurts her the way it hurt Rachel? That would be the final straw, the air escaping with a loud hissing groan from my deflating balloon of sexuality.

She must sense my insecurity. "Nathan," she whispers, facing me earnestly. "I want you. You want me. Let's do this."

I nod, visualizing the Nike swoosh in my head. *Just do it. Just do it. Just do it.*

I boldly lift up to my knees and she scoots closer, her legs gloriously spread for me. I take myself in my hand and slide it over her. I can't believe she's so wet. She really wants me. She must. She looks up and nods with determination.

I take a deep breath and now leaning over her, I begin to push, tentatively at first but once her warm wetness envelopes me my confidence grows.

Oh my God, this feels so amazing; she's incredibly aroused. Halfway in, I pause, stopping my eyes from rolling back long enough to focus.

She's panting, and her face is flushed.

"Are you okay?" I ask concerned.

"I never," she groans, "...so full, so damn good. More...I want it all." And the way her legs tighten over me, I know she means it.

The sensation overwhelms me. I pause and take a deep breath, then another. She stills and waits, understanding. "I just..." I stutter.

"I know, I know," she says gently. "It's okay...just whenever you're ready."

"Oh, Brooke..." I start the slow sinking of the last few inches. When our hips finally meet, I gasp. She's pulsing around me, and there is no question that this is the best feeling in the entire universe. I mean it was great when her mouth was on me, but this is great times a trillion. My head falls back and we both moan in unison.

"Ahhh," she groans, as she struggles to catch her breath.

I still, and study her face, which looks slightly strained. "Does it hurt?" I'm compelled to ask, hoping I don't kill the moment.

The strained, focused expression melts into bliss. "This is heaven. I'm in heaven." Her eyes meet mine, and they are warm and soft and so happy.

"Oh...oh," I moan as she grips me hard.

"And let me now state for the record, that size does matter. Oh yeah, it matters." She grins.

"Yeah?" I ask, starting to feel more confident. I concentrate as I shift my hips up, pulling partway out, and then push back down.

"Oh, yes. Do that again harder."

I lift up, her tightness fighting my release. I grit my teeth and pause, hanging on before I push back hard. The flush spreads across my chest as I do it again.

She's moaning, her hips rising and falling as her head rolls side to side.

I want to growl from this raw male thing rising out of me. Brooke is under me, and she wants me to take her hard.

"Oh, my God...so good," she cries out as I thrust again.

She winds her fingers in my hair and pulls me towards her. I feel her lips skim my neck until they press against my ear. "Do you understand what you're doing to me?" she whispers.

"Oh, Brooke," I moan.

Her eyes are almost violet and hypnotizing in the gray morning light. I pull out even further then push harder back in, a current of supreme pleasure coursing through me. *There are no words to adequately tell her how incredible this feels.*

"Nathan," she whispers, smiling as she suddenly realizes something. "You did it...we're doing it!"

Yes, we did, and *we are,* and it's friggin' great. Let's bring out the marching band and a skywriting plane to spell it out... *We're doing it!*

And even though I'm about to come...far too soon...before I could flip her over or hang her upside down, or that crazy stuff they do in porn films...I now know what's possible.

I can't believe it. I'm inside Brooke and she likes it...a lot.

Animate Me / Chapter Fifteen / A New Man

"Don't talk to me about importance! Because of you, the future of this entire universe is in jeopardy!" ~Buzz Lightyear to Woody[xiv]

My face is pressed against her neck as I try to remember who I am. *Oh my God, that's right, I'm Nathan, and I just had the best orgasm of my life.* A moment later, however, I realize that I'm probably crushing the woman who put me in this blissful state.

"Brooke?" I ask, my voice heavy with concern as I regretfully lift up and move off of her. The withdrawal of my manhood from its happy new home is particularly jarring.

"Are you okay?"

"Oh yeah," she purrs as she settles on her side, up against me.

We lie silently for a while. I'm spooning her from behind, holding her tightly, grateful that I seemed to satisfy her despite my past history. I don't think there's ever been a time I was more curious to know what she's thinking. I just can't wait any longer...I need to know. I clear my throat.

"Are you sure you're all right?" I whisper. "Was it okay for you? Was that too hard?"

"No, it was perfect. It was all perfect." She lets out a long sigh.

"Then why are you so quiet?"

"I'm just thinking."

"About?" I run my fingertips lightly along her arm.

"Was it what you imagined?" she asks quietly. "Was it what you hoped for?"

"Actually a million times better," I respond. "I can't tell how many times I've dreamt of it being like this."

"With Dani?" Her voice is soft and tender.

She knows the answer to this question. Maybe she wants to know if I'm brave enough to admit it. I take a deep breath. "No, with you," I admit.

I can feel her body shift even though she stays quiet for a minute. I hold my breath waiting. Embarrassed, I decide to deflect the question back to her. I take a deep breath for courage before planting kisses along her shoulder. "Have you ever imagined doing that with me?" I try to stay calm despite my pounding heart; I desperately want to hear her answer.

Say yes, Brooke...say that you dream of me making love to you every single night.

"Yes, I've imagined it. I'll tell you a secret," she says softly. "Sometimes at work I want to lure you from your cubicle into a conference room. Then I imagine pushing you down into the chair at the head of that long table, undoing your jeans..."

"Yes?" I gasp, as I excitedly wait to hear the next part.

"...and then sinking to my knees and taking you in my mouth."

I swallow hard. *Whoa...in the conference room?* "Well, that could be arranged," I say.

"Would you like that?" she asks in a raspy voice.

"Yeah, I'd like that a lot," I sputter, thrilled to know she's fantasized about me too.

We continue to talk, undoubtedly both of our minds racing with the information we've shared. But after a few minutes the conversation shifts, I feel her soften into my embrace and then she speaks up again.

"Can I ask you something, Nathan?"

"Anything."

"Tonight, the way you looked at me...the things you've said. This feels like it's more than sexual attraction. It almost seems like you're falling in love with me."

For a moment I can feel the worry start to bubble up somewhere deep inside but I try to calm myself enough to respond to her.

Be brave...

"What if I am?" I say softly.

She's so still, probably in shock. Well, I'm in shock too.

Please answer, Brooke. Say something...anything.

"You're so important to me…but I'm so afraid to complicate things… mess this up."

Complicate things? That sounds like a problem with a business deal. That doesn't sound like love. My heavy heart falls.

"Everything with you is different, Nathan."

"Different?"

"There are things I've never felt with anyone before. Sometimes I don't know how to handle it, and it scares me."

I pull her closer. I can't help wondering how much of this is about Arnold. "Do you love him?" I ask, trying to mask the sadness in my voice.

"Arnauld?"

I can't even speak; I just nod my head against hers.

"In the beginning I felt something I thought could have been love. But actually, now I understand that I never felt that way about him."

Be brave…deep breath. "Do you think you could ever fall in love with me?"

There's a long pause. I know this isn't easy for her. I brace myself, in case her words crush me.

"I have so many feelings about you…as I said, I'm scared. I need to sort them all out. But you've got stuff to sort out too."

Not really. I know my love for her is permanently etched into me, like a tattoo on my heart. But she's still thinking of Dani and all the fiction I created while trying to build a bridge between our worlds.

It suddenly occurs to me that maybe this is too much for her…her fear of commitment may ultimately cause her to push me away. I can't let that happen. I decide to soften the edges. I know she just needs time to get used to the idea of us.

"You won't pull away from me, will you? I can still see you, be with you?"

"Yes, yes," she sighs and pulls me closer. "I need you Nathan. Don't worry, I won't let you go."

I skim my lips along her ear and into her hair. "Okay. Please don't, Brooke. I need you too."

We hold each other until the room grows brighter. She finally speaks up. "Hey, are you hungry?" She asks shifting to face me.

"Starving," I smile, trying to keep things light.

"Pancakes?"

"Oh yeah…I'll help."

We tumble out of bed and pull our nightwear on before heading off to her kitchen. We're sitting close at her breakfast table, our feet criss-crossed together.

"These are so good," I say happily as I finish off my first stack.

She nods happily. I take a sip of coffee and look at the clock. Seven, I don't need to be at work for another few hours. I help myself to more pancakes and settle in. It occurs to me that every morning could be like this if Brooke ever chooses me.

When we're done I carry our dishes to the sink and start washing. She presses up behind me. "Oooo, I love a man who washes dishes."

I press back. "I love a woman who makes me pancakes."

"When you're done you wanna watch cartoons?" She asks grinning.

"You need to ask? You pick. I'll watch whatever you want."

I can't even imagine feeling happier than this.

When I finish the dishes we crawl back in bed, curling up together to watch *Toy Story*. Even though I imagine I'm more like Woody, I always root for Buzz. I love his unwavering confidence in his abilities. It almost doesn't matter that he can't actually fly as long as he believes he can.

When it's finally time for me to leave, I pull on my tuxedo slacks and white undershirt, and sling my jacket and shirt over my shoulder. I look like one of those wild party boys the morning after…after he was up all night long in bed with a beautiful, sexy woman.

Hell, yes.

At the front door Brooke wraps her arms around me and I run my fingers through her hair. It kills me to leave her and the little cocoon we've wrapped ourselves in.

"What time are you going in?" I ask.

"I'm not sure I'm going in today," she admits. "I might just take the day off and rest. It was a big night, you know."

I grin. "Yeah, I'll say. When can we talk then?"

"I'll call you in the afternoon before you go to Starbucks."

"I do home deliveries," I tease.

"I'm sure you do," she teases back as she opens the door. She leans into me and kisses me. "Thank you."

"Please don't thank me. Last night my whole life changed. You gave me an experience I was starting to think I'd never have. So if anyone is going to be giving thanks it's me."

She smiles shyly, takes my face in her hands and kisses me once more.

I regretfully move away from her, towards my car. But despite my reluctance to leave her, I'm energized knowing I'm a new man as I walk out the gate, a better man than I was when I entered just over twelve hours ago. And it's all because of Brooke.

• • •

With everything on my mind, I've forgotten about my new haircut. Combined with my new glasses, my look is definitely different. But I'm reminded of this fact, as I pass the check-in desk in the lobby of Sketch Republic. The receptionist's eyes widen and her mouth falls open as I walk past.

Honestly, it's rather unnerving and I fear the worst when I finally face my gang. Unfortunately my trepidation was not unfounded.

"Ooooo look who got cleaned up for the Emmys," Andy drawls as I turn the corner into production.

"You wish you could look this good, doofus," I shoot back.

"Preet-taaay!" howls Joel.

Damn.

Genna peeks out of her cubical. "Wow, Nathan. You look really great with that haircut. I love the hot glasses too."

I blush. "Thanks Genna."

Just then Nick steps out of the break room and eyes me warily.

"Hey, Nick."

He folds his arms over his chest. "How was the big night?"

If he only knew. "Oh, the Emmys were all right I guess, if you like that sort of thing."

"New haircut, new glasses…it looks like you're trying to impress someone. Am I right?"

I can't imagine why he looks worried about me. With his piercing blue eyes and longer, wavy blonde hair he's always been the golden boy here with the ladies. His handsome looks and charming personality insured that he could have had almost any girl in this building.

179

"I didn't want to embarrass Brooke. I had to do something."

"Hmmm," he responds before he turns away. Maybe he and Dani haven't made up yet. He still doesn't seem to trust me. I guess I was less of a threat when I looked like a weirdo.

As I watch him walk away I realize that if this is the worst of the fallout from my makeover, then I can handle it. I'm sure there will be some caricatures down the road, but how bad can they be?

When I get to my cube I realize that my cell phone is still turned off and when I check it I see that there is a call from Dad's lawyer. I listen to my voicemail and am surprised to hear that Sharper Edge Comics sent over a proposal Friday. They must really be ready to move on our deal. He asks me to call and discuss details after lunch. I smile to myself. Everything is looking up.

At noon a bunch of us head over to Subway. I lag behind to walk with Dani whose spirits seem a little low.

"You okay?" I ask.

"I guess," she replies, looking down and picking at her blue nail polish.

"Nick?"

She makes a face. "I don't think he wants me, Nathan. When he took me home from the get together he didn't even kiss me and come inside."

"Did you ask him to come in?"

She grins. "Yes, as seductively as I know how." But then her expression falls. "He must be over me. He's probably into someone else now."

"No. He would have told me that." I say with conviction. "He wants to be with you. I think he's just afraid that it may not work out again."

"Yeah, well to hell with that! Why is everyone so goddamned afraid? Sorry, but I'm getting really tired of pussy men who don't just say what they want and go for it. The bottom line is that women need to know they're wanted."

Could it really be as simple as Dani says it is?

Just then we reach Subway, and I pause before I pull the door open for her. "Shall I tell Nick that?" I ask as I try to imagine what Brooke would say to all of this.

"Be my guest," she says, looking determined. "He only has so many more chances before this ship sails." I'm not sure if she actually means that. With the smile she gives me, it's hard to say for sure.

Women can be such a mystery.

• • •

I call the lawyer, Walter, right after lunch and go over the proposal. I'd already prepped him with my insistence of holding onto my character rights. I agree however to give them exclusive publishing rights for three years and their production company first look for any television or film deals. All of that sounds ridiculous to discuss at this point, but Walter insists that it must be determined up front or we'll regret it later. By the time we get off the phone I can't imagine this deal getting settled, but it's certainly worth a try.

At three-thirty I get a text from Brooke.

No coffee for me today handsome, I'm still in bed.

Handsome? I grin ear to ear and text her back. *No special delivery?*

That's very tempting, but I'm sure you should be at work.

Well, Joel is waiting to see this scene :- (

Yes, you be good. There will be other times to be bad :-)

Okay, rain check then?

Yes, and I'll call you tonight. xoB

My heart soars as I sign off, so happy that she not only remembered to contact me but she flirted with me as well. My bliss lasts for a solid hour until it is shattered with a phone call from the ice princess, Alana, Arnold's assistant.

"Arnauld wants to see you right now."

"Now?" I question. "I'm supposed to meet with Joel to go over my scene."

"Do I really need to repeat myself? Arnauld wants to see you *now.*"

"Okay, I'll be right up."

"Hurry," she snaps before hanging up.

So many emotions surge through me as I ride up the elevator that I'm sure I'm flushed by the time I reach Alana's desk.

"He's waiting," she hisses. "Go right in."

This is bullshit. I'm not going to let him intimidate me.

I half step into the royal chambers. "You wanted to see me?"

He gives me the Arnold glare. Who does he think he is, Lex Luthor? *Hey, he sort of looks like him, now that I think of it.*

He flicks his wrist and points to one of the chairs in front of his desk. "Sit," he commands.

So now I'm a dog. *Careful Arnold, I may bite.*

I fold my arms over my chest as I sit down. "What's up?"

He shifts in his seat and the door magically closes behind me, just like it did my last visit here.

"How'd you do that? I ask pointing to the door.

He ignores my question. So I lean over to peer under his desk and notice a foot pedal not far from his fancy shoes. Ah…so he is the Wizard in his own little Oz, pretending he has magic powers but in reality it's smoke and mirrors.

"What'd you do to her?" He growls and I sit up quickly.

What the hell? "What do you mean, what'd I do to her? Is something wrong with Brooke?"

He studies me carefully, and I'm getting the makeover stare. He narrows his eyes. It's ironic that he doesn't seem to like the change with my haircut and new glasses since he's the one who prompted it.

He finally speaks up. "She's not coming in today, and she never misses work."

"I didn't do anything to her," I state firmly. "She just seemed really tired when I left. That was a big, stressful night for her. She was nervous."

He raises his eyebrows. "Well you sound like quite the expert on Brooke's feelings. You better not be fucking with me, Evans."

He knows my last name.

"Have you talked to her?" I boldly ask.

"Of course I've talked to her. We're having dinner tonight. I'll find out then what you aren't telling me."

I sit quietly and wonder if Brooke will tell him everything. How does an open relationship work exactly?

"You didn't try anything with her, did you?"

Screw you, hairy back. I'm not giving him anything. I want to protect Brooke.

"Would it matter if I did? As you pointed out before, I'm a total dweeb. She'd never want to be with me. So what are you worried about? Who am I compared to you…the president of this company?"

He eyes me suspiciously and flips his computer screen toward me. "Explain this."

I study a picture that was taken of Brooke and me right before we went inside for the show. She's so beautiful and I'm frankly stunned to realize how good we look together. I want a copy of this: first so I always have proof that it happened, and secondly so I can frame it for my bedside table.

Yet on the other hand, I can't get past the fact that it's creepy that Arnold tracked the picture down and has been studying it. I guess the way Brooke and I are gazing at each other with adoration doesn't help the situation.

Wow. We really look like a couple in love. Worried, I try to play it off cool. "What about it? That's right before we went into the auditorium for the show."

"What the fuck is she doing in that dress? That isn't the one I picked out for her."

"You're really asking *me* why she's wearing that dress? Shouldn't you ask her that?"

"Oh, you can bet I will," he glowers.

I lean in towards his screen. I know I shouldn't but I open my mouth anyway. I just can't resist.

"What the problem anyway? I think she looks really great."

I get the death glare again. *He's really good at that.*

"You know Evans, a good friend of mine was at the Emmys and he didn't like the way you were looking at Brooke."

"What did he mean by that?"

"He said you looked like you wanted her," he states, an ugly edge to his voice.

I don't like any of this. I can't let him intimidate me. "Really, like I want her? All that in a look that he observed at a big packed event?"

"I just want you to know that I'm watching you. Every move you make. I know you've been Brooke's cute little project, and she loves your computer help, and how you bring her coffee every afternoon. But bottom line—you're distracting her. I don't like it, and if I decide to, I will stop all of it."

My stomach drops. "Stop it?"

"I don't want Brooke distracted. I need her focused. So just be aware that you've been warned. Time to make other plans for your Starbucks playtime."

"But…" I start.

"That's it." He says abruptly, cutting me off. "Get back to work."

I rise with hesitancy. I want the last word, but I know I can't have it. He has control right now over the two greatest passions in my life, Brooke and my work. He can easily crush me. So as I stagger out of his lush office and back down to my crappy cubicle I vow that somehow, someway I will change things so Arnold no longer holds in his grubby hands all that I consider most precious. I have to figure out how to protect the two parts of my life I know without a doubt that I can't live without.

Thirty minutes later I'm still flip-flopping my cell phone back and forth across my desk as I draw. I still have five drawings to do before I leave and my focus is completely shot. Maybe I need to call Brooke and tell her what Arnold said. Maybe I shouldn't. I would rather do it in person, but she's seeing Arnold tonight…there is no time. Maybe, maybe…I agonize until I can't take another moment, and I pick up the phone and tap on her name.

"Ha, you caught me! I'm watching more animation!" She laughs.

I smile, despite my inner agony. *God, I love that girl.*

"What are you watching?" I ask.

"*Despicable Me.* Have you seen it? It's really good."

"No, but I've been meaning to. You'll have to loan it to me. What's it about?"

"It's about a really bad guy, who becomes good and does the right thing."

I think of Arnold. If only life were more like cartoons: we could drop anvils on people's heads, wear roller skates with rockets, and really bad guys, like Arnold, could magically become good.

"If only…" I moan.

"What's wrong? Did something happen?"

My fingers grip around the phone. "Arnold called me into his office."

"Why? What did he want?"

My mind races...how do I explain how testosterone fires up a Neanderthal when another caveman wants his woman?

I decide to underplay it so she doesn't worry, but at least knows he talked to me. I don't want her surprised in case he brings it up at their fucking dinner.

"I think he just wanted to know how things went at the Emmys."

"Really?" she asks, sounding suspicious.

"I don't think he cares for me much. He didn't seem to like my haircut either."

"I'm sure he didn't," she scoffs. "He doesn't tend to like guys who are better looking than him."

How does she do this to me? I'm unsettled, and she still makes my spirits soar. She thinks I'm better looking than Arnold, who I know is considered very handsome.

She falls quiet again.

"What Brooke?"

"It's just weird, why didn't he wait to ask me? We're having dinner tonight. I'm curious if he'll mention talking to you."

"Are you going to tell him about last night?" *Please say no, please say no.* I know if she does it's all over.

"Well, we normally tell each other everything...no details, just the general idea. But I need to see what he's up to first. I'm not sure what I'll do."

This time I get quiet.

"Nathan?"

I don't answer, the fear choking me, taking my breath and words away.

"Nathan," she says softly. "I know this looks bad to you, but I'm not going to let Arnauld tell me what to do. If he doesn't like it, that's his problem."

"But you warned me. You told me it's complicated."

"Yes, I did. But if it were so easy, how worthwhile would that be? I thought about you a lot today. Do you believe in me?"

"So much, Brooke...so much."

"Good... then I want a Buzz Lightyear drawing on my cup tomorrow. Okay?"

I smile while my heart thunders, and I imagine she can hear that too. "Okay."

But when we say our goodbyes and I hang up, I curl over my desk as my fear flares, a burning torch on a dark desolate street. Only hours ago I finally held all my dreams in my arms...I just can't lose her now.

Animate Me / Chapter Sixteen / Santa, the Easter Bunny and Brooke

"Aw, the poor puddy tat! He fall down and go... BOOM!" ~ Tweety Bird[xv]

The thing is...she said she would call me tonight. Not tomorrow, not the night after, not sometime...but tonight. So when she doesn't, I start to freak. I just have a bad feeling because of how my meeting went with Arnold. I know after the amazing and intimate night Brooke and I had, that she wouldn't just disregard me like this.

I pace through my house for over two hours, before finally forcing myself into bed at midnight with my phone on my nightstand. The ringer is turned on high so it'll wake me up if she calls while I'm asleep. But as it turns out, the high volume isn't necessary; I can't sleep, and she doesn't call.

I try to play it cool at work. Too paranoid to call upstairs looking for her, I just force myself to draw until it's time to defiantly leave for Starbucks. *To hell with Arnold, telling me I can't bring Brooke coffee.*

I know Brooke didn't forget to call me, something happened: like every one of her phones died and she was pulled into an endless all-day meeting as soon as she arrived. I'm so worked up that my Buzz Lightyear sketch on her Starbucks' cup is half-hearted. She deserves better, and I know it.

As I head up the elevator I wonder what I will say if Arnold sees that I have completely disregarded his "orders" to quit my coffee time with Brooke. But as it turns out, I didn't need to consider the potential fallout. For when I approach her office my worst fears are confirmed. Her office is dark and Brooke-less. I turn to Morgan and she nods silently. She seems to know something is up in that creepy secretary way.

I hand Morgan the coffee. "Where is she?"

"Arnauld took her on a surprise trip to Bacara, that resort just outside Santa Barbara."

"On a Tuesday?" I ask, bewildered.

"Monday night actually. Freaky huh? I knew they were having dinner, but I knew nothing about this trip. Alana didn't either," she confides.

"So how did you find out?" I ask, gripping the edge of her desk so I don't fall over.

"I got a weird email from her blackberry at nine p.m. last night. She said he was taking her to celebrate the Emmy win. She then gave me a list of meetings to cancel. They won't be back in the office until Thursday."

I look at her stunned.

"The other weird thing is that Arnauld gave Alana instructions to throw a big party this Saturday for the whole company to celebrate the win. You know, our first Emmy in two years."

"Poor Alana, she's going nuts...I mean a party for four hundred people by Saturday. I'm trying to help her. I've got all of these lists going." She fans her hands over several printouts that are striped in different colors of highlighter.

She suddenly picks one up and moans. "Damn, I'm sorry Nathan. I was supposed to call you." She points to one of the items on the list.

"What does it say?"

"Please contact Nathan right away and tell him I'm sorry I couldn't call, but we'll talk when I get back. Shit...she said to contact you right away. I had it in my head to tell you when you came up for Starbucks time. Sorry, I screwed up."

I want to strangle her, but I stay as calm as possible. "Yeah, I was worried when I didn't hear from her," I admit. Of course, I can't tell her that I'm far more worried now.

I should've never underestimated Arnold. The crafty bastard didn't crawl to the top of his profession by being slow-witted. He obviously is not one to be outdone.

"Have you heard from her since that email?"

"No," she says without hesitation. "But it's a romantic getaway—I'm not expecting to."

Damn, just kill me now and put me out of this misery. My Brooke is at a fancy resort with hairy back, being wined and dined, massaged and pampered. What does she get from me? Fumbling foot massages, paper cup drawings and In-N-Out. I don't stand a chance and I'm starting to wonder why I ever thought I did. Before the despair fully kicks in I decide to make a quick exit. "Okay, thanks Morgan. If you hear anything else, will you let me know?"

She takes a sip of Brooke's coffee, her fingers carelessly covering the Buzz drawing. I turn my head so I don't have to watch.

"Sure, Nathan."

I don't even remember the walk back to my cube.

Once back at my animation desk I consider my options. I obsess on the idea of driving to this Bacara place. What I can't figure out is what I would do once I get there…run into them casually at dinner? *Yeah, I just happened to be in the area and heard the food here was really good.* Would I spy on them by the pool while perched up in a tree? Probably not…with my luck I'd get flustered seeing Brooke in a bikini, and plummet to my death—or worse, survive only to face public humiliation via Mojo Jojo.

It's not like Brooke was kidnapped. As much as I love the idea of saving her, I can't break down the door to their suite, pull him off of her, beat him to a pulp and then carry her away in my arms. I do, however make a note to save this idea for future wanking fodder…especially the manly *carrying her off in my arms* part.

No, Brooke went of her own free will. Maybe she was even excited about it. He *is* her boyfriend after all. Romantic getaways sound like something girls really like. I'd like one too if it were with Brooke, even if there weren't a comic convention involved.

I rest my face in my hands and lean over a really bad Bernie drawing. *Damn Nathan, this obsessing isn't helping anything.*

In desperation I grab my cell phone, and reach out to Curtis, hoping I catch him during one of those very brief periods where he isn't completely distracted by Billie.

"Curtis," I groan when he answers his phone.

"Hey dude, you sound like crap. What's wrong with you?"

"Brooke's been kidnapped," I say, not hiding the devastation in my voice.

"What the fuck? Are you serious?"

I realize that wording may not have been wise. "Well actually, by her boyfriend. He suddenly took her to Santa Barbara for some mid-week romantic get-away."

"Dude, do-not-do-that! I was getting amped up to go all Rambo and help you hunt down whoever kidnapped her."

"I'm sorry. I just can't handle this, Curtis. I don't know what to do. Can we go get a beer or something?"

"I'm supposed to pick up Billie at her store soon to go get burgers. Why don't you come?"

"I don't want to mess up your date, but a female perspective might be helpful with this too."

"Okay, I'll call and warn her you're coming. Why don't you meet us at her shop at six-thirty."

I rush to finish my work so that I can sneak out a little early. My favorite comic book store sounds like the most comforting place in the world to be right now.

When I pass through the doors I take a deep breath and feel instantly calmer now that I'm in one of my happy places. Billie is on the phone, so I wave to her and head over to the *New Release* section to check out the latest *Thor* issue. I'm several pages into the story when Billie comes up behind me.

"So Curtis says you've got it bad, Nathan."

I sigh and put the book back on the rack before turning to her. "Yeah, Billie…real bad."

"So he wasn't toying with me? You really are in love with Brooke, and were doing this thing with Dani to stir things up?"

"Something like that," I admit.

"That was sure stupid," she says, matter-of-factly, her fists perched on her hips.

"Yeah, well, I never claimed to be good at this love stuff. I don't know what I'm doing. It's amazing I've gotten as far with her as I have."

"Did you do it?" she asks, her eyes wide and disbelieving.

I look down, my cheeks burning. But I realize that I'm not going to get good advice unless I'm honest. "Yes, we did. And now she's doing it with her boyfriend at some fancy resort."

"Oh, bummer, dude."

"I don't even know now why she did it with me."

"Shut up, Evans. I don't want to hear you talking like that. You're such a catch and you're just too stupid to realize it. I used to think that your cluelessness was kind of charming, but now it's getting old."

Billie thinks I'm a catch? I scratch my head, bewildered.

"So how was the sex? Was it good?"

"I thought it was amazing."

"Did she ask you to spend the night?"

I nod.

"Morning sex?"

"Yes," I admit, embarrassed.

She folds her tattooed arms over her chest and tips her head up, like she's calculating something.

"Here's the deal. Brooke is falling for you, but it's complicated."

I blanch. It's eerie she repeated Brooke's exact word: complicated. I nod briskly, encouraging her to tell me more.

"Arnauld is her boss, and you're making her realize that he doesn't give her what she needs, but her life and work are built around him. He's now realized what's happening and he's doing damage control to protect his assets. He's probably brain-washing her as we speak."

"Arggg," I moan. "Yes, yes. He's brainwashing her, that's exactly what I'm afraid of. What do I do, Billie?"

Just then Curtis walks through the door and saunters over to us, pulling Billie into his arms.

"Hey bro," he says as he holds her.

"You've got one brilliant girlfriend Curtis," I tell him, gesturing towards Billie.

"Don't I know it," he laughs. "She's sure as hell smarter than me."

"Damn right," she agrees, smiling.

We head over to Mo's Café and over beers and burgers plot my strategy to pull Brooke out of Arnold's web.

"Be chill when she gets back dude, don't act like a crazy obsessed stalker cause that will turn her off for sure," Curtis advises.

I turn to Billie. "Did you really mean what you said at the shop, that Brooke is falling for me?" I want to believe that so much it hurts.

Billie nods. "But you've got to let her figure this out in her own time. If you push her it will backfire."

I take a swig of my beer and give myself a silent lecture to allow Brooke some space. As desperately as I want her back in my arms, I have to look toward the future. I have to be the together, loving person she would want to be with. Not the wound-up, desperately in love man, I really am.

• • •

The next day, when I step into the break room, there's a crowd gathered around a large flier on the bulletin board.

"Par-tay! I know just what I'm going to wear!" Dani calls out. "Wait until you see how hot I'm going to look Saturday night."

I catch Nick rolling his eyes, but I also see him fighting a smile.

"I can't believe they rented the Palace," replies Genna. "That must have cost a fortune."

"Palace? Is this thing in the kingdom of Far Far Away? Will we be in the presence of royalty?" Andy snickers. "If so, I'll make sure and wear a clean T-shirt."

"No, idiot," Joel responds. "It's that club in Hollywood. Do you ever get out of your man-cave?"

"Only when I'm out of brews and Cheetos."

"Our noble leader must be spending a fortune. We didn't even get cost of living increases this year, what's he trying to prove?" asks Kevin.

"Word is that he's trying to impress his lady, that Brooke chick who does development," Andy chimes in.

I bristle and curl my hands into fists. It offends me deeply to hear her name pass through Andy's slobbering lips. Never mind that I almost threw up in my mouth after hearing her referred to as a chick let alone Arnauld's "lady."

"Well, if he wants to impress her he could take what he's spending on this shindig and pay for a wedding. That would make more sense. They could have kids and start their own animation dynasty."

"Oooo, maybe it's a surprise royal wedding and we're all invited!" squeals Genna.

"If that's the case I'm not bothering to pull out a clean T-shirt. This one will do," Andy grumbles as he pulls down the hem, so we see Charlie Brown's stretched face.

Dani looks over at me. I can see the concern on her face, but I keep my expression calm even though I'm getting more nauseated as each second passes. I slowly work my way over to the counter and pour myself another coffee, before heading out of the break room. Dani catches up with me in the hallway.

"Are you okay, Nathan?" she asks gently.

"Not really. But what can I do? He took her out of town and I can't talk to her to know what's going on. Until they get back from their trip I'm driving blind, hoping I don't crash."

"Are you coming on Saturday?" She asks.

"I don't think I can avoid it, but I'm sure not looking forward to it."

"Well, I'll be there if you need a friend to hang with. We can go together if you want."

"Thanks, Dani. You're a good friend."

The rest of the afternoon is tantamount to Chinese water torture. Horrible thoughts drip with a consistent pace through my mind, while I pray for my sanity. Drip, drip, drip, drip…only time will tell how long I can hold on.

That evening I try to work on my comic book but the first line I draw of B-Girl undoes me. I end up resorting to hard liquor and watching bootleg versions of the censored wartime cartoons to numb my mind until I finally pass out in a Looney Tunes stupor.

Thursday I hear through the grapevine that Arnold and Brooke are back and there's a meeting first thing with his team about Saturday's event. Genna's friend is the CFO's assistant so we get all of our info directly through her.

Evidently it's going to be a full on party: there's going to be a DJ with a dance floor, catered food, open bar…the works. I didn't think animators danced, but I'm sure the assistants and accounting staff will make up for us uncoordinates, and get out there and boogie. The whole thing sounds like a major pain-in-the-ass production and we're all expected to go.

I'm so anxious to talk to Brooke but I'm not sure if it's a good idea to head upstairs until I know more. *Maybe I can drop by her house after work?*

After lunch I force myself to get into the cartoon groove and work on animating a new scene. I'm drawing away and listening to my iPod when I sense someone's watching me.

I look up to see Brooke just inside my cube. She looks rested and has pink cheeks. She also looks apprehensive about being here.

I peel out my earbuds and set my pencil down. "Hi," I say softly. I'm so relieved to see her, but nervous as well.

"Hi Nathan." She smiles at me sweetly, but it seems edged with sadness. I immediately realize that she isn't going to hug me. *Maybe it's cause we're at work, and she's afraid someone will see.* I try to tell myself.

"How are you? Did you have a good time in Santa Barbara?" I'm trying to not obsess over the idea that everything feels different between us now, and not in a good way.

She nods. "Yeah, it was nice…really beautiful there. Have you ever been to Barcara?"

"No, but I considered it once." I leave out the part where "once" means on Tuesday when I found out she was there with Arnold.

"Well, the time away gave me time to think about things."

"Things?" I ask nervously. This isn't going well.

"Yeah, and I think it may be a good idea not to do the coffee visits anymore, so I thought I should drop by and tell you before you go." She looks down.

It was one thing to hear this from Arnold, but something else entirely with Brooke. Doesn't she realize how much this will hurt me?

Well, she must have no idea. She didn't even warn me before she ripped the Band-Aid for my obsession off, and now here I am with my disappointment exposed between us.

I just stare at her with my mouth twisted. I can't form words, and finally I turn away.

"Okay, sure," I finally reply once I'm facing my animation table and not her huge sad eyes. My head has fallen forward and it almost feels like I'm talking to the Bucky drawing I just finished, but he's distracted because his head's on fire. I push the drawing away from me and lean into my elbows.

"Nathan," she insists, trying to regain my attention. "Don't act that way."

"Act what way?"

"Like I've disappointed you." Her expression's worried, taking away all the happy pink coloring from her restful getaway.

"Oh."

I leave it there—no lace trim, or creamy filling…just *oh.* It's one tiny word that holds much more than its weight in despair. *You don't think you've disappointed me, Brooke? Well, try climbing into this broken heart and tell me if you like the view.*

"Come on, Nathan…I came down here to see you and make plans."

"Plans? What do you want to do?" I try a fake enthusiastic voice. I'm battling a weird unsettled feeling. I can't help it. I turn back to face her.

"Are you free early Saturday? I have to pick up something at Fred Segal's and I thought we could get outfits for the party together…then have lunch or something."

Pick outfits together? I break into a cold sweat. We slept together and now she wants to go shopping?

Maybe she thinks I can be her BFF for our own episode of *What Not to Wear.* I've seen that show at my Mom's house, and I fear she will make me stand in front of those horrifying three way mirrors. I don't need that experience to know I don't dress right. Besides I loathe clothes shopping.

But what stings much more is knowing that I am now merely her shopping buddy. I assume I'm no longer her Starbucks bearing, beer drinking, couch cuddling, cartoon compatriot, buddy/lover. To say that my manhood just shrunk, both metaphorically and in actuality, would be a vast understatement. I try to regain my equilibrium.

She tips her head wondering why I haven't responded. Thank God she can't hear this conversation in my head. Something occurs to me and I speak up.

"Who's Fred Segal anyway…is he a friend of yours?" *Hell.* Maybe she's planned a gay set-up. I must have been much worse in bed than I could've ever imagined.

"A friend?" She laughs. "Oh, man...I've missed you. No, Fred Segal is a chic store in West Hollywood that has all the hippest stuff. A lot of music and film people shop there."

"Why would I want to shop there? I'm not hip," I point out.

"No, but you could be," she encourages.

Oh. Is that it? I'm not hip. Suddenly everything becomes clear, yet still feels dirty. Where'd my beautiful Brooke go who didn't care so much about that stuff? A few days with Mojo and this is where it leaves us?

I don't want to be hip, Brooke. I don't care about being hip. I just want you.

"Is this what you want?" I ask quietly.

"Yes, I want you to come with me. I want to spend time with you. Besides, we'll have fun."

I nod, my resolve outweighing my concerns. "When should I get you?"

"How about eleven. I'll be home from my Zumba class and showered by then."

I'll miss the yoga pants, I realize with despair. I agree because what choice do I have? As wrong as this feels right now, I can't give up yet. Not at least until I learn what's really going on in her mind and if I still have any chance at all.

Damn Brooke, evidently while you were away I lost my mojo, and you seemed to rediscover yours...your very own hip Mojo Jojo with the furry back and apparently impressive mind-control abilities.

• • •

For dinner that night I make tuna fish on Ritz crackers with cherry tomatoes on the side because I like the way those little red balls explode in my mouth. I'm trying to have a good attitude but even my favorite dinner doesn't cheer me up. I'm just about ready to go to my studio when the phone rings.

"Hi Nathan."

It's unusual for her to call during the week so I am a bit alarmed. "Everything okay, Mom?"

"Yes, everything's fine. I was just thinking about you and wanted to see how you're doing."

Moms and their intuition. If she's going to ask, I'm not going to hold back.

"Well remember that scene where Sylvester thinks he's flying up to Tweety's nest and he gets so excited, but then he remembers that he can't fly, and in despair, crashes to the ground? Well I'm Sylvester, and that pretty much sums up how things are going for me."

"Oh no, that doesn't sound good at all. What happened with Brooke?"

"She just came back from a romantic few days with her boyfriend and now we can't have coffee together anymore in the afternoons. It's the beginning of the end."

"But Nathan, you knew from the start that she was with that man. Why are you surprised?"

"I just thought we were getting closer and had something special. But I must've been wrong."

"Those things aren't necessarily mutually exclusive, Nathan. She may care about him and you too. I could tell she really likes you and I would imagine you've gotten even closer since I saw you two together."

"Yeah, you could say that," I offer as I think about her asleep, curled up against me in her bed. My world felt perfect at that moment.

"Hasn't she been with him a long time? Isn't he her boss?"

"Yes," I whisper. *Don't say it…don't say it…*

"It's complicated Nathan."

Damn. She said it.

"And you know what?"

Don't say it…don't say it…

"You have to have faith."

Ugh. She said it. I knew she would.

I believe in Pixar, the tenacity of Walt Disney and number two pencils. I'm not so sure about a God who didn't give me the skills or appeal to win my true love.

"But Mom, what kind of God would present me a Brooke and then take her away? And then she ends up with a damn monkey, not even someone who deserves her."

"A monkey?" she asks bewildered.

"It's a long story. Never mind."

"Look Nathan, there's a reason you both are going through this. I don't know what it is but I do know it will make you stronger and even better if you finally get together. If you can find your faith it will get you through."

"I wish I could believe that," I moan.

"You'll still see her around work, won't you?"

"Not really, we're on different floors. She did ask me to go shopping with her Saturday. What do you think that means. Do you think she thinks I'm gay?"

"No. She knows you're not gay. Where do you come up with these things, really! It means she wants to spend time with you away from that Arnold's world...some place you two can just be, without any pressure or people watching."

"Really?" I suddenly feel more hopeful realizing she may be right.

"Yes," she confirms. "I really think this can still work out, Nathan. So make the most of your shopping date. Be sweet and kind with her. Be yourself."

I hold onto my mom's words; they wrap around me and hold me up. She makes me want to believe in Santa, the Easter Bunny and my future with Brooke.

So for added motivation, after I crawl in bed, I wire myself up for the Dr. Wayne Dyer recording about relationships. I don't fall asleep until he's convinced me that I can take my destiny into my own hands. I can't give up yet.

• • •

Saturday morning I get up early and take a run, eat some Fruit Loops and then shower and shave. I give myself a pep talk as I put on some of that cologne my mom gave me for Christmas. I'm looking my best and ready to go see Brooke.

When I pull up to her place she's waiting by the gate. Either she's really excited to see me or she doesn't want me to go inside. I try to convince myself the former when I see the big smile on her face.

"Hey you!" she says as she slides into her seat. "Looking forward to our outing?"

"Well, I'm looking forward to being with you," I reply smiling.

"What's this?" She asks, pointing to the cup holder section of my car.

"Well, I know I can't get you your macchiatos at work anymore, but that doesn't mean I can't other times," I insist.

"Oh, Nathan," she sighs happily, wedging her foamy drink out of the cup holder to take a sip. "You even did a drawing for me!" She holds it up and studies it with a big grin on her face.

"Yeah, it's me post-shopping at the hip store."

"Oh, it's great! You're so clever. Thank you."

"Guess what else?" I grin as I reach in the back, grab the bag and set it on her lap.

"Krispy Kreme doughnuts!" she squeals.

"You didn't...how could you? Now all my Zumba-ing is for naught." She tears open the bag and pulls out a doughnut, immediately taking a bite.

"Sorry," I mumble, grinning. But as I watch her close her eyes in anticipation of that warm sugary rush of perfection, I'm not sorry at all—not one little bit.

"Mmmm." She closes her eyes as she chews. She has the most sublime expression on her face. "So good…"

As we wind down the hill towards the land of hip, she feeds me bites, in-between hers. I watch her lick her sticky fingers, her eyes dancing as she reaches into the bag for more to share.

I feel alive again, like a remastered cartoon print where every color is brighter and more vivid, every detail sharper. We laugh and joke in our own bubble, sugar flakes falling over us like snow on this brilliant California day.

Animate Me / Chapter Seventeen / Magic Jeans

"I was hiding under your porch because I love you." ~Dug, from Pixar's *"Up"*[xvi]

"So you're trying on a 'cute' outfit at this Fred place?" I ask as we turn onto Melrose Avenue. "'Cause if they have dressy yoga pants, that'd be my suggestion." I grin, and as I glance over, I see she's grinning too.

"Hmmm, maybe they have some stretchy black velvet ones," she teases.

"Yeah, fancy ones like that. Now, we're talking," I agree.

"Well, my personal shopper picked a few things so we shall have to wait and see."

"Personal shopper? What does that mean?"

"If left to my own devices, I would wear jeans and hoodies everywhere. So Arnauld has this woman who works at Fred Segal's put things together for me. It annoyed me at first, but I have to admit that it saves me time because I don't like shopping for clothes much."

Svengali Arnold strikes again.

"Well, that makes two of us," I agree. "My idea of clothes shopping is stuffing a few things in my cart at Target on the way to the video game aisle."

"So is that why you looked so thrilled about this outing when I first asked?"

"Well, let's just say I can think of other ways I'd rather spend our time together, but I'll get through it."

• • •

"What do you think?" Brooke asks as the salesman holds up a pair of men's jeans with really narrow legs. I'd be very irritated with how close this guy is standing to Brooke, but when we approached his area he was practically grabbing another guy's butt, so I'm not overly concerned. Besides he spent a little too much time assessing my body to figure out what style and size would work on me, so I'm pretty sure he's pitching for the other team.

I'm having trouble focusing because there are so many distractions here in Fred's collection of individual boutiques. To start with, our salesperson's name in this one is not Joe or Bill or Dave, but Ransom. *What the hell, kidnapper dude?* I really wish he was out somewhere on a casting call rather than trying to help Brooke make me hip.

I turn back towards her to see that she's holding up a tiny pair of jeans.

"Is that one of those pairs of skinny jeans? Seriously, I get claustrophobic just looking at them. I may as well just wear tights and go for the superhero look."

Brooke makes a face at me.

The salesman, who confuses me again by being the straightest looking gay guy, gives a wry smile. "I don't blame you. They're a bit restrictive. I don't care how stretchy the fabric is." He reaches for another style and checks the tag for sizing. "What about these? They have a great fit. They're True Religion."

"Holy jeans? Well, that's a new concept. But they're still too small looking."

"You always wear your jeans baggy, Nathan," Brooke says. "This is a chance to try something new. Besides, they'll show off your great butt."

Great butt? She really likes my butt! I can't help smiling.

The salesperson nods with conviction, and I pretend I don't notice. He also hands me a dress shirt to try on.

"Okay, I'll try them on *for you*, Brooke."

When I tentatively step out of the dressing room I can tell by their expressions that they're pleased. I'm not sure about the fancy looking shirt with colorful stripes and this freaky print with weird little shapes lining the collar and cuffs.

"Why are there amoebas on this fabric?" I ask, showing her the cuffs. "It looks like something under a microscope."

"Those are paisleys." She laughs. "You weren't joking about not being into fashion."

"You can say that again," I say to Brooke. At least she looks pleased… actually, really pleased. Her expression makes me think she'd like to join me in the dressing room for some fun. Well?" I ask holding out my arms. "Is this what you had in mind?"

Ransom lifts his hand and makes a motion. "Turn," he says. As I pivot and am halfway around, he stops me and lifts up the bottom of my shirt. "Perfect fit," he concludes.

I'm guessing my butt looks great.

"Yes," Brooke agrees with a heavy sigh. "You look so handsome, Nathan. None of the girls will be able to resist you tonight."

Great, the girls won't be able to resist me. What about you Brooke?

My nerves are completely frayed. I have no idea what's really going on.

"Okay, we're done." I say to Ransom. "I'll take them."

He nods briskly as I head back to the dressing room. I don't even care at this point what this will cost me, I just need to get out of here and away from Fred's shrine to fashion. If Brooke keeps admiring me I'm going to pull her into the dressing room so we can make out, and send all the over-priced jeans hanging around us tumbling to the floor.

Luckily Brooke's shopping seems less traumatic for her than my experience. She refuses to let me see what she tries on, so her personal shopper, Noelle, sends me to the gift boutique where they have an eclectic selection of art and design books to occupy me. But as I notice her enter the gift shop to find me, it's evident that she wasn't in the dressing room too long before she picked something out. *Nothing better than a decisive woman,* I think to myself.

"Can I buy you lunch?" She asks coming up alongside me as I flip through a book about deviant art.

I turn and smile at her, relieved that the earlier heaviness has lifted. I put the book back on the shelf and linking her arm through mine, she pulls me to the café in the next area. We set our bags alongside the table, open the menus, and get situated. As soon as we're settled, I turn towards her.

"Can I hold your hand?" I say.

She smiles softly at me, and I feel her hand graze my thigh under the table until it finds mine. Her fingers curl into my hand and I gently rub my thumb across her soft skin. I feel instantly calmer, happier.

The waiter comes up and I'm grateful to be able to order a burger, even if it is infused with pesto. Brooke orders one of those girly salads and despite the distraction, doesn't let go of my grasp. I study her face and the way her lips turn up when I gently squeeze her hand.

"Brooke, can I ask you something?"

She nods at me, wide eyed.

"Is it really important to you how I dress?" I point at the bag with my purchases. "'Cause no matter what I wear, it's still me inside. You know I don't care about clothes and stuff like that."

She looks surprised by my declaration. "I'm not trying to change you, if that's what you think," she replies. "You just never seem to understand how attractive you are. I thought maybe wearing something special tonight would make you feel good. You were so confident at the Emmys in your tux."

"Screw the clothes. What makes me feel good is when you look at me the way you did that night, and just now when I stepped out of the dressing room."

She tips her head, considering what I've said and a look of worry shadows her expression. "I should be more careful. It's just hard for me to hide my attraction to you."

"But I liked the way you looked at me, it made me feel wanted…it felt good," I argue.

"But I was going to start controlling myself. Until I get my situation straightened out, my attraction to you and our physical relationship just confuses everything." She gently eases her hand out of mine and places it on the table, then fiddles nervously with the silverware.

I feel frustration fire up in me. I know this is Arnold's influence. "But I don't want you to stop being with me."

She looks down nervously and takes a sip of water as I persist with my point.

"Remember when our friendship got off track and you wanted to stop touching me before? I couldn't stand not seeing and being close to you and you missed me too…didn't you?"

She nods solemnly.

"Well, that just didn't work, and it won't now either," I insist.

I can't resist asking the obvious. The timing of her new reticence about us immediately followed her getaway trip. "Is all of this because of Arnold? Did he say something to you while you were in Santa Barbara?"

"Yes," she admits, her expression getting very dark.

"And..."

"Nathan, listen to me. I'm trying to work some things out and you can't be in the middle of it. But meanwhile you need to stay as far away from Arnauld as possible. Promise me."

"I wish you'd tell me everything and let me help you. I'm not afraid of him."

"Well, you should be."

"What's he holding over you Brooke because frankly I don't understand why you're with him at all? What aren't you telling me? Did you even want to go to Santa Barbara?"

"No, and I should've refused. We ended up arguing most of the time."

"So it wasn't romantic?"

"Hardly," she huffs.

"You know Nathan, the honest truth is that since we've met, all I've done is distract you and pull you into my mess with Arnauld. Here things were moving along with you and Dani and suddenly I'm the one you're spending time with, opening up sexually with. I'm comfortable for you, an older woman involved with another guy, showing you the ropes. But I'm not the type of girl you really want, the kind of girl who'd be good for you."

I'm stuck on the idea that she thinks she's just a distraction. I look at her bewildered.

"And as this progresses, I'm doing things without thinking of the ramifications for both of us. Ever since we made love, all I can do is think about when we will do it again. I swear, I wanted to follow you into that dressing room earlier. For goodness sake, I was thinking about you the entire time I was in Santa Barbara."

I can't even feel the thrill of her declaration because of the question lingering in my mind. "Did you tell Arnold that we slept together?"

"No, I just couldn't. Honestly, the way things were going, I was afraid to."

I look down, twisting the napkin in my lap. Everything is so simple to me; I love Brooke and she should be with me. But as everyone in my life points out, I need to not pressure her, because for Brooke, this is very complicated.

"Arnauld has also accused me of losing my edge at work. I really need to get my shit together."

She looks stressed and it makes my heart heavy. I want to hold her and make it all go away, but I fear it will only make things worse.

"Can I ask you one thing, Brooke?" I say.

She nods, her eyes sad.

"Why are you so sure you're not the right kind of girl for me? You've got to understand how much I care about you."

"Because I know you Nathan, you want a girl, one special girl to split that little foil packet of Pop Tarts with. You want a nice, sweet girl who will always be by your side—a solid relationship like your parents have…a marriage and kids, who hopefully like cartoons more than soccer."

"Am I that transparent?" I ask.

"You're wonderfully transparent and so sincere. It's one of the things I love most about you." She smiles tenderly. "But you have to know, I've never been that kind of girl. I've never had a good relationship, and I'm not sure I'd even know how. Also, I'm so into my career I'd probably make a terrible mother, and besides, I'm selfish."

"No, you're not, Brooke," I insist, refusing to let her say that about herself.

"If I weren't selfish, Nathan, I wouldn't have dragged you into my mess."

I realize in that moment that I believe in Brooke more than she believes in herself. I want to shake her and make her see that these feelings she has for me are all sign posts pointing to the road she should head down… the road that I'm waiting for her on. But she isn't ready yet—I'm not so completely dense not to see this. I need to calm and placate her and try to buy more time.

"What do you want from me, Brooke? Just tell me."

She looks at me with a twisted expression somewhat like gratitude, mixed with discomfort.

"Arnauld told me that you're taking Dani to the party tonight."

"How the hell did he know that?"

"He has his ways. He seems to know quite a bit about you and Dani."

"What does he say he knows? Nothing has happened between us. He's just messing with you because he knows I care about you too much."

Brooke suddenly looks very tired and defeated. Something's really weighing on her and I wish she'd tell me what it is.

"Will you just really try to have a good time with Dani tonight? Focus on her. Give her all your attention."

My heart drops but I'm not surprised. Perhaps she thinks it will solve something if Dani and I actually get together, but I know it won't because it's never going to happen. I decide to lighten things up because I sense she isn't going to tell me anything more today and she looks so defeated. "But I'm going to still talk to you tonight." I insist. "I want you to show me your new fancy yoga pants."

She smiles and shakes her head. "Oh, Nathan…"

The only thing I know when we finally finish lunch and get up to leave, is that tonight is going to be a test of not just my acting abilities, but my self-restraint as well. When I see Brooke on Arnold's arm, it's going to take everything I have not to go mad.

• • •

"Who are you, and what'd you do with my Nathan?" Dani exclaims after she sees me at her door.

"Very funny, Dani. Can you just let me in, or do you want to humiliate me a bit more first?"

"No, that was enough," she asserts, opening her door wider.

"What?" I ask, getting irritated with her gaping mouth.

"It is pretty amazing how much you've changed. I wasn't kidding about barely recognizing you. You're kind of hunky now."

"Hunky?" That is a word I was certain would never, ever be attached to me. I don't even know how to process that idea in my geek brain.

"Yeah, and where did you get that outfit? Cause I know for a fact that they don't sell Cavalli at Target."

"Brooke took me to that Fred Segal's place today." I state matter-of-factly.

"You were shopping at Fred-fucking-Segal's?" she exclaims.

Clearly that has significant meaning to people of the fashion persuasion.

"Yup," I admit.

"Damn," she grumbles. "I wish Nick loved me the way you love Brooke. You'd do anything for that woman."

I let out a long, sigh. "Yes, I would."

Looking at her sad expression, and knowing what I know about Nick, I can't help but encourage her.

"Don't be so sure Nick doesn't feel that way too, Dani. You just have to give him a chance to show you."

When we walk into the Palace, for a moment I forget that I'm a geek. To an outsider it could almost look like I'm a hip guy out with a hot girl, the night lying before me ripe with the promise of plenty of booze and hot sex. But when I trip on the way in, I am reminded to both myself, and the entire nightclub crowd, who I really am. You can wrap a package any way you want, but that doesn't change what's inside.

I pause to gather myself before we move into the main room for the party. I can't shake the weight of worry knowing what's at stake tonight. Frankly it's a relief that Dani is searching to spot Nick as hard as I am looking for Brooke. She finds him first, and grabs onto my arm. His angry eyes pierce through me as he watches us walk in. Since he and Dani started talking again he seems to have lost his tolerance for seeing us together. But Dani isn't going to stop this game until she's at least kicked a field goal.

"Come on, Nathan," Dani says, pulling on my hand. "Let's go get a drink."

Most of the Beaver gang is here already, huddled around a table close to the bar. It's weird to see everyone all dressed up and in a party mode. Despite his threats of wearing a dirty T-shirt, even Andy's wearing a relatively unwrinkled button-down shirt with no stains. Although I'm pretty sure there will be stains by the end of the evening.

Joel seems particularly animated this evening. He's brought an outside girl with him and he introduces her as his new girlfriend, Laura. Who knew? Joel is quite taken with this new girl who is Japanese with long black hair and a beautiful face. She seems to have a nice low-key demeanor, which is a good balance to his frenetic energy.

Laura tells Dani that she works at a doctor's office and met Joel while taking his blood. He almost passed out and she had to tend to him.

"With extra-special care," he explains, smiling as he wraps his arm around her waist. She smiles at him in response.

How romantic. Only Joel could hit on a girl while she's draining him of his life force. But regardless, it's rare we have non-toon people penetrate our covert little world so she adds some intrigue to the evening.

Despite my wandering eye, I still haven't spotted Brooke and her absence unsettles me. Shouldn't she be here already? Maybe Mojo has kidnapped her again and is sucking out *her* life force like he tried to do in Santa Barbara. Next time I see her she may be a zombie, devoid of any traces of the girl I fell in love with.

Unnerved, I push my way up to the bar to get my much-needed second beer. This is going to be a very long night.

I have rejoined the group with Dani's Diet Coke, trying to ignore Nick's glare as I hand it to her. I don't know why the ass doesn't just make his move with the girl he obviously loves. But then I reprimand myself: Big talk from the pussy who can't even come clean with Brooke. I look down at the ground and try to drum up a Wayne-ism to pull me out of this funk I'm spiraling into.

But when I lift my eyes Wayne is the furthest thing from my mind. Brooke steps into the room, and she's a vision. Never mind the fact that she's with the monkey, her beauty outshines everyone around her. She's wearing some very fitted black jeans, almost as good as yoga pants. Her fancy purple velvet-looking top is lower cut than I've seen her wear before and the long sleeves sweep down dramatically. I also notice a necklace sparkling around her neck.

Her eyes scan the crowd and when she sees me standing next to Dani her eyes flicker, and she smiles sweetly. Just when I smile back, Arnold wraps his arm around her waist and pulls her aside. Mojo fury flares up inside of me for messing up my moment. If I were Marvin the Martian, I would've blasted him with my x-ray gun without a second thought, leaving Brooke with far fewer complications in her life, and Arnold, a little pile of cinders on the floor.

I try to refocus on our group's conversation as I down my beer. Andy keeps cornering the people carrying around trays of tiny food, and before we know it, we've eaten the equivalent of a meal. I finish off a third beer a little too quickly as I watch Brooke and Arnold work through the room.

In my overwhelmed and beer-edged stupor I notice the music get louder, and I get nervous as I see Dani start to bounce to the beat. She had her hard limits with our arrangement. Well, mine is dancing. *No, just no…it's not going to happen.*

Minutes later she shimmies up close to me.

"It's time to boogie, Nathan," she croons.

"I can't dance Dani," I insist.

"I'll teach you," she responds, forcefully pulling me toward the dance floor. For a small thing, she's powerful and irritatingly determined.

She leads me to the middle of the floor so the non-dancing lookie-loos won't notice us as much. She takes my hands and then has me mimic her, stepping side to side. She's so enthusiastic that it's hard to stay mad and before I realize it, she's moving our arms together so it almost looks like I'm dancing. *What do you know? I guess I actually am dancing.* I'm no John Travolta, but I'm still moving in sync with the pounding bass. It must be the magic, butt-hugging jeans Brooke talked me into buying.

Once I get more confident, Dani lets go of my hands and let's loose. *Damn, that girl can dance.* Her sexy moves are drawing a lot of attention, most notably from Arnold and Brooke, who I suddenly realize are dancing nearby. Never one to miss an opportunity, when Dani realizes that Brooke's watching she begins to drape and grind herself all over me.

The whole thing sets off a scene straight from an episode of *Friends*. Brooke starts looking territorial, which arouses me, thereby making me dance funny. Arnold reacts by doing something akin to dirty dancing with Brooke (with an astounding sense of rhythm, I might add) which of course, makes me want to kill him. Meanwhile it's pretty clear that Nick is getting ready to strangle me. Just when things look like they're going to implode, the DJ shakes things up, and puts on a slow, romantic song. We all stop, stunned and try to quickly regroup.

Arnold takes the lead by pulling Brooke into his arms. Dani responds by wrapping herself around me, and Nick grits his teeth. I know this isn't going to end well. I take a deep breath, place my hands on Dani's hips and prepare for the worst.

I feel his hand on my shoulder first. Nick pulls me away from Dani and then steps between us.

"Thanks Nathan, I'll take over from here," he says simply.

Dani's eyes blaze, as he pulls her into his arms.

I pause, unsure for a moment as to what's the right thing to do.

"I can't take another minute of this," he says to Dani.

She tips her head, watching him, as I stand there like an idiot.

"You belong to me, baby," he tells Dani, loud enough for me to hear. There's a still moment where their eyes meet and everything shifts. Even I can feel it.

"I do?" she asks softly, looking up at him. There's so much love in her eyes.

"You always have, always will, and I'm going to do right by you this time." He gently runs his fingers along her cheek. "I love you, Dani," he insists.

The next thing I know they're moving slowly, in perfect synchronicity, under the hot blue lights. They sway together for a moment before he tips his head down to kiss her. Once he does they're lost to each other and in their own world.

It's clear that the game is over. I can't even panic about the fact that it's happening here in front of everyone, I'm too overwhelmed with a strange mixture of envy, yet happiness, to see them back together.

I step away, hoping to go unnoticed, but there's no way I'd be that lucky. When I look in the distance, I see Brooke watching Nick kiss Dani. She looks surprised, and worried at the same time.

Great. Fucking great.

She looks over at me, her concern evident, but she can't do a thing to help me when Mojo's arms are wrapped around her.

I stand still, as bodies move around me. I want Brooke. I need Brooke. And Brooke doesn't belong to me.

I turn on my heel and frame by frame, I move away from a scene only a fool could animate. All I know is that I've earned this moment with my lies and deceit.

This script is hopelessly flawed. Stop the sequence; put your pencils down. It's time to go back to the drawing board.

My head's pounding as I head straight down the hall. I feel like I can't get a breath...that if I don't get some fresh air I just may lose it.

I push my way out the glass doors to the balcony and curl over the rail, attempting to suck in the cold night air. My mind races as I figure out my exit strategy. At this point no one will miss me anyway, and Nick will be taking Dani home. I turn to head back inside and towards the club entrance when from the corner of my eye, I see the door open.

I turn slowly. *Brooke.* She's come to check on me. My heart surges to know she cares enough about me to leave his side.

She looks worried. "Are you okay?" she says softly.

"I don't know what I am," I answer honestly. "This is a weird night for me."

"Do you feel bad about what happened with Dani and Nick?" she asks.

"No. I think they are meant to be together. I always did, really."

"You did?"

I nod my head slowly. "And Nick's a good guy."

"He is, but you're better, Nathan. You're the best...I hope you know that."

"Well, I know that you make me feel that way."

She smiles softly but doesn't say anything.

I take a deep breath. "I wanted to be the one with you tonight Brooke. I can't stand to see you with Arnold."

"Oh, Nathan..." She sounds despondent. Maybe she's apprehensive and thinks I'm on the rebound or something.

It's time. I've got to do it...

"Brooke, we need to talk. There are some things I need to tell you."

"Okay, but this isn't a good time or place. I just needed to make sure you're okay. I really have to get back inside."

I swallow hard. Maybe she really doesn't want to hear what I have to say. I'm not sure I'll be able to handle it if she rejects me. I just nod, as I watch her, my eyes wide and searching.

"Come on...let's get back," she urges.

"Actually, I'm going to leave now. I think I've had enough excitement for one evening. Can we get together tomorrow to talk?"

"Wait…you're leaving now? Are you sure? You're going to miss my speech; I think it's next. I really want you to hear it since you helped inspire it."

I help inspired her speech? Wow.

"Okay, yeah…I wouldn't want to miss that. So I'll stay for your part and then I'll take off."

"Okay," she says sadly. "Hey, can I give you a hug?"

I smile and step towards her and when her arms wrap around me, everything feels better. I even feel hopeful for a moment until we are interrupted.

"Brooke."

Arnold's voice is dark and heavy in the cool night air. Every muscle in my body tenses.

"It's time," he insists.

She pulls away from me and looks into my eyes. "Come on," she whispers.

I nod silently.

She turns and approaches Arnold, and he flashes me a dirty look over his shoulder, as they step back inside.

Before I follow, I close my eyes for a moment, and take a slow breath trying to calm myself. But when I open my eyes they're gone, swallowed by the inky darkness of the club.

Will I go after them? Will I fight for her? Or will I give up my Brooke dream and slide back into my little life?

This decision is what it's all come down to, as I face the harsh reality of Arnold's hold on her. One moment Brooke is a satellite circling my heart, the next she's lost to me in another galaxy.

Animate Me / Chapter Eighteen / How to Woo a Girl

"I never look back, darling. It distracts from the now." ~ Edna Mode[xvii]

There's an eerie sense of déjà vu as I focus on the stage from my anonymous position at the back of the crowd. Mojo is blathering on about the Emmy win, neglecting to mention that he blew it off to watch two testosterone cases pummel each other in the city of sin.

I was with her, you ass. I was the one she beamed for when they announced the winner.

But as soon as Brooke approaches the mike I realize why I feel this way. I am transported to the first moment I saw her, in the big auditorium at Sketch Republic. I was sitting in the back, preparing to take my usual meeting nap when Brooke stepped onto the stage and it lit up like a summer sky. It was love at first sight.

And now, despite the journey I've taken with Brooke, as close as we've become, I find myself at the back of the crowd once again. But this time, I'm not accepting the idea that I don't matter, that I'm just an anonymous face in the crowd. So as she begins to speak, I instinctively start to push my way towards the stage.

Halfway through the crowd, I'm close enough to see her fingers graze the mike stand. Her brows knit in contemplation before her clear voice starts to echo across the floor.

"When *Danny Deletes* was announced as the winner for Best Animated Series, I felt incredible pride… not just for helping Lazlo bring his brilliant creation into production, but to be part of this exceptional team here at Sketch Republic. Each of you contributes with your talent, ideas and hard work to help make us one of the most innovative studios in the world."

For a brief moment I glance around me and realize everyone's quiet and watching her intently. She has charisma, and I'm not the only one under her spell.

"Animation is hard work, at times it's grueling. There are crazy schedules, challenging budgets, cutbacks and network constraints. Sometimes things can become a grind, and it's easy to lose track of how we fell in love with cartoons in the first place."

I notice Brooke scanning the crowd, but when her eyes rest on mine, she smiles and stops searching.

"Recently, I've had the opportunity to be reminded why I fell in love with cartoons. I've been taught that if your mind and heart are open, true passion will inspire you to do greater things. This has been the greatest gift for me and I will carry it with me always."

My heart's pounding. Have I really inspired her? Have I shown her how to open her heart? I smile at her and she smiles back, her eyes sparkling under the lights.

"And so I challenge each of you to do what you can to keep your passion alive so you'll be inspired to do your best work. Lazlo refused to give up on his dream and was working two desk jobs when I convinced the studio that *Danny Deletes* was worth developing. His determination inspired me to never give up on his project.

"So what inspires you? Do you watch old classic cartoons, go to museums, and draw stuff that has nothing to do with your job? Or maybe you read comic books and remember how the stories and characters used to make you feel.

"All that's important, but this is what I hope inspires you most of all…Every time you lift a pencil, or move that mouse, remember those little kids in front of their TVs watching our shows, and quoting their favorite lines over and over. When they go to bed at night they'll be holding their stuffed Danny, Lucy and Bernie dolls close to their hearts. They deserve our best."

I hear a soft sniff and turn to see Genna brush a tear out of her eye. I quickly turn back towards the stage. *Does she have any idea how inspiring she is? How these guys need to hear this?*

How much I love her?

She looks down, takes a deep breath, then looks up again.

"Your creativity and brilliance touches kids all over the world. Be proud of your work and never forget that you are the keepers of the magic. I'm incredibly honored to be part of your team."

The crowd erupts in applause and cheers. I push myself forward, but then freeze as I see Arnold pull Brooke into his arms and embrace her. He's never shown this kind of affection towards her publicly, and it's shocking to everyone, most of all me. A silence falls over the room, and from that point on everything moves in slow motion. When they pull apart, Arnold tucks Brooke under his arm and grabs the mike. He must've had a few because he definitely has a buzz going.

"Do you love this girl or what?" he yells enthusiastically.

Everyone cheers as he grabs her tighter.

I want to break his hairy arms.

"'Cause I do. What do you think? Isn't she the best? I'd say she's a keeper!"

Brooke rolls her eyes, but in a playful way like she's trying to keep things light.

Arnold gears up again. "What do you think guys? Should I marry her?"

Is he fucking serious? Did he just shout that out to the entire company?

As he pulls Brooke close and kisses her again, I hear, *yes!* and *marry her!* being yelled in between hoots and whistles from the crowd. At this point I'm outside of my body and just observing the whole scene. As hard as I try, I can't get a read on Brooke's expression. Is it shock? She doesn't look thrilled, but she doesn't push him away either. Her numb look and compliance stirs up everything I fear. I may be an emotional idiot, but could Brooke's vague statements at lunch, along with Arnold's declaration suggest the possibility that their ship's getting ready to sail? If so, I'll be left behind, clinging on to a capsized lifeboat.

Arnold pulls her offstage and the music starts up again. Everything's blurry, a swirl of colors and light. The music's deafening when layered onto the screaming inside my head. I sway uncertainly before I feel an arm hook through mine and pull.

"Come on," the feminine voice says with determination. "I'm getting you out of here."

"I have to talk to Brooke," I mumble frantically as she drags me through the crowd.

"Not now…later," she asserts. She picks up speed so that by the time we reach the front door of the club we blast through it.

I fall forward, my hands clutching my knees as I try to suck in air. She waits patiently as I try to straighten up. "I've got to go back in and find her. Please, Morgan…help me find her," I beg.

"This isn't a good time for that, Nathan," she insists as she squints and scans the street. "If you confront her now all hell's going to break loose, and it will only hurt you and Brooke. I know Arnauld well enough to know when it's time to steer clear."

She loops her arm through mine. "Come on, you need a drink."

Yes a drink, and then another. Everything's suddenly in super high-definition focus, and I need it to get blurry again.

She pulls me down the street to a place ironically called The Frolic Room, a retro-cool small bar that looks like it's been around since the fifties. When we go inside, there are only a few customers and a bartender who looks like he's seen everything and then some. She deposits me in a booth where the upholstery crack has been sealed with duct tape. I don't remember telling her I wanted whiskey, but somehow that ends up in front of me. I guess this is the opening scene of the B movie of my life. If only I didn't have to star in it.

We sit silently while she stirs her olive on a miniature sword around her martini, over and over and over. Finally she lifts it out and pulls the olive off with her teeth. I silently watch her in despair, taking long sips from my drink.

"Love is a rough game," Morgan finally says definitively.

I half expect her to snap her gum, and pull a cigarette out of the top of her stocking like they did in those forties movies.

I finish my drink with two gulps, then grab onto my hair and pull hard.

"I love Brooke," I confess.

"No shit, Sherlock," she replies.

"You knew?"

She rolls her eyes. "Of course. It's glaringly obvious."

"If love really is a game, Morgan, Arnold isn't playing fair."

She smirks at my new name for Arnauld.

I look at the little sword now abandoned on her cocktail napkin and realize that if Arnold were an action figure, this would be the perfect size weapon to behead him with.

"Yeah, that's where the rough part comes in. He knows it's war now. He's either going to try to make himself look really good, make you look really bad, or some combination of the two."

Her words ring true, and I squirm at the idea of it. There are endless ways to make me look bad.

"You weren't a threat at first because he completely underestimated you. He won't make that mistake again."

Billie's words from several weeks ago ring in my ear, how I'm going to get tossed to the curb like a cheap hooker. I don't care about my job as much as I care about losing Brooke.

"But he's all wrong for Brooke," I insist.

"I know, but he's made her believe that her career is in his hands. And sadly, I think she believes it."

"I hate how he tries to control her. I would never do that. I'm good for Brooke," I counter.

"I know that, Romeo, but you guys became friends what…a month ago? She's been with Arnauld for over three years."

"He's never gonna give her up, is he?" My fists curl over my knees.

She raises her eyebrows and gives me a stern look. "Did you really think he would? He sees his prize drifting away, and he wants to secure it. I don't even think he intends to marry her; he just wants to make sure she doesn't end up with you or anyone else."

"Really?"

"That's how it looks to me."

"And what about Brooke? What do you think she wants?" I ask nervously.

"I'm not sure. Before she met you, I thought her career was all she really cared about. I've never seen someone work so hard. She was obsessed. Now I'm not so sure."

"Really?" I ask, hopeful. But then I picture Arnold and Brooke on the stage tonight and I plummet back into despair. "But what if she marries Arnold?" I ask, as I motion to the bartender for another drink. He nods and pulls the bottle off the mirrored shelf.

"Well, you just can't let that happen."

I don't remember how much longer Morgan and I stayed at The Frolic Room. I have a vague recollection of lying with my cheek pressed down on the Formica tabletop, moaning as the warbly old jukebox played Frank Sinatra and Peggy Lee ballads. It seemed the properly pathetic conclusion to the worst evening of my life.

"Come-on, Cowboy," she says finally pulling me out of the booth. "I'm sure the coast is clear now. I'm driving you home."

"My car," I mumble.

"Give me forty bucks," she commands. "We'll pay off the parking attendant so you don't get towed. You can get it tomorrow."

I hand her my wallet and watch her pull out the cash. She drags me to the lot and deposits me in her car before fast talking the head attendant. Even in my drunk stupor, I realize that Morgan's a force to be reckoned with.

Gratefully I don't toss my cookies on the drive to Burbank, even though the air freshening thing dangling from her rear-view mirror is making me gag. I hang my head out the window and let the air slap my face as Morgan weaves along the Cahuenga Pass that carves through the Hollywood Hills towards the valley.

I manage to remember my address and once we arrive she takes my arm and walks me to my door like some kind of backwards date. I drop my keys fumbling at the front door, so she picks them up and helps me get the door open.

"Morgan…" I start and she holds her hand up to stop me.

"No, Nathan. No need to thank me. Just do me a favor and don't let that fucker win. Okay?"

I stand up straighter. It's like she's slapped me in the face. I'm alert again. "No, he can't win," I agree, tightening my hands into fists.

"Now you're talking!" She grabs my fancy shirt by the collar and shakes me. "Look it may get worse before it gets better, but you can't give up. You have to convince Brooke that she deserves real love."

"I'll do my best," I assure her as I watch her pivot and march down the walkway.

"Thank you, Morgan," I call after her.

In her final grand gesture, she doesn't look back but lifts her hand and waves once. It's like a salute from my very own general in this fight for

Brooke. Tonight may have required a retreat, and Arnold may have won the battle, but somehow, some way…I've got to win the war.

I have one final thought before I tumble inside and deposit my hip-fail of an outfit into the bottom of the clothes hamper:

Damn, I'm lucky to have Morgan on my side.

• • •

"Dad?" I say softly, trying to find my voice. Each moment since I woke has felt like being dragged across a bed of gravel. My head's throbbing and my skin feels raw.

"Son, are you okay?"

"Yeah, but I need to ask a big favor. I need a ride into Hollywood to get my car, and I can't get a hold of Curtis. I could call a cab but I'd rather have back up if there's a problem."

This isn't the kind of call my Dad's ever gotten from me, so he knows to take it seriously. "I'll be there shortly," he responds without a pause. "I calculate between twenty and thirty minutes barring any unforeseen traffic issues."

"Thanks, Dad."

Twenty-three minutes later when I get in his car he studies me carefully. He appears relieved to see no obvious signs of bodily harm, but he must sense my heart's wounded.

"Hollywood?" he asks.

I give him directions the way he likes them, precise and without extraneous information. He has verbal and visual total recall, so I know I won't need to repeat myself.

"Exactly what are the circumstances for this unfortunate state you find yourself in? It is clear that copious amounts of alcohol were involved."

"Yes, I had a friend drive me home last night since I was too intoxicated to drive."

"Well, if you're going to have a bender, at least you used wise judgment."

"Well, my friend did, but I'm sure that I would've come to that conclusion on my own."

"I'm don't want to pry, Nathan, but is this about Brooke? I deduce you are crestfallen, and I fear that there's been a setback."

"You could say that," I admit quietly. "Last night Arnold announced he plans to marry her."

"I see," he says. "That's a most definite setback…a chink in the armor, a fly in the ointment, a monkey wrench thrown into the mix."

"Yeah, I'd like to stick that damn monkey face first in the ointment," I growl.

Dad gives me a puzzled look and then refocuses on the issue.

"I must ask this, Nathan and answer it honestly. Does she want to marry him? Does she love him?"

I shake my head vehemently. "I don't think so. He's changed, and not for the better over the course of their relationship. I can't even figure out what she still sees in him other than job security."

"I see," he replies thoughtfully. "Okay then, let's get to work with some basic analysis. Grab the pad on the back seat and there are pens in the glove box."

I know better than to question Dad when the pads come out. In his mind, every problem requires a list and extensive notes to examine. It's how he makes sense of the world.

"Okay, draw a line down the middle—a column for you, and a column for him."

My line is shaky. I scrawl Nathan and Arnold on the top line.

"Age relative to Brooke?"

"I think he's in his late thirties or early forties, and she's thirty."

Dad lifts his eyebrows but doesn't comment. "Write the subject on the far left, then minus four for you and plus ten for him."

"Career?"

"Animator, versus company president." I dutifully write out the details.

"Financial Standing?"

"Well, he makes a lot more than me, that's for sure. But I do okay."

Dad nods towards the pad so that I write it down.

"Education?"

"I heard he has an MBA from Harvard. I have an art degree." I cringe at how pathetic that sounds.

"Level of attractiveness from a female's perspective?"

221

"Geek, versus Adonis," I scribble down, my spirits falling further. "Physique?"

"I'm in good shape, but he's in great shape."

Dad frowns. Something occurs to me.

"You know what though? I think I'm bigger. I mean I think my, well you know…" I point down at my crotch.

"Your penis?" Dad questions matter-of-factly, like I'm comparing beaker tubes in a lab.

I take a deep breath. "Yeah, I'm pretty sure my penis is much bigger than his. Brooke only had regular sized condoms at her place which wouldn't fit me."

He finally grins with this victory. "Well, you are an Evans, Son. Besides, statistics show that well-endowed men have greater success securing their desired mate. Take my word for it; that's a definite asset."

Okay then. Finally, one for the home team.

"So while we are on that subject, how about sexual prowess?" he asks.

"Well that's like comparing Pee Wee Herman to Warren Beatty in his day."

He coughs. I'm impressed that Dad can keep a straight face.

"Sharing common interests with Brooke?"

"I think I win there, hands down. I don't even think Arnold likes cartoons."

"Okay, that's good. And finally, some of the most significant attributes…personality? List five qualities each."

"Devoted, determined, awkward, inexperienced, hopeful…versus powerful, pseudo-charming, confident, persuasive…ASSHOLE."

He pulls the car over and takes the pad out of my hand. "Okay, let me review and summarize." He studies the two columns, his brow furrowed in concentration. He sets the pad on the console and turns towards me.

"You two couldn't be more different. Brooke must be terribly confused. Here she's with this Arnold person for how long did you say?"

"Three years."

"Yes, and then you come along and seismically impact her world." He taps the pencil down the list. "You are young, inexperienced, less successful, less attractive…"

"Thanks Dad, I'm feeling like a million bucks right about now."

"Let me finish, Nathan. What I was trying to say is that despite all of these shortcomings, she's undeniably drawn to you. There must be an extremely powerful chemistry between you."

I nod enthusiastically.

"And you love her."

"With all my heart."

"Well then prove to her that you can be strong and confident too. Even the most successful women want to know that you can be their equal. You can do it, Son. Just think, you are about to make a deal with your comic book that could lead to significant life-altering success. You're the most defiantly determined person I know. Your entire life I've watched you single-mindedly and tenaciously go after anything you really wanted."

I nod. He's right. Once I set my mind to something I can never give up until I achieve what I want, or get what I need. And I want Brooke. I need Brooke.

"Most importantly you need to claim her, as man has claimed his woman throughout the ages. This is not rocket science, Son; it's human primal instinct. Make her understand that she should be with you… quite simply, she *is* your chosen mate. You need to be hers. We're a highly developed society, but in the end we're all animals. And it's still a jungle out there."

I smile as I picture Brooke and I as Simba and Nala from *the Lion King*, running side by side along the animated savannah.

He lifts up the pad, and waves his hand over my writing as he continues.

"And all of the scientific data, statistical facts and empirical evidence can't compete with the indefinable heart's desire. For if in the end, she loves you, and she chooses you…none of the rest of this will matter."

He tears the sheet off the pad, wads it up and tosses it in the back seat.

Stunned, I look in behind us and then back at my dad. I've never seen him discard the facts…ever. I didn't think that man had a recklessly romantic bone in his body. Boy, was I wrong. I can't help but grin.

Before he moves back into traffic he gives me a firm nod. "Looks like you've got some serious wooing to do."

Happily my Mini-Cooper is waiting patiently for me when we pull into the deserted lot, the lone surviving soldier from my hellish night. I give Dad one of our awkward hugs and thank him for not just the ride, but also his advice. He looks pleased that his pep talk seems to have inspired me.

When I get home, I fire up my computer. My task is very specific as I get on the internet, my fingers flying over the keyboard.

Google search: *definition of woo*

Results: *Woo: To seek the affection of with intent to romance.*

I return to the Google page looking for another form of help. I type in *How to Woo a Girl*. The results flash in a mere second, and fifth item down, I find just what I'm looking for on WikiAnswers.

How to Woo A Girl

The list starts out rather uninspiring. I was hoping for magic potions, spells or at least instructions as to where I can buy pheromones to physically draw her to me like a huge magnet that never releases its hold.

*Show interest…look in her eyes when you speak to her…be sensitive and caring…be assertive, and lead…*yeah, yeah, yeah

I scan further down. What's this?

Whisper in her ear… That's weird, but certainly easy. Do they mean all the time? That would be ridiculous. I continue on.

Dress nicely… Shoot, not with the clothes again.

Be nice to your young relatives in front of her… I don't have any young relatives. Maybe I could borrow some? Shit, this stuff is complicated.

Help others in front of her, like the poor and needy…

Make her laugh… I'm assuming not when you're helping the poor and needy.

For holidays like Valentine's Day be sweet and thoughtful instead of cliché…

blah, blah, blah

*Don't be overtly sexual…*well, it's too late for that one.

*Learn to dance, take ballroom dancing lessons…*seriously? That has disaster written all over it.

Be spontaneous!

And finally, *take the first step. If you're ever going to win the prize you have to tell the prize you want it.*

Now that makes the most sense to me of all the suggestions.

Wow. There are so many things to consider that my head's spinning. Did Arnold do all this stuff for Brooke? I mean I really doubt that he whispered in Brooke's ear or helped others, but I know for a fact that he's a good dancer.

I read the list three times, jotting down ideas on note cards. I then tape up everything on my bathroom mirror so that I can review the suggestions often. The last card I wrote I hang in the most prominent location, right at eye level:

If you're going to ever win the prize, you've got to tell the prize you want it.

I take a deep breath and nod at my reflection. It's time.

While I still have the nerve, I march out to the kitchen and grab my phone, then quickly dial Brooke's number. I'm frustrated when her phone goes directly to voicemail, but I attempt to leave a message anyway.

Hey Brooke, it's Nathan. I'd like to take you to dinner tonight so we can talk. How's seven p.m.?

I pause for a moment. Was that too pushy, or appropriately direct? *Damn.* I better finish this up.

So give me a call... okay thanks... bye.

I stare at my phone for a moment and then remember that I haven't hung up, so I nervously hit the *end* button. It occurs to me that maybe I should text her too since I can control my words better, and not sound like an idiot.

Hi Brooke, just left you a voicemail about dinner tonight. Let me know if seven is good.

I hit send. Moments later I get a reply.

Sorry, can't do dinner, at Arnauld's now.

Damn. A wave of panic washes over me, and my woo-ing plan takes a back seat to my fear. My fingers shake as I type crazy words I shouldn't text.

Just needed to let you know that I'm not going to let you marry him.

There... I said it. I feel sick and triumphant at the same time. I can't believe I just texted that.

Is that so?

225

Thank God she isn't mad at me. But her calm reply just fuels my fire.
Are you going to marry him?
You just told me that you weren't going to let that happen.
But would you have tried?
I'm curious now…what would you've done to stop it?
Ride up on a horse and carry you off in your wedding gown.
Very dramatic.
I mean it. You can't marry that ass.
The ass is getting off the phone. Can we talk about this tomorrow?
Tonight. I insist.
I don't know how long this argument will take. Tomorrow…please Nathan, I will explain everything then, I promise.

And just like that she's gone. I watch her words fade back into the screen, the blue background a cold infinity I can't penetrate.

Instinctively my fingers move over the tiny keyboard, willing the words I had wanted to tell her to materialize. Slowly, deliberately, I spell out my truth as if each letter is a sign I'm posting on the road of this twisted journey.

i l o v e y o u b r o o k e

I get overwhelmed as I reread my message for her. I thought we had more time than this. I'm fighting back waves of frustration to know that she's with him even if they're fighting. Couples fight and make up all the time, and there are still enough pieces of their puzzle I'm missing to make me uneasy. There's a devastating fear of what may never be mine…with the absolute understanding that the only thing I really want, is the one thing I may never have. I keep typing, adding on.

i l o v e y o u b r o o k e w i t h a l l m y h e a r t

I study the words, rubbing my finger across the screen over and over, wishing she could understand that she's everything to me.

But instead of hitting send, I delete the message and close the screen. This is so much bigger than a text. I need to face her with my truth. Tomorrow will be the day.

Animate Me / Chapter Nineteen / Stalking 101

"Look Mack, just what's going on around here?" ~ Daffy Duck[xviii]

Is five a.m. too early to call? That seems like a perfectly respectable time to call, even if it's still dark out. I pace back and forth in my kitchen, glancing at my watch every minute or so. I picture Brooke curled up asleep like an angel, and it's the only thing keeping me from hitting the send button on my cell phone.

At six a.m., after choking down a Pop Tart and my second cup of coffee, my resistance finally fails. With my hands shaking I text her:

Hi Brooke, can I take you to breakfast? I'm craving pancakes. How about you?

Yeah, that sounds good…kind of casual…not like I'm foaming at the mouth from the idea that she may be with Arnold making wedding plans. Maybe they're online right now setting up one of those gift registry things. Yeah, sure, at six in the morning…maybe I'm losing my mind.

I set my phone in the middle of the kitchen table, and proceed to stare at it for fifteen minutes. There's no response.

By eight-fifteen I'm dressed for work but a little edgy. Yeah, just a bit. I've already worn a path in the rug that runs down my hallway. It occurs to me that maybe she's lost her phone. I've never heard of Brooke losing anything, but it could've happened. It's not impossible. Before I get in the car I call her, reminding myself that if she's lost her phone, she won't answer.

"Hey Brooke, are you free for lunch? There's this great little place in Toluca Lake I'd like to take you to. How's noon, or even better eleven-thirty?"

Good, that was direct. Now I better figure out a great little place. It sure as hell can't be Taco Bell. It occurs to me that she usually doesn't eat until one p.m. but I'll go stark raving mad if I have to wait that long to see her.

When I pull into the parking garage, Mojo's car's there, but not Brooke's. Did she ride in with him? Or does he have her tied down, drugged up and locked in his attic so she can't return my calls? I consider knocking on the lid of his trunk to make sure she isn't in there. I don't find my fears unfounded considering the last time she didn't return a call, the monkey had kidnapped her, forced her to go to Santa Barbara, and proceeded to brainwash her.

Upstairs, before I've unloaded my workbag, I pick up the office phone and dial.

"Hi Morgan."

"Hey, Nathan. What's up?"

"Hey, thanks again for your help on Saturday. I really appreciated it."

"Glad to do it," she replies. "So, are you doing okay?"

"Yeah, I'm okay. But I'm wondering is Brooke in yet? I wanted to ask her something."

"No, she's not in yet…but it's still a bit early for her. You want me to tell her that you called?"

"Yes, please do…as soon as you see her."

At nine thirty I sneak out the front and check the parking lot again. Her car still isn't there. Nine forty-five I text her:

Hey Brooke, are you having car problems? Do you need a ride?

Nothing.

At ten twenty Morgan calls me.

"I just heard from her. She's not coming in."

"Did she say why?"

"No, and she sounded really stressed out. Did you talk to her yesterday?"

"No we texted, but she was busy with Arnold, so we couldn't talk."

"Weird…I wonder what's going on," Morgan says.

Her tone makes me even more nervous.

I'm not sure exactly when I lose all semblance of rational thought and control, but the texts start flying fast and furious. Her phone must be on fire with all my attempts to reach her, each text about fifteen minutes apart.

Hey Brooke, how about a late lunch? In-N-Out? I know you can't turn that down.

Are you feeling okay? Did Arnold feed you some bad fish or something?

Can I bring you some chicken soup? How about some nachos?

Have I done something wrong? Is this some kind of weird test?

Is there a reason you're avoiding me? Am I in the doghouse?

I'm freaking out. Can you please text me back?

I'm about to follow that one up with an even more desperate text when I hear someone clear their throat. I look up and see Nick watching me.

"What's up, dude? You're suddenly a texting fiend. I've been hearing that little *beep, beep, beep* all morning."

Defeated, I lay the phone down on my drawing table and hang my head. "I've been trying to reach Brooke."

"I see. Well…has it occurred to you that maybe she doesn't want to be reached?"

"But I haven't done anything to her," I point out. "I don't understand why she won't talk to me."

"Maybe she's avoiding everyone, not just you. That was quite a scene at the club on Saturday."

I just nod my head.

"Was that for real?" Nick asks. "Is she going to marry him? I mean I just can't see it…he seems so completely wrong for her."

"I haven't been able to talk to her to find out." I rub my hands over my face.

"No wonder you've been texting so much. I'd be going nuts too."

"I don't want to lose her, Nick," The despair weighs heavy in my voice.

He studies me for a moment, with a concerned expression. "Hey, come to lunch with me and Dani," he says, waving his hand in a motion to follow him as he takes a step out of the cubicle. "We'll go to Tin Horn Flats and get beers with our burgers."

It almost sounds good, but I shake my head. "You guys just got back together. You need to be alone, not with me tagging along."

"Come on, I insist," he says, grabbing my arm. "Besides you and your antics are responsible for getting us back together."

I can't hide my surprise. "She told you?"

"Sure, we told each other everything. You know that was a really stupid idea, Nathan."

"Yeah? Well, it worked out for you."

"Yes, it did." He smiles and steps behind me and gently pushes me forward. "Now let's get your shit figured out too."

Over my second beer, I watch Dani get a faraway look in her eyes while she drums her fingers on the weathered wood tabletop.

"I know, I know…he has that excess hair problem right? My brother's a genius with equipment. Why don't we get him to jerry-rig the electrolysis machine at the place Arnauld goes to so that they fry the fucker next time he gets his fur removed!"

I almost spit up my beer. "Ha! That's brilliant!" But then my smile falls. "Only that won't work because he gets the fur waxed."

"Waxed?" Nick asks, horrified.

"Even better, we will give new meaning to *hot* wax!" Dani exclaims.

"Isn't her devious mind a wondrous thing," Nick says as he gazes at her lovingly.

Dani's face lights up again with a new idea.

"I know! Remember that shit he said to Brooke about her figure? Let's hire some skinny bitch actress with ginormous silicone tits to interrupt an important board meeting and accuse Arnauld of giving her VD."

"Yeah! And we'll dress her in a stripper outfit with her huge tits hanging out!" Nick chimes in.

Dani gives him the look, the one with one eyebrow cocked. I guess girls can suggest stuff like that, but not boyfriends unless they want to get into big trouble.

"I don't know you two," I respond. "That would reflect poorly on Brooke too since she's been involved with him. So that's not such a good idea."

"I guess you're right," Dani agrees. "Okay, give me a little time. I'll come up with some other ideas."

"That's my girl," Nick says proudly.

Back from our rowdy lunch, the beer buzz and lingering humor holds me over for almost an hour before the panic sets in again. Like a drug addict fresh out of rehab, I weaken and surrender to my next hit. I pull my phone out of my pocket with shaky hands.

Three twenty-two pm:

Hey Brooke, I just wanted you to know that I'm not going to text anymore. So you can have all the space you need today.

Three thirty-eight:

Unless of course you actually want some company, but are afraid to ask for it. Then I'd be happy to text you.

Four-o-two:

I know I said I wouldn't text, but we're gathering to go to Starbucks. Are you sure I can't bring you one?"

Four thirty-seven:

I bought your drink just in case, and I just did the best drawing ever. You want to see it?

Five fifteen:

This cup should go in the Starbucks hall of fame. Seriously. You're missing out Brooke.

Five seventeen:

Nick just came over and said he's going to break my fingers if I text you again.

Five fifty-nine (texted from the parking garage)

Leaving work now—I'll be home soon if you want to talk.

• • •

The crazed beating on my front door is the first indication that this won't be a pleasant visit.

"What's wrong with you?" Brooke screeches, waving her hands dramatically as soon as I pull open the door. "Have you lost your mind? Why did you call or text me every fifteen minutes today? Aren't I under enough stress without you stalking me?"

I step back stunned.

Great...I used to be attentive and caring...now I'm a stalker.

I've never seen this side of Brooke and it scares me. With her hands jammed on her hips as she lingers on my doorstep, she looks kind of wild. Despite this, I still feel relief to see her. Angry Brooke is better than no Brooke.

Is this our first fight?

"But, I needed to talk to you right away," I implore.

"Right. I think I got that. But did you take your head out of Toon Town for just a minute to think what I've been going through since Saturday? That maybe I needed some space and silent support, not more pressure?"

Yup, I'm sure of it. This is our first fight. Her face is really red. This must be the Buttercup side to her personality she warned me about.

I take a moment to think about what she's trying to say.

Toon Town? Been going through? Silent support? Is this that cryptic girl talk I've heard they revert to when they're angry?

I've never had a girl be this angry with me before. I'm compelled to defend myself. "What about what I've been going through since Saturday night? Have you considered that? You could've just responded to any one of the texts and told me that you needed some time," I explain carefully. "Then I wouldn't have gone crazy with worry."

She just stares at me dumbfounded, like I have three heads.

"Right. And you would have given me that time?"

"Maybe not," I admit. *Damn. I am a stalker.*

"Exactly! Look, I don't mean to be a bitch, but I'm over the edge here. Everything I've worked for is ruined. I'm a joke to everyone."

"What are you talking about?" I ask baffled.

"Saturday…Saturday! I mean for fuck's sake, my boss and quasi-boyfriend announced to the entire company that he was marrying me like I'm some idiot mail order bride. No conversation ahead of time, no warning…just parading me around like some damn door prize. I'm so humiliated. I don't know how I can show my face there again."

"People don't think of you like that, Brooke," I say softly.

"You have no idea, Nathan…no idea. I've been busting my ass trying to find another job, so I could finally get out from under him, and every opportunity mysteriously vanishes before the deal is struck. Well, now I'm the laughing stock of our industry. Look at all the fucking emails I've already gotten wishing us the best."

She holds up her blackberry.

"I'd rather not," I whisper.

My mind is reeling…another job…out from under him? What have I been missing?

"And you!" She pushes me on the chest.

Uh oh, she's getting physical. Wow, it's kind of hot. I try to focus so I don't get aroused. That would be really awkward and weird right about now.

"You're the one who's stirred everything up. You and your damn pedestal, treating me like I'm sooo perfect...like I deserve more. You don't realize what that does to me."

"I thought it's good to be admired," I say, trying not to feel bad.

"But don't you see...I'm always worried that I'm going to let you down. All along you've thought you weren't good enough for me. When will you figure out that it's me who's not good enough for you?"

"How can you say that?" I ask, baffled.

"I'm a mess, Nathan. I don't even know who I am anymore. The sooner you figure out what a sorry mess I am, and that I'm not anywhere close to perfect, the better off you'll be. You can go find the girl who really deserves you."

I realize there are tears steaming down her face. Confused, I hold my hands out, palms facing up. "Find the girl, what girl?"

"*The* girl," she says, her voice breaking. "You should go find her."

"What makes you think she couldn't be you?" I ask.

There are little sobs now in between the crying. It's breaking my heart.

"No, not me," she cries.

I never would imagine she could be like this. She always seems so powerful, so sure of herself. I'm seeing another side of her and it's a revelation. I realize it's my turn to be strong. I clear my throat so my voice will be sure and steady.

"I'm not going anywhere, so stop saying that Brooke." I pull her into my arms. She feels so fragile, and it makes me want to protect her.

"Besides, even if you are a mess, you're my perfect mess."

She bucks and fights my embrace. "Quit saying that! I'm not perfect Nathan...not even close."

I decide to try a new tactic. "Oh, I know that... believe me!" I tease.

"You do?" She sniffles, the crying slowing down.

"Sure. What you don't understand is that despite the fact that your coffee drinks are disgustingly sweet, you like Strawberry Shortcake, and that you have questionable taste in men, you're still perfect to me."

She sniffles against my chest, and I feel her relax a tiny bit into me. I rub my hand over her back slowly.

"You think my coffee drinks are too sweet?" She asks quietly, sniffle-free.

"Oh yeah! When I order them my teeth hurt."

"Then why do you get them for me? You could try to get me to order something less sweet?"

"I wouldn't do that, Brooke. I don't want to change you. I just want to make you happy."

She takes a deep breath that shivers from the leftover tears.

"Oh, Nathan. Whatever am I going to do with you?"

"Whatever you want to," I reply.

She pulls away just enough to look up at me and smile.

"Thank you," she says softly.

"For what?"

"I actually feel a little bit better."

I smile back. "Good. See if you'd let me take you to breakfast at six this morning, you could have avoided all this heartache," I tease.

"Yeah, six in the morning. If you could see me at six in the morning on a work day you'd know that would never happen."

"See, yet another way you aren't perfect...the list is getting long now." I give her a crooked smile.

She grins, and then looks embarrassed. "I'm sorry I yelled at you."

"And pushed me," I remind her.

"Yes," she agrees, looking down ashamed.

"I'm not. I think you needed that. I think we both did. Besides, I'm just really, really glad you're here. Are you going to be sweet to me now?" I ask, half teasing, half not.

She smiles softly. "Yes, I'm going to be very sweet with you." She studies me for a moment, and then wipes the tears off her cheek. "Ugh, I'm a mess. I need to wash off my face. Where's the bathroom?"

"First door on the right, in the hallway."

"Okay, I'll just be a sec."

I watch her walk away, and although I'm still worried about her, I'm so glad she came over. I step to the window and gaze out to the back garden and think about all the things she's revealed to me.

She's been trying to leave Arnold, she wants a new job, she thinks she's a mess...wait...wait!...oh God, no!

It all hits me like an icy wave, and a panic shoots through me that I've never known. The time I almost got hit by a minivan when I was riding my new bike Christmas day doesn't even compare.

Because at this moment Brooke is in my bathroom…the bathroom where the instructions on *How to Woo A Girl* and all my note cards are posted. My emasculation will be so profound if she reads that stuff, I'll never recover.

I want to die.

I rush to the door and knock. "Brooke, Brooke. I need to get in there."

Silence.

I try to turn the knob, but it's locked. I rattle the handle in frustration. "Brooke. Please, please let me in."

Silence.

I press my hands and forehead to the door, and say a prayer that she'll let me in.

Please Brooke.

My humiliation is so big I can't wrap my arms around it. There's no way she will ever be able to see me as anything but a loser idiot. I have lost every bit of gain I ever made with her with one simple mistake.

It was bad enough when I thought I was losing her to Arnold, but this…

"Please, Brooke. Please."

Her silence tells me everything.

It's done. It's over. I might as well put the polo shirt with the bow tie and pocket protector back on. My heart feels like it's melting right out of my chest.

I turn and walk back to the kitchen and straight out the back door. I need the sun and air of the backyard, because if I stay in that house another moment I think I will climb the walls.

I pace across the grass, thinking of what I will say. *I'm sorry I'm such a loser?* There are no elegant words to explain how much I want her, and the lengths I'll go to be the best man I can be for her. How can I explain that I needed a jumble of inkjet printouts and note cards to give me a glimmer of hope.

I'm not sure how long I've been outside mumbling to myself, but I finally get the balls to go inside and get her out of the bathroom. It's time to face the music. But once inside, I see that the bathroom door's wide open. I warily approach the doorway and peek in, confirming that my guide to avoid being a loner pathetic idiot is still plastered all over the mirror, and Brooke is no where to be seen.

"Brooke?" I call out panicked. I can't believe she just left without saying goodbye. The loser manifesto must have really freaked her out.

"In here," she calls out weakly. It sounds like she's in the bedroom. I look inside and see that she's lying on my bed, white as a ghost.

"I hope you don't mind," she offers. "You don't have a couch, and I got dizzy and needed to lie down."

"Oh no. Are you sick?" I ask concerned, stepping closer.

"No, and don't worry — I'm not pregnant."

Not pregnant? Oh, but can you imagine how beautiful a baby Brooke would be? I try to keep my eyes from bugging out of my head while she continues.

"It's stupid, really. I'm so freaking stressed out that I didn't sleep last night, and I haven't eaten either…so it all caught up with me. I think I'm dehydrated too. Would you mind getting me some water? "

"Of course." I quickly head to the kitchen, relieved for the distraction. I quickly grab some stuff and head back.

I watch her push herself up into a sitting position as I unscrew the cap for her.

"Here, drink up."

She takes a sip and then looks at the plate I set on the nightstand. "What's that?"

"Crackers with Cheese Whiz and a little box of raisins. I think you should eat something."

"Cheese Whiz?" The edges of her mouth turn up. "I didn't think they made that anymore."

"Oh sure. I get mine at Seven-Eleven." I watch her eat a few raisins and take a tiny bite off a cracker. I can tell she's tentative about the Cheese Whiz. "Don't worry, it's still good. That stuff never expires."

"Precisely," she says, wrinkling her nose. When she finishes most of the water she lays back on the bed. "I'm so tired," she says softly.

"Why don't you nap?" I suggest, desperately hoping she'll stay.

"Okay, but only if you lie with me," she says, her voice already fading.

I kick off my shoes and crawl up on the bed, settling in on my side facing her.

"I didn't sleep either. Maybe I'll nap too."

She reaches over and our hands link. My heart surges somehow sensing that despite whatever she learned during her visit to my bathroom, that she still accepts me. She isn't going to cast me out.

I take a deep grateful breath. I feel so much calmer with her here next to me, her hand tethering me to her. I start to surrender to the exhaustion.

Right before I close my eyes and fall away from the waking world, I say a silent prayer of thanks. There must be a geek-loving angel with a tender heart looking over me and my girl.

I blink slowly, taking in the lavender light. Brooke is nestled under my arm and I sense her stirring. What time is it? How long have we been asleep?

"Nathan?" she whispers.

"Yes," I whisper back.

"You're awake."

She gently squeezes my arm and then rolls over and grabs the water bottle. I get up to use the restroom, and when I'm done I carefully pull all the papers off the mirror and shove them in the bottom drawer.

When I return I see she's eaten several of the crackers and the rest of the raisins.

"Feeling better?" I crawl back up on the bed and study her face.

"Yeah." She rolls over to face me. "Hey Nathan? Can we talk about something?"

"Sure," I respond, immediately nervous.

There's a silent minute where she seems to be considering her words. She looks troubled, and I try to steel myself for whatever she's about to say. Finally she smoothes out a wrinkle on the bedspread and looks up at me.

"There's stuff we've been keeping from each other, isn't there?"

I nod slowly. *Oh no, where's she going with this?*

"I've known for a while that there was something up with your thing with Dani, but I didn't want to say anything. I guess it sort of gave us a buffer, a comfort zone. You know what I mean?"

I just nod and look down, afraid to admit any specifics yet. I need to tell her I love her, but it hasn't felt like the right time. I'm not sure I'm ready for all of this.

"And I know there's something about your comic book that you don't want me to see. You're afraid I'm not going to like something, aren't you?"

"Yes," I whisper. "You could say that."

"And there's a lot I haven't told you about my situation with Arnauld. I've only told you parts because…well, I guess because I needed a buffer too."

"Yeah," I guess so. "So you're really not going to marry him?"

"No." She smiles. "I never would've married him. Even if I'd never met you. I wouldn't have married him, I swear."

I nod, taking a deep breath and letting the relief seep through me.

"This is the deal," she explains. "I've been so stressed, so worried…I mean you have no idea of the hell that it's been inside my head."

Her face twists up in pain and she runs her hand across her forehead.

"I'm sorry," I say quietly as I inch closer to her. "Can I do anything?"

She lies still for moment thinking, and then her expression fixes somewhere between hope and fear. "You know what I need? I need a week of no worries, just fun, just happy. Yeah that's what I need…happy twenty-four, seven."

"Okay," I stammer, having no idea how I can facilitate that.

"Here's the thing. Arnauld is leaving for New York tonight. He has meetings there all week that he couldn't get out of. I told him last night that I wouldn't marry him, and he insisted that I take the week to think it over. We are meeting the night he gets back."

"So you're going to think about it this week?"

"No, like I said, I have no intention of marrying him, but I agreed to talk again because it was the only way he'd get off my back. We rehashed everything last night for hours. He just wore me the fuck out."

I can see the price she's paid by the exhaustion in her expression.

"And that's my point…I don't want to think about anything for a while. I need a goddamn break from agonizing over how to get out of this mess, the things he's doing to sabotage my job search, and how to salvage my career. The worst part though is my guilt from pulling you into this disaster, then worrying about how I can protect you from him."

She looks up at me, the concern and care she feels so evident in her expression as she continues. "It's just all too much. So I just want to be free from any heavy thoughts for a few days.

"Okay, so what can I do to help?" I ask hopeful.

"I want to have fun….fun with you. I'm always happy when I'm with you. You make me feel special and appreciated."

I smile widely. "I'm so glad, Brooke." I guess I've done a few things right.

"And I want to make you feel the same," she says softly.

Wow.

She runs her fingers up my chest and looks up at me. "You know what I really want from you?" She gives me the sweetest smile. "…I want to be wooed."

My breath catches. She didn't just say that.

"You want me to woo you?"

"Yes, but for the record, I don't want to meet any small relatives yet, and I'd like to take the ballroom dancing lesson with you. I don't want you dancing with some middle aged woman in Lycra."

I grin. She wants me to woo her. "So a week of woo…I think that can be arranged."

"Good, and *woo week* starts now. I want just happy times—no heavy conversations. We can have those talks next week. Just fun for now, okay?"

I nod enthusiastically despite my anxiety of the looming Arnold and B-Girl reveal. This isn't the time to worry about worst-case scenarios.

I reflect back over all she's said and I can't believe it…she wants to be with *me*.

"So to start, can you read this to me?" She has a coy smile as she reaches into her back pocket and pulls out something folded up. I watch her beautiful fingers pull the folds apart and press it out against the bedspread. When it's as smooth as possible she hands it to me.

I hold it up in the dim light, and recognize my writing. It's the note card I wrote and taped on the mirror, just after I called her this morning. It's written in bold letters, all in caps.

TODAY IS THE DAY I WILL TELL BROOKE THAT I'M IN LOVE WITH HER

Oh, my. Here we go…

Animate Me / Chapter Twenty / A Two-Way Woo

"Forget them, Wendy. Forget them all. Come with me where you'll never, never have to worry about grown up things again." ~Peter Pan[xix]

My fingers are trembling, as though they're trying to hold up the weight of all of the longing I've ever had for Brooke. "You took this off the bathroom mirror." I observe quietly, full of apprehension.

"Yes, I did," she admits, not looking the slightest bit guilty.

"I would've told you, you know," I protest. "The day isn't over yet."

"Are you going to read it to me or not?" she teases.

"But I thought we weren't going to talk about anything heavy."

"This isn't heavy. If you mean it, it's full of light and happiness...the most beautiful feeling ever. It's completely woo-worthy." She says with her eyes closed and a dreamy smile.

"Oh, I mean it," I affirm solemnly, trying to work up the courage to look her in the eyes.

"Then tell me; read it," she encourages. "I want to hear you say it."

I hold up the note card but I don't need to read it. The sentiment is etched in my memory. "Today is the day I will tell Brooke that I'm in love with her." I curl the card in my hand.

She grins happily, taking the note back and pressing it against her chest, right over her heart. "So are you going to tell me? I'm really ready to hear it."

I look into her eyes and try to be brave. "I'm in love with you, Brooke," I whisper so softly I'm not sure she's heard the words.

"Like you mean it," she pushes playfully.

I can't help but laugh, she is so infuriatingly demanding. "I'm in love with you, Brooke," I state with strength and confidence, "completely, utterly, overwhelmingly in love with you."

She scoots closer and places her hand over my pounding heart.

"You've just made me so happy." She is beaming brightly, all the earlier exhaustion gone.

"Can I ask you something?" I ask carefully.

"Okay, but remember, no heavy questions."

"Just one...please?"

"Oh, okay." She bites her lip and watches me.

"Do you think you could ever fall in love with me?"

She smiles, like she is holding a secret in her hands. "Yes, I do. Absolutely. How do you know I haven't already, Mr. Woo?"

My huge grin comes from the inside out. I take her hand in mine. *Oh wow, is this really happening?* I don't want push to ask for more details. This is already so much more than I could have hoped for.

"Why don't I show you how I feel about you?" she offers.

"Show not tell?"

She nods as she curves into me. "I want to make love to you."

Good lord. This woman...what she does to me...

"But *I'm* supposed to woo you," I point out. I think I remember the woo list saying I was supposed to take control. But my head's spinning, so I'm not completely sure.

"It's a two-way woo," she whispers right before she settles against me and presses her lips to mine in the sweetest kiss. "You'll make love to me too."

Wow...who cares who's in control...

"Make love," I repeat smiling, noting how much better that sounds than sex or screwing. "Yeah, that sounds perfect to me."

I study her, noting a subtle shift with everything about her. Layers are peeling back like pages fluttering in the wind. Her heart is opening; I just know it.

"I've never felt this way before, Nathan." She says softly, as she starts to crawl over me.

"Never?" I ask, my heart soaring.

"No....so this is just you, and me, and this feeling. Let's go slow. I want to feel everything," she whispers in my ear before feathering kisses down my neck. She lifts herself up and straddles my hips right over where

I'm already aroused for her. "Yes," she whispers as she slowly rocks, her gaze tender yet hungry. "You want me."

"I always want you, Brooke...always." I breathe her scent, and feel her heat as the warmth radiates through me.

Brooke, don't you know how you've turned my world upside down?

I watch her slowly unbutton my shirt. She is ceremonious; as each button pulls apart she leans down and kisses the skin that's revealed. My hands rest on her thighs, slowly stroking, every touch fanning the fire. When she finishes the bottom button, she spreads the shirt open and runs her hands over my chest.

"I love touching you. I love how strong you are," she says softly as she pushes the shirt off my shoulders. I can feel my neck and chest flush from the way she's admiring me.

"Can we take off your shirt?" I ask. The way I'm lying under her, I need her help. "I want to see you too."

As she starts to slowly lift it off, I run my hands up her sides. It's better than sliding across silk because of the warmth and life just beneath my fingertips. She starts to lower one of her bra straps and I stop her.

"Slow," I remind her. I pull her into my arms and kiss her slowly, letting my hands wander. "You're so beautiful...so beautiful, and I can't believe you're here with me."

"Well, where else would I be?" she teases as she steps off the bed, and pushes her jeans off. I watch her. Wearing only her very sheer bra and panties, she climbs back over me.

I've daydreamed this exact scene countless times. It's my very own Victoria Secret catalog come to life—only Brooke's body is much sexier than those women. I rest my hands on her soft hips, feeling so grateful that I'm the one she wants. "You know, I thought I'd lost you. I thought you had chosen to be with him. And now you're here with me...and... well...I just can't believe it."

"Well then, I'm going to keep showing you how I feel until you believe everything."

Her seductive smile really gets me going. I don't know how much more of this slow stuff I can take.

I think Brooke's aware I'm beyond excited. She smiles knowingly as she undoes my fly and starts to pull my jeans and my boxers down. Following the denim, she kisses another trail down my hips and thighs, only detouring to give my erection several long licks from base to tip. I shiver with pleasure.

"Brooke." I moan as I watch her unhook her bra and pull until it falls away. My hands reach up to cup her breasts as we gaze at each other, having entire conversations with our eyes. It occurs to me that this is the least awkward I've ever felt. I just want to please her, to show her what we can be. Her nipples harden under my fingertips and the softest blush moves across her cheeks.

"Oh, Nathan, the way you look at me. What are you thinking?"

"That I'm the luckiest man in the world."

"And why is that?" She knows, but I sense that she needs to hear it tonight as I hold her.

"Because I found the girl I'm meant to be with," I say with certainty. "A girl so amazing that I couldn't have conjured her in my wildest dreams. But you're here, and you're real…and you want me."

"Yes, I do," she says smiling. Her warm hand grasps me firmly, with gliding movements, fluid and smooth. The visual of her hand gripping me, her full breasts, wet lips and dreamy eyes, is just too much.

And with that, I roll so I am on top of her, pressing down hard. We move together, grabbing, rubbing and kissing like teenagers making out for the first time. But then she pulls her luscious thighs apart and asks for more.

And I want more too. She's taught me that one does not need to supplicate to truly express devotion. I pull off her panties and settle between her legs so I can taste her again. My cheek grazes her inner thigh as I move in closer to kneel at the sacred altar of Brooke and prepare to worship. My lips hold the memory of every touch that drove her wild. So my tongue moves over her softness, as her hips roll in response. Her hands twist in my hair, pulling me closer, and she whispers my name over and over and over again.

When she cries out I press my palms inside her knees and gently push her open that much more. As she gasps for breath, I press one final kiss over her and look up into her eyes.

"Beautiful," I whisper, feeling even more confident.

"Nathan, please," she motions for me, her arms reaching. "I need you inside of me… *now*."

Her need is my sexual call to arms, and I'm ready. Every sensation sparks as I breathlessly move over her. My need to take her is primal and raw like I'm a caveman getting ready to claim his woman. "Do you belong to me now, Brooke?" I surprise myself by asking, gasping as I grind against her.

She nods, the corners of her eyes twist with mirth, but I sense she likes caveman Nathan. "I'm only yours," she says with satisfaction. "No one else." Her eyes are hooded. This is really turning me on.

"Mine," I kind of growl, playing it up as I loom over her. I can tell this is turning her on too.

"Is that what you want?" she asks, pulling me closer.

"It's what I've always wanted," I assure her. Meanwhile my arousal has taken on a life of it's own, probing for heat sensors, searching for the happy place of love. My mind twists as every science fiction proclamation passes through my consciousness…stuff about the *force being with me, boarding the mothership,* and *boldly going where I've never gone before.* Making love is a science fiction-worthy, spiritual experience.

Brooke wants me.

Me.

With our eyes locked she takes me in her grasp and brings me to her. "I need this so much," she gasps. "I need *you*, Nathan."

A surge of pride and protectiveness moves through me. I want to take care of Brooke in every way. I want to give her what she needs.

I still for a moment and take her face in my hands.

"I need you too," I admit without hesitation.

As I gaze at her I see tears pooling in the corners of her beautiful eyes. But they aren't sad tears. I can tell.

"Nathan?"

"Yes?"

She pauses and takes a deep breath, as if she's fighting to be brave.

Be brave, Brooke.

"I…"

I wait patiently, stroking her cheeks. I'm still anxious to be inside of her, but that can wait a moment. I sense this is very important.

"I love you," she says gently, but with absolute certainty. She's sweet and sincere, with adoration reflected in her eyes.

She really loves me. For me, loving her was a given. For Brooke, who had closed her heart long ago, this is big…really big.

"You love me," I whisper. She may as well have waved her magic wand at me, and chanted "lumos" for how I've lit up inside. I gaze at her and realize that she's lit up too.

Our kiss is tender and raw as I pull her tightly into my arms. It's time. With laser focus I position and push, slowly sliding myself home as she opens herself to me. She is all warmth and wetness as she arches up, moaning loudly. Every part of her that presses, or wraps around me is an embrace. Our hips are moving, the push and pull of our bodies together. We are electrified with the sheer emotion of our hearts connecting.

I don't know if I was prepared for how those three words would overcome me.

'Cause I'm in love. Big love. Real love. The best love.

I'm overwhelmed with this fireball of passion. And Brooke holds on while I take her for our wild ride. It feels like we are soaring on Disneyland's Space Mountain as I push into her, wide eyes as the stars blur past us in the thrilling darkness.

My hands grasp her curvy hips, pulling her closer as I fill her again and again. Her expression is sublime, a hungry gaze, pink cheeks and parted cherry lips. She is my wingless angel, my Red Hot love.

"Oh, Nathan," she moans, as her legs wrap tighter around me. There is a current flowing through our heated kisses, each deeper and more passionate. I am fighting the urge to completely consume her as I lick and nip my way across her breasts and up her neck.

"Is this what you want, Brooke?" I ask, because I want to get the *making love* part of this right. My heart's so full that I'm pretty sure this is exactly what it should be. I know for sure, it's what I always needed.

"Yes." She moans. "Yes…this is love," she whispers. Her hands suddenly reach upwards, grasping up into the air. I feel her opening, every part of her body deliciously soft and spread. But then the trembling starts and I realize this is a different kind of climax. I hold her in my arms tightly as I push deeper and tell her that I love her over and over.

Something in the way she finally cries out, a soulful sound as her body arcs up, sends me over the edge too. And this time it's Brooke, drawing me out with her words of love as I soar. I call out her name before I fall into the warm embrace of her open arms.

Wow

…just wow.

She's a part of me now, and I finally understand how true love feels.

• • •

The next morning, we both oversleep from the exhaustion of the roller coaster of the day before. Getting up is a rushed affair. She has an important phone conference at nine-thirty, and has to go home to shower and change so I heat up a Pop Tart for her while she pulls on her clothes. She accepts it with an arched brow, but I know she's silently pleased. I mean, who doesn't secretly love Pop Tarts?

When it's time for her to leave I walk her to her car, kiss her goodbye, then hurry back in to jump into the shower and get ready for the day.

Luckily, I'm only a few minutes late. But Joel could yell at me anyway, and it wouldn't matter 'cause I'm on cloud nine. It takes all of my composure not to stand in the middle of the production room and yell out "Brooke loves me!" for all the world to hear.

That afternoon when I bring Brooke her coffee she's on her computer making reservations for Comic Con. Evidently Mojo doesn't like to go, so I'm determined to go with Brooke. She teases me that animators aren't supposed to go on the company dime…as if that could hold me back.

Now that we're in love, it will be the best Comic Con ever. Never in my wildest dreams, did I ever imagine I would walk through those hallowed convention halls with a beauty like Brooke on my arm.

"By the way, if you're planning on dressing up for Comic Con, may I suggest Cat Woman?" I tease.

"You know I dressed up like Wonder Woman at Comic Con once when I was younger."

"You did?" She obviously doesn't understand what that news would do to me, because she looks at me funny when she realizes that my face is flushed and my chest is rising and falling like I just leapt between two tall buildings.

God, I love this woman.

"Can you wear that for me sometime?" I ask, trying to not sound as desperate as I feel.

She looks at me with a twinkle in her eyes. "Sure," she says. "But you have to dress up for me too."

I'm instantly filled with dread at the idea of tights and spandex body suits. "Dress up as who?"

She grins. "I've always had a thing about Indiana Jones."

I breathe a sigh of relief knowing I'm safe from spandex. "Sure," I agree. "How about tomorrow?"

"You're on!"

It occurs to me that I don't have much time to figure out Indiana's costume. Back in my office, I call Billie for a consultation.

"Billie, I need your help. I have to dress up like Indiana Jones for Brooke."

There is a long pause. "Dress up like Indy? Oh, he's the man. Wait, wasn't he getting tied up a lot?"

"I think so," I reply, starting to get nervous.

"That's hot. I like it," she confirms. "So shall I guess that things are on the upswing with Brooke if you've advanced to kinky role playing?"

I suddenly realize that no one in my life knows how things have changed radically over the course of less than twenty-four hours.

"Oh, yes, everything's changed."

"For the good I take it?" she teases.

"So good…Billie, you wouldn't believe how good."

"Glad to hear it…maybe Curtis will finally stop worrying about you."

"He's been worried?" I ask, a lump in my throat.

"I'll say. For a big boy, that guy can get pretty damn emo," she replies laughing. "But enough about Curtis. So what do you need for Indiana?"

"I need one of those safari hats and maybe a whip, and a sheathed knife to hang on my belt…or something to look rugged."

"He doesn't wear a safari hat!" she huffs. "It's a busted Fedora. I have something that will work for that. And of course I have a whip you can borrow, but I need it back by Friday."

I grin into the phone. "And where can I get one of those knives…a sporting goods store?"

"Oh, I've got one of those too."

"You do?" my voice brimming with disbelief.

"Don't ask," she warns me.

"Believe me, I don't want to know," I assure her. Leave it to Billie to be the go-to-gal for all my kinky needs.

Since I'm on a roll, I decide to call Mom and give her an update. "Guess what, Mom?"

"Oh, I like the sound of your voice," she says happily. "Do you have good news for us?"

I pause remembering our last conversation and how she encouraged me. I can't hold back the good news. "Brooke loves me," I state with a full heart.

"Oh my God, wait, wait…let me put your Dad on the phone too!"

I smile as I hear her yelling for Dad to get on the phone.

"Yes?" I hear him say with a concerned tone, as he picks up the line.

"She loves him, Arthur!" Mom says.

"Nathan?" he asks, still not sure what's going on.

"She's not going to marry him, Dad. She loves me. She told me so."

"Oh, that's excellent news. What did I tell you, Son? Logic and statistics don't mean a damn thing when it comes to love. I'm so glad, Nathan. So, how did this Arnauld react?"

"He's on a business trip this week, but before he left she told him she wouldn't marry him. She's going to finalize everything Monday, and then we'll figure things out from there."

"So does she know about Dani and the comic book yet?" Mom asks cautiously.

"Not exactly, we agreed to a week of just being together, and we're going to deal with all the hard stuff next week."

"I see," replies Mom, sounding unsure.

"We're having a week of woo," I explain.

"You followed my advice," Dad says proudly. "Well, as we discussed, historically wooing has always been a favorable way to secure your mate. So what do you have planned for tonight?"

Damn. I've been so swept up with the day that I hadn't thought that far in advance.

"I haven't planned anything yet," I admit nervously. "Everything's been happening so fast. But don't worry; I'll think of something."

There's a pause. "Arthur?" Mom says, "Can we?"

"Yes, Diana. It's perfect…woo-ing with a capital W."

Their shorthand talk always baffles me. "What're you guys talking about?"

"We have tickets for the Hollywood Bowl tonight. I just finished packing our picnic dinner, complete with an excellent bottle of wine. You should take Brooke, Nathan, it's the perfect night for it."

I'd forgotten they always have season tickets with great box seats. The Hollywood Bowl's an experience like none other. "But you guys already had your evening planned," I try to persuade, half-heartedly.

"It's Harry Connick Jr. doing the classics, Nathan. You'd be a fool to pass this up," Mom stresses.

"Wow. That would be super woo-worthy. If you're sure…that'd be amazing."

"We insist," Dad says firmly.

"Thanks. You guys are the best. This really means so much to me."

"We know, Son. Mom and I are behind you two hundred percent. It doesn't take a forensic scientist and inter-personal sociologist to clearly determine that you're meant to be with this girl. We want you to have a stellar time."

Brooke is thrilled when she gets my call.

"I love the Hollywood Bowl…and Harry Connick Jr…wow! You're taking the wooing up a notch."

Win!

"So, let's leave right at six, and I'll follow you home so you can get a jacket and something warmer to wear," I explain.

I splurge on valet parking, and we slowly wind our way up the hillside, surrounded by happy faces and arms laden with food and wine. It's a beautiful clear evening as we settle into our prime box seats facing the famous clamshell shaped theater.

Just the look on Brooke's face when I unpack mom's basket, spreading the cloth over the little fold-down table, makes everything worth it. While I uncork the wine bottle and fill our glasses, Brooke carefully opens each container and fills our plates. We even have cloth napkins and silverware. I'm so happy I can't stop grinning as we eat and sip wine. There are berry tarts for dessert. The sun slowly falls behind the hill and the purple cast of twilight falls over us.

Later as Harry serenades us, Brooke curls up under my arm and I wrap the blanket around us. It feels like he's singing just to us.

Brooke nuzzles my neck then whispers in my ear, "Thank you for tonight, Nathan. I don't know when I've ever been so happy."

"Me too, Brooke," I reply and then gently kiss her, realizing this is one of those moments I'll never forget.

I look up into the night sky, sprinkled with stars and as I hold my girl in my arms, the music surrounds and lifts us up, while Arnold and the weight of the last few weeks falls away. I never would have believed I could feel like this, my heart so full that it's going to spring out of my chest in a big cartoony gesture.

We are in our own world now, my Red Hot and I. The title of the next number sums it all up perfectly…"It Had to Be You."

Animate Me / Chapter Twenty-One / Master of the Woo

"It's my turn now and I've got to make it." ~ Speed Racer[xx]

"You really outdid yourself, you know," Brooke sighs as she curls into me. The alarm clock's gone off but we're doing our best to ignore it.

"Yeah, that was a great evening," I agree. "But I have to tell you, I have a whole support group behind me; Team Woo is leading me to victory."

She laughs. "You're just so damn charming that everyone wants to help you. Who got you those Hollywood Bowl tickets on such short notice anyway?"

"My parents," I admit.

"Awww," she croons. "Remind me to thank them. That was so sweet."

"They really like you," I share, hoping that makes her happy.

"I like them too. I see so much of them in you."

I pull her tighter into my arms and kiss the top of her head. She sighs happily then lifts up to face me. "So don't forget I have a late meeting tonight."

"That's right," I say. "How late do you think it will go?"

"I'm not sure, I'll call as soon as I get home."

"Okay. What would you like for breakfast?"

"Can we have Pop-Tarts?"

"Strawberry or brown sugar?

She laughs. "Both!"

On the way to work, my cell phone rings.

"Hey Dad. Thanks again for last night. It was completely perfect."

"I'm glad, Son. We were happy to do it, and the reward is hearing it achieved the desired effect."

"I'll say," I agree, remembering not just the concert, but also the rest of our night with the physical manifestation of the woo. Before my thoughts get too X-rated though, I try to focus back on the conversation.

"By the way, I just finished going over your contract for your comic books. Nathan…wait a minute, are you driving? Is your headset on? Because the statistics of accidents due to cell phone usage while conducting a vehicle are staggering."

"Headset's on, Dad."

"Excellent," he says sounding relieved. "So regarding the contract, I'm not concerned about the points you asked me about…pretty much standard legal-speak. This looks pretty solid to me."

I breathe a sigh of relief. Knowing Dad is good with the Sharper Edge Comics deal means a lot to me.

"I do have one question though, Son. How are you going to manage these obligations for Sharper Edge, do your job at Sketch Republic justice, and have a romantic relationship all at the same time? Don't get me wrong—you're highly capable. But men traditionally are not multi-taskers. Evolution really left that in the hands of the female of the species, and their ability to excel at it convinces me that they'll eventually rule the world."

"I can multi-task," I insist, imagining myself stepping out of a phone booth and ripping my shirt open to reveal the big Super N on my chest.

"You're already under the hypnotic spell, I see. With new love, when the surge of hormones hits you, you're so euphorically distracted and blissfully unaware of the world that your house could burn down around you and you wouldn't notice."

I'm so flustered that I swerve the car a bit before I regain my composure. "Dad, can we please not discuss hormones hitting me?"

"But do you understand the ramifications of my point? Sharper Edge has very high expectations for you and your comics."

"Of course. Look, my plan is to give it my all and go without sleep for a while until B-Girl gets established and hopefully succeeds. Then I will quit my day job and devote myself to Brooke and B-Girl full time."

"Quit your job?" he asks thoughtfully. I can tell he's making complex financial calculations in his mind.

"Hell, Arnold may fire me before then, and I'll get unemployment. That could work to my benefit."

"Being fired is never a desirable option, Nathan. Your industry is small. The stigma could follow you if you wish to re-establish yourself in animation."

I start tensing up. Thinking about fucking Mojo just does that to me. It's a relief as I pull into the parking structure not to see his car and be reminded I won't see his car or his hairy ass all week.

"Dad, I just arrived at work…gotta go."

Dad is patient with the brush-off. He knows I can only take so much advice at once. "Okay, Nathan, I'll call Walter and let him know you'll sign the documents and get them out today. Congratulations, Son. I'm proud of you."

I feel a thrill realizing that this is good to go. I'm going to sign that darn contract as soon as I get in my cube, and be one step closer to my dreams coming true.

• • •

At lunchtime Dani agrees to order me a sandwich so I can drop the contracts at Fed Ex, before meeting up with them to eat.

"So it's a done deal?" She nods at the contracts on my desk as I pull money out of my wallet and hand it to her.

"Yeah, I still can't believe it," I admit, shaking my head. "Everything's working out so much better than I could've hoped."

"Everything?" she asks, her eyebrows raised.

"Can you and Nick keep a secret?" I know I can trust them, and I feel like I owe them the truth after what we all went through together.

"It's on with Brooke?" she asks, smiling and looking hopeful.

"It's so on." I grin like a fool.

"I knew it, I knew it!" She bounces on her heels excitedly. "Nick owes me twenty! I could tell—your whole vibe was so different yesterday, even if you were trying to hide it. We have to go out for drinks soon so we can hear the whole story."

"Okay," I agree. "But meanwhile we have to be on the down low until the Monkey gets back and she tells him," I explain.

"Well that'll be an interesting day at Sketch Republic," Dani states. "But fuck him. He's getting just what he deserves. And even if he's an ass and gets nasty, you have something else already lined up."

I nod, because it feels good to hear Dani so confident about my future.

That afternoon Joel walks in on me as I'm doing a drawing on a Starbucks cup. He doesn't say anything—just rolls his eyes, and walks out of the cube. I vow to stay later tonight and get some extra work done to show my thanks.

I'm happily buzzing as I sketch out Brooke posed as a modern day Juliet on her home's balcony. Of course, I'm below…one hand reaching up to her, the other placed solemnly over my heart.

I finish it up with a few details and then hold it up proudly and shake my head. My Dad's right, the hormones have rendered me insane…but damn, am I a happy fool.

Morgan gives me a look I've never seen before. She seems genuinely impressed with my apparent progress. She gives me a thumbs-up as I pass her on the way into Brooke's office.

But when I step inside my girl looks tense as she tersely says something into the receiver, then slams the phone back down in its cradle. She leans over the desk and drops her face in her hands. It's obvious she hasn't seen me yet.

"Brooke?" I ask, tentatively.

She looks up startled. "Hi," she replies weakly. "How long have you been standing there?"

"I just got here. Who was that you were talking to?"

She gives me a pained look. "It was Arnauld."

Anger fires up in me. "What did he want? I thought he was supposed to leave you alone and give you space for a week."

"Exactly," she agrees. "He was interrogating me as to what I've been doing, who I've been with…"

"Did you tell him?" I ask, twisting my fingers together.

"No, of course not…so he threatened to come back early."

My stomach drops. "But this is our time," I say, trying to hold back my frustration.

"I told him that if he came back now, I wouldn't even talk to him, so he may as well stay and take care of business. I think he got the message loud and clear."

"So he isn't coming back early?"

"I really don't think so. He still has a lot of work to take care of. And I swear, I'm not going to let him mess up my woo week, damn it."

I stare at her all flushed and wild looking. I can't help it; I want her. I'm getting more distracted by the moment.

"Have I ever told you how incredibly sexy you are when you get mad?" I ask.

"Really?" She looks at me and almost smiles, and then finally notices that I'm holding coffee. I feel her mood instantly shift.

"Is that for me, Mr. Woo?"

"Yes, it's especially for you, Ms. Woo."

Brooke has a coy smile as she approaches me. She reaches for the cup anxiously as if she knows this is going to be a special one. I proudly hand it to her. I'm feeling good…confident… *like I'm the master of the woo.*

She oohs and runs her finger gently over the image as if she's holding a masterpiece.

"Nathan," she whispers.

I smile at her, basking in my masterfulness.

"This is my new favorite cup!"

"I puff my chest out proudly. But when I see her eyes have glazed over, I tone it down. "Remember, I told you how much you inspire me."

She suddenly turns and picks up her phone and taps a button.

"Morgan, I need to have a private conversation. Can you make sure that I'm not interrupted?" She then walks over and shuts the door quietly, carefully setting the lock.

Oh my

As she turns, she gives me the look, and it only gets more heated as she walks back into my open arms. Her lips find mine, in an insistent, insatiable way. My arms wrap around her tightly as one of her hands works its way through my hair.

"Whoa, Brooke," I gasp when we finally part. She pulls off my heavy black glasses and sets them down with such energy that they skid across her desk.

"Nathan…how will I get through today without having you?" she asks, pressing into me.

I can tell that the frustration over Arnold's call has made her reckless. She seems to need my full attention right now.

I press my hands over her and pull her against me so she understands how much I want her too. "I'll be thinking of you like this all day," I whisper, my lips on her neck, my hand edging up towards her breast. "But we'll be together later tonight and we can have fun then."

"That's too far away," she sighs. "I can't wait that long."

"Brooke, what are you doing?" I ask, as she starts to undo my belt buckle. *Holy shit.* I remember her office-sex fantasy. It's looking like her fantasy could be mine too. "In here?" I ask nervously, gesturing to her office door and the walls with offices on either side. "There are people working all around us."

"Is this too much?" she asks, when we stop to catch our breath. "I know I can get loud."

"Well, it's obvious how much I want you but are you sure? The gossips around here would love nothing more than having something to talk about. I don't care about me, but I don't want to put you through that."

She holds onto me and sighs. "Oh, you're right…that would be really bad."

I nod my head and kiss her forehead. She knows I'd do it if I could figure out how we could get away with it. I'd make love to her anywhere, anytime.

That's how much I want this girl.

Amped up and inspired, I head right over to the Outer Limits when I get off work. I don't see Billie at first, so I get lost in the graphic novels section of the store.

Moments later I feel a tap on my shoulder. "Hey Nathan!"

I didn't even hear her approach. "Hi Billie."

"I have your whip and other shit in the back. Hold on a sec and I'll get it."

As she walks away I watch the tattoos flex on her calves as she moves. I marvel at the idea that Billie is practically a sister now. Who would have thought?

She returns, handing me a black shopping bag full of my props. The brim of Indy's fedora peeks out of the top of the paper sack.

"Hey, thanks so much, Billie. I really appreciate your help."

She shrugs. "Sure no problem."

She walks over to the new releases part of the store. "Hey, we got your new book in today. I loved the new monkey-man villain. Is that who I think it is?"

I grin and nod.

"You play a dangerous game, my friend."

"But that's the last book," I warn her.

"What do you mean the last?" she demands, her eyes squinting as if she's angry.

"Well, the last *I'm* publishing. I signed my deal with Sharper Edge Comics today. They'll be publishing the next one in about eight weeks. I'm submitting the pages tomorrow, and they really work fast."

She throws her arms around me and hugs me tightly, before stepping back and placing her hands on her hips.

"That's so awesome, Nathan! Mother fucking Sharper Edge, Dude! This is going to be huge...I just know it."

"Thanks, Billie. I don't know about that, but I'm never gonna forget that you supported me and B-Girl from the very start."

"Awww. Hey, I know! Let's have a big party here when the first book launches. What do you think?"

"That'd be great," I assure her. I think about Brooke and imagine that everything will be settled then and she will be my special guest that night...my real life B-Girl.

• • •

At seven Brooke texts to ask if I mind her having a drink with her girlfriend Jenn, who was at the meeting. They rarely get to see each other. I assure her to take her time and have fun. It's almost nine when she calls me from her place.

"Hello, Nathan." She sounds very flirty and I like it.

"Hi Brooke, are you home safe?"

"Yes, I am and guess what?"

"What?" I ask.

"I told my friend Jenn all about us. I think I bored her. I couldn't stop talking about you."

"What'd you tell her?"

"That you're the kindest, sexiest, most talented, loving, brilliant man I've ever known. I also told her you're an awesome kisser."

"Just kisser?" I ask, teasing her, since I'm already flying high with the "sexiest" comment.

"Alright, I didn't want to be crude, but after a few lemon martinis I told her you were the best lover I'd ever had, and that I'm madly in love with you."

Best lover ever? I can't help being skeptical, but I sense she means it. Maybe it's because she's never made love to someone who adores her as completely as I do.

"Wow, you should have drinks with her more often if these are the reports I get back. What did she say to all of that?"

"She was rather shocked. She never thought I would fall for someone this hard."

"Not even when you were with Arnold?"

"Who's Arnold?" she asks playfully.

I know she's kidding, but she has no idea what those two words do to me.

Yes, who the hell is Arnold?

It reminds me of that Looney Tunes cartoon where Daffy is Duck Twacy and Eraser man tries to "rub him out" by erasing the crazy duck away completely. I'm going to get Brooke a big-ass eraser and together we will rub Arnold right off our page. With one careless sweep of my hand, his little, pathetic eraser crumbs will tumble to the floor.

"So did you really tell her that I was the best lover you've ever had?"

"Yes, handsome. And I meant it."

I swallow and take a deep breath.

"Brooke, I just want you to know that I'm really wanting to drive you wild right now."

There's a long pause.

"How wild?" she finally asks, all breathy and hot.

"Really, really wild. I know it's late, but can I come over?" I try not to not be too pushy, but there's definitely urgency in my voice.

"How fast can you get here?" she asks. She sounds urgent too.

"Really, really fast,"

"Well then…Go Speed Racer, go," she chants into the phone.

The spirit of Speed Racer's with me as I fire up my Mini-Cooper, Mach 5. I race through the streets of Burbank knowing the sooner I get to her place, the sooner she'll be in my arms. Tonight I will make wild Speed Racer love to my Trixie-Brooke. I sing the theme song at the top of my lungs, all the way back up that hill.

"Go Speed Racer, go Speed Racer…go Speed Racer, goooooooo!"

Animate Me / Chapter Twenty-Two / Indy Gets His Princess

"The choice to lead an ordinary life is no longer an option." ~ Kevin Parker[xxi]

"When I was a kid I saved my allowance to buy a vintage Speed Racer slot car set." I grin as she takes a sip from her Speed Racer-styled Starbucks cup. In the drawing she's driving his Mach 5 racing car and has left tracks where she's raced round and round her cup.

"You're such a guy, Nathan." She laughs.

"And aren't you glad," I tease back.

"Are you still coming over tonight, Indiana Jones? I noticed you haven't shaved."

"Hell yes," I reply, thinking about my costume and props laid out on my bed.

"And you're sure you want to see Wonder Woman tonight?" she asks.

"Brooke…" I state categorically. "Do you really think I would pass up a chance to see you dressed as Wonder Woman?" I fold my arms over my chest, and shake my head in mock disbelief. "Really woman, I thought you knew me better than that."

She laughs and throws her hands up in surrender. "Okay, okay... the little blue panties and red bustier will make an appearance tonight exclusively for you...seven o'clock sharp!"

As I head out of Brooke's office Morgan calls me over.

"Nathan?"

I stop in my tracks, and turn back towards her desk.

"Yeah, Morgan?" I ask, smiling. But I'm always smiling when I've just seen Brooke.

"I don't know what in the hell you've been doing...sprinkling fairy dust in her macchiatos, or whatever...but do me a favor?"

"Anything...just name it."

"Please, just keep it up. I've never, ever, seen her so happy."

I grin widely. "Really?" I can't help asking.

"Yes, really," she offers, smiling.

"It's a deal," I agree.

Her expression becomes serious. "You know you'll need to be careful when Arnauld comes back. So if I can help in any way...well, I just want you to know that I've got your back."

Even though she bursts my bubble, reminding me about the monkey's highly anticipated return, I'm very touched by her sentiment.

"Thanks, Morgan. That means a lot to me."

She nods.

"And if I can ever do something for you, will you let me know?"

"Sure thing. But no bullshit...Brooke's the best boss I've ever had by far, so it makes me happy to see her this happy."

• • •

After work I head home and get my costume together for my big date with Wonder Woman. When I finally pull the hat on my head and look in the mirror, I have to smile and admit to myself that I look pretty good. The look is right, but that's only part of the effect. So all the way up the winding road to Brooke's I give myself a pep talk to get in character for my girl.

I am the man...I am Indiana Jones!

The sun is low in the sky as I stride up to my Wonder Woman waiting in her home's open doorway. It takes my complete focus to maintain my Indiana Jones bravado when all I want to do is stop and bask in her super hero glory. From her majestic gold headpiece, all the way down to her sexy boots, she is everything I'd hoped for and more. With great concentration I manage to carry off my swagger as I move close to her.

"Hey, Wonder Woman," I say in a low voice, tipping my hat. "You're looking mighty fine."

Wow, the way she's looking at me…it's kind of wild…

"Indiana," she says in a low seductive voice. "I always knew someday you'd come walking back through my door." She reaches out and runs her fingers along the edge of my shirt. "You have no idea how long I've waited for you."

Hot damn.

There's so much pent up desire fueled by our private fantasies that between the flush moving across her chest, and the way she's gazing at me, I can tell she's excited already. I sweep her into my arms and kiss her with everything I've got. My hat falls off my head and tumbles to the ground. Moments later, we're grinding together against her door jamb, not even caring who might pass by and see us. At this point I just want to make love to her until she sees stars.

When I grope her breast over her costume, and bite her neck, she gasps, "Let's go inside." I kick the door wide open and carry her towards her living room. I feel this unbelievable surge of adrenaline…*I am Indiana Jones, sweaty and rugged, ready to take my woman!*

I stop in the hallway and press her against the wall so I can kiss her again. She wraps her legs around my waist, locking them at the ankles and pulling me close.

Damn, we really should've done this dress-up stuff sooner.

I take her cuffed wrists and secure them high above her head, pressing them firmly against the cool plaster. Her abundant cleavage is spilling out the top of her costume. With one quick yank downwards, I set her breasts free.

She's panting as she gives me a wild look. She's unbelievably sexy, her desire wrapping around us like a cape. Her naked breasts are so beautiful. I tease her nipple with my tongue as she watches.

"Are you trying to overpower me?" she asks, her voice heavy with want. Her wrists are fighting against my grasp.

"I already have," I reply with confidence. Moments later, my eyes quickly scan her living room as I gruffly pull her toward the couch.

"Are you going to take me, Indy?"

I give her a dark look. "Yes, Wonder Woman...Diana...Princess of Themyscira...I'm going to take you. I'm going to take you hard."

Whoa, that was good.

Despite the fact that I'm dragging her into the living room, I can tell she's impressed I've done my Wonder Woman homework. My rewards are the lusty moans she cries out as I wrap my arms around her, and pull her back so she's pressed against my front.

"Do you feel what you do to me?" I chant in her ear as my arousal pushes against her round bottom, tightly bound in little blue panties sprinkled with stars.

"Jesus, Nathan...I mean Indy," she groans. "Yes, I can feel everything."

That's all I need to hear. My trembling hands almost give me away, as I slide my fingers inside her waistband and pull her blue panties all the way down. She quickly steps out of them, and they fall to the floor. Between her red corset and boots, and the way her naked bottom sways before me, I'm barely holding on.

With one hand I fold her down over the edge of the couch, with the other, I slowly start to yank apart my belt strap and buckle.

I pull off my belt accessorized with the whip and knife and drape it across the chair to my right. When I place my hands back on her hips, I feel her softness as she arches her back, lifting her ass towards me.

"What are you thinking about?" I ask, my hands stroking her silky skin.

"I'm thinking about how good it's going to feel when you take me, Indy."

I swallow hard, trying to calm myself. This is even better than I'd imagined.

"But first I have to know," she asks demurely. "What were you going to do with that whip?" She taunts me with a look before glancing over at the belt.

Brooke, oh Brooke…does my girl want to get naughty?

I remember my scouting days and get an idea. I reach over and separate the whip from the belt.

"You want it rough, don't you?" I demand.

"So rough." She moans wantonly, but then pauses, as if in thought. "Well, sorta rough," she offers, gently correcting herself as she looks at me nervously.

I grin back at her before getting stern again…*as if I could ever hurt this girl.*

"Well, then you need to remember that I'm in control," I demand in my best Indiana Jones voice. "Stop squirming and put your hands forward."

"Have you been talking to Billie?" she asks, sounding concerned.

"Don't worry, Princess, this isn't going to be like that."

I step around her, pull her arms forward, then carefully wind the narrow end of the whip around her wrists. It only takes seconds for me to secure her with a two-half-hitch knot I learned in Boy Scouts.

I would feel creepy about this if Brooke didn't look so thrilled. She seems less nervous now.

"So now that you've got me just how you want me, what are you going to do with me?" She wiggles her butt a little side to side. "Are you aroused, Mr. Jones?"

"Hell yes, woman. If I were the Tasmanian Devil, I would've ravaged you by now."

She looks back, arches her brow and shakes her head at my cartoon slip.

"But I'm not Taz, I'm Indiana Jones!" I exclaim, correcting my serious lack of continuity.

She brings us back into focus with a super hero command. "Show me how aroused you are." I notice her furrowed brow; she's looking like she means business.

I undo the zipper, push my pants and boxers open, and free myself. Her eyes grow wide as she watches. I give her one of those Harrison

Ford smirks as I grab my hard-on, "This is what you do to me Wonder Woman."

"Oh, God," she moans. "I want it."

"And you're going to get it," I assure her as I step behind her delicious *derrière*—a bottom worthy of a super hero. I slide my boot in between hers and ease her legs further apart.

As I push into her, my eyes roll back in my head. Who needs the Lost Ark when you've got Wonder Woman bent over and begging, her blue spangled panties wantonly discarded on the floor?

What would the people who know us think? Wonder Woman, Princess Diana of Themyscira is mating with Indiana Jones of Princeton, New Jersey…We are sexually and spiritually united in something akin to a bad fan-fiction crossover in our very own X-rated production.

• • •

When we finally conclude our most daring lovemaking yet, I pull her into my arms. We settle down, and although our costumes are askew, we're completely satisfied.

We decide to get into her Jacuzzi tub. She pours some stuff in the water, making the bathroom smell like the Sherwood Forest. I recline against the back of the tub, while she settles in between my legs leaning into me, as the Jacuzzi bubbles move around us.

"Oh, that was so damn good," she says, letting out a satisfied sigh.

"Mmmm," I agree. "You sure inspired me in all your Wonder Woman glory."

"And you, my God…I think you should dress up like Indy, at least once a week."

I smile and kiss her behind her ear, until an unsettling feeling starts creeping up on me. "Hey Brooke?"

"Yes?" she asks, pulling my arms tighter over her.

"You know how you encouraged me to change my look: new glasses, haircut, clothes? And now, with this dress up stuff, I have to wonder. Do you think that me, just plain old me, is going to be enough to keep you interested?"

She pushes away and turns around to face me. I can see she's stunned by my question.

"It's just that I'm not that exciting," I continue. "What happens if you start getting bored with me?"

"Bored? First of all, let me make myself perfectly clear," she states firmly. "I know you don't realize it Nathan, but you're the least boring person I know. I always have the best time with you. Then to top it off you're so gorgeous just looking at you gets me going. And in some ways the fact that you are clueless about it is so endearing, in another it's maddening. And if that isn't enough, there's your body."

"What about my body?"

"Hello? Your body is so damn hot, all lean and long, but strong and defined. Don't you know what you do to me? Jeez."

I smile as she runs her hands over my shoulders and across my chest.

"Now, as a lover you are everything I could want. Let's not even discuss how incredible you make me feel."

I grin widely. "Oh, yes, let's discuss that."

"You're the best lover I've ever had because of how passionate and enthusiastic you are. And how long have you been at it? My God, I can only imagine what the future holds."

"Really? The best?"

"Yes, the very best. You make me feel like a goddess, like I'm the most beautiful woman in the world."

"Well you are," I point out. I'm grinning like an idiot now. My happiness can't be contained.

She slides closer to me in the tub and rests her hands on my chest, right over my heart. "But most of all Nathan, most of all…it's your heart that has captured me body and soul. I didn't even think anyone as strong yet tender, tenacious yet sensitive; someone with such an open, warm heart even existed. But here you are and you're mine."

"Yes, I am…and you're mine too," I say, pulling her closer.

She leans forward and presses her forehead against mine. "I am. So does that answer your question?" she asks, as she gently kisses across my eyebrow and down my cheek.

When our lips meet, it's sweet and slow. "Completely," I say grinning.

• • •

The next morning we watch Hong Kong Phooey on Boomerang until I drag myself out of bed. "I've got to get home and get ready for work." I grin and lean over to kiss her.

She gets out of bed too, pulls on a robe and follows me to her front door.

"So I'll see you later," I whisper into her ear, as I hold her tightly in my arms. "I love you."

She grins and kisses me before whispering back, "I love you too."

Back home, I'm about to leave for work, when a feeling comes over me. Something about remembering Brooke as Wonder Woman last night makes me crave a moment with B-Girl. So I go into my studio office and pull out a box that holds final printed copies of the entire series to date. I spread the various issues over my animation table and proudly examine the covers with the fresh eye of time passing and a new perspective.

I pull the first book closer and slowly open it and begin turning the pages. As I examine each layout, I wonder how it would look to Brooke. Would she be flattered to see her persona as a beautiful heroine, a woman capable of changing people's lives and possibly even saving the world?

I smile at this early issue, conceived long before I knew Brooke intimately. Whatever I could learn about Brooke back then, I would weave into the story. Sometimes it was something as specific as a particular outfit I had seen her in at work. Other times it was an expression or mannerism that I observed from afar. It's interesting to me now that I wrote stories with B-Girl musing about people from the dark side, and how her mission in life was to eradicate those whose power grew by belittling others. Some of it feels prophetic now…as if I understood intuitively how Arnold would change and become a blighted shadow across her sunny path.

I remember at the beginning agonizing over her super hero costume design. It needed to showcase her curvy, glorious figure, without looking expected. I wanted the "B" to be cleverly identified as part of her look… so I created a jewel-encrusted "B" pendant that rested gently around her neck. Half rap-star inspired, half shaman-esque, the "B" of the pendant would shimmer when she needed to summon her powers.

If life were a comic book, I could construct a "B" pendant for my girl. Whenever we parted, it would protect and preserve her from the Mojos of the world, until she was back in my arms again.

I glance at my watch, then gently fold the books closed and return them to their box. As I slide the lid back on I realize that next week we will face our final test…Brooke will finally meet B-Girl.

Will she be flattered and moved to know how long she's owned my heart, or will she resent the continual cover-ups and evasion about my big project, and lose her ability to trust me? In the end I believe Brooke will understand why I kept B-Girl a secret and that she will see the character as a reflection of my love for her. Brooke has a big heart and she loves me. I'm certain she will love B-Girl too.

So far our week of Woo has been perfect—a dreamy concoction of love and passion. So as I close my studio door and head towards my car, I'm optimistic. I should send Wayne Dyer a fruit basket or something. His carefully constructed manifesto of self-help has paid off for me in spades. That was the best forty bucks I've ever spent.

Yes, I am a man with a plan, and it looks like all of my dreams are coming true.

Animate Me / Chapter Twenty-Three / Animal Style

"Welcome to downtown Coolsville! Population: us." ~ Hogarth[xxii]

I lovingly push my pencil over the paper, the lead tip stroking her hips and the sides of her thighs. Each line grows darker and more refined as my Wonder Woman comes to life. As my pencil trails around her breasts I remember last night and the way she looked at me as we made love. I shift in my chair and remind myself that this isn't the time or place to get worked up over those memories. Refocusing, I move up to her lovely face where I've already sketched in her features. As I finish up the drawing her lips curl up and her eyes shine as she gazes at me. My fingers gently lift and caress the edge of the paper as I smile back. I gently rub the eraser around the edges of the curves, removing the rough lines.

Good God, it's like I'm making love to a drawing.

I'm so enchanted with her image I don't even hear anyone approach.

"So when did Wonder Woman join the Beaver Patrol?"

I jerk up startled and put my hand over my drawing in a futile attempt to cover the evidence.

"Oh, h-hey Joel," I stutter. *Shit!* "Sorry about that. I'll get back to work. I was just taking a break. I blasted through my first scene this morning."

"Interesting way to spend your breaks, Evans," he says with a smirk. "But actually I came over here to get you. I wanted to talk for a minute." He points down the hall. "Why don't we head into my office?"

I look up surprised, and study his expression trying to figure out what's going on. Before I follow him down the hall, I crack open my bottom drawer to slip my drawing inside. *Have I done something wrong?* I know this isn't about my Wonder Woman drawing since he came to get me before he'd seen it.

His office is smaller than Brooke's but it's still cool. There are storyboards everywhere, and a complete set of maquette sculptures from the show. Joel somehow convinced the budgeting drone to pay to have sculptures made of each character, so the animators could study how the figures looked dimensionally from every angle.

He indicates for me to sit in one of the chairs near the storyboards, and he joins me.

"So what's up?"

"I want to show you something. It's a new idea I'm getting ready to pitch, and I'd like you to be involved."

He hands me a drawing of a young kid. Other than the fact that he's holding a skateboard and looks kind of cool, he's unremarkable. I notice though, that physically he looks a lot like I did when I was young: long and lanky and messy brown hair.

"Who's this?" I ask, studying the character's features carefully.

"He's my main character. His name is Robbie."

I hand the drawing back, baffled as how he expects to center a show around such a normal looking kid.

"Does his skateboard have rockets on it or something? I mean what's unique about him?"

"No, that's the point," says Joel, grinning. "He's a regular kid." Joel leans back and smiles before dramatically reaching over for another drawing.

I appreciate the build…Joel is a master at pitching, and I always learn something watching him.

"And here's his family. The show is aptly called, *Robbie from Romania*."

The elaborately gothic drawing is a cross between *Nightmare Before Christmas* and that show from the late Sixties, *the Addams Family*. When I study the drawing carefully, I notice all the characters have fangs.

"Romania? Oh I get it. It's a family of…"

"Vampires," Joel says excitedly. "Exactly! And he's like the niece Marilyn from that old classic show The *Munsters*. Robbie seems like a regular kid, leading what looks like a normal life…until he gets home to his family, a house full of eccentric vampires."

"Did you get lost in T.V. land again?" I tease him, smiling. "And you're so trendy with the vampire stuff, Joel."

271

"Okay, I admit it," he says with a sour face. "Management has been pushing me to do a vampire show, everyone wants fucking vampires. But I really like this. Think of all the stuff we could do."

We? It sounds like I'm leaving the Beaver Patrol. "What do you mean, we?"

"I really think you're ready for a bigger challenge, Nathan. I'd like you to help me produce the show."

"Produce?" I ask, flabbergasted.

"Yeah, you'd be more involved in the story and character development, possibly even direct a couple of episodes. You'd get your own office and more money. How does that sound?"

Office? With a locking door? I'm liking that idea. Wow!

Of course, my Dad's words about "how I'm going to manage everything" ring in my head. Why is life always like this? Nothing, nothing, nothing…and then everything happens at once. I pause another moment considering what I should say.

"That's such a cool offer, Joel. But I need to let you know that my comic got picked up by Sharper Edge and that's going to keep me really busy in my off hours. I just worry that I may not be able to manage everything."

"Yeah, I heard about your books. Congratulations by the way. It's great and all, but seriously dude, I still think you need to remember that comic books are dying a slow death. I really wouldn't put all my eggs in that basket. I mean, look at Comic Con…there are only a few aisles left of comic book vendors. People just don't read anymore."

But I still read comics…

Joel easily stirs up the apprehension I've had all along and he knows it. I nod my head. "I know. I'm not expecting too much from it."

"That's smart, then no matter what happens you'll be happy," he says patting me on the shoulder. "And you still love working in animation, right?"

"Absolutely," I say deciding on my strategy. "I'd like to work on this idea with you."

"Great, I'll have Anna set up a meeting next week to start planning, and I'll let HR know too so they can work out all the gory details."

On my way out I notice a framed picture of the girl he brought to the party, between the stacks of books all over his desk. "Hey, how's it going with…was it Laurie?"

"Actually, Laura." He grins happily. "It's going great. I'm crazy about her." He studies me for a moment. "You know we've got to find you a girl, Evans. It's been far too long."

My eye starts to twitch, and I nod nervously and shrug my shoulders, figuring it's safest not to say anything. As I silently head back to my cube, I feel great frustration not to be able to tell others about my relationship with Brooke yet. I want the whole world to know that she's my girl.

• • •

Kevin offers to drive a group of us to Sharkey's for lunch. As we approach the open elevator to head down, I see Brooke's already in the elevator having an intense conversation with a man I've never seen before. As soon as she sees our group, she turns towards us. When our eyes meet, she smiles sweetly.

"Hey guys," she says. "This is the creator of *Danny Deletes*. I'd like you to meet Lazlo."

Lazlo turns to face us with a wary look. He looks rugged, like he lumbers timber wherever the hell he lives, when he isn't drawing a little boy computer genius, that is. He reacts by stepping closer to Brooke, and I don't like it…not one bit. He turns back to her and whispers something in her ear before any of us can introduce ourselves.

The ass is whispering to my woman. I grit my teeth so hard I'm surprised they don't crumble in my mouth. Kevin looks at me and rolls his eyes before taking another sideways glance at them.

Brooke takes a step away from Lazlo and addresses us again. "So where are you guys headed to?" She asks brightly.

"Sharkeys," Andy replies happily. Of course the rotund man-boy is blissfully happy. As long as he's eating fast food or playing with his life size doll, he's perfectly content.

"Do you want to join us?" I ask my girl, looking directly into her eyes. Of course, I mean just Brooke, but I know I can't really clarify that at this moment.

The mute lumberjack is shaking his head vehemently.

"No, we're meeting the producers at Prosecco's," Brooke quickly responds. "But you guys have a great time."

I clench my hands into fists as I imagine him at a fancy lunch with Brooke. He probably takes a handful of toothpicks to chew on when he leaves the restaurant.

When we get to the lobby, we part ways. But right before we pass through the door Brooke looks back at me and winks. Of course the man-boy, Andy, notices and almost squeals as he turns to me.

"Dude, did you see that? She winked at you! I'd tap that hard if I were you."

"Shut up, Andy," I growl.

But despite his gross outburst, I must admit Brooke's wink did me a world of good. I know she did it to reassure me, not caring who else would see. I carry that wink with me well into the afternoon.

Just after four I call her office directly to tell her that I'll be late getting coffee since I was finishing up a scene on deadline.

"Are you done with Mr. Personality yet?" I ask, immediately second-guessing the wisdom of my nasty tone.

There's a long pause.

"Mr. Personality? What exactly are you alluding to, Mr. Evans? You weren't impressed with Lazlo?"

"Not exactly," I admit.

"Aww, he's not so bad. I actually really like Lazlo, except that he eats with his mouth open, and he's a breather."

"A breather?" I ask, getting more agitated by the moment. What the hell does that mean? Was he breathing on my Brooke?

"You know those pug dogs with the squishy faces? He wheezes like one of those."

"Did he breathe on you?" I can't help but ask.

"What?" she questions, sounding baffled. "What do you mean, did he breathe on me?"

"Never mind," I huff, feeling very discouraged.

"Are we jealous? Is that what this is about? Because you can't possibly be jealous of Lazlo?"

"Why can't I? Isn't being jealous and over-protective one of my jobs... being your boyfriend and all?"

There's another pause.

"Boyfriend?"

"Yes," I say boldly. "That only makes sense since you're my girlfriend."

"Girlfriend?" she repeats.

I'm not sure if we're getting anywhere here.

"And that also makes you mine, not the breather's," I clarify.

"Oh, really?"

"Yes," I reply without hesitation.

"For the record, I think it's sexy, Nathan, when you go all possessive and dominant on me like this."

"Dominant?" I ask, my mind reeling with images. Maybe she's trying to tell me something. *What does dominant mean to her?*

She seems to sense my anxiety. "Don't worry, I'm not talking about that kind of dominant, where you have to tie me up and throttle me. Sometimes it's just about being direct and demanding what you want. You know, like Indiana Jones."

"Oh, I see," I say, even though I don't really understand the practical applications of that yet.

"It's like you pushing me down to my knees and telling me to take you in my mouth, because you need that from me."

I pull the phone away from my ear and examine it like it's faulty. Did she just say that on the work line?

"Geez, Brooke. I'm not sure I could do that. Push you to your knees? That sounds inappropriate, like something that I'd never do."

"But could you say, 'I want your mouth on me,' if you desired that?"

I know I'm turning bright red; if anyone walks by my cube now they'll think I've got a sunburn.

"Well, I always desire that, but honestly, I'd be too embarrassed to ask you like that."

"I see. But don't you think it's okay if your woman wants you to say it? If she wants to do that for you?"

"Is that what you want?" I ask, nervously.

"Yes, definitely it's what I want, and what I need. Actually, I want it now. I'm all flustered and hot just thinking of being on my knees for you."

"Oh, good God, Brooke…"

"I know…I'm naughty. See, it reminds me of when you were Indy and how commanding you were."

"But we're leaving in an hour?" I say quite unconvincingly, more like a question.

"Oh, that will be more than enough time. Say it Nathan; I want to hear you ask for it."

"Really? Now?"

"Yes, now. Come on…I know you can do it," she encourages.

I stand up and look over the top of my cube. Andy has his ear buds in and appears to be rocking out to one of his metal bands as he works. I sit back down in my chair, and cup my hand over the speaker part of the phone. I take a deep breath and speak in a low, firm voice.

"I want your mouth on me, Brooke." My heart's pounding. This is crazy shit…but I'm definitely getting off on it.

There is a long pause where all I can hear is her breathing, and I imagine I see the wheels turning in her head. She sounds breathy when she replies. "Listen, take the elevator up to the nineteenth floor. When you get off make a right and walk to the end of the hallway where you'll find a conference room. I'll meet you there in five minutes."

Just then, Kevin steps into my cube and firmly motions that he has to talk to me.

"Ugh, hold on," I say to Brooke.

"What's up?" I ask Kevin, relieved that he doesn't seem to notice how flustered I am.

He looks irritated. "You're late for the production calendar meeting." He points to the production room down the hall.

"Do we have a meeting scheduled? I didn't hear about it."

He nods.

Shit, I must be losing it…now I'm forgetting meetings.

I hear Brooke sigh into the phone.

But I know my priorities. "Hey Kevin, can you take notes for me. I have an important issue with…" My mind reels. "…with my insurance and HR needs to talk to me right now."

"Yes, it's a very important issue" Brooke echoes in the phone. "….a critical meeting. Don't be late, Mr. Evans."

Kevin nods, and walks off.

"I'm on my way," I assure her.

My pulse speeds up as I wander down the abandoned hallway. I think these offices were used recently when we had two other shows in production. Although our posters still hang on the walls, now this place is a ghost town.

But when I peek my head in the last room, I see Brooke standing in front of the big picture window, looking out over the view. "Brooke," I call out just loud enough for her to hear. It's weird to be in this huge conference room, especially since I know what kind of meeting this is going to be. I'm fully aroused in anticipation.

She turns and points to the chair at the head of the table. "Why don't you have a seat?"

I step closer, watching her eyes as they move over me. At this point, my excitement's quite evident, and although she doesn't say anything, her eyes do widen at the sight of me.

As I approach the chair, she slowly passes me and closes the door, then turns the lock. The clicking sound when the lock settles makes my heart skip. I settle into the chair and wait. Every hair on my body is standing on end.

She strolls back very slowly, considering me. She steps close enough to almost graze my knee, then leans back, her ass on the edge of the table. She folds her arms and gives me a business-y look that confuses me.

"Is that look on your face burning desire or are you still agitated about my meeting with Lazlo?"

"Maybe some of both," I admit.

"I want to ask you about your reaction to him again. I wasn't flirting with Lazlo. It was business. So why were you jealous?" she asks.

"Are you trying to provoke me?" Her demeanor reminds me of a kitty batting around a mouse with her paws before she pounces.

"No, I really want to understand."

"I didn't like the way he was looking at you," I reply simply.

"Really? And how was that?"

"Like he wanted to breathe on you and chop down your tree."

"Chop down my tree?"

"He looks like a fucking lumberjack."

"Oh, Nathan." She smiles and slowly shifts her legs towards me. "But don't you understand you're the only one I want. I'm going to be doing business with men; it's what I do. But that doesn't have any reflection on my love and desire for you."

"I guess I forget sometimes," I admit.

"You're always so nice, so accommodating. I think it's time for you to toughen up."

I feel like we're talking about something else all of a sudden. Like Brooke is subtly training me for the battles we may face up ahead. She studies me for a moment, but then her expression shifts to a warm gaze. "Besides, it's hot to see this side of you. You know it's okay to be more assertive about what you want. It's good for you."

"Okay...I'm going to be assertive from now on."

"Good, handsome. And you know what else?"

"No, what?"

"It makes me kinda crazy for you...right now I feel like I'm burning up inside."

If she's burning, I'm a raging fire. I swallow hard and try to calm myself.

She gives me a sexy smile. "So, tell me...what do you want...right now?"

"I want what you want...this," I fumble, gesturing between us.

"This?" she asks, like she needs clarification. "I want you to be more specific."

I look back at the conference room door, making sure it's still closed. *More specific...okay, here goes.*

"Well for one thing, I want to see more of you," I say smiling as I gesture towards her chest. I look up at her to gauge her reaction. She's completely non-flustered.

Brooke looks pleased as she glances down at her shirt and nods. "You know this shirt has snaps. Why don't you just rip it open?"

"Really?"

She nods and gives me the look. "I want you to rip open my blouse... come on...do it, Nathan."

I lean in toward her and press my fingers into where her shirt comes together. I curl my fingers over the fabric, imagine I'm Superman and pull with force. The shirt explodes open and I hear her take a sharp breath.

I swallow hard. "Wow," I whisper. I look up at her and she has a sultry expression. It's clear she's excited. My gaze trails down to her breasts, so hypnotizing in the sheer shimmering bra. My fingers flex anxiously wanting to touch her, but I realize that I should ask for something else. I picture Brooke in my mind, running her hands over her curves, cupping her softness as she gazes at me.

"I want *you* to touch your breasts," I say boldly.

Brooke makes a show of it as she glides her fingers over her creamy skin. I notice her nipples harden under her circling fingers. She lets out a low moan as she watches me intently.

"Like this?"

I nod. *Just like that.*

As she pinches her nipples she looks up at me and drags her tongue along her bottom lip. "And what would you like me to do now?"

I reach up and place my hands at the top of her arms, not sure the best way to ask. I pause, and look down before I finally find my courage.

"I want you on your knees," I say in an unsteady voice.

As she sinks down, I press lightly on her shoulders. But really she's the one controlling the momentum. Once she's on the floor she looks up at me, waiting for me to continue.

"Touch me," I whisper, struggling not to be embarrassed.

She gently runs hers hands up my thighs and then settles over where I'm hard and pressed tight against my jeans. When her fingers press down, I shudder.

"Brooke," I moan.

"Can I open this up?" she asks, as her fingers linger over the fly. "I need more."

"Uh huh," I respond, my heart pounding.

She teases, working slowly until her hand pulls the fabric apart and she grasps my hard-on. I close my eyes as her hand moves over me. With my eyes shut, I'm acutely aware of the symphony of sensations: the warmth of her fingers, the softness of her breasts pressed against my knees, and the quickening pace of her breath as her hand tightens and finds its slow rhythm.

She suddenly stops and waits, still as can be.

"Well, aren't you going to tell me?" she challenges.

"Tell me?"

"Tell me what you want." She looks determined, unyielding. "Or maybe you aren't so sure what you want."

Why's she challenging me? But then I start to understand that she needs this from me. It's important for her to see how strong I can be with her, without my costume on. "I know what I want," I assure her. "I always know what I want."

"Really?" she smirks playfully.

"I've always wanted you," I point out.

"Anything else?"

I know my face is bright red, but I try to ignore the flustered feeling of being embarrassed to ask for things that keep me up at night in my ever expanding world of Brooke fantasies. I clear my throat and look her in the eye. "I want your mouth on me."

She looks pleased, like a kid who got exactly what she asked for on Christmas morning. I see a flash of lust in her eyes before she takes me in her mouth. She circles her tongue over me until I have no sense of time or space, just Brooke. But then she pauses and continues with the damn talking. "See that wasn't so hard?" she points out as she shakes her head defiantly.

She asked me to be assertive and dominant, so here we go. "More…" I insist as I reach out and cradle her head, running my fingers through her hair. I guide her towards me until I'm back in her mouth.

She hums with delight, before she pulls me in deeper.

I'm mesmerized, watching her. Her eyes are half-mast, heavy with pleasure, and she moans each time I rock my hips. I reach over and brush her hair away from her face, but my hands remain and I give in to the temptation of pulling her even closer.

I could've never imagined being like this with her, but at this rate I'm not going to last much longer. Something primal flares in me. I need to be buried inside of her, and I need it now. "Wait, I need you to stop," I warn her as I ease her back. "Can you get up?" I ask, as I think of what we should do next. "Can we…?"

"Yes?" she asks, watching me carefully.

"I want you bent over the table," I answer, more sure of myself.

She looks intrigued as she lifts up. I put my hands on her hips, and she playfully pushes them off. "You have to tell me what you're going to do." She insists.

"I think you know," I put my hands back on her hips and turn her around. "I sure as hell won't be pitching a show or conducting a storyboard meeting."

"Glad to hear it," she teases.

It just confirms my earlier thought; she needed to know I could take control. I rise and step right behind her, so that my erection presses heavy against her. I see her fingers spread flat against the wood grain of the oversized table as she waits for me, legs spread wide.

I lean over her so that my chest brushes her back, and speak low into her ear. "Is this what you fantasized about?"

She turns her face slightly towards me. "Yes," she sighs. "This is exactly what I fantasized about." I push her skirt up and see that she's naked underneath.

I swallow hard. "Wow…where are your panties?"

"In my purse," she whispers. "I wanted to be ready for you."

"Thank you." I moan as I run my hand over her soft skin.

I press her down towards the table with a firm hand. "Okay then. I'm going to take you now, Brooke."

"Yes," she whispers with a ragged breath.

She lies with her left cheek pressed against the table and her eyes closed as I push into her. I start really slow, focusing on every sensation but when she starts to touch herself I'm overcome . The harder I thrust, the louder she moans until I realize we've forgotten where we are. This is way hotter than I could have ever dreamed.

There's a haunting eroticism about being in this public place in our most private moment. As I move against her, the images of our week fill my mind and fuel my fire. She's Wonder Woman, my enchantress willing to sink to her knees to please me.

She belongs to neither the monkey nor the lumberjack. She belongs to me, and she's so much more than I could've ever hoped for.

My thrusts build hard and fast, as I try to consume her. When she starts to climax, she sparks the Looney Tunes fuse on my ACME bomb. My heart's thundering, my breath a gasp, as I arc back…and then…Kaboom! For a moment, the room fades to black and I see swirling stars in my eyes.

"Nathan?" she squeaks.

I open my eyes and gasp for air. I think I blacked out for a moment. She calls out again, more urgency in her voice.

"Nathan…you're too heavy. I'm having trouble breathing!"

I quickly lift myself up. I must have collapsed on top of her. "I'm so sorry, Brooke. Are you alright?"

"I am now!" she sighs as she pushes up. "And I was more than alright a few moments ago."

I slowly pull out of her and lower her skirt, suddenly feeling very decadent. I can't believe we just did that in a public conference room. "Wow," I say awestruck, as I pull her upright. "I sorta lost control." I adjust my glasses that are askew.

She nods. "I'll say. That was even hotter than my fantasy."

"Really?" I ask, grinning.

"See…you showed me you can be bold and get what you want," she assures me with a happy, dazed expression.

"It wasn't too rough? You liked it…really?" I ask uncertainly, as I tuck myself away and pull my jeans closed. I feel the old Nathan in me returning and I'm a little nervous. That dominant stuff is hot, but it really isn't me.

She pushes me playfully and gives me a mock stern look. "How can you even ask that? Wasn't my pleasure pretty self-evident?"

I nod, with a sheepish look. "I guess so."

"You know, this has been the best week ever," she says.

"I agree." Suddenly the idea of going back to work is pointless. "Hey, can we just take off now? I'm starving!" I announce, as we work our way out of the room, and approach the elevators.

"Sure," she agrees. "How about burgers at In-N-Out?"

"Animal style?"

"Is there any other way," she asks grinning.

Animate Me / Chapter Twenty-Four / The End of the Woo

"They can't order me to stop dreaming." Cinderella[xxiii]

The next morning, Brooke wakes up and looks troubled.

"What's wrong?" I ask, stroking her cheek.

"It's our last day of woo week," she says sadly.

She has no idea how the dread of tomorrow is creeping up my spine.

"Don't remind me. I don't want it to end. Let's not end it…let's just keep it going," I reply, trying to sound upbeat.

She smiles softly. I can tell there's nothing she'd like more. "By the way, I'm making dinner for you tonight," she informs me.

"Really? You're cooking?" I guess the look of disbelief on my face is a bit off-putting.

"Watch it!" she warns me. "I can cook…I can bring home the bacon *and* fry it in the pan, you know."

I smile at her. "And I love that I'm learning that about you."

"Besides," she continues. "I haven't wooed you enough. You deserve a lot of woo, world-class woo."

My girl wants to woo me. I reach over and gently squeeze her hand.

"Okay, Ms. Woo, dazzle me."

When I leave her place it hurts to drive away. It's a physical pain, like I'm being pulled apart. Everything feels wrong the whole way home.

So I spend my afternoon with B-Girl, doing the digital color work over the inked lines for the new issue. I'm going to hate when I get so busy that I'll have to give up this part of the process, because every time I color in a page, I feel like I'm bringing B-Girl to life.

It's not long now before Brooke meets her. However nervous that makes me, I know in my heart she'll adore her just as I do. B-Girl is the physical manifestation of my love and admiration for her. I think Brooke also understands by now that with her strength, kind heart and goodness she'll always be a super hero to me.

• • •

Incredibly impatient to be with her again, I break Curtis's dating law and show up early for our dinner. Instead of peonies, I've brought roses from my garden, and a bottle of red wine. When she opens the door she's barefoot and wearing an apron, her cheeks flushed.

"I thought I'd come a little early and help," I offer as I step inside.

"I bet it's because you missed me so much you couldn't stay away," she teases.

"Am I that obvious?"

She turns and kisses me.

"Yeah," she acknowledges laughing. "It's one of the things I've always loved about you."

She directs me to open the wine while she stirs and fusses over the stove. The salad and garlic bread require her attention as well. After I pour the Chianti, she lets me taste the Bolognese sauce. It's so good that I moan happily, and she grins. My girl can cook...*damn*.

For a moment I glance around and wonder if she'll let me move in...like, tonight. With Brooke, wherever she is, is where I want to be.

She makes me wait while she carries everything outside to the patio. The last thing she does is take my roses, now nestled in a little vase, out to the table.

"Come on Mr. Woo," she coaxes, pulling me by the hand.

I smile and follow as she leads me to her little wonderland. The table is tucked under a canopy of twinkly lights, with the Harry Connick CD playing. The food smells wonderful.

"Wow, Brooke," I sigh.

"See, I can woo too," she says grinning as we take our seats.

"Thank you...for this."

She smiles sweetly, unfolds her fancy napkin and smoothes it over her lap.

My heart's so full as I watch her refill our wine glasses. It's all the little details of what's she's done for me that tell me so much.

We take our time and savor dinner, despite a nervous buzz. There's a current of electricity crackling through us only slightly muted by the wine and her soothing touches. Woo week has been everything I'd hoped for and more…but with heavy hearts, we both know it'll soon come to an end.

When our plates are pushed away we finally face the looming elephant on the patio. "How are you feeling about tomorrow?" I ask, trying to mask my anxiety.

She looks down and I see the darkness move over her expression.

"Not great," she admits.

"What are you most worried about?"

"Well, obviously I'm not looking forward to my conversation with Arnauld. It's not going to be fun."

I nod and wait for more.

"He doesn't like it when he doesn't get his way."

I sit silently, staring at my wine glass before taking another sip.

"What do you think he'll say?"

"I'm not sure. His manipulation can take different directions."

"Are you ready for that. I mean, you're sure of what you want, aren't you?"

"Yes, of course." She takes my hand in hers. "I've just got to deal with him and get it over with."

I suddenly picture Brooke with Arnold and my stomach falls. A seed of fear is planted, growing through me wild and untamed. What if he says something that scares her just enough?…enough so that she's not so sure after all?

Feeling edgy, I push my chair back and get up, walking to the railing. I take a deep breath trying to calm myself as I gaze at the view.

I feel her settle next to me. "Are *you* okay?"

"I'm nervous," I admit. "I don't want you to have to go through this. It makes me crazy how he tries to manipulate you."

"I know," she admits. "But I need to finish this conversation with him so we can move forward."

I turn and look at her. She needs to understand how serious this is for me. "Brooke, you know how much I love you, and now that I know you love me too, everything's changed. I can't share you with him or pretend to the world that you're not my girl." I take a deep breath and imagine life moving on as it was, as if nothing happened. I shake my head. "I just can't."

"I don't want that either," she says quietly.

I know what has to be said. "This has to be it…an end for Arnold, and a beginning for us. If it isn't…"

"Yes?"

"I can't just sit back and watch you with him, knowing you love me. You have to make a choice. It's the only way for me."

She steps into my arms and rests her cheek on my chest.

"Well, of course I choose you," she says softly, with no trace of hesitation.

My breath catches as I pull her tight against me. When we kiss, the emotion is raw as if each fear we had buried this week has broken through the soil and come to light. Every feeling is heightened and dramatic like it's the last time we will be together, even though we both know that isn't the case.

Pulling me inside to her bedroom, she's rendered in gold from the cast of the twinkly lights outside the window. She kisses me again, but this time soft and slow, like butter melting.

"Brooke," I moan as her fingers purposefully unbutton my shirt, and slide it off. She leans into me, kissing my shoulder, and tenderly feathering her lips up my neck.

I'm silent, yet my heart speaks to her as I hold her close.

Love me

I sense somehow she hears me. She pulls back enough to look up into my eyes.

"Oh, Nathan," she whispers. "Don't you realize how much I need you?" Her voice has a desperate edge, her grip tight on my arms.

Show me

Her shirt peels off easily, a white flag waving before it falls. My lips trail across her forehead and into her hair. Hands reach, skimming bare skin, but it's not enough. Insatiable, I crave more and more...I desire everything...every part of her.

"I need you too, Brooke, more than you know." I run both hands through her hair and pull her into a kiss.

Choose me, my heart murmurs.

Her hands pull my jeans open and I sigh as her fingers slowly dip inside.

"I want *you*, baby," she says softly.

Another deep kiss, there's a sharp pull from my heart to hers.

"I'll always take care of you...cherish you," I say gently.

Believe in me.

"You promise?" She moves my hand to her breast, now bare.

Cross my heart

"Yes, yes," I assure her, fingers circling as she leans closer.

Be with me...forever.

She pushes her skirt off her hips, until it puddles around her feet. She's glorious in her bare beauty, curves to graze with my tongue, my fingers, my soul.

Her lips press against my ear, the soft whisper. "Make love to me."

Yes. She is mine.

Up on the bed, I'm on my knees with her soft hips cradled in my hands. I pull her closer slowly. The sense of fullness once I'm completely inside of her is overwhelming. She's a vision as she moves with me. Even in the faint light I can see her eyes look straight through me.

I love you, Brooke

"Nathan," she whispers, again and again as I touch her tenderly.

Never stop calling my name...especially when you're in my arms

"Is this what you need?" I ask, my fingers sliding, full of intention while I continue to rock into her. I watch her carefully, every stroke an attempt to make her tremble.

"No one has ever made me feel like this." She tightens and sighs, then opens deeper.

We are meant for each other, Brooke

The way her hair fans across the sheets is startling, a silk headdress, worthy of a queen.

"Do I feel good to you?" she whispers, then moans.

I can't...I can't find the words for her perfection

"Jesus, Brooke."

Shining eyes. "...oh, my love," she whispers.

I curl over her, and her legs trail mine as my strokes go deeper, harder, pushing us somewhere we've never gone. She gasps with each thrust and I feel her sigh of surrender right before my movements become desperate and hard.

"I love you...so...much," I stutter.

She cries out and pulls me close as we climax. The world falls away as we hold each other tightly in our own mysterious and unending galaxy.

Our bodies seem to stay connected long after we finally pull apart.

• • •

I wake just as dawn breaks and slowly realize where I am. Brooke's wrapped around me like a starfish on her rock and I sigh with contentment. The memory of the night before fills me with hope and resolve.

In the quiet I conclude that it's a waste of time to worry about our future. It is certain and destined, even if we have to crawl out of the jungle to shed a monkey on our journey. Brooke will find another job, I have B-Girl and plenty of savings...but most importantly, we will be together.

By the time Brooke wakes, my positive attitude is solid and it rubs off on her too. We watch the DVD collection of Gumby and Pokey episodes over coffee, toast and jam. When it's finally time to head out, I keep it light agreeing that I'll text her mid morning. I resolve to listen to Wayne Dyer on my iPod as long as possible while I visualize Brooke and me, united in our own little world.

• • •

I try to focus on work and get a fair amount done. I'm proud I've lasted until almost eleven before I finally text her.

Thinking about my girl...how's it going? Have you seen Mojo yet?

I'm fine, love. No, he's been in closed-door meetings all morning so I haven't had to deal with him yet.

Okay. I'll check in with you later. I love you.
I love you too. XO

I take a break from Bucky and take some time to study Joel's Robbie model sheets for the new project when I suddenly hear my name.

"Nathan?"

I think I recognize her from HR. She always has a fake happy look on her face.

"Yes?"

"I need you to come with me."

"Where are we going?"

"We need to talk to you."

"We? Can you tell me what's this about?"

"Please just come with me," she insists. The happy smile is gone.

So this is how it's going to go. I turn off Wayne Dyer silently hoping that he stays with me even if I have to leave my iPod behind.

I follow her to the elevator. It's the most nerve-wracking ride I've ever had, the silence is like a deafening scream. As soon as we step off I realize that we're heading towards Arnold's office.

"Why aren't we going to HR?" I ask, trying to manage my nerves.

"It was decided to have this meeting here." She says simply likes she's giving me directions to the mailroom or something.

When she pulls open his office door I pause at the threshold, realizing that there isn't a single thing inside I'm ready for. Curtis taught me that in football a blindside is when you are tackled without seeing it coming. My instincts tell me to run the other direction, but I know a man must face things head on.

I am Brooke's man, and I will not run.

I step inside and scan the room. The main HR lady is in the first seat, sitting so upright she looks like she has a metal rod up her back. Then there are two suits watching me carefully, another strangely familiar looking guy sitting just outside the pack and then finally Arnold, seething like a monkey who's had his banana taken away. The death glare he gives me would totally derail me if Wayne and his affirmations didn't have my back.

Brooke is gloriously absent from this train wreck and I'm so glad. It's the one bright spot of relief in this cheery gathering.

"Please have a seat Mr. Evans," suit lady directs and points to the chair facing the firing squad. "These are our lawyers, Mr. Ruiz and Mr. Felton," she informs me as she points to the suits on my right.

Damn.

I have two thoughts. The first is that I'm pretty sure I'm not here to get a promotion. I have to fight off a smile at my humor in the face of disaster.

The second is that they can fire me for some bogus reason and blast me out of here on a rocket. It's not going to change anything that matters to me.

Fuck them...every single one of the soulless fuckers.

I move to the chair, sit down and fold my arms over my chest defiantly. Let's get this done.

I'm ready, you raving assholes.

Bring it on.

Animate Me / Chapter Twenty-Five / What's Mine is Yours?

"Hurry Cecil, he's wrecking our terribly happy magic kingdom!" ~Beany Boy[xxiv]

"Nathan Evans?" Suit lady asks.

Is this a trick question? My sullen audience regards me warily. I glance around the room and note that Mojo only has framed posters of Sketch Republic shows up and the show pictured in front of me was canceled last season. He really should get that replaced.

"Yes?"

"Are you familiar with the employee conduct rules that you agreed to when you were hired here at Sketch Republic?"

She holds up the rule book they gave us at orientation.

"Sort of. I mean I didn't read it, but I know the basics; don't kill your co-workers, stuff like that."

"This is serious, Mr. Evans."

I just stare at her with my game face. She must not want to play. Well, I really don't want to play either. "Yes, I think I understand the rules pretty much."

"Note that on page seventeen it clearly addresses the rule against excessive fraternization on company property."

"Excessive?"

A disturbing feeling crawls through me. Where the hell is she going with this? As if I wasn't unsettled enough, the guy lurking just behind Arnold is staring me down. I look back over to the HR lady, the confusion evident in my expression. My arms loosen where they are folded over my chest, and fall down to my sides.

"Are you aware that there are security cameras in our conference rooms?"

Cameras in the conference rooms…filming what? Oh my God.

Fuck

Fuck, no

My stomach is now somewhere near my knees. I suddenly feel naked, in front of Arnold and the suits, no less. "No." I admit with great reluctance.

"What was that, you fucking pervert geek?" Arnauld yells.

"Hey!" I yell back. It's bad enough knowing he must have watched the footage, but if I'm getting fired anyway, I'm done with his crap.

"Arnauld," one of the suit men barks, holding their hand up like a stop sign.

My mind goes blank but for one thought.

Brooke

We had sex in that room, never realizing we would unknowingly acquire an audience who doesn't appreciate the allure of Brooke bent over the super-sized conference table. I know I'm flushed crimson, and I hate myself for it. I clear my throat. "I see. No, I'm pretty sure that wasn't okay according to the employee guidebook."

"I'm going to take you down, you little fucker," Arnold growls.

"Arnauld! Do we need to step outside for a moment?" the bigger suit asks.

"No," he barks. "Let's get this done."

"So I'm fired. Anything else?" I scoot to the front of my seat. I just want to get out of here, and protect Brooke from what's sure to come… the sooner the better.

"I don't think you understand how serious this is Mr. Evans." The smaller suit advises. "We're very concerned because it appears that some level of force was used in the activities on the video from the conference room recording."

Holy shit.

Force? What are they saying?

The scenes that afternoon start to flash through my memory: pulling Brooke down to her knees, pushing my cock into her mouth. This is what the camera saw, but it must not have heard Brooke asking me to do those things…telling me she wanted it that way.

The blood drains out of my face as it occurs to me how bad this would look on camera. Could they be thinking I took Brooke with aggression against her will? I feel my breakfast rise up in my throat and I choke it back. Surely, once they talk to her they will realize they misunderstood the events. Right?

"Now Mr. Evans, I would strongly advise you to speak with your lawyer before you comment. This is an extremely serious situation."

"It wasn't like that," I insist, ignoring his warning. "It was completely consensual. I swear. Ask Brooke."

"Again, I advise you to wait for your lawyer, Mr. Evans."

"Brooke would never want that," Arnold fiercely insists. He looks like he's going to beat the crap out of me. I hope he doesn't have a gun in his desk drawer because I wouldn't put anything past that fucker.

Despite his fury, I can't hold back. "Like you'd know," I retort.

His fists curl and he looks like he's going to explode. "I'm going to..."

"Arnauld," the bigger suit looks angry.

The whole room's starting to spin. Jesus, I have to get out of here. I turn back to the Human Resources woman. "So what are you going to do to me now?"

"You will be released from employment and escorted from the building. Do you have a lawyer?" She asks.

I nod silently, thinking about my parent's long time lawyer, Walter, who's been helping me with my Sharper Edge contract. I'm sure he'll help me with this.

"Okay, you need to make arrangements with your lawyer, and tomorrow we'll meet with both of you to determine if charges will be pressed. We'll be speaking with Ms. Tobin shortly."

Speaking with Brooke...Escorted from the building...

A sick feeling of dread washes over me, so with trembling hands I reach into my pocket and pull out my cell phone, then turn on the texting feature.

"What's he doing? Take his fucking phone away!" Arnold demands.

"I'm texting my lawyer," I insist.

"Arnauld, it's his right," someone says as I look down to focus on my phone.

I tap out the long message as fast as I can, indicating three receivers. Meanwhile I can hear the firing squad discussing me in the background.

To: Morgan, Dani and Nick

293

HELP. I've been fired and soon will be escorted from the building. Morgan please warn Brooke-conference room has a camera. D&N go get the drawings out of my bottom drawer NOW and save them for me. PLEASE

I hit send. When I look up they are still quietly discussing something in cryptic shorthand among themselves so I wait, my knees bouncing wildly. Less than a minute later my alert goes off.

THAT IS FUCKED-don't worry, Nick's getting them. They're safe with us.

Well, that's something at least. But the next message from Morgan is a blow.

Too late-they already have her.

I'm snapped back to attention.

"Now, Mr. Evans, there's another matter we need to discuss."

"Another matter?" I ask weakly. I'm not sure I can take anything else.

He opens up a file folder and pulls out a document and sets it on the coffee table we're sitting around. It looks like one of the many forms I signed when I started here. Even from this distance, I recognize my signature at the bottom.

Next he opens a large manila envelope and pulls out a stack of comic books. The moment he lays them on the table and fans them out I break out into a cold sweat. In perfect order he has laid out every copy of B-Girl.

"Why do you have those?" I ask, panicked. "They don't have anything to do with Sketch Republic."

"I'm afraid you're wrong, Mr. Evans. They have everything to do with Sketch Republic." The lawyer turns to HR lady. "Okay, we're ready for her."

I look up at Arnold and I can't read his intense expression. Whatever he's up to, it's going to be far worse than anything I've feared. Hate doesn't begin to describe the way I feel about him. It's a good thing I don't have a gun either, because now I'm afraid I'd use it too.

In my stupor, I have a vague sense of HR lady moving outside the room and a moment later the door opening again. I turn just in time to see Brooke step inside the office. To say she looks stunned would be an understatement. She looks rigid with fear.

Her eyes scan the crowd. She calculates each face and who they are, and by the time she gets to me her expression has fallen. I see sheer terror on her beautiful face. When our eyes connect there's a tenderness in her expression, but just then Arnold taps the chair next to him.

"Brooke, come sit here."

She doesn't know about the conference room yet. Her vulnerability in the face of this terrifies me. I wish I had mental telepathy or something so I could let her know what's happened. I sense if I yell something out anyway, it will only make things worse for her. She's a deer in the headlights. Is she the next one to be sacrificed?

I note that she scans the setting again as if she's looking for another place to sit, but it's the only empty seat. She moves to it slowly, with great hesitation. Her gaze fixes on the lurking guy, and it's as if she suddenly understands something I don't.

She starts to get her bearings as she sits. "What's this about?" she demands with authority. "Why is Nathan here?"

"This meeting is about him and some of his activities while an employee of our company," explains the suit named Ruiz. "You've been brought into this particular discussion because it involves you."

"Really?" she asks with confidence. "How?"

Ruiz picks up the first issue of B-Girl from the pile and hands it to her. I want to dive over the table and take it back. This isn't how I wanted her to meet B-Girl. This isn't how it was supposed to happen.

"Do you know what that is?"

"Well, clearly a comic book. What about it?" She doesn't look down. She seems to understand that when she does everything's going to unravel.

"Can you please examine it, Brooke, and read the title to me."

She looks down and studies the cover, not just the title but the center image of B-Girl, where she undoubtedly sees her own reflection looking back at her. She doesn't react with recognition, pleasure or anger; she just closes her eyes and drops her head.

All my worst fears about her meeting B-Girl have just been realized. My heart falls.

"Read it," Arnold demands.

She opens her eyes and studies it again warily. "The Adventures of B-Girl," she says softly.

"B... Yes, B-Girl," Ruiz says. "And who does she look like?"

There's a long pause.

"Brooke?" Arnold insists.

"Me." Her eyes close again. "Me," she echoes quietly.

The suit turns to me. "Mr. Evans, when did you start self-publishing this comic book?"

I pause. I can't lie, the issue date is right there on the cover. "Two years ago," I answer.

"And how long have you been an employee of Sketch Republic?"

"Three years."

"Yes, and how long have you been *friends* with Ms. Tobin?"

"A couple of months," I say softly. *We are more than friends, asshole.*

He turns back to Brooke whose eyes are still closed. The look on her face is killing me. "Have you seen these comic books before?" he asks, waving to the pile and copy in her hands."

She opens her eyes and shakes her head slowly, like it's so heavy it may fall off.

"Please respond, Brooke."

"No."

"So you weren't aware that Mr. Evans clearly was obsessed with you and had exploited your image for over two years?"

"It wasn't like that," I call out. "I would never exploit Brooke."

"I must point out Mr. Evans, that you already did. This is absolutely exploitation." He then turns to Brooke and starts in on her. "Ms. Tobin, since you are friends, can you explain to us why he never told you about the books. This is an important detail to not share."

She sighs. "Does it really matter now why he didn't tell me? He just didn't. He had his reasons."

She sounds like she doesn't care and I can't understand why.

"It's not a big deal," she continues. "Artists take inspiration from everywhere."

Not a big deal?

"This is more than inspiration, Brooke. This is a violation of your person, your image. You're an important woman in this industry, and he's made a mockery of you," says Ruiz.

Great, just great...now they want her to think I was making fun of her.

"I don't see it that way," she says. "It doesn't mean a thing to me. I mean, who still reads comic books anymore anyway." She gives him back the comic like she couldn't be bothered.

"And since you are unaware of your identity being used, shall I assume that you were also unaware that the president of our company was mocked in this comic...mocked and vilified by one of his employees?"

"No, I was not aware of that. How was Arnauld mocked?"

He picks up the most recent book at the bottom of the pile and fans through the pages until he finds what he's looking for. "Here." He holds up the comic. "The last issue had the introduction of Monkey Man, who rules a factory of mind-controlled minions."

Oh, fuck. These assholes are thorough. Should I be flattered that they obviously read all the books?

She purses her lips together tightly and shakes her head. "No, I was not aware of Monkey Man either."

I search her face for a glimmer of something, anything, but she's stone-faced. My Brooke has left the building.

"Brooke." Arnold suddenly speaks, his voice cracking. "Please, tell me honestly...you really didn't know about this?"

She turns and faces him square on. "I promise you, Arnauld, I did not know we were in his comic."

His face softens. "I'm sorry, baby. I'm sorry he did this to you...to us."

She drops her face and closes her eyes again. I notice that her fingers are white as they dig into the upholstery of the chair's arm.

"Okay, that's all we needed to talk to you about, Ms. Tobin," the lawyer announces.

She slowly opens her eyes and for a moment they rest on the document the lawyer pulled out of the folder when this discussion began. Her eyes suddenly fill with fear and I see them shift to Arnauld, before shooting back to the document.

"What are you going to do?" she asks in a tense tone to no one in particular.

I'm trying to not fall to my knees as I realize that there's a horror lurking I don't yet understand.

"I'll explain at dinner, baby. Don't worry. We have it all under control."

"I want to know now," she demands, her voice haunting.

"We must ask you to leave now, Brooke," Ruiz insists in a tone that says everything. Arnold might think he has her back, but the lawyer's not an idiot. He knows her loyalty can't be assured.

"I'm not leaving," she says loudly, digging in her heels. "I want to know what's going on here."

"Brooke, we must insist you leave. Please don't make us call in security," the suit says firmly, making it clear he means business.

"That won't be necessary," Arnauld says smoothly.

"Brooke, don't make him bring in security," the Monkey says gently. "I'll explain everything later."

She curls over in her chair with her eyes closed, and we all sit silently waiting. It kills me that she looks so broken. It's all hitting me that I'm the one who's put her in this position. I am just as bad for her as the Monkey. I just didn't see it.

HR lady stands and gestures to Brooke. "Come on, Brooke, there's another issue we need to discuss over in my office. They're waiting for us."

Brooke finally looks up, her expression completely blank. She slowly rises and moves towards her as they head for the door.

I'm overcome, it feels like everything is shattered, as if I've fallen into the center of the earth and I'm not coming back out. "Brooke," I call out right before they reach the door. The devastation in my tone surprises even me. I almost don't recognize my voice.

She stops suddenly to my cry and pauses. I hold my breath as the seconds pass, praying for her to turn and face me, but instead she never turns. She just keeps moving, out the door, away from me.

Away from us... and that's when I die inside.

For most of the rest of the interrogation I am Charlie Brown with a bunch of adults surrounding me going, "wa,wa,wa,...wa,wa...wa,wa,wa." I'm not sure what they're saying and I really fucking don't care. But finally something catches my attention, and snaps me out of my stupor.

"To be clear, we own B-Girl, as stated in your employment agreement."

What in THE FUCK are they talking about? Employment fucking agreement? Own B-Girl?

This must be about the document Brooke noticed before she left. It finally hits me. My mind recalls the standard form I've signed for Sketch

Republic and other freelance work I've done before I start their projects. It maintains their ownership while I work on their properties.

"That's for stuff I do here at work, not on my own time at home," I insist. I ball my hands into tight fists.

"I'm afraid you have misinterpreted the agreement if that's what you think," Ruiz says calmly.

"B-Girl is mine," I state clearly.

"Not anymore," Arnold says smugly.

"Over my dead body," I assure him. "I will fight this as long as it takes, no matter the cost."

"Well I hope you're a very wealthy man, Mr. Evans. Because these cases are extremely expensive, and Arnauld's prepared to take this all the way."

I think of dad and my family…my creation and my dignity are what I have to fight for. They wouldn't let me back down.

"I have the resources," I insist. "I'll fight it all the way too."

"Good, I love a fight when I know I'll win," Arnold says casually. "Meanwhile, we've contacted Sharper Edge Comics and given them the details. So be aware that your deal is now on indefinite hold until our potentially long case is finished. But I'm sure that they'll be more than happy to deal with us directly when we've won…we're professionals after all."

I glare at him, wishing his fur would burst into flames, and he'd die a slow painful death.

"And while we have fun in court, I think I'll use someone on staff to start redesigning B-Girl to my liking so that we can hit the ground running after we win. Maybe I'll get your old team involved."

"Arnauld," Ruiz warns. He must be able to tell that I'm about to snap.

"Is there anything else?" I ask, trying to neutralize my voice.

"Nope, that's all. Right, Ruiz?"

"We're done for now. Have your lawyer contact me directly so we can discuss how we're going to proceed."

When I go to stand my knees almost give out on me. I falter for a moment, but somewhere inside I find the strength to stand tall and gather myself. I turn towards the Monkey.

"I know I have what you want, but you're fooling yourself if you think money and lawyers are going to make what's mine, yours. You have underestimated me before, and I assure you, you haven't seen anything yet."

I don't wait to see his reaction or hear his response. I'm done. I try to remember to breathe as I head out the door. I need to pass the threshold before it does an Alice in Wonderland and the doorway suddenly shrinks to a tiny size or turns sideways.

I'm so stunned that I just start walking down the hallway...so disoriented that I'm not even sure where the elevators are. I wish someone, any one of my friends, was nearby so that they could help me.

"Mr. Evans, you need to stop." I turn to see Cathy, the HR woman who assisted me once with straightening out vacation days, rushing after me, a security guard only a step behind her.

"I need to get out of here," I say out loud, not specifically to her but more to myself.

"Yes, yes, the guard will walk you out. But do you need to gather any personal items from your cubicle? We can make arrangements another time for you to do it, if that would be better."

I think of my iPod, books and my figurines. I fear they'll all disappear by Mojo's mandate if I don't take them now.

I turn towards her. "No, I want to get my stuff." I'm right on the edge of my sanity, but I need to keep it together. Once I get the hell out of this building I can have my breakdown...but not now. I try to shift into autopilot, pushing all my devastation and panic behind a closed door in my mind.

"Okay, I'll come downstairs with you. The guard will need to be there as well. When you're done, he'll escort you out."

"Is that really necessary? I'm not going to do anything. I swear; I'll just leave."

"I'm sorry, Nathan. It's policy," she confirms pointing towards the elevators.

During the ride down I wonder where Brooke is and how I'm going to reach her. They said they were going to interrogate her. She's probably in there right now hearing the horror of it all. I think I'll go mad if I don't get to talk to her soon and understand how she's feeling. I couldn't get a clear read on her at all in Arnold's office. Was she upset and angry about B-Girl, or trying to pretend that it didn't matter to deflect the situation from me? Why didn't she even look at me after she heard the news?

As we approach the production area I see the team gathered in the hall near Nick's office. They all turn and gawk at me and my entourage before quickly disbanding.

Andy heads back to his work area several steps behind us.

Once I'm inside my cube he peeks over the top of our shared wall. "Whoa dude, what'd you do anyway? Did they catch you doing on-line porn at work or something?"

He looks genuinely concerned, not just for me, but it appears for himself, too.

"No, it wasn't on-line porn, Andy, and if you don't mind, I'd rather not talk about it."

"Sure," he says, seeming to understand that I need my space. "But I'm sorry man, whatever it was. I'm going to miss having you around."

I look up at him and his face is distressed. Who would have thought that the butterball's a softy? He's the last person I expected that from. "I'm sorry too, Andy," I reply, realizing that I'm really sad to leave my team this way. They'd become like a second family to me.

I look sideways and realize that HR Cathy is standing outside my cube, and she's pulled out a pad and pen. She sticks her head inside.

"Sorry, Nathan, but before you leave I have to write down what you take."

"Really?" I say, irritated as all fuck. *Now I'm a goddamned criminal.* The guard hands me an empty box, and I slam it on my desk.

"Spiderman," I call out tauntingly, waving it in the air for her before sticking the figurine inside the box. "iPod…Daffy Duck mouse pad…" I rattle off the titles of my reference books, and she gives me a suspicious look. "Hey, I brought them from home."

"They're his," an angry voice responds, supporting me.

I turn to see Joel standing in my doorway.

"Nathan?" he asks, his hands straight out, palms turned upwards. He looks like he's in pain. "What happened, dude? I *need* you here. What the hell?"

"I know, Joel. This is so messed up." I look down and shuffle my feet.

"What can I do? I'll go upstairs and fight this bullshit, whatever it is."

"There's no fighting this," I say. "I'm sorry. This is really, really bad. Believe me; I never would want to let you down like this."

"Fuck," he curses, looking down. "You were my best guy, Nathan. And besides that, I liked working with you."

"Me too," I agree, feeling worse by the second.

He turns and looks back at Cathy and steps closer. "Hey, I'll give you a call later, and we'll set up a time in the next day or so to go out for drinks. Okay?"

"Yeah, sure. Thanks man."

He punches me lightly on the shoulder and then steps back. "Damn."

"I know." I nod sadly.

"Okay, later, Nathan."

I try to refocus, quickly riffling through my drawers and shelves for anything I don't want to leave behind including my black Darth Vader shaped coffee mug and joke-of-the-day flip calendar. I pull open the bottom drawer, and I feel a huge surge of relief to see it's completely empty. They never would have let me carry those drawings out of the building now. Nick and Dani came through for me.

I stand back up, and realize that I'm finished here. This part of my life is over.

"I'm done," I tell Cathy and she looks relieved there hasn't been more of a scene. But just then Dani and Nick push their way past Cathy and the guard.

Nick gets to me first. He pulls me into a hug and leans into my ear, speaking in a low voice, "We've got you covered, Nathan. Where are you headed now?"

"I don't know…" I answer, because I really don't.

"We'll meet you at your house in about an hour." He quietly states.

As he pulls away, I see Dani looking at my box and crying.

"It's okay, Dani," I say, pulling her into a hug. "I'll be okay."

"It's not okay," she argues. "This is so fucking wrong."

"Excuse me," Cathy interrupts. "He was just leaving."

Dani gets a fierce look on her face and squares her shoulders. "Hey… back off! Do you understand that this is an outrage? He doesn't deserve this, and you should be ashamed to be a part of it."

Cathy starts to respond and then seems to think better of it, taking a step back to talk to the security guard.

"Dani, believe me, I'm better off getting the hell out of here, after what went down. I'll fill you in later, okay?"

She nods solemnly, wipes the new tears away, and gives me one more hug. "Later," she whispers.

I grab my box and head out. As the guard and I walk towards the elevators, Genna and Kevin step forward. I'm not sure how much more of this I can take. I'm barely holding it together.

"I'm so sorry, Nathan," Genna says softly. "We're really going to miss you."

"Me too," I offer, giving her a weak smile. "Hopefully I'll see you guys around."

Finally in the elevator heading to the lobby, I look at the security guard. He's new to Sketch Republic. I've only noticed him around for a couple of weeks. This must be a really shitty part of the job.

"You seem like a nice guy," he comments during our descent. "This must suck."

I realize that he's too green to understand he shouldn't be sympathetic to the fallen. "It does suck," I admit. "I've never been fired before."

He shakes his head. "Wow. And that was a good job I bet."

I nod. "And you know what else? You're right...I'm a really nice guy. I guess that didn't get me far."

"I guess not," he agrees. He follows me into the parking garage, watches me load my box into my trunk and drive off.

I'm in a surreal haze coasting down the street when my missed call prompt goes off. I pull over, and look at the phone's screen: Morgan. I shut off my car and hit send.

"Hey, Morgan, it's me, Nathan."

"Damn, are you alright?"

"No, not alright at all," I say. "Do you know where Brooke is?"

"That's why I called, to see if you knew what was happening with her. She came running in here a while ago, grabbed me and pulled me into her office. She was crazed."

"Fuck," I swear. "What happened?"

"She took this tote bag out of her closet, opened her locked file drawer and stuffed some files and two flash drives in the bag."

"Did she say why?"

"That's the thing. She was shaking and rambling about only having a minute before she had to get back. Something about her telling someone she was sick to her stomach and was going to throw up, so she could get away to take care of this."

"Oh, Brooke," I sigh.

"So she gives me her car keys and tells me to immediately go lock this bag in the trunk of her car. That I needed to be very casual so that no one notices what I'm up to...then come right back up and just do my job like nothing's happened."

"Do you know what was in the folders and on the flash drives?"

"I have no idea. I'd never seen them before. But another thing she did before she left was open up a cupboard and stack up every one of those Starbucks cups you did for her and then put them in the bag. I didn't know she'd kept them. Did you?"

My heart thunders with hope at this simple, yet significant gesture. "Yeah, I knew."

"And then this is the last thing she said to me before she tore out of here, 'Morgan you have no idea what's in these folders or on the drives...I never showed them to you or talked to you about it. Do you understand me?' She was so intense that she totally freaked me out. And then just like that, she was gone."

"Damn," I groan. "So what did you do?"

"I got the bag in her car and came back up like she asked. And now I'm waiting for her to return from HR. What's going on Nathan? I'm completely freaked out."

"Arnold's trying to destroy me, and he's trying to use Brooke to make it happen."

"She won't stand for that," Morgan states emphatically.

"I know, but he may not need her to do it. He seems to be doing pretty well on his own."

"No," she gasps. "It's that bad?"

"That bad," I confirm.

"Fuck. Fucking Arnauld. Mother fucking Arnauld."

"Exactly." I take a deep breath. "So Morgan, please do me a favor. I'm going to leave Brooke a message on her cell phone, but as soon as she comes back from HR have her call me. I desperately need to talk to her and they escorted me off the premises. Will you do that?"

"Of course...whatever I can do to help, Nathan."

"Thank you."

"Brooke will figure this out. She's smart as hell and she loves you."

"I hope you're right," I say softly. *On the first and last counts,* I think. For as much as I can't stand it, I have to be realistic. After the bomb that was dropped on Brooke today, I can't be so sure of her feelings for me anymore.

I sit in my car for a minute trying to calm myself down, before giving up and tapping her name on my screen. Her phone goes straight to voicemail. I clear my throat and begin to stutter.

"Brooke...it's me..."

I pause, my mind racing to think of how to explain what's in my heart.

"I'm so sick with worry right now...I'm panicked, and I desperately need to talk to you, hear your voice....I need you."

My free hand grips the car door handle tight. "By the time you get this you will know about the camera in the conference room. Fuck it all...I don't even know what to say about that. I'm just sick as hell that all those fuckers saw us like that. They can accuse me of whatever they want, all that matters to me is that you're okay."

I feel myself start to break down and my voice cracks with my next words. "I need to know that you still love me..."

I can feel my eyes fucking tearing up. I feel like such a loser.

"Knowing you still love me is the only way I'm gonna get through this.

"You do, don't you?...you know...love me? 'Cause the way you acted in his office...well I'd be lying if I said I wasn't worried."

I take a deep ragged breath.

"I'm so sorry about B-Girl. I wish I'd told you that the character was you in the very beginning. But I was so afraid you'd think I was a creepy freak for worshiping you from afar so long. Was I wrong about that?"

My stomach flips over. *I hope I was wrong. Was I?*

"Anyway, I can't undo all of this shit, and now I've messed up not just my life, but yours too. Damn…I can't believe this is happening. Everything was so perfect last week and now it feels like the end of the world.

"I love you so much, and I'm here waiting for you.

"I need to see you. I need to hold you.

"Please, Brooke…

"Call me."

Animate Me / Chapter Twenty-Six / Calling on Wonder Woman

"Kill my boss? Do I dare live out the American dream?" ~ Homer Simpson[xxv]

"No, fucking way!"

Dani looks like she's going to kill somebody, well, Mojo to be precise.

"Can he do that?" Nick asks, looking sick to his stomach.

"I'm not sure. If I fight it—even if he doesn't win the lawsuit—it sounds like he's going to drag me through court for a long time. I think he'll keep it going until he breaks me financially and emotionally."

They both stare at me with horror etched across their faces.

"But in some ways he's already broken me. If you could've seen Brooke's face..."

"Fuck," whispers Nick, shaking his head.

"And the asshole is like, 'Brooke I'm so sorry for what this sniveling loser has done to you...' like he's going to comfort her from my freaky exploitation and abuse."

"Mother fucker," Dani gasps. "You've got to fight this Nathan!"

"I will," I say with determination. "What choice do I have? If he wins and steals B-Girl I don't think I'll survive it."

"What's Brooke say about it?" Nick asks concerned.

"I haven't been able to talk to her yet. They must still be talking to her."

"Talking? You mean breaking her down," throws in Dani.

"And I've called her several times but her phone's still off. Morgan's on alert to call me as soon as she's out of there. I just need a chance to explain everything to her." My head falls. "I need her."

"I know, man...I know," Nick says. "She loves you. No matter how bad it looks right now, she'll come around."

"I hope you're right," I say, trying not to crumble inside. "I know Mojo is going to keep messing with her, and that kills me."

"The mother fucker needs a message," Dani announces cryptically.

Nick lights up. "What we talked about earlier?"

"Yes, yes. Let's go see my brother after we leave here. This will be right up his alley."

"You're a genius," Nick says with admiration. "The army is building as we speak. It will be epic."

"I know," she acknowledges. "And together we will rock this thing."

"What are you talking about?" I ask warily. "What are you going to do?"

"Nothing you need to know," Dani informs me.

"You guys…seriously, I don't want you getting into trouble on my account."

"It's not just you, Nathan; although of course your situation has inspired us. This is for all the artists and creative people who get fucked over by the suits. This is for all of us."

"Okay, just be careful," I implore. "I can't take anymore guilt right now. If you lost your jobs too, I don't think I could handle it."

"We are super-sleuths, we are ninjas," she hisses. "By tomorrow…"

"Honey, realistically we're thinking the day-after-tomorrow…"

"By the day after tomorrow," she continues, "Mojo will see his future with the very people who make his worthless ass look good, and believe me, Nathan, it won't be bright."

After Nick and Dani leave I call my Dad and give him the bad news. As if it wasn't horrible enough to tell him about Arnold stealing B-Girl, my humiliation is complete in having to describe Brooke and my conference room antics. He asks about Brooke, and I explain that I haven't talked to her yet, that I'm not sure how she feels about me after the big reveal. With a heavy heart I finally tell him about her lack of response when I called out to her before she left the meeting.

I'm grateful he doesn't lecture me, just remains quiet as I try to rationalize my reckless stupidity. When I'm done, he offers to call Walter on my behalf. I can sense how worried he is about me when not even a single calculation or deduction is worked into his quiet words.

Only moments after we hang up, my phone rings. I answer it so quickly I don't even check my screen for who it is.

I hear the cries first and my heart clenches. My fingers tighten over my cell phone.

"Brooke?" I gasp.

"No…Mor…gan," she stutters.

"Are you alright, Morgan? What's happened?" I ask, worry flooding through me. Our tough friend has cracked. This is bad.

She takes a deep ragged breath. "Everything's fucked, isn't it Nathan?" she asks.

"Yes," I admit solemnly.

"Brooke's gone," she offers. "She left and I have a feeling she isn't coming back." She starts to cry again, and I feel sick with worry for her and for me.

"Where are you?" I ask. "Do you need me to come get you?" I have to get to Brooke, but I need to take care of Morgan too.

"No, I need to stay here and watch the fort for Brooke just in case. They just came and took her computer."

"Fuck." This is really happening.

"What did you mean, Morgan…when you said she's gone?"

"She gave me her phone and said she was going to disappear for a while. She told me that she considered me a cherished friend. And that she was going to miss me." She starts crying again.

Why would she give Morgan her phone before she even called me back? Did she even get my message?

"Disappear? What did she mean, 'disappear'?"

"I'm not sure. I've never seen her like that. She was crying. She looked awful and scared… like she was about to walk through fire."

"Brooke…" I whisper.

"There was something about them being able to track her with her phone."

Oh my, God. My Brooke's scared, really scared. I have to get to her. But in the same moment I realize that without her phone, I have no way to reach her, to find her. She's lost to me too. "Did she tell you where she's going?" I ask.

"No, she said I couldn't know, but that she would contact me on my cell phone as soon as she could."

It's not like Brooke to be paranoid. This is freaking me out. "Do you have any idea where she would go?"

"Not really…" Morgan sniffs, then continues, "…because from the sound of it, she won't go somewhere obvious like her friend, Jenn's. It sounds like she doesn't want to be found."

It also doesn't sound like she's coming to me and that realization kills me. She knows I'd do anything for her, but I'm not the one she wants right now.

Still on the phone, I stand up and grab my car keys. I'm halfway to my car before I realize that I didn't even close my front door. I force myself to sit on my front step, realizing that I have to calm down and focus. I can't drive in this state or I'll be unsafe to others. I take a deep breath.

"Okay, Morgan, let me think for a minute. Let's go back a few steps. How long was she in HR?"

"Well, over an hour," she says calming down once she hears I'm trying to stay calm.

"And then?"

"She came back here white as a ghost and really agitated. She told me to get that head lawyer from legal, Ruiz on the phone. Then she went in her office and closed the door."

"Okay, so she talked to the lawyer…" I prompt.

"And then after a few minutes I see her extension's light on my phone go off. So I wait a bit, and when she doesn't come out I knock on the door. She doesn't answer, so I crack the door to peek in."

"And?" I ask anxiously.

"Damn, Nathan, she was curled over her desk with her face down, sobbing…just sobbing. Oh, God. It was awful. So I let myself in, closing the door behind me. I went to her, but I wasn't sure what to say, what to do…so I just offered her a bunch of Kleenex."

"Did she say anything?"

"She just kept chanting, 'it's my fault…because of me…he's ruined.'"

"Ruined?" I feel like I just got punched in the stomach. I know she's talking about me.

"I'm so sorry, Nathan. What did they do to you?"

"Arnold's stolen my comic book and taken ownership."

"Fuck…no! I knew it was something really bad. I knew he'd get revenge somehow for Brooke falling in love with you."

"Yes, I knew he would too. I just never dreamed it would be this."

"Well, that would explain what she said next. She told me to tell you that she was going to do everything she could to stop it. That she couldn't face you again until she fixed this somehow."

"Did she say how she was going to fix it?"

"No, I couldn't even tell if she had a plan, or if she was just rambling in despair."

"Did she say anything else?"

There's a long pause.

"What, Morgan?"

"Shit, Nathan, I don't want to tell you this…"

"I need to know everything. Please."

"Then she told me that she knew all along she wasn't good enough for you, and this just proves it. You'd be so much better off without her fucking up your life."

"What?"

What?

I'm almost angry at her…furious. How can she say that after everything we've shared together? I need her right now more than ever.

"Maybe she was just being dramatic, Nathan. She was so distraught."

"I'm going to go to her house, and see if she's there. She would have to go get stuff if she's leaving for a while."

"Hurry then," she warns. "I'm sure she won't be there long. She's been gone for at least an hour now. I couldn't get away to call with all the computer stuff going on. And before that, Arnauld stormed over here and yelled, then interrogated me because I was supposed to call his office the moment she returned from HR"

"The fucker yelled at you?"

"Yeah, evidently he wasn't done with her yet. And you know what? I don't care if he fires me. Dealing with him just then was the last thing she needed."

I feel a powerful surge of gratitude towards Morgan. "You did the right thing. Thanks for always looking out for Brooke," I say reassuringly.

"Of course."

"Okay, I better go. I'll check in with you later."

"All right. Hey, Nathan?"

"Yes?"

"I'm so sorry. I'm sorry for all of us."

. . .

I put all my focus into driving since my mind and spirit are shot. I keep my cool until I get all the way around Lake Hollywood only to find that they have the road closed due to a movie location shoot. The location cop informs me that unless I can wait about forty-five minutes, the only thing I can do is retrace my steps and then come up from the front, through Hollywood. That alone will take almost thirty minutes or more because of traffic. And that's when I lose my cool.

I turn my car around like an Indie 500 driver and gun it on the windy road around the lake. By the time I hit Barham Blvd. heading towards Hollywood, I'm completely amped up.

She can't just fucking leave me when I need her most. She told me she loved me. She told me it was forever. It was one thing when I thought she was mad at me about B-Girl, but this is something else.

I'm mad at this weak Brooke who slinks away from me when things get rough. I want my strong Brooke, who will stand by me in battle. We could fight this together.

As soon as I pull up to her place I can tell she's already gone. I let myself in the gate, then futilely ring the doorbell over and over and peer in the front windows. There's no sign of her.

I've never felt more defeated. I sit on her doorstep with my head in my hands trying to figure out what to do next. "Don't do this to me, Brooke," I whisper. "Please don't do this to me."

I'm almost back to my house when my cell phone rings.

"Where are you?" Curtis asks, forgoing formalities.

"Driving home."

"Come to Billie's store. Dad called and told me what's going on. We need to talk."

"I don't think I can, Curtis. I'm a wreck."

"Brooke was here not long ago. Billie tore into her."

"I'll be right there."

When I finally arrive at the Outer Limits, Billie has a worried expression as they approach me. Curtis nods an abbreviated greeting.

"Curtis says Brooke was here," I say directly to Billie. "What happened?"

Billie stops right in front of me and rests her fists on her hips defensively. Her expression morphs from concern, to stormy, to fierce.

"I told her to get the fuck out of my store."

I groan and pull my hands over my face.

"Why, Billie?"

"Curtis had just called me with the lowdown, how she didn't come to your defense in the meeting…and then she showed up here. She was trying to buy a complete set of your comics and it pissed me off. What if she's taking them to that asshole Arnauld guy?"

"I assure you. He already has a set."

"And then she started to cry like a baby, and babble that it isn't what I think. Plus, some bullshit that she wants to help you. "So I asked why she wasn't with you when you needed her most. Didn't she understand what it meant to be loved like that? Enough that you would create a character in her name and show her all the love in the world? I mean what the hell?"

"Oh, Billie," I say defeated.

"She blubbered about not being good for you, that you would be better off without her."

I shake my head in despair.

"So I told her that if she was that big of a wimp, in my opinion, she's right…but that you would never see it that way. If she abandons you, it'll kill you."

"What did she say to that?"

"She just cried harder. What an emo."

"Billie!"

"So I told her to take the books and that I didn't want her money. I just want her to do the right thing by you."

I look at Billie. She's right, and she's wrong about Brooke. Either way I'm fucked.

"What? If she's going to abandon you when you need her most, then I'm done with her. I'm sorry Nathan, but it's wrong."

"It's not what you think Billie. She also told her assistant that she's going to try to help me. Even if Brooke is mad about B-Girl, I need to believe she still cares about me. I swear, she wouldn't just let Arnold take me down without trying to do something. Can't you see that?"

"I'm only looking at what's right in front of me. And you should too."

Her words haunt me the entire drive home and with each passing hour it gets worse.

Brooke could have reached me by now. I don't care if it was by a damn payphone or telegram. If she knows me at all she'd know how desperately I'd need some reassurance about now.

Even if she can't handle the fact that I'd obsessed about her so long and hid B-Girl from her, she owes it to me to at least talk about it. A stream of anguished thoughts loops in my head, playing over and over and over until I think I'm going mad. I make a calculated decision to surrender to alcohol to numb my tortured, hopeless thoughts.

• • •

It's a long dark night with my silent cell phone clutched in one hand, an iceless, amber filled glass in the other as I wander aimlessly through my haunted house. I'm a ghost, my deep sighs painful echoes, as I fear the loss of the life I'd always wanted.

I see Brooke everywhere…her shimmering mirages taunt me. But every time I reach for her, my shaky fingers grasp nothing but air.

The next morning, the bright light in the bathroom scorches my eyes. I stand with a slight wobble before I adjust and approach the sink.

What day is it anyway? Ah yes, Tuesday…the day after the worst day in my life.

I glare at my reflection. Good thing Brooke isn't seeing me now. This would pretty much seal the deal.

"Hey Nathan, did you know that Jack Daniels is not a good substitute for Brooke?" I ask myself aloud.

"No?" I answer.

My reflection in the mirror is blurry. It's probably not a good sign that I'm talking to myself.

"But last night I sure thought the Jack Daniels was worth a try."

In the mirror I watch my hands lift in a gesture like I'm explaining my reasoning. I then scowl and shake my head disapprovingly.

"Back to the drawing board, Nathan."

I lean over the sink and splash water across my swollen face and puffy eyes.

I thought only crazy people talked to themselves. So now I'm a crazy fucker.

Morning is a cold, hard bitch.

With considerable inner conflict, I answer the phone call from my Dad. Apparently my zombie-like responses to his questions discourage him.

"Nathan. Pull it together. Have you eaten anything, or did you just imbibe last night?"

"Do you really want to know?" I ask, disheartened.

"Ah, Son. I'm coming over there. But first there's good news. Walter just called, and they aren't pursuing the conference room issue. Seems that yesterday Brooke convinced them it was consensual, that she encouraged the aggressive behavior. She also told them that she absolutely wanted to copulate with you while bent over the conference room table."

"Dad. Stop. I really don't want to hear it." I can't even feel relieved.

"Well, I am extremely reassured that this predatory Lothario issue has been put to rest. But have I taught you nothing, Son, about risk aversion? Next time, take a moment to factor the hazards of exposure, versus the fleeting, yet euphoric moment of physical release. Practicality will win out every time."

"Yes, I'm an idiot. Noted," I slur, slightly. "Are we done?"

"Are you still drunk?"

"Maybe."

"Take a shower, and get dressed. I'm on my way over."

Minutes after we hang up I hear bells ringing again. The mother fucking noise needs to stop. I realize in my stupor that it's my phone and I finally answer it.

"Nathan?"

"Yes, Walter?"

"I need you to go through all of your art, and look for any examples of how you could have been developing these characters before your time at Sketch Republic."

"But I didn't develop them until I was at Sketch Republic."

"I don't think you're understanding me Nathan. Do you want to win or not?"

As I hang up I feel a jolt of reality. Do I want to win? Is he fucking kidding? I have to win. Despite my pathetic state of despair, I haven't lost sight of the fact that Brooke and B-Girl are everything to me. I sink into the living room chair and imagine my life without my two best girls, and my throat starts to tighten until I feel like I can't breath. My eyes scan across the cases of collectibles, and note that each figurine and action figure is stoically posed and still as if waiting for their command for our upcoming battle. Are they worried about me? Do they miss Brooke too? I have to imagine they do...who wouldn't?

I get up to find my phone and decide to leave a message on the land-line at Brooke's house.

"Brooke, if you ever come back to your house and listen to your answering machine, and if you ever care about me and what I think again, will you call me? I thought this was it — you and me, true love and all that stuff. Now you're gone, and I'm lost."

"I'm dying here. Can you call me?"

• • •

Dad finds me in the backyard, sitting in a lawn chair in my Scooby PJ bottoms and no top. The near-empty bottle of Jack Daniels is on the ground next to me, but the large bottle of water is my drink of choice now, as I slowly take sips and stare at the shrubs.

He sighs with resignation, and pulls up a chair across from me. He just sits quietly for a while and observes me. Finally he clears his throat and starts to speak, but before he gets the words out, I hold up my hand to stop him.

I shake my head firmly, and he leans back silent. Another minute passes.

"Maybe it was all a dream?" I finally offer.

"Yesterday?" he asks.

"No, yesterday was very real. Maybe everything before yesterday was a dream…the part where Brooke was in love with me. I had a great job and a comic book deal…because now they've all evaporated into thin air, so maybe they were never real."

He looks me directly in the eyes. "Son, the only thing gone is that job. And as it was, you were ready to move on from that. The rest is still abundantly real. They are still yours to have. You just have some fastidious work to do."

"I'm not sure I have it in me, Dad. I don't know if I can fight my way through this without Brooke."

Dad pulls his fingers through his hair frustrated. I think I'm making him crazy, but I'm beyond caring at this point.

"You must pull yourself together and fight, Nathan. You have to do it for yourself, and you have to do it to show her what you're made of."

"But maybe she doesn't love me anymore. Maybe I'll never make it up to her. Maybe I'll live the rest of my life alone."

"I'll tell you what. I'll put up with this peevish whining today, considering the state you're in and what you've just been through. But then, enough. You need to find your confidence and potent strength for battle, Son, not just wallow in your disappointments."

"I have every right to wallow," I moan, leaning forward with my face in my hands. My elbows dig into my knees and the pain almost feels good. "I could be the fucking king of wallow."

"Nathan, what do you imagine Brooke would think if she saw you like this?"

"That I'm a loser not worth her time."

Dad clears his throat and there's a long moment where I can tell he is weighing his words, making mental flowcharts of my potential responses and the appropriate counter argument for each one.

"Son, have you forgotten that Brooke is on some type of mission to help you? Does that mean anything to you? Her actions regarding secrecy and walking away from her carefully honed position shows her unwavering commitment to you. It also ensures she won't make you any more vulnerable to Arnold than you already are."

"I can't imagine why she's doing anything. I think she hated B-Girl."

"You have no way of knowing that. Just because she acted disinterested with a group she knew were counting on a dramatic reaction, shows she's cunning and fast on her feet. I refuse to underestimate her abilities, and if I were you I wouldn't either."

"Really?" I ask weakly.

"You will never know how she really feels about B-Girl until you are together alone and have a chance to talk it out. I sense that won't happen until she knows you are safe from his treachery."

"I guess," I say uncertainly.

"Give her some time, Son. She will come to you when she's ready. Remember she was hit hard yesterday too. It also doesn't sound like she has a support system like you do. She was exposed and humiliated from the conference room footage. She no longer has a job, whether by her volition or not. Finally she found out that the man she was in love with, kept a very large secret from her, that involved her, for their entire relationship."

His words hit me hard, my angry outer shell cracking and falling in small pieces around me. I take a swig of water and sit a little taller in my chair. "What do I do now?"

"You need to focus on your defense and cooperate with Walter. Go through all of your art and look for anything at all that could help your case. Take rigorous care of yourself during this time of extreme stress… no more binge drinking. Your electrolytes must be completely out of equilibrium."

"Everything's out of whack," I admit, rolling my eyes.

"You need to structure your day, work out fastidiously and eat healthy."

Damn…my Dad and his practical insanity can be incredibly annoying at times.

"Eat healthy?" I stretch out my legs and notice the Scooby-Doo on my right shin must have gotten doused with scotch at some point last night.

Dad stands. "Look, get in the shower and I'll find something in the kitchen for you to eat. When you're done, you need to start going through your archives. We're meeting with Walter in the morning."

At first the hot shower feels like a thousand needles penetrating my skin, but after a minute it actually soothes me. By the time I get out and dry off, I start to feel human again…still miserable, but at least human. When I step into the kitchen I smell brewing coffee and peanut butter.

Arthur looks stern as he shakes his head. "Your cupboards are practically bare, Nathan. The best I could do is peanut butter and jelly. There's barely evidence here of two major food groups, the other three are completely missing. I'm surprised you aren't showing signs of malnutrition."

I shrug. "I love peanut butter and jelly. And I usually have milk here for my Lucky Charms cereal, but Brooke and I were so busy this week and I ran out. That's another food group…three outta five, Dad."

He just shakes his head, as he pushes the plate towards me and then pours a mug of coffee.

He joins me at the table and like a papa bear, watches me slowly eat. We don't talk, but we're comfortable in the silence. As my head starts to clear I can't help but appreciate that he's here trying to help me.

When I'm done I push the plate away, and briskly rub my face. "Okay," I say, trying to assure him I'll be all right, even if I'm not so sure myself.

"Okay," he responds relieved. "So are you going to get to work now?"

I nod.

"Good boy."

I smile at him, and he smiles back when he realizes how that sounded.

He stands to leave. "I'm going to call you later and if I don't hear progress, *I'll be back*," he warns grinning.

Did my Dad just do a Schwarzenegger-Terminator impression? I can't help but smile. "Okay. Thanks Dad."

He pulls me into a hug. "I love you, Son. We're going to get through this."

"I believe you, Dad. And I love you too."

• • •

As I pull open the first drawer in my home office, my internal struggle starts. I close my eyes wincing. I'm just not sure I can do this right now. I open my eyes and briefly look at the neat stack of drawings. Every sketch makes me think of Brooke, and Starbucks cups, Arnold taking B-Girl, and Sketch Republic going on without me. Resisting the urge to flee, I look over to the window and notice my Wonder Woman figurine perched on the nearby shelf. I get up and walk over to her, admiring her majestic stance.

With a sudden impulse, I pick her up and carry her back to my desk area. I pose her on top of the bookcase facing where I'm trying to work. A feeling comes over me.

"Hey, Wonder Woman," I say in a quiet voice. "I could use a little motivation right about now. Could you help me out?"

I don't even feel like the freak I am as I study her, waiting patiently for her response. "If you could talk, I bet you would tell me to be strong… wouldn't you?"

I reach over and tip her head forward like she's nodding.

"Can you share a little of your super powers with me? And as long as I'm going down crazy lane, can I ask one other thing?"

Her little eyes gaze at me intently.

"Can you look out for Brooke too?"

I don't even have to nod her head for her, because just then the light from the window shifts and she kind of glows. I might be imagining it, but it gives me comfort nonetheless. She's going to help show us the way.

I reach into the open drawer with new resolve. My heart may be shattered, and I still fear I may never hold my Brooke again, but I've got to prove to myself and Brooke what I'm made of. I'm gonna try to fight for my B-Girl like any superhero would.

I look back at the little heroine and nod. "Okay, Wonder Woman, let's get this done."

Animate Me / Chapter Twenty-Seven / Persuasion

"As long as these pants are square and this sponge is bob, I will not let you down!" ~Spongebob Squarepants[xxvi]

I'm already awake and have finished my Pop Tarts when Morgan calls.

"Whoa, Nathan…the inmates have taken over the asylum!"

"What do you mean?" Morgan needs to get better at this phone stuff. She keeps freaking me out.

"I'm calling to hear if you knew about the artist uprising at work today?"

I think back to my conversation with Dani and Nick. *Oh no. What the hell did they do?* "Uprising?" I ask, the fear evident in my voice. "No, what's going on."

Morgan sounds completely gleeful. "I just got a call from my friend in accounting. She went in a little early cause her month ends are due, and said there are posters of Arnauld as a monkey all over the building. It's some kind of pro-creative propaganda statement. Maintenance was trying to take one out of the elevator as she rode upstairs to her floor, but it's completely glued down."

Arnold as a monkey? I remember the caricature I had done of him a while back, swinging through the rain forest holding a very small banana. That drawing was in the stack Nick and Dani rescued for me. *Fuck…they didn't…*

"Holy shit," I gasp.

"You don't know the half of it," she says excitedly. "Go turn on your computer, and go to the Sketch Republic homepage."

"The public homepage?" I ask, filled with a twisted combination of thrill and terror.

"Uh huh," she says smugly. "I've got it open on my blackberry. I must say, it's a fitting tribute to our noble leader."

I rush into my studio and flip open my laptop. "Okay, it's on and warming up." I can sense her impatience over the phone.

"So is the homepage open yet?"

"No, wait a sec." My fingers fly over the keyboard as I type the web address in my browser. I feel the blood leave my face as the image comes up. It's my drawing all right, and they've added bits of accent colors. The brightest spot is the hot yellow of Monkey Man's tiny banana. But it's the copy accompanying the drawing that takes my breath away.

Welcome to Sketch Republic...where they steal ideas from their artists for your viewing pleasure. Enjoy your stay, but watch your back on the way out.

I move my cursor over the screen, but none of the links to shows or promotions work. The perpetrators have frozen out the world for anything but their foreboding message.

"Oh good God, Morgan," I exclaim. "I can't believe they did this."

"Oh, I can. I could feel the angry energy in the building since Monday. And it's not only because you were so well liked, and he's trying to fuck you over. It's that everyone hates him and what he stands for. Monkey Man's not going to be very happy today."

I'm horrified but completely awestruck with the sheer brilliance of it. I'm also incredibly honored and inspired that my friends and whoever helped them, did this as a reaction to my downfall.

Dani...clever, clever Dani. Who knew she had hackers, and such ninja skills with perfect timing, up her sleeves? It must have taken a deviously calculating mind to get all those posters up with security cameras apparently everywhere.

"I'm just pulling into the parking structure," Morgan says. "I'll send you a photo of one of the posters as soon as I can."

Over the next few hours my phone is on fire. Images are coming from everyone.

There is even a caricature of B-Girl strangling Monkey Man with her lasso. That one makes me laugh out loud.

But Morgan manages to get my favorite picture: one of Arnold's office before his arrival. Tiny bananas, real ones...hundreds of them, are lying across every possible surface in his grand office. There's also a paper adhered to the top of his chair that states, *Monkey Man Sits Here*, with an arrow pointing down.

Nice. *Really nice.*

Before lunch I hear more evidence as to how well-planned this was. Evidently poor little Demon Spawn-Alana's car was somehow blocked at her apartment building by an abandoned junker. So the poor thing was late to work...too late to warn the monkey and prevent him from slipping on that stray peel while entering his banana-clad domain. I'm told that his howl could be heard all the way down to the next floor.

Karma's a bitch, you asshole. And comic karma, never ends; it just gets more animated.

I'm giddy. The whole drive to the lawyer's office I grin as my phone buzzes over and over with new messages and jpegs.

My tone gets more serious, though, as I enter the fancy office building and head to the floor that's completely occupied by Walter's law firm. Mom and Dad are waiting for me in the reception area, and we're quickly escorted into his intimidating office suite.

Walter's all business as we sit down and start our discussion. He eyes the folder I've placed on the table. "How did your art search go, Nathan?"

"Well, I found some good stuff that might help." I open my portfolio folder and pull out drawings I had done of female superheroes over the years. There are even sketches from high school and earlier. I guess I've always been obsessed with the idea of heroic women with special powers.

But by far the most compelling works are the drawings I did after seeing young women dressed as Wonder Woman at Comic Con years ago. In the series of sketches, I begin to play with her outfit that clearly shows the beginning of my B-Girl ideas. I put them away so long ago; I didn't realize how relevant they could be for this case until I unearthed them.

Mom and Dad examine the sketches thoughtfully and then slide them to Walter. I study his expression as he goes through the pile and picks out the best of the post Comic Con drawings to fan across the table's polished wood surface.

"You were always so talented," Mom says proudly to me as we watch Walter pick up one of the sketches and compare it to a B-Girl comic cover.

"Good work, Nathan," Walter says and Dad nods. "This will definitely help." He studies the work closely. "How interesting that you always dated your work."

"I read once that you should do that. The writer said it was a sign of genius when people archived and documented their early work as if they knew it would one day be considered significant. I know I'm not a genius or anything, but that sounded smart to me."

"You *are* extremely smart, Son," Dad states proudly.

"Well, whatever the reason, that will definitely help us," Walter says. He turns to my parents. "With this and our other case research, things are looking good."

"You're going to hit them hard, correct Walter?" Mom asks in a firm voice. "I want them to understand that we're not playing around. That little Arnold person will regret messing with our son."

I smile inwardly, witnessing the power of Diana Evans. *Do not mess with Diana's family. She will take you down.*

People sometimes make the mistake of assuming she's a mild-mannered Pasadena housewife, when in actuality she oversees the business side of Dad's work. I heard through one family friend that they're an incredible team. She stays on top of the business end so Dad can stay focused on what he does best. Evidently she's a lioness when people don't treat Dad or his work with respect.

"Absolutely, Diana" Walter responds. "We're bringing the team to the meeting in force, and we'll put the fear of a counter-suit in him. I suspect the holding company for Sketch Republic doesn't know about his plans, and I'll make sure he understands how much they will appreciate this misdirected and self-indulgent lawsuit. I went to law school with David Stern, one of the members of their board. I see him on the golf course from time to time. We belong to the same Country Club."

Mom leans back in her chair grinning and Dad smiles as well, then turns towards me.

"See Son, there is more than enough reason to hope for the best."

I take a deep breath and let some tension seep out of me.

"So Nathan, we have our first meeting with them on Monday. Did Elli give you the details yet?"

"Yes," I respond. "It's here, right?"

"I insisted," he confirms. "You shouldn't be subjected to going back to the Sketch Republic building after what they did to you."

I'm sure glad to have Walter and my family on my side.

• • •

I decide to follow Mom and Dad home so I can hang out with them for a while. Mom has promised me a home cooked meal, and I could use some more time away from my empty house.

Once home, Dad insists we take a brisk walk, and I decide not to fight it. He's probably right that I need to start working out again...something about the endorphins lowering stress levels.

As he charges forward I follow silently. He slows for a moment and turns back towards me. "Are you okay, Son?"

"Yeah, I'm encouraged about the lawsuit, but I just wish I'd hear from Brooke. I know you said to give her time, but it's making me crazy. What if she doesn't want me anymore?"

"Then you'll have to put work into convincing her that she does."

"I don't think wooing is going to do it this time, Dad."

"With your current relationship concerns, you are beyond basic wooing now, Nathan. Don't get me wrong, there must be continual woo-maintenance in a relationship. But a crisis like this calls for something more substantial and dramatic...riding in on a horse, breaking down her door, climbing to the edge of a cliff to catch her before she falls...you get the idea."

"Horses kinda freak me out but I'd ride one to Brooke if I knew where she was. No one knows."

"But she's going to contact her assistant. Didn't you say so yesterday? You could leave word with her for Brooke. That would be a primary step."

"I could try that. But you know what's weird? I'm also mad at her. I'm angry that she's decided on her own that she's no good for me. What the hell? I need her right now."

"I'm disappointed with her too, Nathan. But what this has confirmed for you is that she's not perfect. At her core, she has insecurities she hasn't resolved. You always gave her too much power, so now she's surreptitiously taken on all the blame. I fear she will never get over the guilt of making you vulnerable to Arnold's unscrupulous scheming unless she really faces her insecurities and issues and works on them."

"Yeah, she must have been screwy in the head to fall for me in the first place."

"Nathan," Dad corrects me with a stern voice. "I don't want to hear you talk like that. You know you're a loving and devoted partner. She wouldn't have fallen in love with you otherwise."

"All right, sorry." I look down and kick some leaves gathered on the sidewalk. "I guess you're right, I *am* a good partner."

"That's more like it," he agrees.

"You know while you are waiting for her, why don't you write her a letter explaining how you feel. It could be cathartic. And once you're done you can consider whether you want her assistant to give it to her or not."

I nod my head and listen as he continues.

"I think you need to start at the beginning and explain to Brooke not just why she inspired you, but your fears all along in telling her the truth."

His advice makes sense and I nod in agreement. It's time to tell Brooke the whole truth. Even if it's too late…it still must be told.

As we continue to walk, Dad changes the subject, and we talk about the cases Walter has already uncovered that support our position. Everyone seems optimistic, and it gives me hope. Walter has also contacted Sharper Edge and established a relationship with their lawyer.

Some comic book companies of late, have begun giving more rights and recognition to the artists who create their characters, while also giving them freedom to develop their own properties on the side. That bodes well for my case, considering any work I did on B-Girl was always at home and not at all related to the shows I worked on.

"Are you really hopeful, Dad, or am I just wasting money fighting this?"

"I'm not going to sugarcoat this, Nathan. This could be an ugly, extended battle in court. But we'll support you through the case, not just emotionally but however you need us to financially, because we know it must be done."

"But Dad, I don't want to take your money…"

"We want to help. I think you know Mom and I have dealt with several lawsuits over the years regarding my inventions. If you don't fight for your creations, believe me, people will walk all over you…but even worse, it will kill your creative spirit."

I nod. Dad's right. I doubt I'll ever have the heart to create again if I don't get B-Girl back and Arnold does what he wants with her.

Later at home, I check the calls I've missed and marvel with each new round of information from the dramatic day at Sketch Republic. Nick's message informs me that in the afternoon all four hundred and seventeen Sketch Republic minions were marched into the auditorium to be yelled at. Despite management's threats, no one got called out, nor did anyone step forward. The whole execution was so flawless that not a single person is identified as mastermind, instigator, accomplice, or implementer of the grandest gesture in the history of animation studios. I conclude that it's a day that will live in infamy; a story that will be passed on from cartoonist mothers and fathers to geeky sons and daughters, for generations to come.

• • •

Despite the encouraging things that happened earlier, that night as I lie in bed, the melancholy sets back in as I recall how different my life was just a couple of weeks ago when I still worked at Sketch Republic and got to see Brooke and my friends every day. I feel so isolated now.

I also longingly remember how it felt all the times Brooke was here with me. Sometimes I would just run my hand along her sides, and over her hips, filled with disbelief that she was actually here in my arms. I coveted those moments, every one of them.

I toss and turn, dozing off and then fretfully awakening with a start, gasping the still air of my darkened room. The dreams that torment me are fragments, flickering animation frames interspersed with images of Brooke that shift from Black and white, to color and back again. After the third nightmare jars me from sleep, I give up and finally get out of bed.

I continue my sick ritual of checking my cell phone every hour for messages, and the crushing disappointment when there aren't any. Whatever she's going through, I just desperately wish she'd call.

After turning on the TV, I make some coffee and fire up the remote, flipping through all the channels and trying to find the most distracting show possible to watch. Despite the magic of satellite, there still isn't much compelling to watch at four-thirty in the morning.

As I sprawl on the couch I look through a sketchbook that had been left on the coffee table until I find an empty page. Remembering Dad's advice, I slip the cap off a pen and consider the blank slate. There is so much to say that I hardly know where to start.

Dear Brooke...

I sit with my pen suspended in mid-air until I finally give up and lay it down.

How do I explain that it hurts to breathe without her here? That as much as I had initially admired and desired her, I had no idea how truly spectacular she was, and is, until I held her in my arms.

As my thoughts tumble, I grab the pencil lying next to the pen, and start moving it over the page as I think of her. The lines are loose, but I keep circling back until a sketch of Brooke and I at the Hollywood Bowl comes to life. I smile at the happy memory.

I hold it out in front of me, studying the image. Inspired, I continue on, tightening the drawing and adding a few background details. When it's to a place I'm satisfied, I write underneath:

Although I always had a dream for us…this was the night I realized a future with you was truly possible…that it was unfolding right before my eyes.

I feel a surge of emotion as I study it again and suddenly it comes to me. There's no better way for me to show Brooke what's in my heart.

I grab my coffee and head to my studio. The whirl of the pencil sharpener ignites me as I flip to the opening page of a new sketchbook. I write the words first.

There was once a boy, who longed to meet a special girl. He desired to find his true love, yet he couldn't find her…

…that boy was me.

As I stroke my pencil across the page, a rendering forms of a younger me perched at my drawing table. In the sketch, my hand cups my cheek as I lean forward and daydream out the window.

I turn to the next page.

Every girl I met was too hip, or mean, or not appealing…or just not for me.

I started to wonder—would I ever find my girl?

This sketch is more animated. I look flustered in the drawing where I'm in the middle of the page with a question mark over my head, while surrounded by little caricatures of different types of girls. Judging from my expression and body language, none of the girls are to my liking.

But one day, while I sat in the audience at a big company presentation, the most beautiful girl walked across the stage.

The drawing is of a stage with Brooke approaching the podium. The audience in the foreground is dark, with simple lines indicating the people in their seats, except for one seat where there's more detail. It's as if a beam of light shines down on me, and from my expression as I watch her, it's obvious I'm enraptured.

She was smart, and funny, warm and charming…and so, so beautiful.

I happily sketch a close up shot of Brooke at the podium, smiling as only Brooke can do.

And in that single moment, I fell in love...
From then on, everything was you, Brooke.

The page features a close up of me, my eyes wider than my glasses as I watch her. There is a thought bubble over my head where she is in my arms and little hearts float around us.

So every day after I would watch you from afar, trying to get the nerve to approach you. But what I saw was how other men admired you. Your charm was undeniable. What would I say if I ever got to talk to you? I couldn't imagine you would ever want to date a guy like me.

I smile as I draw Brooke chatting on her cell phone, while standing next to a sign that states, "All Brooke Admirers Wait Here." A collection of men in line go to the very edge of the page.

When I finally accepted that I'd never have a chance with you, I took all my passion and dreams and put my energy into creating a character in your likeness. Finally, you were part of my world...

And B-Girl was born.

B-Girl stands majestically in the middle of the page, with sparkling eyes and flowing hair, just as I'd always envisioned her.

I dedicated myself to B-Girl, making her strong, brave and beautiful... just like you, Brooke.

The rendering is of me back at my drafting table, but now enthusiastically working, a finished B-Girl comic at my side.

And then one day, when I least expected it…you walked into my world, and it was as if a door had opened…I will remember that day for the rest of my life.

Grinning in my bow-tied polo shirt with the pocket protector, I'm showing Brooke her Geek World purchase. She's smiling at me too.

And I knew I finally had my chance. I made up my mind that I wouldn't ever give up again until you were mine.

A fine drawing of me presenting Brooke with her first macchiato Starbucks cup drawing follows.

Page after page, my pencil follows after me as I relive our journey in a storyboard style. There are the ups and downs, the coffee break visits, the Dani farce, the hidden comic books and an annoying monkey lurking in the background. As the story progresses I increasingly add bits of color to the sketches until the drawing where Brooke hands me the note card the night we professed our love.

The memories of that life-changing moment overwhelm me. How do I make her understand that she's made me a better man? She's taught me how to love with my whole heart, so intensely that there's a profound longing every time we're apart. I can't beg, but I don't know how to go on without her. Nothing means as much to me without her in my life.

The final drawing of the group is of me alone in my studio holding a drawing of B-Girl and thinking of Brooke. My despair and longing is tangible in my drawn expression. As I study it I know this can't be the last frame of our story…it just can't.

The next time I look up, it's noon and the studio is flooded with light. As I finish and close the sketchbook, I feel a surge of promise. Somewhere deep in my heart I know that when Brooke sees this, it will help her find her way back to me.

For the first time since my world with her fell apart...I feel hope again.

Animate Me / Chapter Twenty-Eight / Home Delivery

"Golly, I sure wish I had a girl." - Cecil the love-sick Sea Serpent[xxvii]

I've just brushed off the cover of my sketchbook for Brooke when my phone prompt goes off. I feel a surge of hope seeing Morgan's name on the text line. Maybe she's heard more from Brooke.

Hey Nathan. I'm leaving for lunch now. Are you around? Can we talk in ten minutes?

Yes! I reply.

"Shit, all hell is breaking loose," Morgan says dramatically.

"What's going on?" I ask. My grip on my cell phone is tight.

"Brooke's computer is back, but they went through her office last night. They weren't even clean about it. It was obvious as soon as I went in to leave mail on her desk. Then Arnauld was yelling at someone like a wild man this morning. I could hear it all the way down here."

"Damn." I take a deep breath.

"But the big news is that I finally talked to Brooke this morning."

"She called you?" I ask as I try not focus on the fact that it's so messed up it wasn't me she called.

"Yes, and the first thing she did was ask about you…if I'd talked to you or heard anything about you."

"What'd you tell her?"

"That I wish she'd call you. I hope you don't mind, but I told her I thought you were really hurt that she hasn't called you yet."

My heart sinks with the truth of it. As much as I'm trying to stay positive, the fact that she hasn't called is eating away at me. "Yeah, I don't mind that you said it. It's true. What'd she say then?"

Morgan's voice gets sad. "Well, it sounded like she was crying, and she mumbled something about needing just a little more time. I didn't know what to say, so I quickly changed the subject. I asked her when she's coming back to work."

The idea of Brooke back at Sketch Republic with Arnold makes me want to double over, but I don't let go of the phone. "*Is* she going back?"

"Actually, she was really surprised I asked. She thought HR would have talked to me already about another position. Evidently, Tuesday she called and told them she was taking an extended leave."

"Really?" I ask hopefully.

"Yes, but I'm thinking she's just stringing them along until she has her showdown with Arnauld."

I hope she never returns to Sketch Republic, but I can't be sure what she really wants. It's so frustrating not to know any of this firsthand.

"And since then I think Arnauld's gone over the edge. Knowing his ego, he probably assumes she's just doing this disappearing act to upset him, and that she will come to her senses sooner or later. I mean, right before I called you, I called HR and they confirmed that nothing about my position has changed. And yesterday, Alana said Arnauld had her make reservations for him and Brooke Saturday night at The Ivy. He even had her get his favorite jewelry story on the line."

I feel sick hearing his desperate plans. He's either deluded or fighting for his last chance with Brooke. The one thing I'm sure of is that even if she doesn't want me anymore, there's no way Brooke would go out to dinner with him now.

"So I'm going to meet her after work today to take her some of the industry files she asked for. Luckily those were still in her file drawer."

"Can I come too?" I ask, knowing the answer.

"No, she told me not to tell you where we're meeting. She's not ready yet."

My anger flares. "Not tell me? She doesn't think she's ready yet? What in the hell does that mean anyway? Well, you tell her that I'm mad at her for not talking to me. This is making me crazy."

"Please don't make me tell her that. She's not well, Nathan. I know it doesn't seem fair, but you need to give her some space just a while longer."

"She needs space? What about what I need?"

"She has it in her head that she has to finish something before she can face you. If you ask me, she's sounding a little crazy now, too."

Great... just great. "Honestly, Morgan. Should I be even more worried about her than I already am?"

"No, I'm not saying that. Just please give her a little more time. She still loves you so much, I can hear it in her voice."

Her words break down my anger just enough, and I remember the sketchbook in my studio. "Morgan, I have something I need you to give Brooke. If I bring it to you after work, before you meet her, will you do that?"

"Of course."

Later, when Morgan opens the door to her apartment, she gives me a curious stare.

"What?"

"You just don't look as bad as I expected. I'm surprised."

"Gee, thanks."

"Well, considering what you've been through," she tries to explain.

I wave my hand at her. "It's okay. No worries. I took a long run this afternoon to clear my head. I also listened to stuff on my iPod. It's helping me keep my spirits up."

"Good for you. Take care of yourself, and don't let this stuff get to you too much."

"If I fall apart now, it's just one more thing that asshole took from me. I'm not going to let that happen."

She nods and gives me a small smile. "Well, I applaud you." She reaches her hands out. "Is that what you want me to give Brooke?"

"Yeah." I hand it to her.

"What's with the package of colored pencils?"

"I left the last page blank. She's the only one who knows the ending... so I want her to show me what it is." I point to the envelope pressed against the sketchbook in the clear plastic bag. "The note explains it."

Her smile gets bigger. "I see. Okay, I'll make sure she's gets it, Nathan."

I step back to leave. "Thanks, Morgan. Hey, will you call me after you see her. You know...just so I can hear she was okay."

"I will. Hang in there," she says. "I know this is going to work out for you guys...I just know it."

"Well, she may have given up on us, but I haven't. I'll just have to be positive and fight for both of us." I nod my head goodbye and turn to leave.

• • •

"Curtis?"

"Hey man, I've been worried. Why haven't you answered my calls?"

"There's so much going on," I reply. "Honestly, I'm trying to handle one thing at a time."

"I get it. This whole situation sucks."

"Yeah. Besides, Billie really threw me when she went off on Brooke. I'm still not sure what to say about it."

"Yeah, she was a little worked up."

"I'll say. Do you think you can work on her so she gets over being so furious with Brooke?"

Curtis sighs. "Yeah, my fiery girl was a bit too intense. I think she's very protective of you. It's really sweet. Don't you think?"

"Sweet? No, I wouldn't say that was sweet."

"Yeah well, she's still mad, but she's calmed down a lot. So does this mean you and Brooke have talked?"

"No. But we're going to…and it will be soon. I just sent her a message through her assistant and I'm hoping she won't be able to resist reaching out to me."

"That must be some message," he says, his tone edged with skepticism.

"I have had my low moments this week, Curtis…but I know she still loves me. I just have a feeling…"

"Well, I hope you're right. Maybe you'll hear from her, and this crap will be over soon. Then you guys can start over."

"Yeah, we can start over. Besides, I'm still planning on marrying her one day. It's going to be a drag if Billie doesn't like her. I bet she won't even come to our wedding."

"Marry her? Dude, your woman has left the building, and you're talking about marrying her? You sound as loony as you were the first time we talked about her. Remember that? She was going to be your girlfriend, and she barely knew who you were yet."

"I remember," I respond, smiling to myself. Dad's right, I'm pretty determined when I make up my mind about something.

"Are you listening to those crazy CDs again about manifesting your future and that kinda crap?"

"Don't knock Wayne, Bro. He got me where I am today."

"Well, right now, where you are today isn't that impressive. I hate to say it, but face the facts."

"But this is just one faulty step along my path. I'll overcome it and be better for it. And I will marry Brooke one day…it may take a while. But just you wait and see."

"Sure you will."

"And you'll be my best man."

"And Sgt. Pepper will be the band at the reception."

"I mean it Curtis."

"Of course you do. And despite my giving you shit, I want to believe it too."

• • •

Just before I leave to meet Joel for burgers and beers, I finally hear from Morgan again.

"How was Brooke?"

"Well, she looked like hell. She needs to get on your Pollyanna plan. But she seems determined. She said her lawyer has set up a meeting with Arnauld tomorrow."

"She's going to meet with him?"

"Yes. She wouldn't tell me why, but if her lawyer is with her, it must be pretty serious. That isn't Brooke's style."

"Did you give her my sketchbook?"

"Of course. Once I handed it to her she clung onto it like a life raft. She didn't even let go of it to drink her coffee."

"Thank you for taking care of that for me."

"Of course. You know, Nathan, I'm worried about her. I hope whatever she's doing tomorrow goes the way she wants it to."

I realize that if whatever she's planned with her lawyer doesn't work, she may never be able to get past her guilt. What will that mean for us and

Ruth Clampett

our future? Even if I'm willing to forgive her for not being by my side this week, will she ever be able to forgive herself for all she feels responsible for?

Will she be willing at all to try to work things out with me? Can I keep waiting, knowing her reluctance? I take a deep breath and respond to Morgan's hope for Brooke.

"Me too."

• • •

"You're dating Brooke Tobin? *The* Brooke Tobin in development... Arnauld's girlfriend?" Joel gasps, completely stunned.

I look around the dive burger joint in Sun Valley to make sure no one we know hears us, and then realize that no one we know would ever come here.

"Ex-girlfriend," I correct him.

"How in the hell did that happen, and how could I have not known?"

"We kept it quiet."

"But wait a minute; he can't fire you for dating her."

"No, but he can fire me for doing the wild thing with her in a conference room. They got it on video."

"Dude, no."

"Yes."

"Have you lost your mind?"

"I guess I've lost my mind over her...I'm in love...does that count?"

"If I wasn't so pissed at you, I'd be impressed."

"I hope you know, Joel, the last thing I wanted to do was to let you down. I really wanted to work on *Robbie from Romania*. It spoke to me, you know?"

"I know...I know." He takes a sip of his beer and then suddenly looks inspired. "Hey, why don't you get a DBA, set up a business with another name and your parents' address, and I'll hire you freelance. They won't even know."

"Isn't that risky for you? I would feel like crap if you got in trouble."

"Why don't you let me worry about that?" he says with a confident look. "This show has to be great. I need the best...I need you."

339

Joel saves the uprising talk for when Nick and Dani join us, so when they storm into the place at seven-thirty, it's like an explosion.

"Nice place!" She jabs Joel, while sliding into the booth next to me.

"We're safe here," he replies with a shrug.

"How's my buddy?" she asks, grinning at me.

"Hi, Dani," I say, giving her a hug.

Nick nods. "Hey man." He smiles as he slides in across from her.

"It's the dynamic duo," Joel says. "Ready to stomp out evil at every turn."

"Damn right," Dani agrees.

"You are unbelievable, my friends. People are still sending me updates and pictures. I am in awe of your talent," I say.

"I know, right?" she agrees. "The execution was close to flawless. I swear my brother is a genius."

"I doubt we could have pulled any of it off without him," Nick chimes in. "He hacked into the security system so that a constant loop of previous footage played on screen. The security guards, who probably were asleep anyway, would've never known what was happening."

"Whoa…impressive," I say with a low whistle.

"I was wondering how no one noticed the set-up," Joel responds.

"But what was even more impressive is that he hacked into the website. They had to pull the site down once they figured out what was on their homepage, and they still can't get it fixed and back up live."

"Well, it was up for a while, but just for giggles. Before they took it down he rigged the Danny Deletes contest that was going on so that *everyone* who entered won a new laptop. They have a big fucking mess on their hands now."

"Your brother must be a genius," I say, incredibly impressed.

"He's brilliant," acknowledges Nick.

"Did you hear about the rest?" Dani asks, delighted.

"No," I answer slowly. "There's more?"

"Some of the stuff today was managed by other people. We alerted the media. I can't wait to see if the news covers it."

Joel nods, and Dani winks at Nick, and in that moment I feel so grateful for my friends. I hope they know that I will always stand up for them, just like they have for me.

I stop drinking after my second beer realizing that I don't want to drive with a buzz. I've got enough trouble without a DUI to deal with.

When we finally head out to the nearly empty parking lot, I agree to meet my friends for Kevin's birthday gathering at the miniature golf place in Sherman Oaks a week from Saturday.

"Please stay out of trouble," I say sternly to Dani as I give her a hug.

"And miss all the fun?" she teases.

"Please watch her, Nick," I say.

"Don't worry, I'll keep an eye on this one," says Nick as he pulls her close. "I hope you and Brooke work it out soon," he says.

"Me too. Thanks, man."

"You still haven't talked to her?" Dani asks, worried.

I shake my head no.

"You will soon," she says, hugging me.

"Yeah, good luck with everything," Joel adds, nodding in agreement, and then turns to me.

"DBA dude, DBA...I need you," Joel chants, pointing at me as he slips into his convertible.

I nod, smiling, and give a wave before getting into my car.

I'm home and just letting myself into my front door when I sense someone is behind me.

"Hey...are you Nathan?"

I quickly turn to see a young guy wearing the green Starbucks apron and hat over the usual black pants and shirt, standing in my walkway.

"I've been waiting in my car for you to come home. I'm afraid your coffee is cold," he says, holding the white cup out to me.

I shake my head. *Is this a dream?* I only had two beers.

"Sir?"

"Are you sure you're at the right place?" I ask, confused. "I didn't order any coffee. Besides, I didn't think Starbucks delivered."

"We don't deliver. This was an unusual circumstance," he confirms with a sly smile. "Nathan Evans, right?"

"Yes," I respond. He steps closer and hands me the lukewarm cup. I lift it up, trying to read the markings on the cup sleeve in the dim porch light. "Venti cappuccino with extra foam."

My heart thumps hard. That's the drink Brooke got for me the first time she brought me coffee.

"Who ordered this?"

"I don't know her name," he replies anxiously. He seems in a hurry to finish this up. "She was really pretty, with long reddish-brown hair."

"Big blue eyes and a beautiful smile?" I ask.

He nods. "Is she your girlfriend?"

"I think so," I answer honestly.

"Well, she sure seems crazy about you, if that helps. She begged me to do this for her the moment I got off work."

"Well, thanks," I say, not sure what else to do. I don't even want coffee. I mean, it's time for bed.

I fish for my wallet. "Here, let me give you a tip."

"No, that isn't necessary. Your girlfriend paid me a hundred bucks to do this. I didn't want to do it. I could get fired, and I told her no five times, but man, she was really insistent."

"A hundred bucks?" I ask, incredulous.

"Yeah, and she said I had to keep on my apron and hat and that I had to give you this exact cup."

"A hundred bucks?" I ask again.

"Please don't be mad at me. She wouldn't take no for an answer. My girlfriend and I even missed our movie for you to get this cup of coffee." He shakes his head. "And you don't even want the coffee...I'll never understand the point of this. Can I go now?"

"Okay, sure. Tell your girlfriend I'm sorry you're late."

"It's all right; she's okay about it," he admits. "She thought it was really romantic."

I smile. "Well then, thank her for me."

"Can I take this apron off now too?" he asks.

I laugh and realize that it's the most relieving laugh I've had since Sunday.

"Sure, take it off."

"Well, try to enjoy your coffee. I hope you like it...that's the most expensive cup of coffee in history, I bet."

He nods and rushes to his car, pulling off the apron and hat as he goes.

Once I'm inside, I turn off the alarm and flip on the lights. I'm overcome with curiosity.

There has to be more to this than just a cup of coffee.

I move into my dining room and set the cup down. I begin to study it. I never put the sleeves on Brooke's cups, so I'd have room to draw on them. I carefully remove the lid and gaze inside. Most of the milk foam bubbles have popped and the liquid is a lazy brown. I sniff it and it has the oldish coffee smell from sitting so long, so I snap the lid back on and slowly turn the cup so that I can examine it further. I discover that on the edge of the sleeve she wrote *start here.*

I lean back in my chair and stare at it some more, delaying what I hope is the big reveal. Finally, I lean forward and carefully wedge the cardboard sleeve down to the bottom of the cup, as gently as a man who slides the panties off his lover.

My heart starts pounding. Sure enough, there's a message hidden under the sleeve.

She wrote in small letters in the center of the cup:

I loved our sketchbook story so much. And realizing that despite everything, you still love me. It gives me hope.

"Oh, Brooke, after everything I've said to you how could you doubt that?" I say out loud.

There I go again, talking to myself like a crazy man. At least I'm a crazy hopeful man at the moment. I look back down at the cup and realize there are dots that lead me further around the cup…

There are things I need to tell you. Will you meet me at the Starbucks in Toluca Lake tomorrow at 4pm?

As much as that first line scares me, at least she's finally ready to see me. Finally…I almost can't believe it. Of course I'll meet her—wild horses couldn't keep me away.

One more twist of the cup reveals the best part of all.

See you tomorrow. Love, Your B-Girl

Love…my B-Girl.

My eyes instantly well up and I take a deep ragged breath. It feels like the first full breath I've taken all week. I cradle the cup in my hand and gently turn it to reread her words again and again.

Tomorrow I will see Brooke. She knows everything now and she still wants to see me.

She still loves me.

When I finally rise to go to bed, I stop in the kitchen, pour out the coffee and carefully rinse out the inside of the cup. I finish by gently patting it dry with paper towels. Before I crawl in bed, I set it on my nightstand so it's the last thing I look at before I close my eyes to sleep.

It may have been the world's most expensive cup of coffee, but it was worth every cent.

Animate Me / Chapter Twenty-Nine / Wounded Soldiers

"You needn't be out there on the edge anymore. You needn't be alone."
~ Batman[xxviii]

Just past seven a.m. I wake up with a start and it takes a moment to remember where I am. The Starbucks cup on my nightstand grounds me, but also reminds me that I dreamed of Brooke.

In the dream, she was trapped in a cartoon and I was trying to get her free. It was like that trippy Aha! *Take On Me* music video that made an impression on me when I was a kid. I take a deep breath and move closer to the edge of my bed so I can read her words again, to remind me that Brooke isn't trapped in a cartoon. I'm having coffee with her this afternoon. I smile and run my fingers through my hair.

I ease out of bed and decide to take a run. I may have a meeting with my lawyer to talk about the challenges in the case, but today there's a reason to feel real hope. I chant my new mantra.

I'm seeing Brooke today.

I'm just tying up my running shoes when Curtis calls.

"Dude, quick! Turn on channel seven!"

I grab the remote and press the buttons. "Why? What's up?" I ask as I wait for the TV to warm up.

"Do you have it on yet?"

I look and as the screen brightens there's a cleaning ad on. "It's just a commercial right now."

"Yeah that's right; now turn the sound up and wait!"

I turn up the volume and just moments later the news broadcaster comes on.

Watch out cartoon fans...there's an uprising in Toon Town! The artists at Sketch Republic are staging a revolt claiming the company's president, Arnauld Roth, has stolen the personal creative work from a young artist, who was employed there, named Nathan Evans. The company's headquarters was plastered with angry posters and the company's public website was hacked with the protestors' message.

The visual switches from the broadcaster to my monkey illustration with Nick's verbiage on the homepage of a computer.

I gasp out loud. I can't believe this is on the damn news.

"Whoa," I hear Curtis gasp. "That fucking rocks!"

The company's twitter account was also hacked. For almost twelve hours, tweets were continually sent to the ninety-thousand Sketch Republic followers from a so-called "monkey man" character who tweeted repeated threats to steal their ideas and claim them as his own, while sucking out the souls of his followers.

I can tell the newscaster is fighting back a smile as she reads the copy.

The twitter sabotage may have gone unnoticed longer if a diligent mother hadn't reported the tweets to Sketch Republic's parent company after her child was traumatized by the threats. Her lawyer says a lawsuit's pending.

I fist pump the air victoriously. I mean, I feel sorry for the kid and all, but this is just brilliant. Arnold is getting it from all sides.

Yesterday evening, several local bus bench advertisements were replaced with posters of the same theme and the resourceful rebels also took over one major billboard in Burbank, all within several miles of the Disney, Warner Bros., Nickelodeon, and Cartoon Network Studios.

They switch to the long shot of a billboard on Olive Ave. just past Warner Bros. It appears that the monkey man poster was reformatted in a long rectangle and pieced together in large printed squares. I can't believe it.

Our inside sources tell us that the perpetrators have not been caught yet, but the entire staff is being interrogated. Meanwhile, the company president is now being investigated for his practices.

Curtis hoots loudly in the background.

We will keep you updated as we uncover further news from this Toon Town mutiny.

"Damn, Curtis!" I gasp after putting the TV on mute.

"Crazy...right? Did you know about all of this?"

"I knew some of it, but not the twitter and billboard parts. My friends masterminded it."

"Well, those are some damn clever friends," Curtis acknowledges. "Boy, I sure wouldn't want them as my enemy."

"Nor I," I laugh. "Wow...that made my day. Thanks for letting me know."

"Sure, bro. If that doesn't inspire you, I don't know what will."

Right after we hang up, I think about my Brooke cup and almost call Curtis back, but then I realize who I want to tell my big news to first. I pick up my phone.

"Hey Dad," I say casually, as if today is just another day.

"Did Curtis catch you in time?" Dad asks. "It's remarkable that your story has made the local news. Your personal experience of being abused by management is developing into a social issue and could impact the future for other artists. What do you think about that?"

"It's unreal...I'll be happy if something good actually comes out of this nightmare."

"I agree."

"And Dad, there's something else, too."

"What's that?"

I can't help grinning as I say the words. "I'm seeing Brooke today. She finally contacted me."

I hear him breathe a big sigh of relief. "That's great, Son. When did you hear from her?"

"She got a message to me last night to meet her at four today."

"Really...she sent you a message? That sounds mysterious and ripe with potential."

"I also know from Morgan that she has a big meeting with Arnold today."

"As I suspected, she didn't want to see you until she had some type of resolution for your predicament. Well, perhaps there will be a plethora of good news today."

"I sure hope so."

"Will you call us?" He asks.

"Yes... yes, I promise."

As I do some stretches for my run I let my mind wander. I try to imagine what it will be like to see Brooke again. Will she want to kiss me, or even hug? She says she wants to talk...what if there are other issues I don't even know about yet? I start to worry, but then force myself to think about other things.

In reality, I'm not even sure what to say to her. Do I tell her how mad and disappointed I've been with her for not contacting me earlier? Do I tell her how low I sank, and the battle I've had to keep my spirits up? Or instead do I try to keep it light?

More determined than ever, I finally head outside and hit a fast pace on my run. My mind spins with thoughts of Brooke, B-Girl, the news report, the Arnold meeting...it's stunning to realize for the first time in my life, I not only don't know what tomorrow holds, I don't even know what this afternoon has in store for me. Whatever Brooke says today could potentially determine how the rest of my life will unfold.

• • •

An hour later, my phone rings.

"Have you forgotten who your leader is in this revolt, Nathan?" Dani whispers into the phone.

"Dani?" I ask. "Why are you whispering?"

"I'm at work. Wait a sec. I'm almost outside. I won't have to whisper in a minute."

I wait patiently until she speaks up again.

"I didn't even get consulted before you called in the media," she huffs. "I saw the news clip online."

"It's online already too?" I ask bewildered.

"Yeah, on the ABC News website. Haven't you seen it yet?"

"No. And for your information, I didn't call the media about all of this. I'm just as surprised as you are."

"I know that, silly man. I called them," she informs me. "But I *am* surprised all the news sites got it up so fast. My brother saw it and alerted me. I forwarded it to Morgan and every one of the troops. Morgan then got it to Alana, who got it to Arnauld right before Brooke showed up with her lawyer. Take that mother fucking Monkey Man!"

Despite Dani's glee, a surge of panic rises through me. Brooke's there with Arnold. I know everything that matters to me rides on how their meeting goes.

"It's viral in the building, and from what I hear, at every animation studio in town. Soon, dear Pinky, we will take over the world!" she says happily, in a voice imitating The Brain.

"Dani…"

"I know, I know…how can you ever thank me. Well, consider us even, since you helped me get my man back. Believe me, Nathan, I'm having the time of my life."

For the next few hours, I try to stay calm and not obsess about how the meeting is going. I listen to Wayne and try deep breathing techniques. All that does is get me worked up since the last time I took breaths like that Brooke's mouth was on me. This isn't calming me at all—just the opposite, as images of Brooke in various states of undress flash through my mind.

Damn, I'm such a guy. Brooke could be in peril, fighting for me in Arnold's office. How can I be thinking about sex at a time like this?

I need to distract myself so I end up resorting to my tried and true…a viewing of the Golden Collection DVDs of classic Looney Tunes. The first DVD starts with *Duck Amuck*, where Chuck Jones has Bugs Bunny at a drafting table animating Daffy Duck in every humiliating way possible. I grin because it reminds me of my Monkey Man drawing and how much it's presence has undoubtedly tormented Arnold.

Next up is Friz Freleng's *Bird's Anonymous*, where Sylvester goes into the twelve-step program to get over his obsession with Tweety Bird. I realize I'll have to join a similar group for lovesick fools if Brooke doesn't come back to me. Robert McKimson's terrific *Gorilla My Dreams* distracts me with Bugs' antics when he's adopted by two gorillas in the jungle.

But my favorite on this DVD is Bob Clampett's *Porky in Wackyland*, a black and white surreal cartoon from the thirties. Porky finds himself falling through a chute into an alternate reality while searching for the rare and illusive Dodo bird. As well-meaning Porky stumbles through the Dali-inspired landscapes, he comes across numerous strange creatures and becomes so exasperated trying to get what he wants most. At some point he's just trying to survive his ordeal. I don't think I've ever related to Porky Pig quite like I do today, because ever since Monday I've been tumbling through Wackyland too.

• • •

At three-forty, I fire up the Mini-Cooper and head to the Toluca Lake Starbucks, right at the edge of the studio side of Burbank. After scanning the place to make sure Brooke isn't here yet, I order our drinks and find a quiet table outside. I don't know when I've ever been so nervous. The entire time my stomach is fluttering and my right eye's twitching.

I try to focus on Brooke's macchiato, and luckily the idea for her illustration comes easily to me. Sometimes the most obvious solution is also the best one. I hold the cup and work carefully while I move my Sharpie over the curved surface. As I carefully finish the sketch, I sense someone settling into Brooke's chair and I look up to warn them that the seat is taken. But it's Brooke, and she's watching me with her huge, somber eyes.

My Brooke.

She studies me carefully, and it's almost more than I can take. As much as I want to jump up and grab her, I have to follow her cues. She chose to sit down quietly without even hugging me first. The realization makes me incredibly sad.

"Hey, Brooke," I say softly.

"Hi." She smiles a sad smile.

We just stare at each other for another moment, taking in everything. She looks tired, not good at all. This is a much different woman than the one I kissed goodbye Monday morning.

"Is that for me?" she asks, pointing to the cup I just finished.

"Yeah," I answer, gently pushing it towards her.

She reaches for it and rotates it slowly until she finds her sketch. She takes a sharp breath and gently runs her finger over the rendering of B-Girl.

A tear works its way down her cheek and she lifts her beautiful hand to brush it away. "I love it," she says looking up at me.

I get up and stand next to her chair. "Come here," I say gently as I extend my arms open.

She blinks back more tears and slowly rises, then steps into my embrace. I fold my arms tightly around her. My heart pounds wildly just to have her close. I'm holding my Brooke again.

"God, I've missed you," I whisper into her hair.

"Oh Nathan. You have no idea…" Her fingers press into me like she's afraid I'll let her go.

"No, I don't. I wish you'd returned my calls. Then I would've had an idea."

"I'm sorry, I couldn't...I just couldn't call, even if I'd gotten the messages. But I thought about you every minute of every day."

She thought of me every minute? If I was in her thoughts...surely, I must still be in her heart. Hope fires up inside of me.

"I've been in the dark all week. If Morgan hadn't at least told me you were all right, I would've gone mad," I say.

"But that's the thing...I haven't been all right. I've been in really bad shape. I pretty much fell apart Monday afternoon."

"But why didn't you let me help you?"

"I'm sorry. I've been trying to come to terms with the fact that I single-handedly wrecked your career. It pretty much pushed me over the edge."

I look down and notice that her hands are trembling. Her spirit seems to be folding inward like a delicate origami.

"I became single-minded," she continues with a glazed look. "Night and day, all I could do was work on my plan to fix it. I had no sense of time or reality. I still can't believe it's been four days since everything fell apart."

I pull away from her and look down on her sternly.

"Brooke, you didn't single-handedly wreck my career. I'm not going to let you take that on. Besides, we both lost a lot that day."

I lead her back to her chair, and once she is sitting again, I go back to mine.

She pulls her fingers through her hair nervously. "I don't care about that job. For me, it was shattering to lose my dignity. But even worse, I lost the belief in myself."

"Oh, Brooke."

"How can you be so calm with me knowing you lost B-Girl and don't have a job, thanks to my supreme stupidity?"

"What do you mean stupidity?"

"Knowing how territorial Arnauld is, I should have known he'd go after you. He's so paranoid I should've assumed he'd have cameras everywhere. It also should've occurred to me that he'd have his guy following us while he was gone. I was just so blissed out with you that I felt like we were in a perfect bubble. I stopped paying attention and left the door open for his menace."

I think back and remember the guy in Arnold's office who looked familiar. *Hell no! He followed us all week?* As my mind races to try to place where I may have seen him, my phone suddenly rings.

I look down and raise my eyebrows. *Walter.*

"Who is it?" Brooke asks as the rings continue.

"My lawyer."

"Answer it, please," she says.

I pick up the phone and press the screen. "Hello, Walter."

"Nathan, I've also got Arthur and Diana conferenced in, as well."

"Good, what's up?" I ask nervously.

"Well, I have big news. I just got a call from their attorney. I'm happy to report that the case has been dropped."

I close my eyes, and reach out to Brooke. She takes my hand and winds her fingers through mine. I hold onto her tightly. Taking a deep breath, I try to still my thundering heart.

She squeezes my hand, and I look up at her. "It's over," she whispers, smiling gently.

"Nathan?" Walter asks into the phone.

"I'm here. I'm just in shock I think. I can't believe it's over. I mean, is it really over? He can't come after me again?"

"No. The agreement that they just faxed us states as much. We have a messenger on the way over with the official signed copy."

"We couldn't be more pleased," Mom chimes in. "Thanks to you and your team, Walter, for everything."

"Well, honestly, Diana, I can't take credit for this victory. It seems Nathan's friend, Ms. Tobin, made this happen. We were just the second string defense if you will. Although I'm sure we intimidated him, it was still too early in the game for us to do our real magic."

"Do you know what Brooke did, Walter?" Dad asks, always the curious man.

"I was able to garner information that evidently Ms. Tobin had some incriminating evidence against Arnauld that she used to barter to get Nathan's property back. In turn, she walked away from her contract and position. She acted very selflessly. Frankly, I've never seen anything quite like it," he admits.

My heart's pounding as I look over at Brooke, concern etched across her face.

"Anything wrong?" she whispers.

I shake my head, lift her hand and kiss it like I'd seen in old movies. She smiles warmly at me.

"Well, sometimes it takes a crisis to test a person's true character," says Mom softly. "And I will always hold a special place in my heart for Brooke, for the way she fought for our son."

"You see why I love her so much?" I ask, not even caring that Walter is still on the line.

I see Brooke's eyes spark hopeful with my words.

"Yes, we do, Son," replies Dad. "And clearly she loves you too."

"Well, congratulations, Nathan, it seems you have a really good woman." He clears his throat. "Tomorrow, we will messenger over the final paperwork for you to sign off on. So now there's just one other issue."

"Yes?" I ask, curious.

"Do you want your old job back? They fired you unlawfully since they didn't fire Ms. Tobin at the same time for the conference room situation. You could demand your job back, and at this point we would probably win."

I think about being at Sketch Republic, in the same building with Arnold, and yet Brooke nowhere near.

"Absolutely not," I say with no hesitation. "My days at Sketch Republic are over. It's time to move on to bigger things."

"Yes!" agrees Dad. "Much bigger things."

"Okay, then. We're done here. Time to celebrate your victory."

"Thank you, Walter. Thank you, Mom and Dad," I say with emotion in my voice.

"We're just so happy, Nathan," Mom says. "And we're very grateful for your help, Walter."

"My pleasure. Now go on and make B-Girl a resounding success, Nathan. That will be your ultimate victory," says Walter.

"Yes, I will."

I look at Brooke, overwhelmed with love and gratitude. My B-Girl, my Wonder Woman, saved me after all. She gave up everything for me. How do I tell her what that means to me?

"Brooke Tobin," I whisper.

"Yes, Nathan Evans?"

"How can I ever thank you?"

She shakes her head in disbelief. "Thank me for picking up the pieces after almost destroying your life and career?"

"No, for saving me...for loving me."

"Saving you? It's the least I could do. Loving you...how could I resist? What choice did I have?" She teases, but yet there is something so earnest in her gaze.

"Come here," I demand, holding my arms out.

She gets up and, blushing like a schoolgirl, sits down on my lap. I nestle my head into the crook of her neck. My arms wrap around her and I smile as she relaxes into me.

"Morgan gave you the sketchbook, so now you know I've always loved you, Brooke."

She pulls back and looks at me, tears in her eyes. "Our storyboard romance that you drew," she says softly and sighs. "It's the most special gift...the most wonderful thing anyone has ever done for me. And it gave me hope."

"I wanted to explain from my heart why I did the things I did. I hope you know that I didn't intend to lie to you, Brooke. I just made some bad decisions because I would've done anything to be with you. I guess I didn't believe in myself enough to know you could love me just the way I am."

"And I do."

I grin. "And you *still* love me?"

"Of course," she says. "More than ever."

"Can I ask you something?"

She looks up at me and nods. "Anything."

"So why did you want to meet at Starbucks? Part of me was worried that you chose here so you could break up with me and make a quick getaway."

She shakes her head slowly.

"You know we kind of got started thanks to Starbucks."

"Anything else?" I ask, convinced there's more to it.

"Actually, I was thinking *you* may have needed a neutral setting so that *you* could make the quick getaway."

"So we're both fools," I point out. I reach toward her and gently run my thumb over her lips. She looks at me with such longing in her eyes that I disregard where we are. I take her face in my hands and pull her close. As our lips connect, I'm struck by the unraveling of raw emotion. We both know how much more we could have lost. Our kiss is everything...a desperate reconnection, a harrowing conclusion immediately followed by brilliant new possibilities.

"This," I say as we part and gasp for air. "This is what I've held on for. This is what I've been living for."

My fingertips curve around her waist just as I'd remembered. My touch cannot forget a single inch of her.

"Take me home," she whispers, soft and unsure. I can tell she doesn't trust herself....trust her need for me.

"Are you sure?" I ask, lowering her feet to the ground and standing up against her.

"Yes, but I'm scared I'll get too emotional. This has all been too much for me," she admits. "Less than a week ago we were on top of the world, and then it all came crashing down. Honestly, I'm still a mess from all of this drama."

"A mess?" I ask gently. She does seem so fragile. I wish I could make her see how strong she has been despite everything.

"I know you hate it that I blame myself for all of this, Nathan, but I still feel raw from all the devastation and humiliation. I'm afraid if we make love I'll end up sobbing or losing it from all my pent up emotion. I can't bear to hurt you any more than I already have."

Oh, Brooke

"I'll go slow, so slow," I offer. "I just need to hold you and talk this out. That can be enough for now."

"Really?" she asks, unsteady.

"We have a thousand days and more for the rest, Brooke. I've waited a long time for you...a little longer is no big deal."

"You're unbelievable," she says, shaking her head.

"This is our beginning." My hand tightens around her waist. "Just never, ever leave me again."

"But..."

"No. I can't go through that again. Whatever you were going through, and whatever you will go through...we can go through it together."

Her head drops for a moment and then lifts up as she faces me. It's as if she's searching in my eyes to understand the source of my strength so that she can learn to build her own resolve.

"Together? Okay, I promise."

She reaches for her cup as I step away from the table and toward our cars. I walk several paces, but turn back when I realize that she hasn't joined me. She's paused, and is gazing at her cup again with new regard. Her resulting joy makes me smile.

I reach out for her, my hand beckoning. "Come on, B-Girl," I tease. "Your presence is greatly anticipated at the house of woo."

She grins and steps forward, until our hands meet and fold together. "Ready?" I ask.

She nods. Her cheeks are flushed, her eyes bright.

We are wounded soldiers finally reunited from our separate battles. We move slowly and with purpose, knowing that each step away from our past takes us closer to our future...together.

Animate Me / Chapter Thirty / Making Magic

Hey, Sulley, I'm baring my soul here. The least you can do is pay attention!
~Mike Wazowski[xxix]

Once we arrive at my house, we wander around trying to figure out where to sit and talk. It's becoming abundantly clear that it was a bad decision not to have a couch.

"Why don't we sit on the bed?" I suggest. "We can angle the back up."

She looks at me with raised eyebrows.

"I promise, I won't try anything…just talk." I'm relieved when she agrees.

After I adjust the bed with the remote, Brooke climbs on and holds one of the pillows in her lap like a security blanket. She still looks broken.

While I wait for her to say something, I act casual, taking a long sip of my still-full cappuccino before setting it on the nightstand. I can tell by her expression that she still isn't sure where to start.

"Brooke?" I finally ask gently. "Can you tell me about the meeting with Arnold? What did you do to make him give up the fight?"

She nervously smoothes the wrinkles of the bedspread out in front of her and takes a deep breath. I suddenly worry I shouldn't have started there, but she surprises me with her first seemingly random question.

"Do you remember Bob Emerson at Sketch Republic?"

"Was he that executive who left last year?"

"Yes, he was Chief Financial Officer and a great guy. He was kind of a father figure to me. He took me under his wing when we worked together, and taught me a lot about financing projects and how the industry ran."

I nod, actually feeling good for Brooke that she had someone besides Arnold teaching her things.

"Well, after a period of time I could tell that he didn't like that I was with Arnauld. He never said why, but I sensed that he had issues with him and thought I deserved much better."

"Good man," I say quietly.

"In the months leading up to his departure he kept suggesting things, encouraging me to get another job, subtly suggesting distancing myself from Arnauld. Then one day we had a closed door meeting, and at the end, he suddenly gave me several files and flash drives and told me to keep them somewhere safe, just in case I ever needed them."

"Whoa." Now we're getting somewhere.

"The next day, he resigned. He still checks up on me once in a while. I'm sure by now he's heard on the news about the uprising that's going on over there."

"You know about that?" I ask, surprised.

"I found out today when we showed up for the meeting. Morgan met my lawyer and me outside before we headed in. She didn't tell me about it yesterday when she gave me your sketchbook. I think she was worried how I'd handle the drama of it all. She knew I was on the edge and working so hard to get ready for this meeting with Arnauld and the lawyers."

"She cares about you so much, Brooke."

"I know. I'm so grateful. She's been an incredible support to me. I knew she had my back, and I knew she was watching out for you, too."

"She is, and she did. She's such a good friend."

"Yeah, today she gave my lawyer and me the lowdown before we went inside. She showed me the news clip."

I smile at her. "Pretty amazing, huh?"

"Well, it helped explain why Arnauld was completely unglued when we showed up. He normally has a powerful game face. Anyway, thank God I took those files out Monday right after everything blew up and before they searched my office. I was an idiot not to take them home the day Bob gave them to me. Will I ever learn, Nathan?"

"You're trusting, Brooke. I understand why you wanted to believe in Arnold."

"I guess so. But I was such a fool." She curls into her pillow looking defeated.

I need her to stay focused. "Come on, tell me…what happened next?"

She nods. "So when I finally picked myself up off the floor Monday afternoon, I called my lawyer, Erika. She's another person like Bob, who I've looked up to and trusted. She's been amazing. She actually insisted I stay at her house this week, even though that seems pretty unorthodox."

"I'm just so glad to know you weren't alone in this."

"I don't know what I would have done without her. You know, after Bob had given me the folders I checked them out, but the first part was financial spreadsheets that didn't make sense to me so I just locked it away. Erika has this forensic accountant guy that went over everything for two long days, and believe me…it wasn't pretty."

"What had Arnold done?"

"All kinds of illegal kick-backs with the broadcasters, and skimming from profits into his personal accounts."

"He could go to jail," I say, trying to contain my delight.

"Well, Erika wanted me to turn him in, but that would've put your case with B-Girl into limbo for who knows how long."

"Oh, no," I say, concerned.

"And I couldn't have that. All I wanted was to get B-Girl back to you, and for Arnauld to be out of my life."

"Oh, Brooke."

I look at her and my heart hurts for all she's been through to try and help me. "So how did Arnold handle the news?"

"Oh, it was as awful as I'd imagined. He wouldn't look at me, but he yelled repeatedly at Erika. And man was she powerful…the louder he got, the quieter and more fierce looking she got. Ruiz had to keep barking at Arnauld to get him to calm down. He was wired and kept getting up and pacing. I was a nervous wreck."

"Were you scared?"

"Yes, but not as scared as I was earlier in the week. As I started to learn about his activities, I became afraid he would come after me to protect himself. I had a lot of crazy thoughts…I mean here's a man I had naively trusted for years, and I couldn't believe what he'd done. With his temper, who knows what he's capable of?"

I'm stunned into silence as I imagine how worried Brooke must have been. If only I could have been there to protect her and make her feel safe.

"But more than that," she continues. "I was really afraid that he'd do something to you if I'd gone to you after the meeting Monday. If he had, I couldn't have lived with myself."

"Is that one of the reasons you disappeared and didn't contact me?"

"The only reason," she says with a sad sigh. "I knew it kept you safe, and he would've done anything to find me, once he thought I wasn't with you anymore."

"How could you even go back to Sketch Republic and see him knowing what you were up against? You must have been so freaked out."

"What choice did I have? Yes, I was panicked, but that feeling was jumbled up with a whole bunch of emotions. I really just wanted to get it over with so I could get out of there for good. Once Erika finished laying it out and our conditions, Ruiz took Arnauld to his office to discuss what they were going to do."

"How long did you have to wait?"

"About fifteen minutes. Luckily, Erika was confident enough for the two of us."

"That must have been the longest fifteen minutes of your life."

"You have no idea…besides the horror of facing Arnauld… I swore I would never go in that building again. Who knows how many people saw that tape with us half-naked in the conference room? It was hard to look anyone in the eye. I'm still so mortified that people would have watched something so intimate that was just between us."

"Oh, Brooke, I'm so sorry."

"Well, Arnauld was very subdued when they came back. It was as if Ruiz had tranquilized him. Thinking it over now, I am sure the uprising at Sketch Republic had really torn him apart. He had deluded himself into thinking he was popular with the staff. So he was coming from a place of weakness before we walked through his door."

"What'd they say?"

"Ruiz stated that they would agree to drop the case and relinquish any claim to B-Girl, but it was under two conditions. The first, of course, was that we would agree to never disclose the information we had presented in our demands. The second was that Arnauld wanted to talk to me privately."

"No," I insist, a little too forcefully. "Please tell me you didn't agree to that."

"Erika didn't like it either, but I just wanted to get it done and leave. Besides, part of me wanted to tell him face to face how much he had hurt me. So she and I stepped outside for a minute and came to an agreement."

"What was that?"

"First, he had to sign the agreements she had brought with her. Secondly, the conversation had to be there in the conference room with the door open so she could view from the hall."

"Oh, I bet that infuriated him. Brooke, if I'd known about this ahead of time I wouldn't have let him be alone with you."

"I know. But wait there's more. As the final insult, Erika wanted his jacket removed."

"She knew he was a threat and wanted to make sure there were no weapons," I think, out loud. "I like this woman. She's damn smart."

"Yes, she is. He was so offended when she made him turn around after the jacket was off…he almost stormed out, but he knew I was willing to walk if he didn't cooperate."

"So what did he say?" I try to keep my voice calm even though my heart is racing.

"You won't believe it."

I don't like the sound of this. "What?"

"He opened by saying that he was hurt that I was scared of him. All he ever wanted to do was make me happy," she says with an edge to her voice.

"Yeah, right," I huff.

"Then he went on to say that he wanted me to come back to him, and back to Sketch Republic. He said something about 'letting the boy go play with his comics' and we would run the studio and be partners in every way."

I just look at her, dumbstruck.

"I know…can you believe it? He's insane."

"What'd you say?"

"Nothing at first. I think the look on my face was like yours just a moment ago. I think he finally understands that everything is crumbling and maybe he needs me more than he realized. He always thought it was me who needed him."

"Well considering how he treated you and everyone else, what did he expect?"

"Maybe he thought I could rally the troops and get everyone to calm down. He isn't stupid. I think he just didn't expect the staff to turn on him. As I said earlier, he'd convinced himself he was well-liked and respected."

"Well, he's beyond deluded," I observe.

"You know, for a moment, Nathan, I almost felt sorry for him. He just doesn't get it and he looked like he was about to lose it. So for self-protection, I tried to be calm and not just go off on him. As much as I wanted to scream at him, I figured if I kept my cool it would be safer. So I bit my tongue and told him that even though I couldn't work with him anymore, I really appreciated the opportunities he gave me, and all that I learned. The minute I softened, he started getting pushy, saying that I owed him another chance."

"You don't owe him a damn thing."

"I know. So I got up to leave and that's when things got ugly."

I can literally feel the hairs stand up on the back of my neck. "What did he do?"

Her head falls, and her cheeks get red. I try not to freak out. "He brought up the conference room."

"What did he say?" I ask tersely, between gritted teeth.

"That we may have had an open relationship, but that he couldn't believe I would act like such a whore under his own roof."

"I'm going to kill him."

"You don't need to, Nathan...I already did. I told him that I wasn't a whore, I was a woman madly in love with a man he couldn't hold a candle to."

I realize that my fists are clenched so tightly that they're losing feeling. With her words, they begin to loosen.

"And I told him he could trash me all over the industry, that I didn't give a damn. I'd give everything up for you without a second thought."

"Brooke," I whisper.

"That killed him. It's like he finally realized I'm completely in love with you, and there's nothing he can do to change it. He freaked out. The next thing I knew he grabbed me by the shoulders and held onto me so forcefully I thought I'd break. He was mumbling incoherently and trying to kiss me. Oh God, it was awful."

"What?" I growl. I can feel the fire explode right under my skin. I want to tear his fucking limbs off.

"I was trying to shove him off of me while I cried out for help, but really it was only a matter of seconds before Erika and Ruiz rushed in and peeled him off. Erika hissed something to them both about a restraining order and we were in the elevator heading down by the time I'd fully caught my breath."

"Mother fucker. Thank God Erika was right there with the door open."

"Damn, he's insane."

"Yeah, he's completely insane."

She nods. "You know, Arnauld just never believed I'd be willing to walk away from him and my career. But that's who he is...it's all that really matters to him. But that's not me. I know that because of you, Nathan."

I reach out and take her hand. It's cold and shaky, so I scoot over and pull her into my arms. We sit together silently, trying to calm down. She's been through so much. I run my hands up and down her arms, over and over, until I feel her settle against me. "Things are going to be okay, Brooke. Let me take care of you," I whisper against her cheek. My need to protect her is overwhelming.

There's a long pause. I can tell something else is weighing on her mind. After the longest minute of my life she finally turns to me.

"I know you want to take care of me, and I love you for that, but that's the point isn't it? I need to stop relying on men to take care of me. I need to carve my own path."

"A path away from me?" I ask, intent on being strong no matter what her answer.

"No, a path alongside yours. Rather than getting another corporate job, I'm thinking about starting my own business. I could start out consulting on projects and hopefully develop shows eventually. It's going to be hard, but I want to figure it out."

"So you'll consult on other people's projects, but still be my girl?" I'm teasing, but there's truth there too. I wish she'd work with me, but I know enough not to suggest that right now. It's hard because the inevitable changes in our lives ahead unsettle me.

"Of course. I'll always be your girl," she says, smiling at me. "I know you'll be supportive through the challenges. I just have lots of work to do as I learn to stand on my own two feet."

"Of course I'll be supportive." I smile back, proud to be with a woman who is strong and able. "Whatever you need from me…just ask."

She sighs and seems to relax before a smile lights up her face. "How about a kiss?"

Yeah, enough with the talking.

I gaze into her eyes before I kiss her tenderly. I hope she feels everything that's in my heart. "I have so much love to give you."

"And I want it all," she whispers.

"You're so demanding, you and your new path," I tease.

"Kiss me again," she insists.

I feel her hands weave through my hair while she pulls me to her. Her lips are soft yet insistent as they move over mine. I surrender to the feeling, and don't hold back. We're intoxicated with sheer desire pent up from our endless days apart.

We kiss and kiss, my body is electrified just having her pressed against me. My hand moves toward her breasts and I ache to touch her, but I stop myself. She pulls my hair and moans in protest. Seriously…how much longer does this woman think I can resist her? It takes all I have not to press her down over the mattress and show her exactly how much I want her. "You're making this going slow thing difficult," I warn her.

"Sorry," she says, looking demure. She pulls back and lies against the pillows. "I know it would be prudent to go slow and be gentle with each other…we've been through so much this week. I've just missed you terribly." She gives me the look…the hungry, insatiable one.

Whoa.

"That isn't helping," I say as I internally fight the ache for her. I know she's still so shaky.

She puts her hands over her face. "I'm sorry," she says sounding as frustrated as I feel.

"I'll tell you what. I'm going to get up for a minute to cool off. I'm going to get some water…I think I'll do that…yeah, that sounds good." Now I sound like I'm trying to convince myself. "Can I get you anything?"

She nods. "Okay, could you get me some water, too? You know, I'm kind of cold so I'm going to wrap myself up in your blanket."

I shake out the blanket and drape it over her. She smiles happily. Once in the kitchen, I pull two bottles of water from the fridge then lean over the sink and splash water on my face.

I have to take a couple of minutes thinking about random stuff until I calm down enough to rejoin her. I'm just about to head back when it occurs to me that Brooke probably hasn't eaten. Before heading back to the bedroom, I root through the drawer full of take out menus from places that deliver in my area. I pull out the Middle Eastern, Italian, and Thai ones to show her. I'm not leaving the house as long as she's here with me.

When I return to her, she's crawled fully under the covers.

"Brooke?" I whisper. She's still as a mouse and her eyes are closed. "Brooke, are you asleep?"

I'm met with sweet silence. I take the remote and lower the bed and she doesn't even stir. I realize as the blanket falls back, that she's holding something. With closer inspection, I realize it's the picture I framed of us all dressed up at the Emmys. It takes some effort to pry it out of her hands and set it back on the nightstand.

Smiling, I kick off my shoes and strip down to my boxers and T-shirt before crawling in to hold my girl.

While she sleeps I hold her tightly, rubbing light circles down her back and pulling my fingers through her hair. For the most part she sleeps peacefully, but every once in a while her body tenses and her expression looks troubled. It pains me to know that for all I've suffered this week, I'm so much better now, yet Brook is still suffering. I fear it will take a long time for her to forgive herself for her part in our drama.

• • •

About an hour later when she stirs, I take it as an opportunity to wake her up. If I don't, she'll never sleep tonight. "Brooke," I whisper, brushing her cheek with my fingertips. "Wake up, sleepy head."

She blinks slowly three times until she realizes where she is. The most beautiful smile lights up her face. "I fell asleep," she says with a yawn and a stretch.

"You needed it. You were exhausted," I acknowledge.

"I haven't really slept all week. That felt so great. Did you sleep too?"

"No, I just watched you. I couldn't have anyway...I've never been more awake."

She smiles. "Are you hungry? I'm starving."

I pull the menus off the nightstand. She eagerly scans them before I order enough Thai food to feed a small army.

We have a picnic right on the bed eating straight out of the cartons. In between bites of Pad Thai noodles she surprises me.

"I guess I should go home after this. I need to start figuring out my plan."

"It's Friday night, Brooke. You can figure out your plan on Monday. Why don't you stay with me this weekend?"

"You want me to?" Her lips curl into a sweet smile. "You're right, we need time to just be together doing nothing," she admits.

"Yeah, just be together. What was the first part of your plan, anyway?"

"Well I need to buy some office supply kind of stuff, get my office set up at home and reach out to some of my contacts. I also have to send a formal letter to all of my Sketch Republic peers about leaving the company to pursue other interests."

I wince for a moment, feeling bad for her. I'm sure that's going to be a hard letter to send. "I'll tell you what, let's go to the office supply place tomorrow 'cause I need to get stuff too. Then we can get you set up so you can hit the ground running on Monday. You can bring your laptop over if you want to work on the letter and send emails before then."

"You'd do that with me?"

"Of course. If you're nice, I'll even share my wireless with you."

She grins, leans over, and kisses me. "Everything's going to be all right, isn't it?"

"Yes. We'll make sure of it."

That's how it goes...I push, she pulls back and then we meet half way.

• • •

The next day, we're at Staples, the office superstore, considering the selection of Post-it notes when she surprises me again.

"I started seeing a therapist," she offhandedly mentions as she throws the three-inch, six-pack in the cart.

"You did?" I stutter. "Where'd you find a therapist?"

"Erika recommended her. Her name is Judy and she's really great."

"I don't know much about that stuff. Do you just sit around and talk?"

We push our cart down to the file folders section while she thinks about my question.

"Well yes, but she directs it, kind of leads me into the stuff I need to work on. You know, issues with my parents that led to my behavior now, that kind of stuff."

"Do you talk about me?"

"Well, I've only seen her twice, but yeah. I talked about you a lot."

"What did she say?"

"That you sounded like an amazing and supportive partner."

I grin. "I like her."

"She's going to help me get over what happened, Nathan. I want to be the best partner I can be for you."

I don't know if it's what she's said, or the fact that we've agreed to share a shopping cart and all that implies, or that I'm a little worked up to see Brooke in yoga pants again, but I grab her and kiss her in the middle of the paper aisle. It's one of those long, endless kisses where the world falls away and she's all that exists. The stock boy, who's trying to get to the neon colored card stock for a customer, has to clear his throat to interrupt us since we're blocking him. Brooke giggles; we scoot over, and continue on.

Later that afternoon we're on my bed again, this time with our laptops and other work related stuff. I'm doing research on the internet for a B-Girl story idea while Brooke goes through her emails looking for a show treatment that she'd been sent a while back. Her phone, which is dangling from the edge of her overturned purse, suddenly starts vibrating. It buzzes through three complete cycles, yet she doesn't respond.

I look up at her. "Aren't you going to answer that?"

She looks over at me and shrugs.

"The voicemail box must be full. That's why it keeps ringing," I explain. "You should at least empty it."

"But what if I'm not ready to hear the messages?" she asks, looking uncomfortable.

"Well then don't listen, I guess." I think about the desperate call I left her. It must be there with all the rest of her calls. "But you're going to have to do something by Monday if you're going to start making business calls. People are going to have to be able to call you and leave a message."

She lets out a long sigh. "I know you're right, I'm just kind of scared of what the messages say."

"Do you want me to listen to them for you? I can be your screener."

She smiles softly. "No, I can't ask you to do that. Besides, this could be a step forward for me."

"Yes, it will be a step forward," I agree.

She studies me carefully. "Will you stay with me, though? In case I need moral support?"

"Of course."

She lies back on the pillow and taps the keys to access her voicemail. I take her free hand in mine, and although I can't hear the messages, I lay back as well, so I can watch her reactions.

As she listens to the first message she rolls her eyes. "My mom," she informs me shaking her head.

"One down…five thousand, three hundred and forty-nine to go," she teases.

The next few seem inconsequential. Then her expression gets dark. "Arnauld," she shares.

My hand tightens over hers. She takes a deep breath. "What?" I ask.

"Nothing really. He's just demanding that I come back immediately. This was Monday right after the meeting. He's so angry."

I nod and watch her expression. Her thumb hits the delete button without hesitation. It's a whole other matter with the next call. She watches me with wide eyes as she listens. When a tear slides down her cheek, she closes her eyes and rolls on her side away from me.

"What, Brooke?" I ask as I move toward her. I notice that she's dropped the phone on the bedspread as she curls into herself. I gently push down on her shoulder until she rolls back toward me.

"I can't believe you left that message and I never heard it," she says, her voice sorrowful. "You thought I didn't love you anymore. It's so heartbreaking."

"I was really freaked out," I admit. "I couldn't understand why you hadn't contacted me."

"I hurt you so much, Nathan."

"Yeah. I'd kind of lost it that day when I didn't hear from you. As each day passed there were points I got really angry, and other times incredibly hurt. The worst part was just not knowing."

"You needed me, and I wasn't there. I wish I'd been strong enough to stay…to be by your side," she says with regret.

"Me too," I respond honestly. "What matters now is that you're here. That counts, and you've promised to work it out and stick by my side no matter what we have to face moving forward."

"But I'll always feel like it wasn't enough. I should've been there for you."

"You did the best you could. For God's sake, the whole week you were trying to help me." I ease off the bed and set my laptop on the dresser, then take hers and do the same. Her phone joins them. When I crawl back on the bed I pull her in my arms.

"Time for a break," I say softly.

"Good idea," she agrees, running her hand over my chest and she cuddles closer. "You know, I don't want that stupid phone anymore. I want a new phone, and I'm picking it out this time."

That-a-girl. "Cool. Let's go shopping tomorrow after brunch with my folks." I look down at her and study her expression. "What?"

"Are you sure they want to see me…I mean, after everything that happened? You said that they know everything."

"Are you kidding? Yeah, they know everything and that's why they're probably building a shrine to you at their house as I speak. They're crazy about you for the kind of woman you are. It's not just because I'm over the moon in love."

"Really?"

"Yes. I promise."

"Are Curtis and Billie coming?" she asks, looking worried.

"No, they're not," I assure her.

"Yeah, well, I want to see your parents. I want to thank them for taking care of you. You know…if I prove myself over time, maybe they'll adopt me."

I laugh. "I think they already have."

Her eyes are wide, and her expression hopeful. "I can't believe how much better I feel than I did yesterday. It's like I'm getting my strength back."

"Now you're sounding like the B-Girl I know and love." I look down and see that she's grinning. "What?" I jiggle her.

"I'm just having a happy moment right now. For the first time in a long time, I feel the thrill of what might be right around the corner. Just think how things could be…B-Girl might be a big hit, I could find work that I love outside of corporate animation, we can take fun trips and be together without anything in our way."

"It's pretty exciting," I agree, loving her positive attitude.

"You know something… you animate me, Nathan. It's as if you've brought the real Brooke to life."

I think of the hundreds of sketches I've done of her as I went from admiration to infatuation, from obsession, to pure and blissful love. The real Brooke was always there, she just needed someone to believe in her.

But will she ever see what she has given me?

Before I met Brooke, I was a shell: smooth inside with jagged edges, a hollow form waiting to be filled. Now I feel a life force surging through me. Her love has made me believe that I can make my life whatever I want it to be.

…and she thinks I animated her.

I run my fingers though her hair. "I could always tell who the true Brooke was. You always have been and always will be my dream girl," I reply, smiling.

My words seem to light her up from within. She climbs up on top of me, straddling me with her hands pressed into my shoulders. "We're going to do great things, Nathan."

She's so excited, so I get excited…but maybe not how I should. I try to shift so she doesn't notice how excited I'm getting. I mean, she's got yoga pants and a tight T-shirt on for God's sake. How much does she think I can take?

"Brooke?" I groan. *Is it my imagination or did she just grind over me?*

371

"Yes," she whispers, leaning forward so her breasts skim my chest.

"I'm getting too excited, you've got to stop. Remember, we're going slowly..." Surely she knows what she's doing to me.

"Maybe I can't stop. Maybe I don't want to," she offers, her mouth pursed in a pout.

"Brooke," I moan. "I'm sure you can tell how desperately I want you." My eyebrows knit together, as it takes everything I have to restrain myself. "I'm trying to be respectful and give you your space and all, but I can't take much more of this."

Evidently my speech only spurs her on. She pulls her shirt up over her head. If this is an endurance test, I'm going to fail. "Brooke?"

She's watching me, almost challenging me to stop her. The bra is discarded next.

Oh my God. Her breasts...her perfect breasts. I feel the fire move from my groin all the way up my chest and across my shoulders.

"Brooke, you can't do this stuff and expect me not to make love to you. That's cruel."

"I know what I said earlier, but I want you, Nathan...so much."

"Like, want me, as in...have me inside of you?"

"Yes, I need to feel you inside of me."

"Are you sure?" I ask. I hesitate, grappling with the physical pain of my need for her, yet wanting to make sure she's emotionally ready.

She gives me a feral look and grinds again. I see strength in her eyes. *She's ready.*

She slides off the bed and I watch her carefully to see if she wavers. She quickly slides down her yoga pants and thong. I pry my jeans off and throw them across the room. Her fierce look of desire is steadfast. Maybe this is just what we need.

"Oh, my," she comments, smiling at my erection once it's free.

"Yeah, I'm a little excited. I've missed you a lot...I've missed this."

She grins. "I've missed this, too."

She wraps her fingers around me and strokes several times before climbing back up to straddle my hips. She bites her lip and her eyes become dark and sultry as she lifts up, then slowly, so slowly...sinks down over me.

"Oh, *oh*," I moan. My heart is beating wildly.

As I gaze back up at her, I realize that her eyes are wet with tears. I wonder if this is too much, but then she takes a deep breath and opens her heart wide.

"I love you, Nathan," she whispers as she curves over and kisses me tenderly.

"Oh, Brooke…"

Before she kisses me again, she rests her hand over my heart. "You're everything to me."

In that moment, I realize that every difficult part of our journey I'd do again if it meant we'd end up here.

"I love you so much. You're my everything, too," I say.

I reach for her, stroking her soft hips with my fingers. I fear if I don't hold on I may shatter from all the emotion as we kiss slowly, languidly, soulfully. I'm overwhelmed with desire and my hips instinctively begin to rock against her. Her eyes roll back with pleasure before she refocuses and gradually starts to move.

Her hips swivel and I'm undone for the heat, and wetness, and look of longing in her eyes. I let out a low moan. I don't know when anything has ever felt so good.

"What, baby?" she whispers.

"I'm just so glad we aren't going slow after all."

She pauses and sighs.

"I just learned something else to tell Judy," she states out of the blue.

"What's that?" I gasp, wondering how she can even think such a thing in the middle of this erotic scene.

"That when it comes to my feelings for you, going slow is not an option."

Perhaps we were never meant to slow down.

"Well, don't fight your natural instincts, B-Girl."

I love her passionately, with all my super powers.

I love her tenderly, still mindful of her fragile heart.

I love her completely, until she understands the majestic way she has filled me, heart and soul.

Our climax unravels what was twisted up, showering us with fragments of light and sensation. She is completely open and brilliant as she pulls me in. I surrender to her open arms, falling deeper into her.

My B-Girl's back...and she's mine.

Animate Me / Chapter Thirty-One / A Picket Fence and Pixar

"There are a lot of choices here, just pick one! Pick one so we can start!" ~Marlin[xxx]

It's a beautiful Sunday morning when I take Brooke's hand and gently pull her toward my parents' front door. As we pass through the threshold, Mom walks down the hall toward us, and calls out to Dad, "Arthur, Nathan and Brooke are here."

She wipes her hands on her apron as she approaches us. "Brooke," she says with reverence. She reaches out and pulls Brooke into her arms.

I can tell Brooke is taken aback, but she welcomes Mom's affection. When they finally move apart Mom takes Brooke's face in her hands. "Darling girl, what you did for my son..." She shakes her head with a wide smile. "I still can't believe how brave you were."

"I don't know if I was brave," Brooke says. "I just had to do whatever I could for Nathan." Brooke lowers her head, like she's still struggling with her role in the situation.

"We're so grateful," Mom says.

"I'm just so glad it's over," Brooke admits before smiling and turning to me.

Just then Dad bounds down the stairs, buttoning the cuff of his shirt.

"Brooke, our heroine!" he booms. His hug is considerably more awkward, yet still heartfelt.

"I agree, Arthur. Brooke's our heroine...our super hero!" Mom exclaims.

Dad nods enthusiastically.

I cringe at their corny effusiveness. I hope Brooke isn't too embarrassed.

"Thank you," Brooke says softly. "You're too kind."

I lean over and kiss her on the cheek, completing the mush in this sappy love-fest.

I've just polished off my second serving of waffles and sausage when Dad shifts the conversation to Brooke's work plans.

"So Nathan said you're planning to open your own company. Will you be a consultant solely, or do you have other ambitions?"

"Yes, eventually I'd like to develop properties into shows and other licensing opportunities. Usually as a consultant, you're brought in as a knee-jerk reaction to a problem with an existing show. Frankly, new work would be more rewarding."

"And you won't miss working with a larger company?" Mom asks.

"No, not to say I didn't appreciate the big paycheck and high profile, but I felt like I was dying a slow creative death there. Every decision was made for financial viability with no regards to quality or conceptual integrity."

"Well, my guess is that you will feel empowered once you rise above the corporate quagmire," Dad responds. "I worked for a large company once, and it brought understanding to that joke about how many executives it takes to screw in a light bulb."

"Yes, that was right after we were married," Mom chimes in. "I felt so bad for Arthur, he was always frustrated."

"And I was lucky because my sweet wife was willing to go without, so that I could try to make a living on my own."

"I've always believed in you...and I knew you would be so much happier forging your own path."

Dad nods in agreement. "It's liberating to be able to make a sensible decision of your own, without having a gaggle of naysayers to offer up their two and a half cents."

Brooke laughs out loud. "Yes, being able to make decisions without a committee is exactly what I need."

I look at my parents and realize I hadn't really heard them talk about this period of their lives around me in years. They've weathered their struggles so well, and it gives me hope that Brooke and I can too.

We all pitch in to clean up. Brooke and I clear the table. Dad's washing the dishes while Mom puts things away. I keep noticing Brooke watching them with wonder. At one point Mom goes up to Dad while he's working and kisses him on the cheek then whispers something in his ear. He laughs, then suddenly turns around and pulls her close for a kiss, his soapy wet hands wrapped around her waist.

Brooke catches me observing them and she blushes. I'm so used to Mom and Dad's affection that I don't think anything about it, but it seems to be a revelation to Brooke.

Before we leave Mom asks me to take the scraps to her composting thing in the back of the garden. Brooke follows me out and seems to be paying particular attention to the look and layout of the garden as I finish my task.

At one point she just stops and takes it all in. "It's so beautiful out here," she says softly.

"It sure it is," I agree. "And now that you're their heroine, they'll want you to hang out here all the time."

She grins. "They like me, don't they Nathan?"

I pull her into my arms. "They love you," I assure her. "But how could they not? My mom told me once that she always hoped I'd meet someone like you."

The kiss that follows lingers as a shimmer of light falls over us through the trees. Everything just feels incredibly right; it's that moment when the final piece of the puzzle slides into place.

We say our goodbyes to my parents and head to the phone store. As we get out of the car, Brooke pulls out her cell phone and examines it. "Arnauld picked this out for me and I think when we're done buying a new one I'm going to run over this one with my car."

"I'll be happy to help you with that," I joke. But I'm not joking as I imagine backing up and going forward, over and over.

Brooke getting a new phone is going to be cathartic for us both. Even though it escapes logic, I feel betrayed by the old phone as it didn't help me reach her during my days of desperate need.

Once inside the store, I stand back and watch Brooke with the salesman as she tries every phone that fits her requirements. She asks all the right questions and makes a confident decision. I make it a point not to chime in like Arnold would. Besides, I love watching my girl in action. She knows what she wants.

I hold her hand while we wait for them to do the data transfer and get her paperwork set. She looks at me bright-eyed. "This is a fresh start, isn't it?" she asks smiling.

I nod and kiss her on the forehead.

"It's funny how the small things can make me so happy," she shares.

I nod. "I'm like that too."

The salesman hands her the bag full of phone stuff, and she turns towards me. "Can we go home now?" She realizes her slip and corrects herself. "...I mean, back to your house?"

I grin. "Sure, let's go."

Back at my place I try to keep the mood casual. While I water the plants in the backyard, Brooke sits out on the back porch working on something. When I approach her to see what's she's up to, she pulls it up to her chest to hide it. I realize she has my sketchbook and the colored pencils I gave her are spread out next to her.

"What're you doing?" I ask in a casual voice.

"None of your concern," she answers, making a face at me.

"Is that the sketchbook I gave you?"

"Maybe," she teases.

"Are you doing a drawing for me?"

"Maybe."

I smile and continue watering the flowers next to the porch.

"Hey Nathan, you know I'm not good at drawing, right?" she asks, suddenly worried.

"Brooke, I don't care if you draw stick-figures, I just want to see us the way you do."

"I think this should be in the future since there's no mystery as to where we are right now."

"That's true." I grin at her words and the certainty in her tone. The reality of our relationship is no longer a question that needs an answer.

"The future's good," I agree. "How about a couple of years from now?"

She tips her head considering, but doesn't seem convinced.

"...or five years or how about ten?" I figure I'm pushing it, but why not? As far as I'm concerned, Brooke owns all of my future.

Her eyes light up like she has a picture in her mind. "Okay," she replies smiling, before ducking her head and getting back to work. But then she looks up again.

"This won't be a masterpiece, but it'll be from my heart."

"That's what matters the most to me," I assure her.

"But your drawings are so amazing," she laments.

"Brooke," I warn her. "What did I say?"

"That the fact that it's from my heart matters most to you." She grins.

"Exactly."

After dinner I ask Brooke if she wants to see a movie, but she has something else in mind. She still hasn't shown me her drawing, but I figure when she's ready to, she will. I watch her expression as she tries to decide what to do.

"Nathan." She pauses and seems hesitant, then finally looks up at me. "Would it be okay if you showed me your studio again...you know, where you work on B-Girl."

I smile inside. "Sure, I'd love to." I guide her by the hand down the hall and into the studio. She's been in this room before, but back then she didn't know about B-Girl. This will be a much different visit. I point to the drafting table. "This is where I've sat endless nights thinking about you and drawing B-Girl."

She smiles sweetly at me, noticing the Wonder Woman figurine overlooking where I create.

Before we start I pull open my flat files and take the current work out and spread it across my drafting table. There's already a full set of the printed final B-Girl issues at the side of the table closest to her.

She looks shy and apprehensive to be here, but I'm excited. She reaches up and slides the top comic toward her. "You've got such a great story sense, Nathan. And you have no idea how much I love B-Girl, and not just because I inspired her...she's a great character."

"You read them already?" I ask, pointing to the stack of comics. "All of them?"

"Yes, I did...of course. I read them all this week and loved every single issue."

I smile at her. She can only imagine how long I've hoped to hear those words.

"Can you tell me about your process?" She asks excitedly. "How do you get your story ideas? Do you write the entire story out first, then go back and illustrate it?"

I love it so much that she's genuinely interested in how I do this. I pull out of the pile loose pages of notes and some rudimentary layouts to show her. "I outline the story first, then do a real rough layout where I start blocking in the type."

"I can't believe you've done all of this yourself," she says with admiration.

"Well, luckily I'm pretty fast. And besides, it's exciting to me. I'm inspired since I've always been in love with my subject..." I grin at her and she grins back. "...and I still am."

She runs her fingers along my arm. "So what are you working on now?"

"I just finished these pages. It's the conclusion of the Monkey Man storyline. I'm retiring him now. I don't think he's relevant."

"Did your lawyer tell you to drop it?"

"No, the agreement Arnold signed protected me against all future claims, but I'm done with him. I want him out of our lives."

"I agree," she responds as she considers what I'm saying. "So how did you end the storyline? Did you kill him off?" Her eyes get wide, her expression playful.

"No, that would have been too easy. Here." I sort through some of the pages. "Do you want to see? It's not pretty."

"Hell, yes," she says in a low voice that isn't entirely playful.

"So the minions had turned on Monkey Man and to enact revenge, he planned to blow up the factory while they're still inside. B-Girl got to him in the nick of time and disabled him with her stun power. The authorities arrived to find him a quivering, drooling mess on the floor."

"Oh yeah," she comments with a dark pleasure.

"And from there he was transported to Primate Prison where he was thrown in the same cell as a massive alpha gorilla named Big Lou. Unfortunately for Monkey Man, Big Lou is in an amorous mood and has a thing for little furry monkeys."

"Oh no...you didn't!" She giggles.

I hold up the drawing. "Yes, I did. See, the last time we see Monkey Man he's clinging to the cell bars crying for help while Big Lou picks the bugs out of his fur and prepares him for mating."

"Oh, that'll be really painful." She laughs mischievously. "Poor, poor Monkey Man!"

"Yeah, my heart just breaks for him," I agree, rolling my eyes.

"You're so clever," she says, sidling up to me.

"Gee, thanks."

"You know I noticed when I was reading that you worked some of my real life outfits and mannerisms into the story from the very first book on."

"You noticed." I'm embarrassed and pleased at the same time.

"You really did pay close attention to me back then."

"I've always paid close attention to you."

She picks up another issue and lays it open on the desk, then points at B-Girl. "See, here's that cute outfit I wore the day we met at Geek World."

"You looked so sexy in that. Will you wear it again for me sometime?"

"How about tomorrow? It's not like I have to dress up for work or anything."

I get excited realizing that she intends to see me tomorrow too and not just throw herself into working all the time. Maybe soon the days and nights will just blend into each other and we'll never be apart.

"Hey, can I watch while you draw B-Girl? Maybe you could draw something for me?"

"Sure." I think about it a moment and then brush my hand over a fresh page of paper in my pad before teasing her by drawing soft, loose lines that slowly build towards an image.

Brooke stands up and leans in, looking over my shoulder. I feel her breasts against my back and I have to push the dirty thoughts out of my head while I work. I can feel her breath against my neck and a tiny moan when she sees B-Girl finally take shape.

Her warmth against me is distracting in the most wonderful way. I can barely keep working and it takes my complete focus to finish the drawing. Finally, I hold the pad up and review the image of B-Girl sitting on top of the world, like it's an oversized beach ball. She looks powerful and sexy…and of course, she's beautiful. I took extra time sketching her hair so it's flowing behind her.

"Do you like it? See…you're on top of the world."

"I love it!" she says happily. "Can I have it? I'm going to frame it."

"Sure," I respond happily, handing it to her.

She kisses my neck and hugs me. "So is B-Girl always alone? Does she have a special someone?"

"Funny you should ask," I reply. "She does. She has a boyfriend who I'm introducing in the next book."

She grins. "Oh good…a boyfriend! So what are his special powers?"

"He's a mere mortal."

"Really?" The look on her face is priceless. "So she's open-minded about such things?"

"Yes, B-Girl's brilliant. She knows that sometimes you find the best things in life where you least expect them."

"Are they happy?" she asks.

"Supremely happy," I assure her. "He worships his B-Girl and would do anything for her."

"I see. And does she worship him?"

"I think so…I hope so."

"I bet she does," she whispers before she swivels me in my drafting chair until I'm facing her. "If he's anything like you, then she worships him completely."

She must know by now what those words do to me. I take a deep breath and try to control my overwhelming desire to push the drawings aside and take her on my drafting table.

Slow, Nathan. Go slow…

I wrap my hands around her hips and slide my chair closer to kiss her, gently at first but then the passion builds. As I reach up and cup her breasts, I remember the first time I held her like this. Just like now, she moaned as I pleasured her, yet my heart was insecure. I didn't know back then if she merely pitied me, or if her lust was genuine.

So now as she chants my name and presses her hand over me through my jeans, there is no question of her true desire. My fingers slide under her skirt, stroking her thighs higher and higher until they slip under her panties. She rocks into my tender touch.

"Take me here, Nathan," she whispers huskily, as she leans back against the table full of drawings.

A low growl escapes out of my tight chest. My dream's coming true... my studio's about to be set on fire by Brooke and her magic ways. I help her pull off her skirt and panties before lifting her up in my arms.

I can't help smiling inwardly. *How many times did I fantasize about taking Brooke on this table where I draw her every night?*

In the frenzy, the Wonder Woman figurine face plants on the credenza while Monkey Man's demise scatters over the floor. The room smells like sweet naked Brooke and lusty sex.

I love it...every part of it. My Toontown office will never be the same.

• • •

Late that night as we crawl into bed she brings the sketchbook with her. I try to contain my anticipation as she cuddles up to me.

"Do you want to see what I drew?" she asks sweetly.

"Sure."

"You know when I thought about what I wanted the final drawing to be, I knew I didn't want it to be about work or our careers. All I cared about was that we'd be together...the rest is secondary."

I smile, realizing how much thought she put into this.

"So I closed my eyes and listened to your suggestion... where would we be in the future—like in ten years...and this is what I saw."

She slowly opens the cover and sorts through the pages until she gets to the back of the book. "Here we are." She carefully flips the pages over the spiral and sets the pad down on my lap. "I hope you like it."

I lift the pad and study it. I can tell she's watching intently for my reaction, and I don't even have to perform. My grin is natural and heartfelt. The drawing is charmingly amateur, but she's clearly put a lot of thought and effort into it.

Brooke and I are on the beach holding hands. She's wearing a B-Girl style swimsuit. There are two small people and something that resembles a dog gathered together, just in front of us at the shore.

"Did you know how much I love the beach? Where is this?" I ask her, avoiding the bigger points of interest.

"Hawaii," she replies. "I want to go there with you. It'd be really romantic."

I make a mental note to call Mom's travel agent tomorrow. "And your swimsuit…it looks B-Girl inspired," I point out.

"Nice touch, huh?" she asks, watching for my reaction.

"Yes. I love that. And who's this?" I ask, pointing to three small figures near the shore."

She carefully gestures as she explains. "These are our children: Walt and Mary, and that's our dog, Pixar."

Pixar.

"We took our dog with us to Hawaii?"

"We take him everywhere. He's a dog with super powers…he protects and babysits the kids."

I laugh. "I see…but just two kids?"

"Well, I went from a firm zero to two with you, baby…so I wouldn't push it."

I take the book and prop it up on the nightstand so it faces us, before pulling her into my arms. "It's perfect. I love your drawing, and I love you."

She looks at me intently. "Really? You don't mind if we only have two kids?"

"As long as I'm with you, I'll be happy with anything that comes our way." But then a thought occurs to me so I pick up the sketchbook again and examine the drawing more closely. "We had kids without being married?" I ask, feigning concern.

"What? Of course, we're married. Why did you assume that?"

I hand the pad back to her. "Well, where are our rings?"

She rolls her eyes. "I see you're a detail man. Do you have a pencil here, or do I need to get up and find one."

"Open the drawer next to you," I instruct.

She finds a pen, and with her tongue peeking out of the corner of her mouth as she concentrates, she carefully enhances her drawing by adding a tiny ring to each of our ring fingers.

"There," she says, satisfied.

"That's better," I agree.

She studies the figures by the shore, and lightly runs her fingers over Walt and Mary. "I'm not sure I'll be a good Mom," she admits. "But you make me want babies, Nathan. You make me want a friggin picket fence and meatloaf on Sundays."

"I make you want meatloaf on Sundays?"

"Yeah, she says, curling into me. "I wanna be your woo-man." She giggles at her joke. "And I don't know how good I'll be at trying to balance having a career and being a mom one day, but I want to try."

She has no idea what this is doing to me. I trail kisses across her cheek and pull her closer. "You'll be great," I say with confidence. "And we'll do it together. We'll be a team."

"The dynamic duo," she agrees.

"Anything else you want?" I ask.

"I want you to hold me tight. You have a way of making me feel like I'm all that matters."

"Because..." I push her to continue.

"I *am* all that matters."

"By George, I think you've got it."

We're wrapped in each other's arms about to doze off when I'm compelled to bring up something that's bothering me. "Brooke," I whisper.

"Mmmm?" she responds, winding her arm even tighter around me.

"Walt Evans?" I ask, as I stroke her shoulder.

"Don't forget his sister, Mary Blair Evans," she insists.

"Mary Blair? The famous illustrator who worked for Disney?"

"Yes," she replies, grinning.

I almost laugh out loud. She's so damn cute...she's killing me with this. "Brooke, love...those are great names. Grand, noble names, but..."

"Yes?" she says, I feel her body tense against me.

"I'm a Looney Tunes guy, Brooke. When you throw in Pixar, we got three for Disney, and a big fat zero for Warner Bros. It's just not right."

"That's true...Disney acquired Pixar," she responds thoughtfully. "Well, what do you suggest?"

"There are a lot of greats of animation at Warner Bros.," I point out.

"For the record, although I love their work, I'm not a fan of the name Friz...nor Chuck for that matter," she huffs.

"Well, there's Carl, or Leon...or how about Robert? There are two Roberts, Clampett and McKimson."

"I like the name Robert," she agrees. "Robert Walter Evans. I like the sound of that."

I grin. *She still got the Walt in there.* "Those are some pretty big shoes for that little guy to fill," I warn her.

"Yeah," she sighs. "But he'll have our toon-genes baby, and all our love to help him along."

"And don't forget Mary. She very well may outdo us all," I point out.

"Mary's going to kick ass," she agrees. "She'll be our little Power Puff Girl."

"Anything else?" I ask. "As long as we're sorting this all out."

"Let's see," she says, thinking out loud. "We've got the love nest with the picket fence."

"Check," I respond.

"Two kidlets, Mary and Robert."

"Check."

"A Golden Retriever named Pixar."

"Golden Retriever? I like those...check."

"Meatloaf on Sundays."

I laugh. "Check."

She pauses.

"Anything else?" I ask as I pull her up over me. All this talk is making me wild. I want her again…badly.

The good news is I think she wants me again, too. She spreads her thighs and lifts up so she's straddling me. "You," she whispers.

"Me? Oh, you've always had me."

She nods, then leans over and kisses her way up my neck. "Yes, most definitely you," she chants; her expression loving as her breasts graze my chest. I reach up and fill my hands with her softness.

"Are you sure?" I challenge playfully, as I give her my love.

The heat is radiating off her. She swivels her hips provocatively.

Oh, Brooke…

She nods, certainty in her big blue eyes.

"You."

The End

Acknowledgements

My first support team for my writing efforts was my spirited daughter Alex, my sweet sister Cheri and dear friend Lisa Fortunato, who cheered me on before I'd even found a single reader. They always made me feel that my efforts were worthwhile-that it wasn't insane to be writing late at night after working long days. I love you guys for that and so much more.

I appreciate that my husband and daughter put up with me as I got lost in the world of my characters. I often forgot about things like dinner and that my Mac didn't always have to be perched on my lap.

I will forever be indebted to the fan fiction community, who welcomed and inspired me as a reader and writer. The amount of creativity, artistry and support I found there changed my life in many ways. I have made friends from all over the world and had incredible experiences I would've never imagined. There are so many wonderful readers who reviewed, blogged and tweeted about my stories and inspired me to keep writing. I'm too afraid to miss someone to list everyone's names, but know that I adore and am thankful to all of you.

In the fanfic community I also found my story support team when I was joined by four exceptionally bright and talented women who pre-read and helped me edit my stories. Love and endless gratitude to my fic sister Azucena Sandoval, Laura Edmonston, Jenn Miller and Kathy Wallace. I've also been lucky to work with Jada D'Lee, a terrific designer, who rendered magic creating promotional banners and trailers for my stories. Elli Reid continually supplied me with amazing imagery to inspire my writing. The generosity of all of your time and support, my friends, will never be forgotten.

When I made the decision to publish a new cycle of editing began. Many thanks to Angela Borda, Susi Prescott, Aviva Layton, Melanie Mueller and Judy Marks who took my hand as we traveled down the tough road of editing for publication. I have learned so much from each of you and I'm very grateful.

Anyone who knows me knows how much I love the artists in the animation and comic world. Words cannot express how much I appreciate the incredible talent and heart of gold of brilliant artist Juan Ortiz, who illustrated all but two of Animate Me's illustrations, including the cover drawing. He went above and beyond what I had hoped for my story and brought a charm to the drawings that made me unbelievably happy.

I am so lucky to have Juan and the terrific men in my life who have helped and encouraged me to chase my dreams. Thank you to Tad Marburg, Michael Senich, my brother, Rob Clampett, David Johnston, Niall Leonard, Vince Musacchia, Alex Costa, Jack Morrisey and Erik Odom.

Hugs to my team at Clampett Studio Collections: Susan Avendano, Susan Barrett, John Murphy and Michelle Smart who welcomed with great enthusiasm and support the news that I'd be publishing fiction. I don't know what I'd do without you guys.

And continuing the theme that it takes a village to self-publish a book, thanks again to Juan Ortiz for the wonderful cover character drawing and Jada D'Lee for the perfect book cover design, both made me cry tears of joy. Many thanks to David Johnston for his flawless cover photography, Skye Moorhead for her photoshop work and Erik Odom and Anais Mendoza for contributing their beautiful hands. Thanks to Kirk Mueller for early development art. With the production of the book trailer, thanks goes to David Johnston and Daniel Peacock for cinematography, actors Michael Senich and Anna Koehler for their enthusiasm and great work, and Renegade Animation for bringing the cup art to life. Thank you to 52 Novels for formatting, and to AToMR and JeantheBookNerd guiding me through book blog tours.

And I'd like to wrap up this novella of thanks with love and gratitude to the amazing woman writers and friends who guided and supported me through the challenges of publishing and life. They never let me stop believing I could do this. I have so much love for my Lost Girls: Erika Leonard, Susi Prescott and Dawn Carusi. Also endless admiration and appreciation for S L Scott, Mary Whitney, Liv Morris, Killian McRae and Judy Marks. You women rock.

It's been an extraordinary journey and I'm so grateful for all of you.

Coming: November 2013

Mr. 365

When reality show producer Sophia is assigned to convince Christmas fanatic Will to be on their holiday special, she imagines him to be an oddball momma's boy wearing a reindeer Christmas sweater. What she doesn't expect is the handsome, mysterious man who captures her attention, and seems determined to win her heart.

Their attraction is undeniable, and as charming Sophia convinces Will to work with her, she slowly unwraps the secrets in his past that make this determined and soulful man still yearn for the childhood he never had.

When the chaos of production starts, will Sophia be able to keep her promises to protect Will from being exploited, or will the bitter truth of reality television be a runaway train of disaster for both of them?

Join Sophia, Will, and his dog Romeo as they enter the world of his enchanting holiday house where stars shine indoors and snow is always falling…365 days of the year.

About the Author

Ruth Clampett, daughter of legendary animation director Bob Clampett, grew up surrounded by artists and animators. A graduate of Art Center College of Design, she has been VP of Design for Warner Brothers Studio Stores and taught photography at UCLA. Today she runs her own studio and as the Fine Art publisher for Warner Brothers Studios has come to know and work with some of the world's greatest artists in the fields of animation and comics.

From this colorful background comes Ruth's first novel, *Animate Me*.

Ruth lives and works in Los Angeles, strictly supervised by her teenage daughter, who helps plan their summer around their yearly pilgrimage to the San Diego Comic Con.

Connect with Ruth:
RuthClampettWrites.com
https://twitter.com/Ruthywrites
https://www.facebook.com/RuthClampettWrites
http://www.goodreads.com/author/show/4115217.Ruth_Clampett

To see the artwork of Animate Me illustrator, Juan Ortiz:
http://www.juanortiz.org/

And check out Vince Musacchia's art on his blog:
http://vincemusacchia.blogspot.com/

End Notes: Chapter Cartoon Quotes

[i] *Pinky & the Brain, "Pinky and the Brain: Pinky Suavo" 1997, Warner Bros. Animation*

[ii] *Pepe le Pew, "For Scent-imental Reasons" 1949, Warner Bros. Animation*

[iii] *Batman & Robin, "Batman Television series: The Cat's Meow" 1967, 20th Century Fox Television*

[iv] *Superman & Lois Lane, "Superman" movie 1978, Warner Bros. Pictures*

[v] *Winnie the Pooh, "Winnie the Pooh and the Blustery Day" 1968, Walt Disney Studios*

[vi] *Hefty Smurf, "The Big Smurf" 1987, Hanna Barbera Productions*

[vii] *Barney Rubble to Fred Flintstone, "The Flintstones Movie" 1994, Universal*

[viii] *Betty Boop, "Baby Be Good" 1935,* Fleischer Studios

[ix] *Wallace, "Matter of Loaf and Death" 2008, Aardman Animations, Ltd.*

[x] *Pokey, "The Gumby Show: Pokey's Price" 1966, Clokey Productions*

[xi] *Velma, "Scooby-Doo, Where Are You: Hassle in the Castle" 1969, Amblin Entertainment, Hanna Barbera Productions*

[xii] *Cheshire Cat, "Alice in Wonderland" 1951, Walt Disney Studios*

[xiii] *Dee Dee, "Dexter's Laboratory: LABretto" 1998, Cartoon Network Studios*

[xiv] *Buzz Lightyear to Woody, "Toy Story" 1995, Pixar Animation Studios*

[xv] *Tweety Bird, "Birdy and the Beast: 1944, Warner Bros. Animation*

[xvi] *Doug, "Up" 2009, Pixar Animation Studios*

[xvii] *Edna Mode," The Incredibles" 2004, Pixar Animation Studios*

[xviii] *Daffy Duck, "Duck Amuck" 1953, Warner Bros. Animation*

[xix] *Peter Pan, "Peter Pan" movie 2003, Universal Pictures, Columbia Pictures & Revolution Studios*

[xx] *Speed Racer, "Speed Racer: The Most Dangerous Race" 1967, Tatsunoko Studio*

[xxi] *Kevin Parker," Spider-Man" movie 2002, Columbia Pictures Corporation, Marvel Enterprises*

[xxii] *Hogarth, "The Iron Giant" 1999, Warner Bros. Studios*

xxiii *Cinderella, "Cinderella" 1950, Walt Disney Studios*

xxiv *Beany Boy, "Beany and Cecil: Beanyland" 1962, Bob Clampett Productions*

xxv *Homer, "The Simpsons: Treehouse of Horror IV" 1993, 20*th *Century Fox Animation, Gracie Films*

xxvi *Spongebob Squarepants, "Spongebob Squarepants: Dying for Pie/ Imitation Krabs" 2001,* Nickelodeon Animation Studios

xxvii *Cecil, "Beany and Cecil: Cecil Meets Cecilia" 1962, Bob Clampett Productions*

xxvii *iBatman, "Batman: The Killing Joke" 1988, DC Comics*

xxix *Mike Wazowski, "Monster's Inc." 2001 Pixar Animation Studios*

xxx *Marlin, "Finding Nemo" 2003, Pixar Animation Studios*

Made in the USA
Middletown, DE
07 December 2020